PRIDE AND PREJUDICE

PRIDE AND PREJUDICE

Jane Austen

edited by Robert Irvine

broadview literary texts

National Library of Canada Cataloguing in Publication Data

Austen, Jane, 1775-1817
   Pride and prejudice

(Broadview literary texts)
Includes bibliographical references.
ISBN 1-55111-028-8

I. Irvine, Robert P., 1965-.   II. Title.   III. Series.

PR4034.P7 2002   823'.7   C2001-902560-2

Broadview Press Ltd. is an independent, international publishing house, incorporated in 1985.

North America:
P.O. Box 1243, Peterborough, Ontario, Canada K9J 7H5
3576 California Road, Orchard Park, NY 14127
TEL: (705) 743-8990; FAX: (705) 743-8353;
E-MAIL: customerservice@broadviewpress.com

United Kingdom:
Thomas Lyster Ltd
Unit 9, Ormskirk Industrial Park
Old Boundary Way, Burscough Road
Ormskirk, Lancashire L39 2YW
TEL: (01695) 575112; FAX: (01695) 570120; E-mail: books@tlyster.co.uk

Australia:
St. Clair Press, P.O. Box 287, Rozelle, NSW 2039
TEL: (02) 818-1942; FAX: (02) 418-1923

www.broadviewpress.com

Broadview Press gratefully acknowledges the financial support of the Book Publishing Industry Development Program, Ministry of Canadian Heritage, Government of Canada.

Broadview Press is grateful to Professor Eugene Benson and Professor L. W. Conolly for advice on editorial matters for the Broadview Literary Texts series.

Text design and composition by George Kirkpatrick

PRINTED IN CANADA

Contents

Acknowledgements

I should like to thank Julia Gaunce and Barbara Conolly at Broadview for their help and great patience, and Karina Williamson for suggesting the project in the first place. Thanks also to Glasgow University Library, Department of Special Collections, for permission to reproduce the image on p. 41; to Oxford University Press for permission to use the extracts from Austen's letters; and, finally, to Tom Carpenter at the Jane Austen Memorial Trust for his assistance.

Introduction

THE continuing popularity of Jane Austen's novels might seem
to require little explanation. Their clever plots, attractive heroines, and wish-fulfilling love-stories have become a paradigm
for romantic fiction. All these features also lend themselves to
adaptation for the cinema or television, which can add a new
attraction missing in Austen's original texts, namely the visual
pleasure of lavishly recreated period dress and interiors. Indeed,
Austen is one of only a few nineteenth-century novelists
(Henry James is another who springs to mind) to have re-
entered popular consciousness as genre screen-writers. Yet on
the other hand, this popularity is deeply puzzling, for the society in which Austen's stories are set is one so very alien to her
modern readers. A provincial, rural England, apparently untouched by the industrial revolution, and untouched too by
democratic politics, is pored over by the readers of urban,
industrial, democratic societies. One can find any number of
clever love-stories which are not embedded in this historically
distant setting; so why do modern readers keep reading love-
stories which are?

Part of the reason lies, I want to suggest in this introduction,
in the way in which this society, hierarchical, rural, pre-industrial, while foreign in *reality* to modern readers, nevertheless
represents a *fantasy* of what England is like that is very familiar
to an English middle-class readership and indeed to others.[1]
I want to argue that this fantasy has its roots in the peculiarly
English social settlement of the eighteenth century, one which
compromised between a system of inherited social status and
the sheer power of money. In *Pride and Prejudice* Austen does
not just represent a pre-industrial idyll into which the modern
reader can retreat. Rather she narrates this historical com-

---

1 It is clearly also a fantasy of Englishness cherished by foreign readers, too, for whom
the concern of Austen's society with fine shades of social class and decorum, and
the sublimation of hostility and desire into witty dialogue, seem both amusing and
quintessentially English (even if their pleasure is accompanied by relief that they do
not have to live there).

promise itself, the compromise between bourgeoisie and aristocracy that created the culture that now consumes her.

1. Social rank and social mobility in Austen's England

None of this should diminish our own sense of the very real gap between England then and now. England in 1813 was a quite rigidly hierarchical society, and *Pride and Prejudice* is in part a novel about the possibility and implications of mobility between status groups in such a society. Politically, that society might be divided into those great landowning families (of "quality" or "rank") whose menfolk inherited political power in the form of a right to sit in the House of Lords, the upper chamber of the British parliament; those whose property in land (the gentry), or membership of a city corporation, gave their men a right to vote in elections for the lower (but more powerful) chamber, the House of Commons; and everyone else. This last group included the vast majority of the population, the propertyless factory workers, miners, subsistence farmers and rural labourers who had no vote in anything. But in the cities it included an expanding urban middle class, a bourgeoisie, whose property took the form of stakes in manufacturing companies or trading concerns. In both town and country, it included *rentiers*, living off interest paid on capital investments, often those who had retired from their own enterprises; and lawyers, churchmen, and officers in the armed services (these professions were the usual destiny of the younger sons of the gentry who did not inherit their paternal estates). Jane Austen's family belonged to the rural version of this professional middle class, and earned its living predominantly in the church (her father George, and her brothers James and, eventually, Henry, were Anglican clergy) and the military (her two youngest brothers became naval officers).[1]

The distribution of political power is only half the story, however. After two centuries of imperial expansion and the consequent steady rise in the importance of colonial trade and

---

1 For discussion of the Austen family's social position, see Terry Lovell, "Jane Austen and Gentry Society" and David Spring, "Interpreters of Jane Austen's Social World."

the financial system that funded it, and in the midst of the world's first and most dramatic industrial revolution, the distribution of *economic* power no longer corresponded to this political hierarchy. A significant proportion of the bourgeoisie had become very wealthy indeed, to the point of rivalling the longer-established rich on their landed estates.

Edmund Burke, looking back in 1790 for the causes of the revolutionary turmoil that had engulfed France the previous year, found one explanation in the absolute social separation there between new wealth and the aristocracy before the revolution. Rigorously excluded from the privileges and power of the landed nobility, this vital, innovative section of society eventually made common cause with the urban poor, and overthrew the aristocracy altogether (see Appendix C). From this perspective, the English could be seen to have developed in a contrasting direction. Even though, as in France, the middle classes were excluded from *political* power, in England they mixed *socially* with the old élites: property, of whatever kind, became as important a social marker as inherited rank. New types of public space (the pleasure gardens and coffee houses of London, the balls and assemblies of the smaller towns) provided a venue for this heterogeneous "general society"; those with no property, the "vulgar" majority, were of course not included in that generality.

With this social mixing went intermarriage. Indeed, through marriage, something like real social elevation was possible. Political power went with the great estates, and estates very rarely came up for sale on the open market: they were usually *entailed* on a particular inheritor, which meant in effect that an estate was already the property of the person to whom it would pass next, and the present landlord merely a tenant for life, without the right to sell it. But if one could not buy an estate, one could *marry* a member of the landed gentry, and gain an estate as part of the marriage settlement between the two families. It is this possibility that is given such importance, in explicit contrast to the French situation, in the Commons speeches against alterations in marriage law reproduced in Appendix A. In Britain in the eighteenth century, marriage had come to be seen as the means whereby new wealth was co-opted into the ruling élite without overthrowing the principles of hereditary power.

However, the social spaces which made this mixing possible had to be governed by some set of rules of behaviour, conventions that allowed people from different backgrounds to recognise each other as "polite" and to meet on equal terms.[1] Insofar as these rules excluded the poor, they went by the name of "propriety," for they distinguished the behaviour that was "proper" to the wealthy from that which was not; insofar as they insisted that the function of society was to give and receive pleasure to and from others, irrespective of background, they went by the name of "politeness," "complaisance," or "civility."[2] The pleasure was to come above all through conversation, but conversation that excluded certain subjects (such as religion or politics) which might lead to pain and insult (by a too-vehement partisanship) that would in turn open up or reveal those particular social divisions that it was the job of polite society to heal. Politeness is what the newly-rich had to acquire to be able to mix with their social superiors.

Pride and Prejudice is deeply concerned with the grounds of this sort of social settlement. The ability of polite society to accommodate the very different types of wealth enjoyed by the novel's characters is shown to be threatened from a number of directions. On the one hand, the Bennet family itself is divided between those members who have mastered these codes of propriety (Jane and Elizabeth) and the others who have not (all the others). On the other, Darcy (to begin with) and the Bingley sisters make the mistake of associating propriety with gentry status, of *explaining* Mrs. Bennet's vulgarity by reference to her bourgeois origins, one brother a country attorney and another

---

1   Adam Potkay sums this up: "In an increasingly commercial, mobile, and variegated society, politeness vies with the traditional aristocratic prerogatives of birth and land for being that which sets the gentleperson apart from the lower orders" (*The Fate of Eloquence* p.87).

2   Lawrence Klein notes that "politeness" is defined (by Abel Boyer in *The English Theophrastus*) in 1702 as "the art of pleasing in company"; and comments, "politeness encompassed technique, norm, and social environment: it was a set of attitudes, strategies, skills and devices that an individual could command to gratify others and thus render the social realm truly sociable" ("The Progress of Politeness" p.190).

a merchant. Hence the importance to the novel of this latter brother, Mr. Gardiner, and his wife; not only because they take Elizabeth to Pemberley in Volume III (as the novel ends by reminding us), but more importantly as living refutations of Darcy's snobbery. Propriety can indeed be observed by the urban middle class. Darcy, as he later realises, has himself broken the rules, by being so unready to give social pleasure to others as the code of politeness demands.

The novel opens with the arrival in a small rural community of a young man, Charles Bingley, and his sisters, whose money comes from trade, not land: the late Mr Bingley was a merchant, but his children now live off the interest accruing on the capital that he amassed. Darcy, who accompanies them, is a different type altogether. Although not a lord, his mother was the daughter of a lord, and his income of £10,000 a year places him among the wealthiest commoners in the kingdom;[1] the Norman-French origins of his name and that of his aunt, de Bourgh, places his ancestors among England's earliest feudal masters. Much about the Bingleys, and thus much about the progress of the story, becomes clear when this difference is kept in mind. The Bingleys are a family putting distance between themselves and the origins of their wealth by acquiring the "manners" of, and alliances with, the landed élite. Austen's narrator notes that the Bingley sisters

> had a fortune of twenty thousand pounds, were in the habit of spending more than they ought, and of associating with people of rank; and were therefore in every respect entitled to think well of themselves, and meanly of others. They were of a respectable family in the north of England; a circumstance more deeply impressed on their memories than that their brother's fortune and their own had been acquired by trade. (p.54)

---

1   When Mrs. Bennet says of Darcy's income, "'Tis as good as a Lord!" (p.377) she is right. Gentry families like the Bennets might scrape by on £1000–£2000 a year, but generally on somewhere between this and Darcy's figure. Compare this with George Austen's income of around £600 a year by the time he retired (most of it from sources other than his salary as a vicar); and a skilled workman perhaps £100 (figures from Spring, and Jan Fergus, *Jane Austen: a Literary Life*, p.48).

Conspicuous consumption, one might note, is a large part of the élite lifestyle that the Bingley sisters have acquired. Their "habit of spending more than they ought" marks them as exactly those daughters of the successful merchant whom Robert Nugent comments are "generally bred up to be good for as little, and to be as proud, expensive, and whimsical as any lady of quality whatsoever" (see Appendix A, p.392). Note also the tension implied here between the "respectability" of the Bingley family and the origins of its wealth. The sisters' thinking "meanly of others," visible in their consistent snobbery towards the Bennets, Philipses, and Gardiners, is a condition of their thinking well of themselves, not because they themselves are of a much higher rank, but because they are not. The Gardiners are different from the Bingleys only in the much smaller scale of their wealth, and because they have put no distance between themselves and their business in a quite literal sense: Mr Gardiner lives "by trade, and within view of his own warehouses" (p.168). Keeping her social distance from the middling sort is a condition of Miss Bingley's ultimate acceptance into the landed elite by marriage to Darcy, or a man like him.

It is in her brother's relation to Darcy, however, that the Bingleys' particular situation has its most direct influence on the plot of this novel. For Darcy is in effect Bingley's mentor or patron, and Bingley's "natural modesty" (p.219), his "diffidence" (p.370: these are Darcy's words), his readiness to accept Darcy's judgment on all matters, without displaying the deference that would openly admit his inferiority, is not simply a character trait but the result of his transitional social status. Darcy acts as Bingley's guide to the fine discrimination of social differences that mark a member of the élite: the difference, for example, between real and assumed humility (pp.84-85); or between a fine girl to dance with at a country ball, and the fine lady that one needs to marry in order to consolidate one's new social position. This latter distinction is the one on which Darcy acts when he separates Bingley from Jane Bennet, falling decisively as she does into the former category.

2. Burkean conservatism and the Longbourn entail

The political importance of this social settlement between old and new wealth, and the codes of politeness on which it depended, was made all the more obvious by the 1789 revolution in France. In 1793, after the execution by the revolutionary government of the French king, the United Kingdom went to war with France, and its government introduced a series of repressive measures designed to flush out sympathisers with the French ruling party, the Jacobins. The reactionary paranoia generated bears comparison with the atmosphere created by anti-Communist witch-hunts in the United States in the 1950s: expressing any of a range of radical political opinions brought one under suspicion, and could lead to social ostracism (the government's efforts to jail suspected subversives usually ended in failure). This was the political atmosphere in the 1790s when Jane Austen began her novel-writing career: a first version of *Pride and Prejudice*, entitled *First Impressions*, was written in 1796-7. When the novel was finally published in 1813, Britain was still at war with France (1790).[1]

The most resonant anti-revolutionary statement, made before the Jacobins' program of mass executions of its enemies ("the Terror") had largely discredited its democratic fervour, was Edmund Burke's *Reflections on the Revolution in France.*[2] Burke's argument against the revolutionaries is one of the classic statements of political conservatism. It argues (to boil down

---

1 Austen's father offered the manuscript of "First Impressions" to the very reputable publishing firm of Cadell and Davies in a letter dated 1 November 1797: they declined even to look it over. Austen revised this text under its new title in 1811-12, and sold the manuscript to Thomas Egerton for £110: see note to Appendix G. Jan Fergus argues, on the evidence of Austen's letter of 29 January 1813 included there ("I have lop't and crop't so successfully...") that the revision consisted mostly in cutting and condensing (p.82), and possibly also in the development of the scenes between Elizabeth and Darcy, which seem more sophisticated than anything else she was writing in the 1790s (p.84). Substantially, however, the novel seems to be a product of the earlier decade, which is also the period in which it is set (see introduction to Appendix F).

2 The Terror touched Austen personally. Her cousin and friend, Eliza Hancock, had in 1781 married a French army captain, Jean François de Feuillide; Capt. de Feuillide was guillotined in February 1794.

a long and complex text) that a successful state, like a successful estate or a successful family, is one that engages the emotions, the instinctive loyalty, of its subjects. Without such loyalty, any social grouping, the nation included, is simply a collection of self-interested individuals, only prepared to give up their autonomy if they get something of equal value in return. But the intelligence of any one individual is a weak and chancy thing, as like as not to misidentify that individual's true interests. The constitution of the country represents a deeper and more reliable wisdom, developed over centuries. It is because of its long continuity and evolution that we naturally feel for it the respect and loyalty we feel for parents. To abolish the state because its practices appear irrational, and then draw up new institutions on the basis of abstract principles (as the French had done) would lead to disaster, for those institutions, commanding no *instinctive* respect, could always be subjected to further rational criticism; and so society would descend into the chaos of perpetual revolution.

To express the relation between each generation and the state, Burke had recourse to an image that has direct relevance to *Pride and Prejudice*. The constitution, he explains, is like an entailed estate: that is, it is inherited by each generation from the last, but hedged around with restrictions on what the new generation can do with it, just as the landowner cannot sell off his land, or cut down all its trees for easy profit, and so on. Rather, such an estate is already in a sense the property of the *next* generation, in that it is *their* interests that govern what we do with it: the landowner is in this way himself the tenant (albeit for life) of his own descendants. Such is the continuity of the British state, says Burke: no one generation has the right to wreck an inheritance such a long time in the making.

As a romantic comedy (understood in the most general terms), *Pride and Prejudice* is concerned directly with continuity, with the reproduction of a society and its values by a younger generation, despite the barriers placed in their way by established conventions and alliances. Jane marries Bingley, Elizabeth marries Darcy, despite the gap between their families in terms of wealth and status. In doing so, like most romantic comedies, it legitimates the established order by showing it to be capable of absorbing the new. Within this generic structure, however, Austen figures the *threat* to social continuity in exactly the legal trope in which Burke figures its guarantee: in the entailment of an estate. *Pride and Prejudice* both literalizes and re-mystifies Burke's trope of inheritance. It literalizes this figure by making the actual entailment of a particular estate the mainspring of the plot: it is because his family will *not* inherit Mr. Bennet's estate on his death that finding husbands wealthy enough to maintain his daughters financially is such an urgent imperative. (That the novel concerns a particular estate does not prevent its taking on the wider, national and political significance attributed to entailment by Burke, as we shall see.)

However, *Pride and Prejudice* also mystifies the Longbourn entail by obscuring the exact nature of the legal settlement that has created this situation. Entailment is such a useful metaphor for Burke because, while it takes absolute control of an estate out of the hands of its present possessor, it does not impose an unchanging set of arrangements down through the centuries from an immemorial past. Rather, the entailment of an estate was something renegotiated by each generation with its predecessor. Burke's trope thus allows, at the national level, for constitutional innovation within the framework of an ongoing tradition. Unalterable entailments, dictating a line of inheritance over which each succeeding generation had no control, had indeed existed in English law, but lawyers had long since found ways of allowing the present possessor of an estate to break such an entail and choose his own heirs. If such was the settlement of Longbourn, Mr. Bennet could easily alter its terms in favour of his daughters. Since it seems that Mr. Bennet cannot do this, the estate must be entailed as part of a "strict settlement," a legal arrangement that had become the standard way of transferring land in England in the eighteenth century. In a strict settlement, the young Mr. Bennet would have agreed with his uncle, the previous owner of the estate and Mr. Collins's father, that on the latter's death he would become only a life-tenant, with limited powers to alter or dispose of that estate. Mr. Bennet is likely to have agreed to this arrangement, when he came of age at 21 or at his marriage, in exchange for some form of income from the estate until the death of his uncle put him in possession. Such a settlement also defines who will inherit after Mr. Bennet: Mr. Bennet's eldest son, and in the absence of a son then the nearest *male* relative, Mr. Collins, rather than Mr. Bennet's daughters (this is what is meant by "entailed in default of heirs male," p.65).

The important point to grasp is that this is not a state of affairs simply imposed on the Bennet family out of nowhere, or nature, or history, the product of some impersonal and implacable determining force. That is how Austen allows it to appear in the novel, largely by giving the loudest complaints of its injustice to Mrs. Bennet. But women were not *automatically* excluded from inheriting property, as the presence of two very grand heiresses in this novel, Lady Catherine de Bourgh herself and her daughter, should remind us. Rather, the exclusion of his daughters from the entail is an arrangement to which Mr. Bennet *agreed*, in exchange for the short term benefit of an income on which he (and perhaps a young wife) could survive. But Mr. Bennet's partial responsibility for the plight of his daughters is only hinted at in the novel:

> "How any one could have the conscience to entail an estate from one's own daughters I cannot understand; and all for the sake of Mr. Collins too! — Why should *he* have it more than anybody else?"
>
> "I leave it to yourself to determine," said Mr. Bennet. (p.160)

Mr. Bennet's enigmatic words here, conspicuous in their position at the end of a chapter, are not an ironic comment on his wife's ignorance of such matters, but an avoidance of personal responsibility of the same kind that later allows Lydia her fatal jaunt to Brighton.

In contrast to Mr. Bennet stands the man who will take his place in Elizabeth's life, Fitzwilliam Darcy, the master of Pemberley. Corresponding to his exalted origins, Darcy represents all the concern for family continuity, all the virtues of responsible and self-abnegating stewardship, which for Burke are central to English national life. At first, of course, the personal and family pride which accompanies this sense of heritage is subject to some satire in the words of the narrator and Elizabeth herself. This pride needs to be reformed, indeed, by Elizabeth's salutary rejection of his proposal of marriage; but the social discomfort that it produces is shown by the novel to be of less consequence than the great good that Darcy's power allows him to do.

Alistair Duckworth and Marilyn Butler, writing in the 1970s, developed a political reading of Austen which foregrounded her deployment of Burkean conservatism. The reform on which *Pride and Prejudice* focuses, in this reading of the novel, is that of Elizabeth Bennet. She must learn that her lively criticism of Darcy, and (by extension) her scepticism towards inherited authority in general, are potentially as socially irresponsible as her father's withdrawal from his family into his library, unless it can be used to renew and revitalise the old institutions of power represented by the Pemberley estate. The marriage of Elizabeth and Darcy thus represents just that negotiation of inheritance with innovation which Burke sees as essential to national continuity.[1] Butler places Austen with Burke among the ranks of more-or-less explicitly anti-revolutionary writers, caught up in a polemical "war of ideas" with the fellow-travellers of French republicanism. Butler claims that for Austen, as for Burke, the eighteenth-century Enlightenment ideal of the rational, questioning mind, distanced from and critical of the society around it, was ultimately to blame for the chaos of the French Revolution and its aftermath. Elizabeth's intelligence appears in this light as itself proto-Jacobin.[2]

The problem with such readings of *Pride and Prejudice* is that Elizabeth's witty refusal to be awed by Darcy as a man is so

---

1 See Duckworth's new introduction to the 1994 paperback edition of *The Improvement of the Estate*, p.xxvi.
2 As Elizabeth's opinion of Darcy begins to change, she jokes that she "meant to be so uncommonly clever in taking so decided a dislike to him, without any reason. It is such a spur to one's genius, such an opening for wit to have a dislike of that kind" (p.241).

attractive, so entertaining, that it is hard to feel that it is funda-
mentally wrong, as Butler herself acknowledges:

> What makes *Pride and Prejudice* especially baffling is that
> the form taken by intelligence in the novel is so seductive.
> The reader cannot help admiring Elizabeth's wit and
> sharing her lively and satirical vision...[1]

Elizabeth, in the end, is awed by Pemberley, and does marry its
owner. But if this novel *ends* by affirming the claims of a hierarchical society over the perspective, rationality and feeling of the
individual, the experience of reading it is nevertheless an
immersion in that perspective, that rationality, that feeling. The
reader is seduced by the glory of Pemberley only because she
has already been seduced by the wit and independence of Elizabeth Bennet, and *her* recognition of the basic rightness of
Darcy's inherited power is one the reader is therefore likely to
take on trust. Social hierarchy is validated here only by being
put to the test of an individual consciousness, the heroine's, and
this sits uneasily with the anti-individualistic "conservative tendency" that Butler sees in the novel as a whole.

3. *Pride and Prejudice* and enlightenment feminism

One explanation for the apparently "subversive" nature of its
heroine might be that this novel is also, and equally, committed
to another set of values, quite different from and predating
those of anti-Jacobin reaction, namely those of (what we now
call) enlightenment feminism. After all, the reason that the
entailment of the Longbourn estate is *not* an image of social
and political continuity is because the Bennet children are
excluded from inheritance by their gender. This use of the
trope of inheritance might then appear as a *critique* of Burkean
conservatism from a broadly feminist point of view: the continuity of tradition which Burke values so highly excludes
women. For Margaret Kirkham and Alison Sulloway, indeed,

---

1   Marilyn Butler, *Jane Austen and the War of Ideas* pp.216-17.

Austen takes her place in a long line of women writers who, since the seventeenth century, had fought for women to be treated as rational beings on a par with men, and in particular for education for the daughters of the propertied classes that went beyond those "accomplishments" likely to improve their chances in the marriage market. In Volume I, chapter viii, Miss Bingley lists music, singing, drawing, dancing, and modern languages among these. Ancient Greek and Latin and their literatures, the traditional mainstay of a boy's education, were dispensed only to a tiny and usually very wealthy minority of girls in the eighteenth century; philosophy, history, and religion, let alone the developing natural sciences, were seen as a distinctly masculine preserve. That is, young women were given the skills necessary to rise in the judgement of men, and thus to secure a husband, rather than to exercise rational or moral judgement themselves. Lydia Bennet has not been brought up to think about anything other than attracting men, with potentially terrible consequences. Without the evidence to the contrary that wider information might have facilitated, of course, it was easy for men to characterise women as *essentially* trivial, irrational, and duplicitous, thus justifying their continued exclusion from the education that might have made them something else.

In Austen's lifetime, the most prominent representative of this feminist tradition was Mary Wollstonecraft, author of *A Vindication of the Rights of Woman* (1792). Wollstonecraft was sympathetic to the French revolutionaries, and had earlier written *A Vindication of the Rights of Men* (1790), a powerful rebuttal of Burke's *Reflections*. However, Kirkham suggests that concern for the reform of female education "cut across other political divisions to a considerable extent."[1] "Our habit of thinking of Mary Wollstonecraft as a Jacobin, and Jane Austen as a Lady Novelist praised by [the conservative Walter] Scott, makes it difficult for us to see connections between them; attention to the 'feminist tradition' of the eighteenth century, in its widest sense, shows that it is by no means bizarre to look for such connection" (Kirkham 40-1). However, by the time Austen came

---

1   Margaret Kirkham, *Jane Austen, Feminism and Fiction* p.xiii

to turn her draft *First Impressions* into *Pride and Prejudice*, posthumous revelations about Wollstonecraft's unconventional private life had been pounced on by conservatives to bring her thoroughly into disrepute. Austen, concerned to preserve that precious respectability that was the only substantial wealth of a clergyman's unmarried daughter, could only express ideas similar to Wollstonecraft's through "policies of thematic and rhetorical caution."[1]

Yet for all this, Elizabeth's story ends with her delighted submission to Darcy in marriage. Gratitude to powerful men is not a characteristically feminist emotion. Yet it is *gratitude* that forms the foundation of Elizabeth Bennet's *love* for Fitzwilliam Darcy: caught in a reciprocal gaze with Darcy's portrait at Pemberley, impressed with the evidence of his social power that surrounds her, Elizabeth "thought of his regard with a deeper sentiment of gratitude than it had ever raised before" (p.264).[2] The love-story element is not, as Sulloway suggests, simply a conventional wrapping that has in itself no political content, disguising Austen's (feminist) political agenda. Desire does not transcend politics in this way: Elizabeth's desire for Darcy is produced by her political situation, and their love-story carries its own political values, values that seem opposed to the feminist interest in which Sulloway and Kirkham otherwise place Austen.

In Butler's reading of the novel as a disguised conservative polemic, it is Elizabeth's lively intelligence that does not fit; in Kirkham's reading of the novel as a disguised feminist polemic, it is her marriage to Darcy. The two critics, reading the novel within radically different contexts, identify the same disjunction at the heart of *Pride and Prejudice*. So long as we read *Pride and Prejudice* within only one of these discursive frameworks, Burkean conservatism or enlightenment feminism, some major aspect of the novel will appear as inexplicable, or as a mistake,

---

1   Alison Sulloway, *Jane Austen and the Province of Womanhood* p.4.
2   I draw this point from Maaja A. Stewart: "Elizabeth's gratitude is a direct response to the excitement of Darcy's power, which she no longer distances but looks at clearly, with an obvious interest in forging for herself a connection to this power through Darcy's mediation" (*Domestic Realities* p.56). Compare Gregory's comment: "What is commonly called love among you is rather gratitude..." (Appendix B. 2).

or as a defeat. Read with Burke, the attractiveness of Elizabeth's independence might seem like an incitement to radicalism; read with Wollstonecraft, Elizabeth's marriage to Darcy seems like surrender to the forces of established authority. But if we instead ask how this novel combines these two political positions, what relationships it creates between its questions of rank and its questions of gender, we will perhaps be getting closer to its true achievement, and the reason for its enduring significance today.

4. Politics and the uses of gender

In the past decade or so, an increasing amount of critical attention has been directed to the role of gender in the political debate in Britain following the French Revolution. The story that has emerged is of an increasing investment by conservative commentators in one particular version of femininity: that of the domestic woman, the wife and mother who is the moral as well as the economic centre of a home, who always put the welfare of husband and children before her own desires. This ideal itself was not an invention of the 1790s. Nancy Armstrong for one has charted its rise from the late seventeenth century as a specifically middle-class ideal, one whose meaning was shaped by its opposition to an aristocratic ideal of the "fashionable" or "elegant" woman, whose overt display of wealth and sexuality was designed for consumption in the public spaces of the court, ballroom, and pleasure gardens of the capital, rather than the private space of the home.

According to Armstrong, at least, the domestic ideal found its most effective expression in the conduct book, a genre of writing designed to instruct young women in how they should behave in society, and there are extracts from three of the most influential, by James Fordyce, John Gregory, and Hannah More, in appendices B and D. But if the conduct books offered middle-class girls another ideal to which to aspire than the aristocratic one, it would seem to cancel out any possibility of rising in rank by marrying an aristocrat, for without engaging in the rituals of fashionable display, how were you going to meet one, let alone attract him? It is into this gap between bourgeois moral code and aristocratic ambition that a particular tradition of the English novel developed, peddling the fantasy that feminine *resistance* to aristocratic manners might in fact be profoundly attractive to handsome aristocratic males. In Samuel Richardson's *Pamela; or, Virtue Rewarded* (1740), a servant girl fights off the advances (including attempted rape) of a master who cannot bring himself to believe that someone of her rank could think her virginity so important; until, that is, he reads her letters and discovers her absolute sincerity, undergoes an astonishing moral conversion, and instead proposes marriage — which Pamela accepts.

Thus such narratives are engaged in the propagation of norms of behaviour on which master and servant might meet, by imagining such norms as produced by a woman's moral reformation of a man. The type of marriage it imagines is one in which the characteristic faults of each gender will be cancelled out by the virtues of the other. Crucial in the propagation of polite culture as a set of moral and social values were the daily papers written by Joseph Addison and Richard Steele in the early years of the eighteenth century, *The Tatler* (1709-11), *The Spectator* (1711-12, 1714) and *The Guardian* (1713). Repeatedly in those journals we find the same concern with the complementary nature of the genders:

> As Vivacity is the Gift of Women, Gravity is that of Men. They should each of them therefore keep a Watch upon the particular Biass which Nature has fixed in their Minds, that it may not *draw* too much, and lead them out of the Paths of Reason…. Men should beware of being captivated by a kind of savage Philosophy, Women by a thoughtless Gallantry.[1]

It is precisely a union of this type that Austen imagines for

---

1 *The Spectator* no.128 (July 27, 1711). In Bond (ed), *The Spectator* vol. II p.8. The "biass" Addison refers to is the warp on a bowl that makes it run in a curve or "draw." Compare Dr. Gregory on the civilizing effects of courtship in Appendix B. 2.

Elizabeth and Darcy: "by her ease and liveliness, his mind might have been softened, his manners improved, and from his judgment, information, and knowledge of the world, she must have received benefit of greater importance" (p.198). But we must remember that, in *Pride and Prejudice* as in *The Spectator*, the compromise being worked out in terms of the sexes is a displaced version of one being sought between the social ranks. Elizabeth's rejection of Darcy forces him to reform his manners to something more congenial to those of a lower rank in general, as well as making him deserving of Elizabeth's love in particular.

Armstrong offers us, then, one way of understanding the interrelation of this novel's concerns with gender and social hierarchy. But she does so by reducing the historical moment of Austen's novels to one episode in a much larger historical process: that of the rise of an apparently monolithic "bourgeoisie." The particular circumstances of British reaction to the French Revolution are then necessarily mere epiphenomena of this underlying historical process. In contrast, Claudia Johnson's *Jane Austen: Women, Politics and the Novel* centres on the reactionary politics of the 1790s. The domestic woman appears here, not as the Trojan Horse of middle-class economic and political interests, but on the contrary as an element in the conservative rhetoric of the anti-Jacobins. The domestic ideal developed by the likes of Fordyce and Gregory were appropriated in the 1790s by Hannah More and others, in novels as well as in conduct books, as the core of the national values which would save Britain from *moral* defeat by the republican French, as her army and navy would save her from military defeat.

> To be sure, women novelists had never been wanting for subjects before the Revolution in France. But after it, those largely domestic subjects, concerning which they had been acknowledged to have some wisdom, were brought to the forefront of national life and were infused with dignity as well as urgency.[1]

---

1   Claudia Johnson, *Jane Austen* p.2.

In the reactionary novels of Jane West and Hannah More, in consequence, the threat of revolutionary subversion is translated into sexual terms:[1]

> With the countryside full of Jacobin riffraff out to ruin English families by seducing women away from fond fathers and rightful husbands, female modesty — that is to say, the extent to which women do not feel, express, and pursue their own desires — is no less than a matter of national security.[2]

This is the type of novel current in the 1790s when Austen begins the novel which will become *Pride and Prejudice*. Johnson argues convincingly that Austen's novels both appropriate and react against this political investment in "female modesty."[3] *Pride and Prejudice* is clearly critical of the conduct books' demand that a woman should not express her own desires, but wait for a man to express them on her behalf. Reading Darcy's explanation of his interference in Bingley's relationship with Jane, Elizabeth realises that Jane's inability to express her feelings was one factor that allowed Darcy to behave as he did: "She felt that Jane's feelings, though fervent, were little displayed, and that there was a constant complacency in her air and manner, not often united with great sensibility" (p.227). While Austen is in many ways a conservative writer, she is, in *Pride and Prejudice* at least, concerned to *legitimate* rather than castigate female desire. As we have seen, this novel's legitimation of the political status quo in Britain is only done *through*, not in spite of, Elizabeth's individual sexual desire: her desire, that is, for Darcy. One can then argue, as Johnson does, that Austen here is brilliantly appropriating reactionary values and using them for her own, femininst, ends, by showing that

---

1   Examples of such fiction include Elizabeth Hamilton's *Memoirs of Modern Philoso-phers* (1800) and *Letters of a Hindoo Rajah* (1796), both available in Broadview editions.

2   Johnson p.18.

3   For an excellent survey of this issue, see Yeazell, *Fictions of Modesty* [in P&P], chapter 4. "Modesty" is a key term in all the extracts collected in appendices B and D.

female desire can be a support, rather than a threat, to the existing order.

> In fact, the "conservatism" of *Pride and Prejudice* is an imaginative experiment with conservative myths, and not a statement of faith in them as they already stood in anti-Jacobin fiction. To be sure, by using these myths, even to hedge, qualify, and improve them, Austen is also, necessarily, used by them. But throughout the course of the novel those myths become so transformed that they are made to accommodate what could otherwise be seen as subversive impulses and values, and in the process they themselves become the vehicles of incisive social criticism.[1]

One should note however that Johnson herself hedges here: to say that Austen is "used by" conservative myths is an odd refusal of agency to Austen herself in the context of a novel whose whole point, according to Johnson herself, is the re-inscription of feminine agency within conservative ideology. The role given female desire in legitimating social hierarchy will tend to reconcile conservatives to a wider scope being given to the female voice within the culture as a whole, but it will also tend to reconcile propertied women to the existing social hierarchy. There is no reason to take this novel's commitment to anti-revolutionary politics as any less voluntary than its commitment to this type of feminism: in *Pride and Prejudice*, they are *mutually* legitimating. If the legitimation of one appears to any reader as the unfortunate side-effect of the legitimation of the other, it does so only because of the political position from which that reader begins.

Johnson's argument, however convincingly it squares the circle between conservative and feminist readings of this novel, nevertheless leaves one question unanswered: how is this "accommodation" possible? What is it about the discursive universe in which Austen is working that allows her to use two apparently opposed political positions to prop each other up? I

---

[1]   Johnson p.75.

would like to finish by suggesting that *Pride and Prejudice* is able to do this by utilising a series of fundamental distinctions, of boundaries, that had only recently been drawn or re-drawn in her society, and which continue to shape our experience today.

5. New identities: class and nation

I began this introduction by distinguishing between the hierarchy of *political* power inherited by Austen's England, and the increasing *economic* power wielded by those engaged in trade, finance, and industry. The social alliance through inter-marriage praised in the debates on the Hardwicke Bill was one answer to this discrepancy. But by the beginning of the nineteenth century, new solidarities and alliances were reshaping the social structure of the United Kingdom. Before, people had tended to understand their place in society vertically and locally, as it were: in relation to a local superior and local inferiors. For the propertied, this position was defined in part by systems of patronage: how far one might get in a professional career, or in politics, was determined by the extent to which local "connections" with the power to do so pushed positions one's way.[1] The clearest example of such patronage in *Pride and Prejudice* is of course Mr. Collins, whose whole identity is defined by the patronage of Lady Catherine, and whose job consists in occasionally attending to the spiritual needs of her tenants; but Darcy's relation to Bingley also carries some of the features of patronage, as we have seen.[2]

---

1 So, for example, George Austen, the orphaned son of a country surgeon, is taken up by an uncle who paves his way towards a scholarship to Oxford; he then is given two church livings, of Steventon and Deane churches in Hampshire, by a second cousin, Thomas Knight.

2 The portraits in *Pride and Prejudice* of men who depend on patronage, namely Collins and Wickham, might suggest that this novel includes an attack on the whole system. But it should be remembered that the resolution of its central crisis, Lydia's elopement, depends on one more exercise of Darcy's power in this regard, by securing Wickham a commission in the regular army. Patronage, male aristocratic power, is redeemed, one could argue, by its use to rescue the marriageability of two young women from the lower gentry, Jane and Elizabeth Bennet. The power-structures that had governed relations between men are given new moral credibility by being transferred to relations between men and women.

Opposing this understanding of social organisation, partly as a result of the increasing concentration of workers in cities, partly as a result of the developing science of political economy, was a new vocabulary of *class*. Workers in factories or mines had no particular bond with those who employed them other than the wage they received for their work; they were more likely to identify horizontally, with other workers throughout the country, than with their superiors.[1] Political economy, in the writing of Adam Smith as later that of Karl Marx, defined people's social position in terms of their role in the economy, the source of their income, rather than the family into which they happened to be born and the connections with which it provided them: defined them, that is, in terms of class rather than rank.

As far as the propertyless are concerned, one can see both types of identification at work in Appendix F. In the account reproduced there of the trial of Lord Bateman, a militia officer, for assaulting a local constable, we find his soldiers taking his side, both in the courtroom and on the streets of the town where they are billeted, *against* the local people with whom, in economic terms, they have so much more in common. On the other hand, the mutineers of the Oxfordshire militia make common cause with the labouring people of Sussex, where they have been stationed, against both officers and local authorities, in order to impose their own prices on essential commodities. It is from such alliances, working across local or regional identifications, that class-consciousness emerges. Behind the eagerness of the *Sussex Weekly Advertiser* to assure their gentry and merchant readers that they could avert such disturbances by lowering prices voluntarily lies a real worry about the consequences of such consciousness for their local power, if they must depend on the regular army to defend them from people previously their own.

---

1   I borrow my terminology here from Harold Perkin, *Origins of English Society*: "At some point between the French Revolution and the Great Reform Act [of 1832], the vertical antagonisms and horizontal solidarities of class emerged on a national scale and overlay the vertical bonds and horizontal rivalries of connection and interest" (177; quoted in Siskin, *Historicity of Romantic Discourse* p. 139).

The eighteenth-century settlement thus comes under threat from an increasing consciousness among the "vulgar" of their own common identity. However, *Pride and Prejudice* is not only about the forging of alliances over class boundaries: it also imagines a new alliance between parochial and metropolitan ruling élites. The gap in lifestyles between the inhabitants of Meryton and the Bingley group is not only produced by the disparity in income between them: it is also produced by their differing relationships to the capital. London, for Darcy and his friends, is home for perhaps half the year, and their initial claim to be arbiters of manners is their familiarity with *London* manners, referred to as "fashionable" or "elegant." For Meryton people, London is a distant and glamorous place, for all its geographical proximity to Hertfordshire.[1] The one local who has briefly entered the court is Sir William Lucas, and he has never really recovered from the experience. We should not lose sight of the fact that the local landed and professional classes, the Bennets, Lucases, and Philipses, were the people responsible for the day-to-day political and judicial administration of England, in their role as counsellors and Justices of the Peace and so on (see, once again, Appendix F section 3). When they refer to "the country," they invariably mean the *county*, the local area, and not England or Great Britain. Sir William was mayor of his town: yet his awe of Darcy marks the deference of the provincial top-cat to his national superior. The Bennets send to a local apothecary when they are ill; the Bingleys call out a London surgeon. The young ladies of Meryton are always in danger of losing their fashionable lovers to the metropolis. Darcy's eventual concession of his role as arbiter of propriety to Elizabeth marks the establishment of a standard which transcends this gap and is thus *national* in a sense that neither local nor metropolitan standards alone could claim to be.

It is thus that the eighteenth-century compromise between

---

1   One should not lose sight of the fact that London itself is two places: Westminster, centred on the Court of St. James and Parliament, in the West, the heart of the fashionable world of Darcy and the Bingleys; and, downstream, the City of London, the financial and trading centre where the Gardiners live, to the great amusement of Miss Bingley. Elizabeth and Jane visit the latter, but never the former.

the ranks of old and new wealth produces a culture that can claim to stand for England as a whole. The common culture forged among the polite turns into what would soon come to be thought of as a "national culture," with "culture" understood in a new sense: not as that which could be acquired to set one *apart* from one's forebears (in the sense that Bingley and his sisters have become "cultured" as their father was not), but as that set of practices, social and aesthetic, specific to a nation, and passed on from one generation to the next irrespective of the individual's aspirations. Culture in the latter sense becomes important in this period as that which guaranteed a continuity of national identity in a period when industrialisation was transforming the country beyond recognition. And as a *national* inheritance, culture is necessarily in the possession of all, and not only the landed élite.

However, in most European countries, including the other member nations of the United Kingdom, concepts of "national culture" emerge using the customs, songs and folklore of the peasantry, of native small-holders and subsistence farmers, as the core of what that culture *is*. So the cooking of Provençal peasants becomes the specifically French *national* cuisine of Paris restaurants; tartan plaid, the dress of Highland cattle-drovers, becomes the *national* dress of Scotland, worn by the bourgeoisie at weddings, and royalty on holiday; and no group of people can claim to constitute a nation without discovering (or inventing) their own heritage of songs and stories transmitted orally through generations huddled round fires of turf or birchwood, henceforth to be performed by small children in national costume on school gala-days.

In England, this doesn't happen. In *Pride and Prejudice*, we see an equivalent national identity emerging, but from the other end of the social spectrum. In England, the "middling sort" plunder the culture of their social *superiors* for signifiers of a national, cultural identity. In opposition to the French Republic's persecution and execution of its aristocracy, the English propertied classes define their nationhood by appropriating their own élite as custodians of national culture. Volume I chapter viii includes a telling exchange between Darcy, Bingley, and the latter's sister on exactly how Bingley should attempt to emulate his friend. The conversation will turn to whether Bingley could build a house to match Pemberley; but the cultural inheritance for which Darcy is responsible, and to which Bingley cannot aspire, rather lies within its walls:

> "I am astonished," said Miss Bingley, "that my father should have left so small a collection of books. — What a delightful library you have at Pemberley, Mr. Darcy!"
>
> "It ought to be good," he replied, "it has been the work of many generations."
>
> "And then you have added so much to it yourself, you are always buying books."
>
> "I cannot comprehend the neglect of a family library in such days as these." (p.75)

Bingley will never be able to build a family library like Darcy's as he might build another Pemberley, and this is one of the first suggestions that there might be more to Darcy than the pride on display at the Meryton assembly. But what does he (and Austen) have in mind by "such days as these"? Here he refers to the specific historical situation of the novel's action, without saying exactly what makes it special; but part of what makes it special must be the books that it produces, books which can take their place on the shelves next to the purchases of his father and grandfather. Darcy's comment brings the story's historical moment into the novel as a cultural situation, as the presence of a militia regiment in Meryton brings that moment as a military and political situation. In neither case are the specifics of that situation mentioned in the text (what war, exactly, is being fought; what books, exactly, are being published). But where the soldiers represent a disruptive force arriving from elsewhere and leaving again in accordance with orders from a national government, the books can take their place in a library as part of a historical continuity of cultural production and consumption. The appearance of the militiamen represents national historical events as the rupturing of traditional, local patterns of life; Darcy's library promises that, under the custodianship of men such as himself, even this moment of rupture can be assimilated, by means of culture, in the ongoing history of a continuous English nation.

I say that *men* like Darcy are now the custodians of national culture; but unlike their political power, this cultural role is one in which *women* can also participate. Hence Darcy's addition, in this same conversation, to the list of the normal conduct book accomplishments required of a woman, of "something more substantial . . . the improvement of her mind by extensive reading" (p.76). This is not only a demand that women need information to fulfil their civilising role in polite conversation; in the context of Darcy's previous comments, it also demands that any future partner in marriage will be capable of sharing his function as carrier of a national culture, the latter understood as essentially separate from the political life that will remain a male preserve. Books are thus to be understood as "aesthetic" objects which transcend the political-historical circumstances of their production, and women's cultural authority will be based on its strict demarcation from political power. And this prospect, held out for Elizabeth Bennet by Darcy's comment, is realised in the person of her creator. Jane Austen's prestige as a novelist, as measured in the praise of periodical reviews such as those reproduced in Appendix H, or in her appreciation by the Prince of Wales, is conditional on the exclusion of overt reference to politics; but as we have seen, the separation of cultural activities from politics has happened for profoundly political reasons.

6. Conclusion: Austen, the aesthetic, and the production of national culture

One can go further. Austen's turning aristocratic life and attitudes into the subject-matter of a novel might itself be seen as an appropriation of the signifiers of their power for her own aesthetic and commercial ends, and if so, then we can see Elizabeth herself adopting the strategy of her author. For twice Elizabeth uses aesthetic categories to turn slights received from her social superiors to her own social advantage. At the Meryton assembly, she turns Darcy's hurtful overheard dismissal of her into a funny *story*, for the entertainment of an audience: "She told the story however with great spirit among her friends; for she had a lively, playful disposition, which delighted in anything ridiculous" (p.51). Pemberley's other great assertion of cultural continuity is its picture-gallery. Miss Bingley uses this to mock Darcy's attraction to Elizabeth by imagining the impossibility of integrating them into the narrative constructed by the family portraits:

> "Do let the portraits of your uncle and aunt Philips be placed in the gallery at Pemberley. Put them next to your great uncle the judge. They are in the same profession, you know, only in different lines." (p.88)

For Miss Bingley, the purpose of art is not to overcome social barriers, as this novel does, but to demarcate them: to celebrate the continuity of Darcy's family and thus display what makes them superior to mere country attorneys. To include the Philipses in this collection would be to submit them to the mocking gaze of their social superiors, alive and dead. Miss Bingley then proceeds to enact this principle of social exclusion physically, by cutting Elizabeth out of a walking party on a narrow garden path. Yet Elizabeth, who has not heard the previous exchange, is once again able to reconcile herself to this slight by deploying aesthetic categories, and turning the group thus formed into the object of her *own* aesthetic appreciation. In response to Darcy's guilty observation that she has been cut out, she says, "You are charmingly group'd, and appear to uncommon advantage. The picturesque would be spoilt by admitting a fourth. Good bye" (p.89). This moment enacts in miniature, I am suggesting, the appropriation of a national élite as an aesthetic phenomenon by a more broadly-based middle-class culture that receives fuller expression in Elizabeth's visit to Pemberley, certainly, but also in Austen's novel as a whole.[1] Not

---

1   I suggest that the vogue for country-house visiting among the middle-classes in the later eighteenth-century represented another example of the appropriation of the aristocratic as an aesthetic effect, as a signifier of national continuity: see Appendix E.

only are the aristocracy to become custodians of a national cul‐
tural heritage, but they are themselves to become aesthetic
objects; not only the contents of Pemberley's library, but the
house itself, and the view from its windows, now represent not
the power of an oligarchy, but a set of values that are essentially
English.

Jane Austen and her time: a Brief Chronology

1775   Jane Austen (JA) born (16 December) at Steventon, Hampshire, to Rev. George Austen and Cassandra Leigh Austen

1776   **U.S. Declaration of Independence**

1783   With her sister Cassandra at Mrs. Cawley's school at Oxford and Southampton

        Peace of Versailles: U.K. recognises U.S. independence

1785–6   With Cassandra at the Abbey School, Reading

1788   **George III becomes mentally ill**

1789   **French Revolution: storming of the Bastille; National Assembly adopts Declaration of the Rights of Man**

1792   Completes *Catharine, or the Bower*

        France arrests royal family, declares itself a republic. Invasion fears: U.K. militia mobilised

1793   Henry Austen, JA's younger brother, abandons planned ordination and joins Oxfordshire Militia

        Execution of Louis XVI: UK declares war on France. The "Terror" in Paris; treason trials of radicals in Scotland

1794   Begins drafting *Lady Susan*

        Detention without trial in U.K.; state trials of radicals in London end in acquittal

1795   Writes "Elinor and Marianne"

        Militia mutinies

1795–6   First serious flirtation, with Tom Lefroy

1796   Begins "First Impressions"

        Spain allies with France

1797   George Austen submits "F.I." to publishers Cadell and Davies: rejected sight unseen

        British Naval mutinies. Franco-Austrian treaty

        JA begins *Sense and Sensibility* (based on "Elinor and Marianne")

1798   **Rebellion in Ireland put down. France invades Egypt**

        Battle of the Nile: a victory for the British fleet under Nelson

1799   Completes "Susan"

        Napoleon becomes First Consul in Paris coup

1800	**French landing in Ireland fails**
1801	George Austen retires and moves family to Bath; Henry leaves militia to become a banker **Irish parliament dissolved in Act of Union**
1802	Harris Bigg-Wither proposes marriage to JA; she first accepts, then withdraws. **Peace of Amiens: a pause in the war.** **Napoleon made Consul for life**
1803	Sells copyright for "Susan" to Crosby and Co. for £10; it is advertised but not published **War resumed. France sells Louisiana territory to the U.S.**
1804	Begins drafting *The Watsons* **Napoleon crowned emperor. U.K. declares war on Spain**
1805	Death of George Austen. **British naval victory at Trafalgar under Nelson;** **France defeats Russia and Austria at Austerlitz**
1806	**Coalition govt. in U.K. France defeats Prussia at Jena**
1807	Mrs. Austen, JA and her sister Cassandra move to Southampton **Abolition of slave-trade in British territories.** **France invades Spain and Portugal**
1808	**The Peninsular War: revolt in Spain, British troops land in Portugal**
1809	The Austen women move to Chawton, on the second son Edward's large estate in Hampshire **Death of Gen. Moore at Corunna; Duke of Wellington commanding British in Spain. French take Vienna**
1811	*Sense and Sensibility* published by Egerton on commission. Reworks "First Impressions" into *Pride and Prejudice*. Begins writing *Mansfield Park* **George III declared insane, Prince of Wales now Regent. Luddite anti-factory riots in Midlands**
1812	Sells copyright of *Pride and Prejudice* to Egerton **U.K. declares war on U.S.** **Napoleon's army suffers massive losses in Russia**
1813	*Pride and Prejudice* (based on "First Impressions"), and a second edition of *Sense and Sensibility,* published by Egerton. *Pride and Prejudice* goes to a second edition

Wellington victorious in Spain; French driven from Holland, Italy, and Switzerland

1814   Begins *Emma*. *Mansfield Park* published on commission by Egerton

Allies invade France, take Paris; Napoleon abdicates, exiled to Elba; Congress of Vienna sets out to restore monarchical European order. Peace between U.K. and U.S.

1815   JA begins *Persuasion*. *Emma* published by John Murray.

Napoleon escapes exile: finally defeated at Waterloo. Exiled to St. Helena

1816   Murray brings out second edition of *Mansfield Park*: it loses money. Henry's bank fails, taking bulk of the family's savings. First signs of illness in JA. "Susan" bought back from Crosby. Finishes *Persuasion*.

Severe economic depression and riots in U.K.

1817   Begins *Sanditon*. Dies (18 July). Henry publishes "Susan" as *Northanger Abbey* together with *Persuasion*.

Detention without trial in U.K.; suppression of democratic societies

A Note on the Text

This text follows the first edition of *Pride and Prejudice* (referred to as A) in all matters, including spelling and punctuation, except for (i) various obvious errors such as missing or misplaced quotation marks, capitalisations, and obvious spelling mistakes, which have been silently corrected in the text; and (ii) at the points noted below. Reference is also made to R.W. Chapman's edition as volume II of *The Novels of Jane Austen* (Oxford: Clarendon Press, 1923), which is the standard collation of all three editions of the novel (the two in 1813 and the third in 1817) published in Austen's lifetime. However, neither the second nor third edition incorporated corrections by Austen herself. Some mistakes from the first edition are corrected by the printer, but some important ones are not (for example in the delineation of speeches at p.46 and p.345, and, especially in the 1817 edition, some new errors are introduced. The first edition is thus as good a copy-text as any. Readers who seek a more detailed textual history should consult Chapman.

p.46 l.19 "When is your next ball to be, Lizzy?"] A puts this on the same line as Kitty's previous comment. But Kitty is unlikely to grant her sister sole possession of a ball by referring to it as "your" ball. This must be spoken by Mr. Bennet, uninterested in his other daughters, and seeking out a way of letting slip his meeting with Bingley. Chapman therefore puts it in a new line, as here.

p.51 l.7 wasting your time] Chapman; wasting your mite A. Not noted in Chapman.

p.82 l.32 and her daughters] Chapman; and her daughter A. Lydia may put herself centre-stage, but Kitty is one of the party too.

p.122 l.11 Bingleys'] Chapman; Bingley's A. The use of the apostrophe very often does not conform to modern conventions, but this is one of the few places where it alters meaning.

p.157 l.31 he proceeded to inform] Chapman; he proceeds to inform A.

p.173 l.36 Miss Lucas paid her farewell] Chapman; Miss Lucy paid her farewell A.

p.234 l.19 "We have dined nine times at Rosings,"]. A puts this on the same line as Elizabeth's previous agreement. But its triviality, and the naming of Elizabeth as the source of the following mental addition in the next line, means this must be spoken by Maria. The emendation follows Chapman.

p.246 l.29 Wherever you and Jane are known] Chapman; Whenever you and Jane are known A. Apart from being more idiomatic, the former reading, from the third edition, makes more sense in the context of the novel's concern with geographical as well as social mobility; and it would be easy to misread an n for an r.

p.249 l.32 on his side] Chapman; on her side A.

p.251 l.35 by carrying] Chapman; my carrying A. The grammar requires *by*: Chapman suggests in his note that it originally read "by my carrying" (p.393: an elision of one word being more likely here than a substitution of one for another).

p.268 l.6 their relationship to herself] Chapman; her relationship to herself A. Not noted by Chapman.

p.317 ll.23-4 a gulf impassable] Chapman; a gulf impossible A.

p.324 l.15 the Little Theatre] Chapman; the little Theatre A. A specific establishment of this name is being referred to.

p.345 l.27 "And how impossible in others!"] This speech is run together with the previous one in A. But as the next line is clearly Jane's *this* one must be Elizabeth's ironic reply. Follows Chapman.

p.362 l.26 sister has resigned it,] Chapman; sister had resigned A.

p.378 l.18 and thinking for *your*] Chapman; and think for *you're* A.

p.378 l.26 you knew no actual] Chapman; you know no actual A.

PRIDE

AND

PREJUDICE:

A NOVEL.

IN THREE VOLUMES.

BY THE

AUTHOR OF " SENSE AND SENSIBILITY."

VOL. I.

London:

PRINTED FOR T. EGERTON,

MILITARY LIBRARY, WHITEHALL.

1813.

marriage plot
female aggression
men as bank accts.

Jane + Elizabeth
vs.
Marianne + Elinor

CHAPTER I.

IT is a truth universally acknowledged, that a single man in possession of a good fortune, must be in want of a wife.

However little known the feelings or views of such a man may be on his first entering a neighbourhood, this truth is so well fixed in the minds of the surrounding families, that he is considered as the rightful property of some one or other of their daughters. *S+S*

"My dear Mr. Bennet," said his lady to him one day, "have you heard that Netherfield Park is let at last?"

Mr. Bennet replied that he had not.

"But it is," returned she; "for Mrs. Long has just been here, and she told me all about it."

Mr. Bennet made no answer.

"Do not you want to know who has taken it?" cried his wife impatiently.

"*You* want to tell me, and I have no objection to hearing it."

This was invitation enough.

"Why, my dear, you must know, Mrs. Long says that Netherfield is taken by a young man of large fortune from the north of England; that he came down on Monday in a chaise and four to see the place, and was so much delighted with it that he agreed with Mr. Morris immediately; that he is to take possession before Michaelmas, and some of his servants are to be in the house by the end of next week."[1]

"What is his name?"

"Bingley."

"Is he married or single?"

---

1   A chaise is a three-seater carriage, designed for travelling, in this case drawn by four horses. Bingley's direction of travel hints at the entrepreneurial origins of his wealth, the north being the cradle of England's successive (water- and coal-powered) industrial revolutions. Michaelmas is the 29 September, and "one of the four quarter-days of the English business year" (*OED*) on which, for example, tenancies and leases would begin and end.

"Oh! single, my dear, to be sure! A single man of large fortune; four or five thousand a year. What a fine thing for our girls!"

"How so? how can it affect them?"

"My dear Mr. Bennet," replied his wife, "how can you be so tiresome! You must know that I am thinking of his marrying one of them."

"Is that his design in settling here?"

"Design! nonsense, how can you talk so! But it is very likely that he *may* fall in love with one of them, and therefore you must visit him as soon as he comes."

"I see no occasion for that. You and the girls may go, or you may send them by themselves, which perhaps will be still better, for as you are as handsome as any of them, Mr. Bingley might like you the best of the party."

"My dear, you flatter me. I certainly *have* had my share of beauty, but I do not pretend to be any thing extraordinary now. When a woman has five grown up daughters, she ought to give over thinking of her own beauty."

"In such cases, a woman has not often much beauty to think of."

"But, my dear, you must indeed go and see Mr. Bingley when he comes into the neighbourhood."

"It is more than I engage for, I assure you."

"But consider your daughters. Only think what an establishment it would be for one of them. Sir William and Lady Lucas are determined to go, merely on that account, for in general you know they visit no new comers. Indeed you must go, for it will be impossible for *us* to visit him, if you do not."

"You are over scrupulous surely. I dare say Mr. Bingley will be very glad to see you; and I will send a few lines by you to assure him of my hearty consent to his marrying which ever he chuses of the girls; though I must throw in a good word for my little Lizzy."

"I desire you will do no such thing. Lizzy is not a bit better than the others; and I am sure she is not half so handsome as Jane, nor half so good humoured as Lydia. But you are always giving *her* the preference."

"They have none of them much to recommend them," replied he; "they are all silly and ignorant like other girls; but Lizzy has something more of quickness than her sisters."

"Mr. Bennet, how can you abuse your own children in such a way? You take delight in vexing me. You have no compassion on my poor nerves."

"You mistake me, my dear. I have a high respect for your nerves. They are my old friends. I have heard you mention them with consideration these twenty years at least."

"Ah! you do not know what I suffer."

"But I hope you will get over it, and live to see many young men of four thousand a year come into the neighbourhood."

"It will be no use to us, if twenty such should come since you will not visit them."

"Depend upon it, my dear, that when there are twenty, I will visit them all."

Mr. Bennet was so odd a mixture of quick parts, sarcastic humour, reserve, and caprice, that the experience of three and twenty years had been insufficient to make his wife understand his character. *Her* mind was less difficult to develope.[1] She was a woman of mean understanding, little information, and uncertain temper. When she was discontented she fancied herself nervous.[2] The business of her life was to get her daughters married; its solace was visiting and news.

CHAPTER II.

MR. BENNET was among the earliest of those who waited on Mr. Bingley. He had always intended to visit him, though to the last always assuring his wife that he should not go; and till the evening after the visit was paid, she had no knowledge of it. It was then disclosed in the following manner. Observing his second daughter employed in trimming a hat, he suddenly addressed her with,

"I hope Mr. Bingley will like it Lizzy."

---

1 That is, less difficult to discover.
2 "Nervous" here refers to a medically-recognised condition of over-sensitivity to the world around one, an ailment to which women were considered uniquely prone.

"We are not in a way to know *what* Mr. Bingley likes," said her mother resentfully, "since we are not to visit."

"But you forget, mama," said Elizabeth, "that we shall meet him at the assemblies, and that Mrs. Long has promised to introduce him."[1]

"I do not believe Mrs. Long will do any such thing. She has two neices of her own. She is a selfish, hypocritical woman, and I have no opinion of her."

"No more have I," said Mr. Bennet; "and I am glad to find that you do not depend on her serving you."

Mrs. Bennet deigned not to make any reply; but unable to contain herself, began scolding one of her daughters.

"Don't keep coughing so, Kitty, for heaven's sake! Have a little compassion on my nerves. You tear them to pieces."

"Kitty has no discretion in her coughs," said her father; "she times them ill."

"I do not cough for my own amusement," replied Kitty fretfully.

"When is your next ball to be, Lizzy?"

"To-morrow fortnight."

"Aye, so it is," cried her mother, "and Mrs. Long does not come back till the day before; so, it will be impossible for her to introduce him, for she will not know him herself."

"Then, my dear, you may have the advantage of your friend, and introduce Mr. Bingley to *her*."

"Impossible, Mr. Bennet, impossible, when I am not acquainted with him myself; how can you be so teazing?"

"I honour your circumspection. A fortnight's acquaintance is certainly very little. One cannot know what a man really is by the end of a fortnight. But if *we* do not venture, somebody else will; and after all, Mrs. Long and her neices must stand their chance; and therefore, as she will think it an act of kindness, if you decline the office, I will take it on myself."

The girls stared at their father. Mrs. Bennet said only, "Nonsense, nonsense!"

---

1   Public assemblies such as those referred to here were regular social events, usually paid for by subscription, involving both dancing and refreshments, held in the public spaces of a local inn or, in the larger towns, purpose-built assembly rooms.

"What can be the meaning of that emphatic exclamation?" cried he. "Do you consider the forms of introduction, and the stress that is laid on them, as nonsense? I cannot quite agree with you *there*. What say you, Mary? for you are a young lady of deep reflection I know, and read great books, and make extracts."

Mary wished to say something very sensible, but knew not how.

"While Mary is adjusting her ideas," he continued, "let us return to Mr. Bingley."

"I am sick of Mr. Bingley," cried his wife.

"I am sorry to hear *that;* but why did not you tell me so before? If I had known as much this morning, I certainly would not have called on him. It is very unlucky; but as I have actually paid the visit, we cannot escape the acquaintance now."

The astonishment of the ladies was just what he wished; that of Mrs. Bennet perhaps surpassing the rest; though when the first tumult of joy was over, she began to declare that it was what she had expected all the while.

"How good it was in you, my dear Mr. Bennet! But I knew I should persuade you at last. I was sure you loved your girls too well to neglect such an acquaintance. Well, how pleased I am! and it is such a good joke, too, that you should have gone this morning, and never said a word about it till now."

"Now, Kitty, you may cough as much as you chuse," said Mr. Bennet; and, as he spoke, he left the room, fatigued with the raptures of his wife.

"What an excellent father you have, girls," said she, when the door was shut. "I do not know how you will ever make him amends for his kindness; or me either, for that matter. At our time of life, it is not so pleasant I can tell you, to be making new acquaintance every day; but for your sakes, we would do any thing. Lydia, my love, though you *are* the youngest, I dare say Mr. Bingley will dance with you at the next ball."

"Oh!" said Lydia stoutly, "I am not afraid; for though I *am* the youngest, I'm the tallest."

The rest of the evening was spent in conjecturing how soon he would return Mr. Bennet's visit, and determining when they should ask him to dinner.

CHAPTER III.

NOT all that Mrs. Bennet, however, with the assistance of her five daughters, could ask on the subject was sufficient to draw from her husband any satisfactory description of Mr. Bingley. They attacked him in various ways; with barefaced questions, ingenious suppositions, and distant surmises; but he eluded the skill of them all; and they were at last obliged to accept the second-hand intelligence of their neighbour Lady Lucas. Her report was highly favourable. Sir William had been delighted with him. He was quite young, wonderfully handsome, extremely agreeable, and to crown the whole, he meant to be at the next assembly with a large party. Nothing could be more delightful! To be fond of dancing was a certain step towards falling in love; and very lively hopes of Mr. Bingley's heart were entertained.

"If I can but see one of my daughters happily settled at Netherfield," said Mrs. Bennet to her husband, "and all the others equally well married, I shall have nothing to wish for."

In a few days Mr. Bingley returned Mr. Bennet's visit, and sat about ten minutes with him in his library. He had entertained hopes of being admitted to a sight of the young ladies, of whose beauty he had heard much; but he saw only the father. The ladies were somewhat more fortunate, for they had the advantage of ascertaining from an upper window, that he wore a blue coat and rode a black horse.

An invitation to dinner was soon afterwards dispatched; and already had Mrs. Bennet planned the courses that were to do credit to her housekeeping, when an answer arrived which deferred it all. Mr. Bingley was obliged to be in town the following day, and consequently unable to accept the honour of their invitation, &c. Mrs. Bennet was quite disconcerted.[1] She could not imagine what business he could have in town so soon after his arrival in Hertfordshire; and she began to fear

---

1 "In town" here as elsewhere means "in London." We learn in Volume II, chapter iv that Meryton is only 24 miles (39 km) from the capital. This can seem a long way to the neighbours of Meryton, however: see the differing perceptions of Elizabeth and Darcy in Volume II, chapter ix.

that he might be always flying about from one place to another, and never settled at Netherfield as he ought to be. Lady Lucas quieted her fears a little by starting the idea of his being gone to London only to get a large party for the ball; and a report soon followed that Mr. Bingley was to bring twelve ladies and seven gentlemen with him to the assembly. The girls grieved over such a large number of ladies; but were comforted the day before the ball by hearing, that instead of twelve, he had brought only six with him from London, his five sisters and a cousin. And when the party entered the assembly room, it consisted of only five altogether; Mr. Bingley, his two sisters, the husband of the eldest, and another young man.

Mr. Bingley was good looking and gentlemanlike; he had a pleasant countenance, and easy, unaffected manners. His sisters were fine women, with an air of decided fashion. His brother-in-law, Mr. Hurst, merely looked the gentleman; but his friend Mr. Darcy soon drew the attention of the room by his fine, tall person, handsome features, noble mein;[1] and the report which was in general circulation within five minutes after his entrance, of his having ten thousand a year. The gentlemen pronounced him to be a fine figure of a man, the ladies declared he was much handsomer than Mr. Bingley, and he was looked at with great admiration for about half the evening, till his manners gave a disgust which turned the tide of his popularity; for he was discovered to be proud, to be above his company, and above being pleased; and not all his large estate in Derbyshire could then save him from having a most forbidding, disagreeable countenance, and being unworthy to be compared with his friend.

Mr. Bingley had soon made himself acquainted with all the principal people in the room; he was lively and unreserved, danced every dance, was angry that the ball closed so early, and talked of giving one himself at Netherfield. Such amiable qualities must speak for themselves. What a contrast between him and his friend! Mr. Darcy danced only once with Mrs. Hurst and once with Miss Bingley, declined being introduced to any

---

1   "Person" here as elsewhere means (physical) figure.

other lady, and spent the rest of the evening in walking about the room, speaking occasionally to one of his own party. His character was decided.[1] He was the proudest, most disagreeable man in the world, and every body hoped that he would never come there again. Amongst the most violent against him was Mrs. Bennet, whose dislike of his general behaviour, was sharpened into particular resentment, by his having slighted one of her daughters.

Elizabeth Bennet had been obliged, by the scarcity of gentlemen, to sit down for two dances;[2] and during part of that time, Mr. Darcy had been standing near enough for her to overhear a conversation between him and Mr. Bingley, who came from the dance for a few minutes, to press his friend to join it.

"Come, Darcy," said he, "I must have you dance. I hate to see you standing about by yourself in this stupid manner. You had much better dance."

"I certainly shall not. You know how I detest it, unless I am particularly acquainted with my partner. At such an assembly as this, it would be insupportable. Your sisters are engaged, and there is not another woman in the room, whom it would not be a punishment to me to stand up with."

"I would not be so fastidious as you are," cried Bingley, "for a kingdom! Upon my honour, I never met with so many pleasant girls in my life, as I have this evening; and there are several of them you see uncommonly pretty."

"*You* are dancing with the only handsome girl in the room," said Mr. Darcy, looking at the eldest Miss Bennet.

"Oh! she is the most beautiful creature I ever beheld! But there is one of her sisters sitting down just behind you, who is very pretty, and I dare say, very agreeable. Do let me ask my partner to introduce you."

"Which do you mean?" and turning round, he looked for a

---

1   Austen's irony plays on different possible meanings of both words: his character (his actual personality) was decided (obvious); and his character (the role that he is to play in the life and gossip of Meryton) was decided (upon, by the locals in their discussion of him). Elizabeth uses "character" in a similar way in her second sentence in the next chapter.

2   Partners usually danced a pair of dances at a time together, as is clear from Mrs. Bennet's description later in the chapter of Bingley's itinerary among the local girls.

moment at Elizabeth, till catching her eye, he withdrew his own and coldly said, "She is tolerable; but not handsome enough to tempt *me;* and I am in no humour at present to give consequence to young ladies who are slighted by other men. You had better return to your partner and enjoy her smiles, for you are wasting your time with me."

Mr. Bingley followed his advice. Mr. Darcy walked off; and Elizabeth remained with no very cordial feelings towards him. She told the story however with great spirit among her friends; for she had a lively, playful disposition, which delighted in any thing ridiculous.

The evening altogether passed off pleasantly to the whole family. Mrs. Bennet had seen her eldest daughter much admired by the Netherfield party. Mr. Bingley had danced with her twice, and she had been distinguished by his sisters.[1] Jane was as much gratified by this, as her mother could be, though in a quieter way. Elizabeth felt Jane's pleasure. Mary had heard herself mentioned to Miss Bingley as the most accomplished girl in the neighbourhood;[2] and Catherine and Lydia had been fortunate enough to be never without partners, which was all that they had yet learnt to care for at a ball. They returned therefore in good spirits to Longbourn, the village where they lived, and of which they were the principal inhabitants. They found Mr. Bennet still up. With a book he was regardless of time; and on the present occasion he had a good deal of curiosity as to the event of an evening which had raised such splendid expectations. He had rather hoped that all his wife's views on the stranger would be disappointed; but he soon found that he had a very different story to hear.

"Oh! my dear Mr. Bennet," as she entered the room, "we have had a most delightful evening, a most excellent ball. I wish you had been there. Jane was so admired, nothing could be like it. Every body said how well she looked; and Mr. Bingley thought her quite beautiful, and danced with her twice. Only think of *that* my dear; he actually danced with her twice; and she was the only creature in the room that he asked a second

---

1   That is, picked out for special attention.

2   On what it meant to be "accomplished," see Introduction, p.21.

time. First of all, he asked Miss Lucas. I was so vexed to see him stand up with her; but, however, he did not admire her at all: indeed, nobody can, you know; and he seemed quite struck with Jane as she was going down the dance. So, he enquired who she was, and got introduced, and asked her for the two next. Then, the two third he danced with Miss King, and the two fourth with Maria Lucas, and the two fifth with Jane again, and the two sixth with Lizzy, and the Boulanger."[1]

"If he had had any compassion for *me*," cried her husband impatiently, "he would not have danced half so much! For God's sake, say no more of his partners. Oh! that he had sprained his ancle in the first dance!"

"Oh! my dear," continued Mrs. Bennet, "I am quite delighted with him. He is so excessively handsome! and his sisters are charming women. I never in my life saw any thing more elegant than their dresses. I dare say the lace upon Mrs. Hurst's gown—"

Here she was interrupted again. Mr. Bennet protested against any description of finery. She was therefore obliged to seek another branch of the subject, and related, with much bitterness of spirit and some exaggeration, the shocking rudeness of Mr. Darcy.

"But I can assure you," she added, "that Lizzy does not lose much by not suiting *his* fancy; for he is a most disagreeable, horrid man, not at all worth pleasing. So high and so conceited that there was no enduring him! He walked here, and he walked there, fancying himself so very great! Not handsome enough to dance with! I wish you had been there, my dear, to have given him one of your set downs. I quite detest the man."

CHAPTER IV.

WHEN Jane and Elizabeth were alone, the former, who had been cautious in her praise of Mr. Bingley before, expressed to her sister how very much she admired him.

---

1 A French country dance.

"He is just what a young man ought to be," said she, "sensible, good humoured, lively; and I never saw such happy manners!—so much ease, with such perfect good breeding!"

"He is also handsome," replied Elizabeth, "which a young man ought likewise to be, if he possibly can. His character is thereby complete."

"I was very much flattered by his asking me to dance a second time. I did not expect such a compliment."

"Did not you? *I* did for you. But that is one great difference between us. Compliments always take *you* by surprise, and *me* never. What could be more natural than his asking you again? He could not help seeing that you were about five times as pretty as every other woman in the room. No thanks to his gallantry for that. Well, he certainly is very agreeable, and I give you leave to like him. You have liked many a stupider person."

"Dear Lizzy!"

"Oh! you are a great deal too apt you know, to like people in general. You never see a fault in any body. All the world are good and agreeable in your eyes. I never heard you speak ill of a human being in my life."

"I would wish not to be hasty in censuring any one; but I always speak what I think."

"I know you do; and it is *that* which makes the wonder. With *your* good sense, to be honestly blind to the follies and nonsense of others! Affectation of candour is common enough;—one meets it every where. But to be candid without ostentation or design—to take the good of every body's character and make it still better, and say nothing of the bad—belongs to you alone. And so, you like this man's sisters too, do you? Their manners are not equal to his."

"Certainly not; at first. But they are very pleasing women when you converse with them. Miss Bingley is to live with her brother and keep his house; and I am much mistaken if we shall not find a very charming neighbour in her."

Elizabeth listened in silence, but was not convinced; their behaviour at the assembly had not been calculated to please in general; and with more quickness of observation and less pliancy of temper than her sister, and with a judgment too unassailed by any attention to herself, she was very little disposed to approve them. They were in fact very fine ladies;[1] not deficient in good humour when they were pleased, nor in the power of being agreeable where they chose it; but proud and conceited. They were rather handsome, had been educated in one of the first private seminaries in town,[2] had a fortune of twenty thousand pounds, were in the habit of spending more than they ought, and of associating with people of rank; and were therefore in every respect entitled to think well of themselves, and meanly of others. They were of a respectable family in the north of England; a circumstance more deeply impressed on their memories than that their brother's fortune and their own had been acquired by trade.

Mr. Bingley inherited property to the amount of nearly an hundred thousand pounds from his father, who had intended to purchase an estate, but did not live to do it. — Mr. Bingley intended it likewise, and sometimes made choice of his county; but as he was now provided with a good house and the liberty of a manor,[3] it was doubtful to many of those who best knew the easiness of his temper, whether he might not spend the remainder of his days at Netherfield, and leave the next generation to purchase.

His sisters were very anxious for his having an estate of his own; but though he was now established only as a tenant, Miss Bingley was by no means unwilling to preside at his table, nor was Mrs. Hurst, who had married a man of more fashion than fortune, less disposed to consider his house as her home when it suited her. Mr. Bingley had not been of age two years, when he was tempted by an accidental recommendation to look at Netherfield House. He did look at it and into it for half an hour, was pleased with the situation and the principal rooms,

---

1 "Fine" here is a synonym for "elegant" or "fashionable": a signifier of status, habitual social circle and the accompanying attitudes, rather than of the speaker's general approbation.

2 That is, in one of the best boarding schools.

3 That is, the manor-house of Netherfield comes with the right to shoot game on its estate: a right fiercely monopolised by eighteenth-century landowners.

satisfied with what the owner said in its praise, and took it immediately.

Between him and Darcy there was a very steady friendship, in spite of a great opposition of character. — Bingley was endeared to Darcy by the easiness, openness, ductility of his temper, though no disposition could offer a greater contrast to his own, and though with his own he never appeared dissatisfied. On the strength of Darcy's regard Bingley had the firmest reliance, and of his judgment the highest opinion. In understanding, Darcy was the superior. Bingley was by no means deficient, but Darcy was clever. He was at the same time haughty, reserved, and fastidious, and his manners, though well bred, were not inviting. In that respect his friend had greatly the advantage. Bingley was sure of being liked wherever he appeared, Darcy was continually giving offence.

The manner in which they spoke of the Meryton assembly was sufficiently characteristic. Bingley had never met with pleasanter people or prettier girls in his life; every body had been most kind and attentive to him, there had been no formality, no stiffness, he had soon felt acquainted with all the room; and as to Miss Bennet,[1] he could not conceive an angel more beautiful. Darcy, on the contrary, had seen a collection of people in whom there was little beauty and no fashion, for none of whom he had felt the smallest interest, and from none received either attention or pleasure. Miss Bennet he acknowledged to be pretty, but she smiled too much.

Mrs. Hurst and her sister allowed it to be so — but still they admired her and liked her, and pronounced her to be a sweet girl, and one whom they should not object to know more of. Miss Bennet was therefore established as a sweet girl, and their brother felt authorised by such commendation to think of her as he chose.

---

1 "Miss Bennet," in contexts which involve more than one of the sisters, usually picks out Jane as the eldest.

CHAPTER V.

WITHIN a short walk of Longbourn lived a family with whom the Bennets were particularly intimate. Sir William Lucas had been formerly in trade in Meryton, where he had made a tolerable fortune and risen to the honour of knighthood by an address to the King, during his mayoralty.[1] The distinction had perhaps been felt too strongly. It had given him a disgust to his business and to his residence in a small market town; and quitting them both, he had removed with his family to a house about a mile from Meryton, denominated from that period Lucas Lodge, where he could think with pleasure of his own importance, and, unshackled by business, occupy himself solely in being civil to all the world. For though elated by his rank, it did not render him supercilious; on the contrary, he was all attention to every body. By nature inoffensive, friendly and obliging, his presentation at St. James's had made him courteous.

Lady Lucas was a very good kind of woman, not too clever to be a valuable neighbour to Mrs. Bennet. — They had several children. The eldest of them a sensible, intelligent young woman, about twenty-seven, was Elizabeth's intimate friend.

That the Miss Lucases and the Miss Bennets should meet to talk over a ball was absolutely necessary; and the morning after the assembly brought the former to Longbourn to hear and to communicate.

"*You* began the evening well, Charlotte," said Mrs. Bennet with civil self-command to Miss Lucas. "You were Mr. Bingley's first choice."

"Yes;—but he seemed to like his second better."

"Oh! — you mean Jane, I suppose—because he danced with her twice. To be sure that *did* seem as if he admired her — indeed I rather believe he *did*—I heard something about it — but I hardly know what—something about Mr. Robinson."

---

1 King George III reigned 1760-1811. For an example of the sort of routine syco-
phancy for which Sir William was thus rewarded, see the extract from the *Sussex
Weekly Advertiser* for May 11, 1795 in Appendix F3; such ceremonies were carried
out at St. James's Palace in London, the heart of court life. Note how the Lucas
family share a bourgeois aspiration to rural gentility with the much richer Bingleys.

"Perhaps you mean what I overheard between him and Mr. Robinson; did not I mention it to you? Mr. Robinson's asking him how he liked our Meryton assemblies, and whether he did not think there were a great many pretty women in the room, and *which* he thought the prettiest? and his answering immediately to the last question — Oh! the eldest Miss Bennet beyond a doubt, there cannot be two opinions on that point."

"Upon my word! — Well, that was very decided indeed — that does seem as if — but however, it may all come to nothing you know."

"*My* overhearings were more to the purpose than *yours*, Eliza," said Charlotte. "Mr. Darcy is not so well worth listening to as his friend, is he? — Poor Eliza! — to be only just *tolerable*."

"I beg you would not put it into Lizzy's head to be vexed by his ill-treatment; for he is such a disagreeable man that it would be quite a misfortune to be liked by him. Mrs. Long told me last night that he sat close to her for half an hour without once opening his lips."

"Are you quite sure, Ma'am? — is not there a little mistake?" said Jane. — "I certainly saw Mr. Darcy speaking to her."

"Aye — because she asked him at last how he liked Netherfield, and he could not help answering her; — but she said he seemed very angry at being spoke to."

"Miss Bingley told me," said Jane, "that he never speaks much unless among his intimate acquaintance. With *them* he is remarkably agreeable."

"I do not believe a word of it, my dear. If he had been so very agreeable he would have talked to Mrs. Long. But I can guess how it was; every body says that he is ate up with pride, and I dare say he had heard somehow that Mrs. Long does not keep a carriage, and had come to the ball in a hack chaise."[1]

"I do not mind his not talking to Mrs. Long," said Miss Lucas, "but I wish he had danced with Eliza."

"Another time, Lizzy," said her mother, "I would not dance with *him*, if I were you."

"I believe, Ma'am, I may safely promise you *never* to dance with him."

---

1 That is, in a hired carriage.

"His pride," said Miss Lucas, "does not offend *me* so much as pride often does, because there is an excuse for it. One cannot wonder that so very fine a young man, with family, fortune, every thing in his favour, should think highly of himself. If I may so express it, he has a *right* to be proud."

"That is very true," replied Elizabeth, "and I could easily forgive *his* pride, if he had not mortified *mine*."

"Pride," observed Mary, who piqued herself upon the solidity of her reflections, "is a very common failing I believe. By all that I have ever read, I am convinced that it is very common indeed, that human nature is particularly prone to it, and that there are very few of us who do not cherish a feeling of self-complacency on the score of some quality or other, real or imaginary. Vanity and pride are different things, though the words are often used synonimously. A person may be proud without being vain. Pride relates more to our opinion of ourselves, vanity to what we would have others think of us."

"If I were as rich as Mr. Darcy," cried a young Lucas who came with his sisters, "I should not care how proud I was. I would keep a pack of foxhounds, and drink a bottle of wine every day."[1]

"Then you would drink a great deal more than you ought," said Mrs. Bennet; "and if I were to see you at it I should take away your bottle directly."

The boy protested that she should not; she continued to declare that she would, and the argument ended only with the visit.

---

1 This "young Lucas" paradoxically evokes a much older image of the masculine gentry life than the one presented by Austen: a life dedicated to hunting and heavy drinking, and hostile to courts and courtiers, most familiar in the figure of Squire Western in Henry Fielding's *Tom Jones* (1749).

CHAPTER VI.

THE ladies of Longbourn soon waited on those of Nether-field.[1] The visit was returned in due form. Miss Bennet's pleasing manners grew on the good will of Mrs. Hurst and Miss Bingley; and though the mother was found to be intolerable and the younger sisters not worth speaking to, a wish of being better acquainted with *them,* was expressed towards the two eldest. By Jane this attention was received with the greatest pleasure; but Elizabeth still saw superciliousness in their treatment of every body, hardly excepting even her sister, and could not like them; though their kindness to Jane, such as it was, had a value as arising in all probability from the influence of their brother's admiration. It was generally evident whenever they met, that he *did* admire her; and to *her* it was equally evident that Jane was yielding to the preference which she had begun to entertain for him from the first, and was in a way to be very much in love; but she considered with pleasure that it was not likely to be discovered by the world in general, since Jane united with great strength of feeling, a composure of temper and a uniform cheerfulness of manner, which would guard her from the suspicions of the impertinent. She mentioned this to her friend Miss Lucas.

"It may perhaps be pleasant," replied Charlotte, "to be able to impose on the public in such a case; but it is sometimes a disadvantage to be so very guarded. If a woman conceals her affection with the same skill from the object of it, she may lose the opportunity of fixing him; and it will then be but poor consolation to believe the world equally in the dark. There is so much of gratitude or vanity in almost every attachment, that it is not safe to leave any to itself. We can all *begin* freely—a slight preference is natural enough; but there are very few of us who have heart enough to be really in love without encouragement. In nine cases out of ten, a woman had better shew *more* affection than she feels.[2] Bingley likes your sister undoubt-

---

1 That is, visited them.

2 The value placed on feminine self-effacement or "modesty" made it difficult for women to signal their desire unambiguously: see John Gregory's comments on this virtue in appendix B.2.

edly; but he may never do more than like her, if she does not help him on."

"But she does help him on, as much as her nature will allow. If *I* can perceive her regard for him, he must be a simpleton indeed not to discover it too."

"Remember, Eliza, that he does not know Jane's disposition as you do."

"But if a woman is partial to a man, and does not endeavour to conceal it, he must find it out."

"Perhaps he must, if he sees enough of her. But though Bingley and Jane meet tolerably often, it is never for many hours together; and as they always see each other in large mixed parties, it is impossible that every moment should be employed in conversing together. Jane should therefore make the most of every half hour in which she can command his attention. When she is secure of him, there will be leisure for falling in love as much as she chuses."

"Your plan is a good one," replied Elizabeth, "where nothing is in question but the desire of being well married; and if I were determined to get a rich husband, or any husband, I dare say I should adopt it. But these are not Jane's feelings; she is not acting by design. As yet, she cannot even be certain of the degree of her own regard, nor of its reasonableness. She has known him only a fortnight. She danced four dances with him at Meryton; she saw him one morning at his own house, and has since dined in company with him four times. This is not quite enough to make her understand his character."

"Not as you represent it. Had she merely *dined* with him, she might only have discovered whether he had a good appetite; but you must remember that four evenings have been also spent together—and four evenings may do a great deal."

"Yes; these four evenings have enabled them to ascertain that they both like Vingt-un better than Commerce;[1] but with respect to any other leading characteristic, I do not imagine that much has been unfolded."

"Well," said Charlotte, "I wish Jane success with all my heart;

---

1 Card-games.

and if she were married to him tomorrow, I should think she had as good a chance of happiness, as if she were to be studying his character for a twelvemonth. Happiness in marriage is entirely a matter of chance. If the dispositions of the parties are ever so well known to each other, or ever so similar beforehand, it does not advance their felicity in the least. They always continue to grow sufficiently unlike afterwards to have their share of vexation; and it is better to know as little as possible of the defects of the person with whom you are to pass your life."

"You make me laugh, Charlotte; but it is not sound. You know it is not sound, and that you would never act in this way yourself."

Occupied in observing Mr. Bingley's attentions to her sister, Elizabeth was far from suspecting that she was herself becoming an object of some interest in the eyes of his friend. Mr. Darcy had at first scarcely allowed her to be pretty; he had looked at her without admiration at the ball; and when they next met, he looked at her only to criticise. But no sooner had he made it clear to himself and his friends that she had hardly a good feature in her face, than he began to find it was rendered uncommonly intelligent by the beautiful expression of her dark eyes. To this discovery succeeded some others equally mortifying. Though he had detected with a critical eye more than one failure of perfect symmetry in her form, he was forced to acknowledge her figure to be light and pleasing; and in spite of his asserting that her manners were not those of the fashionable world, he was caught by their easy playfulness. Of this she was perfectly unaware;—to her he was only the man who made himself agreeable no where, and who had not thought her handsome enough to dance with.

He began to wish to know more of her, and as a step towards conversing with her himself, attended to her conversation with others. His doing so drew her notice. It was at Sir William Lucas's, where a large party were assembled.

"What does Mr. Darcy mean," said she to Charlotte, "by listening to my conversation with Colonel Forster?"

"That is a question which Mr. Darcy only can answer."

"But if he does it any more I shall certainly let him know

that I see what he is about. He has a very satirical eye, and if I do not begin by being impertinent myself, I shall soon grow afraid of him."

On his approaching them soon afterwards, though without seeming to have any intention of speaking, Miss Lucas defied her friend to mention such a subject to him, which immediately provoking Elizabeth to do it, she turned to him and said,

"Did not you think, Mr. Darcy, that I expressed myself uncommonly well just now, when I was teazing Colonel Forster to give us a ball at Meryton?"

"With great energy;—but it is a subject which always makes a lady energetic."

"You are severe on us."

"It will be *her* turn soon to be teazed," said Miss Lucas. "I am going to open the instrument, Eliza, and you know what follows."[1]

"You are a very strange creature by way of a friend!—always wanting me to play and sing before any body and every body!—If my vanity had taken a musical turn, you would have been invaluable, but as it is, I would really rather not sit down before those who must be in the habit of hearing the very best performers." On Miss Lucas's persevering, however, she added, "Very well; if it must be so, it must." And gravely glancing at Mr. Darcy, "There is a fine old saying, which every body here is of course familiar with—'Keep your breath to cool your porridge,'—and I shall keep mine to swell my song."

Her performance was pleasing, though by no means capital. After a song or two, and before she could reply to the entreaties of several that she would sing again, she was eagerly succeeded at the instrument by her sister Mary, who having, in consequence of being the only plain one in the family, worked hard for knowledge and accomplishments, was always impatient for display.

Mary had neither genius nor taste;[2] and though vanity had given her application, it had given her likewise a pedantic air and conceited manner, which would have injured a higher

---

1 By the 1790s, "the instrument" is the piano-forte rather than the harpsichord.
2 Genius here means no more than natural talent.

degree of excellence than she had reached. Elizabeth, easy and unaffected, had been listened to with much more pleasure, though not playing half so well; and Mary, at the end of a long concerto, was glad to purchase praise and gratitude by Scotch and Irish airs, at the request of her younger sisters, who with some of the Lucases and two or three officers joined eagerly in dancing at one end of the room.

Mr. Darcy stood near them in silent indignation at such a mode of passing the evening, to the exclusion of all conversation, and was too much engrossed by his own thoughts to perceive that Sir William Lucas was his neighbour, till Sir William thus began.

"What a charming amusement for young people this is, Mr. Darcy! — There is nothing like dancing after all. — I consider it as one of the first refinements of polished societies."

"Certainly, Sir;—and it has the advantage also of being in vogue amongst the less polished societies of the world. — Every savage can dance."

Sir William only smiled. "Your friend performs delightfully;" he continued after a pause, on seeing Bingley join the group;—"and I doubt not that you are an adept in the science yourself, Mr. Darcy."

"You saw me dance at Meryton, I believe, Sir."

"Yes, indeed, and received no inconsiderable pleasure from the sight. Do you often dance at St. James's?"

"Never, sir."

"Do you not think it would be a proper compliment to the place?"

"It is a compliment which I never pay to any place if I can avoid it."

"You have a house in town, I conclude."

Mr. Darcy bowed.

"I had once some thoughts of fixing in town myself—for I am fond of superior society; but I did not feel quite certain that the air of London would agree with Lady Lucas."

He paused in hopes of an answer; but his companion was not disposed to make any; and Elizabeth at that instant moving towards them, he was struck with the notion of doing a very gallant thing, and called out to her,

"My dear Miss Eliza, why are not you dancing?—Mr. Darcy, you must allow me to present this young lady to you as a very desirable partner. —You cannot refuse to dance, I am sure, when so much beauty is before you." And taking her hand, he would have given it to Mr. Darcy, who, though extremely surprised, was not unwilling to receive it, when she instantly drew back, and said with some discomposure to Sir William,

"Indeed, Sir, I have not the least intention of dancing. —I entreat you not to suppose that I moved this way in order to beg for a partner."

Mr. Darcy with grave propriety requested to be allowed the honour of her hand; but in vain. Elizabeth was determined; nor did Sir William at all shake her purpose by his attempt at persuasion.

"You excel so much in the dance, Miss Eliza, that it is cruel to deny me the happiness of seeing you; and though this gentleman dislikes the amusement in general, he can have no objection, I am sure, to oblige us for one half hour."

"Mr. Darcy is all politeness," said Elizabeth, smiling.

"He is indeed—but considering the inducement, my dear Miss Eliza, we cannot wonder at his complaisance; for who would object to such a partner?"

Elizabeth looked archly, and turned away. Her resistance had not injured her with the gentleman, and he was thinking of her with some complacency,[1] when thus accosted by Miss Bingley.

"I can guess the subject of your reverie."

"I should imagine not."

"You are considering how insupportable it would be to pass many evenings in this manner—in such society; and indeed I am quite of your opinion. I was never more annoyed! The insipidity and yet the noise; the nothingness and yet the self-importance of all these people! —What would I give to hear your strictures on them!"

"Your conjecture is totally wrong, I assure you. My mind

---

1   That is, with pleasure and approval: compare Sir William's use of "complaisance" to mean "readiness to please" in the previous paragraph. There is not necessarily any hint in this usage that Darcy is taking future success with Elizabeth for granted: it occurs again to describe Elizabeth's attitude to Bingley at the start of chapter viii.

was more agreeably engaged. I have been meditating on the very great pleasure which a pair of fine eyes in the face of a pretty woman can bestow."

Miss Bingley immediately fixed her eyes on his face, and desired he would tell her what lady had the credit of inspiring such reflections. Mr. Darcy replied with great intrepidity,

"Miss Elizabeth Bennet."

"Miss Elizabeth Bennet!" repeated Miss Bingley. "I am all astonishment. How long has she been such a favourite? — and pray when am I to wish you joy?"

"That is exactly the question which I expected you to ask. A lady's imagination is very rapid; it jumps from admiration to love, from love to matrimony in a moment. I knew you would be wishing me joy."

"Nay, if you are so serious about it, I shall consider the matter as absolutely settled. You will have a charming mother-in-law, indeed, and of course she will be always at Pemberley with you."

He listened to her with perfect indifference, while she chose to entertain herself in this manner, and as his composure convinced her that all was safe, her wit flowed long.

CHAPTER VII.

MR. BENNET's property consisted almost entirely in an estate of two thousand a year, which, unfortunately for his daughters, was entailed in default of heirs male, on a distant relation; and their mother's fortune, though ample for her situation in life, could but ill supply the deficiency of his.[1] Her father had been an attorney in Meryton, and had left her four thousand pounds.

---

1   For a discussion of entailment, and a comparison of the various levels of income enjoyed by characters in this novel, see introduction. Mrs. Bennet's "fortune" is an income "settled on" her as part of the marriage agreement: that is, one deriving from a fund set up by both families and held in trust for her (married women being legally incapable of holding property in their own right). Such settlements offered women their only financial security in the event of a husband proving spendthrift, going bankrupt, or indeed dying first without a son on an entailed estate.

She had a sister married to a Mr. Phillips, who had been a clerk to their father, and succeeded him in the business, and a brother settled in London in a respectable line of trade.

The village of Longbourn was only one mile from Meryton; a most convenient distance for the young ladies, who were usually tempted thither three or four times a week, to pay their duty to their aunt and to a milliner's shop just over the way. The two youngest of the family, Catherine and Lydia, were particularly frequent in these attentions; their minds were more vacant than their sisters', and when nothing better offered, a walk to Meryton was necessary to amuse their morning hours and furnish conversation for the evening; and however bare of news the country in general might be, they always contrived to learn some from their aunt. At present, indeed, they were well supplied both with news and happiness by the recent arrival of a militia regiment in the neighbourhood; it was to remain the whole winter, and Meryton was the head quarters.[1]

Their visits to Mrs. Philips were now productive of the most interesting intelligence. Every day added something to their knowledge of the officers' names and connections. Their lodgings were not long a secret, and at length they began to know the officers themselves. Mr. Philips visited them all, and this opened to his nieces a source of felicity unknown before. They could talk of nothing but officers; and Mr. Bingley's large fortune, the mention of which gave animation to their mother, was worthless in their eyes when opposed to the regimentals of an ensign.[2]

After listening one morning to their effusions on this subject, Mr. Bennet coolly observed,

"From all that I can collect by your manner of talking, you must be two of the silliest girls in the country. I have suspected it some time, but I am now convinced."

Catherine was disconcerted, and made no answer; but Lydia,

---

1 For the nature of the militia presence in southern England in this period, see Appendix F.

2 "Regimentals" are British army uniform, almost always involving a scarlet jacket, the "red-coat" of Mrs. Bennet's later comment. An ensign was the lowest rank of commissioned officer.

with perfect indifference, continued to express her admiration of Captain Carter, and her hope of seeing him in the course of the day, as he was going the next morning to London.

"I am astonished, my dear," said Mrs. Bennet, "that you should be so ready to think your own children silly. If I wished to think slightingly of any body's children, it should not be of my own however."

"If my children are silly I must hope to be always sensible of it."[1]

"Yes—but as it happens, they are all of them very clever."

"This is the only point, I flatter myself, on which we do not agree. I had hoped that our sentiments coincided in every particular, but I must so far differ from you as to think our two youngest daughters uncommonly foolish."

"My dear Mr. Bennet, you must not expect such girls to have the sense of their father and mother. — When they get to our age I dare say they will not think about officers any more than we do. I remember the time when I liked a red-coat myself very well—and indeed so I do still at my heart; and if a smart young colonel, with five or six thousand a year, should want one of my girls, I shall not say nay to him; and I thought Colonel Forster looked very becoming the other night at Sir William's in his regimentals."

"Mama," cried Lydia, "my aunt says that Colonel Forster and Captain Carter do not go so often to Miss Watson's as they did when they first came; she sees them now very often standing in Clarke's library."[2]

Mrs. Bennet was prevented replying by the entrance of the footman with a note for Miss Bennet; it came from Netherfield, and the servant waited for an answer. Mrs. Bennet's eyes sparkled with pleasure, and she was eagerly calling out, while her daughter read,

---

1 That is, conscious of it.

2 Most small towns had a circulating library, often attached to a bookseller, from which, for an annual subscription, books could be borrowed a volume at a time. The core of their business was novels: Mr. Collins makes this equation towards the end of chapter xiv of the present volume. But as Miss Watson appears nowhere else in the novel, the significance of the officers' altered habits remains obscure.

"Well, Jane, who is it from? what is it about? what does he say? well, Jane, make haste and tell us; make haste, my love."

"It is from Miss Bingley," said Jane, and then read it aloud.

"My dear Friend,

"IF you are not so compassionate as to dine to-day with Louisa and me, we shall be in danger of hating each other for the rest of our lives, for a whole day's tête-à-tête between two women can never end without a quarrel. Come as soon as you can on the receipt of this. My brother and the gentlemen are to dine with the officers. Yours ever,

"CAROLINE BINGLEY."

"With the officers!" cried Lydia. "I wonder my aunt did not tell us of *that*."

"Dining out," said Mrs. Bennet, "that is very unlucky."

"Can I have the carriage," said Jane.

"No, my dear, you had better go on horseback, because it seems likely to rain; and then you must stay all night."

"That would be a good scheme," said Elizabeth, "if you were sure that they would not offer to send her home."

"Oh! but the gentlemen will have Mr. Bingley's chaise to go to Meryton; and the Hursts have no horses to theirs."

"I had much rather go in the coach."

"But, my dear, your father cannot spare the horses, I am sure. They are wanted in the farm, Mr. Bennet, are not they?"

"They are wanted in the farm much oftener than I can get them."

"But if you have got them to-day," said Elizabeth, "my mother's purpose will be answered."

She did at last extort from her father an acknowledgment that the horses were engaged. Jane was therefore obliged to go on horseback, and her mother attended her to the door with many cheerful prognostics of a bad day. Her hopes were answered; Jane had not been gone long before it rained hard. Her sisters were uneasy for her, but her mother was delighted. The rain continued the whole evening without intermission; Jane certainly could not come back.

"This was a lucky idea of mine, indeed!" said Mrs. Bennet,

more than once, as if the credit of making it rain were all her own. Till the next morning, however, she was not aware of all the felicity of her contrivance. Breakfast was scarcely over when a servant from Netherfield brought the following note for Elizabeth:

"My dearest Lizzy,

"I FIND myself very unwell this morning, which, I suppose, is to be imputed to my getting wet through yesterday. My kind friends will not hear of my returning home till I am better. They insist also on my seeing Mr. Jones — therefore do not be alarmed if you should hear of his having been to me — and excepting a sore-throat and head-ache there is not much the matter with me.

"Yours, &c."

"Well, my dear," said Mr. Bennet, when Elizabeth had read the note aloud, "if your daughter should have a dangerous fit of illness, if she should die, it would be a comfort to know that it was all in pursuit of Mr. Bingley, and under your orders."

"Oh! I am not at all afraid of her dying. People do not die of little trifling colds. She will be taken good care of. As long as she stays there, it is all very well. I would go and see her, if I could have the carriage."

Elizabeth, feeling really anxious, was determined to go to her, though the carriage was not to be had; and as she was no horse-woman, walking was her only alternative. She declared her resolution.

"How can you be so silly," cried her mother, "as to think of such a thing, in all this dirt! You will not be fit to be seen when you get there."

"I shall be very fit to see Jane — which is all I want."

"Is this a hint to me, Lizzy," said her father, "to send for the horses?"

"No, indeed. I do not wish to avoid the walk. The distance is nothing, when one has a motive; only three miles. I shall be back by dinner."

"I admire the activity of your benevolence," observed Mary, "but every impulse of feeling should be guided by reason; and, in my opinion, exertion should always be in proportion to what is required."[1]

"We will go as far as Meryton with you," said Catherine and Lydia. — Elizabeth accepted their company, and the three young ladies set off together.

"If we make haste," said Lydia, as they walked along, "perhaps we may see something of Captain Carter before he goes."

In Meryton they parted; the two youngest repaired to the lodgings of one of the officers' wives, and Elizabeth continued her walk alone, crossing field after field at a quick pace, jumping over stiles and springing over puddles with impatient activity, and finding herself at last within view of the house, with weary ancles, dirty stockings, and a face glowing with the warmth of exercise.[2]

She was shewn into the breakfast-parlour, where all but Jane were assembled, and where her appearance created a great deal of surprise. — That she should have walked three miles so early in the day, in such dirty weather, and by herself, was almost incredible to Mrs. Hurst and Miss Bingley; and Elizabeth was convinced that they held her in contempt for it. She was received, however, very politely by them; and in their brother's manners there was something better than politeness; there was good humour and kindness. — Mr. Darcy said very little, and Mr. Hurst nothing at all. The former was divided between admiration of the brilliancy which exercise had given to her complexion, and doubt as to the occasion's justifying her coming so far alone. The latter was thinking only of his breakfast.

Her enquiries after her sister were not very favourably answered. Miss Bennet had slept ill, and though up, was very feverish and not well enough to leave her room. Elizabeth was glad to be taken to her immediately; and Jane, who had only

---

1 Mary begins by reproducing the terms of eighteenth-century moral philosophy, in which moral action is prompted by natural sympathy or feeling rather than by reason; her last comment shades into conduct-book inanity, however, and she seems not to notice the incongruity.

2 Claudia Johnson (1988, p.22) notes that Elizabeth's "activity" here repeats but redeems the unseemly, petticoat-muddying "energy" of the "mad feminist" caricature, Brigetina Botherim, in Elizabeth Hamilton's reactionary novel, *Memoirs of Modern Philosophers* (1800; ed. Clare Grogan, Peterborough, ON: Broadview, 2000).

been withheld by the fear of giving alarm or inconvenience, from expressing in her note how much she longed for such a visit, was delighted at her entrance. She was not equal, however, to much conversation, and when Miss Bingley left them together, could attempt little beside expressions of gratitude for the extraordinary kindness she was treated with. Elizabeth silently attended her.

When breakfast was over, they were joined by the sisters; and Elizabeth began to like them herself, when she saw how much affection and solicitude they shewed for Jane. The apothecary came, and having examined his patient, said, as might be supposed, that she had caught a violent cold, and that they must endeavour to get the better of it; advised her to return to bed, and promised her some draughts.[1] The advice was followed readily, for the feverish symptoms increased, and her head ached acutely. Elizabeth did not quit her room for a moment, nor were the other ladies often absent; the gentlemen being out, they had in fact nothing to do elsewhere.

When the clock struck three, Elizabeth felt that she must go; and very unwillingly said so. Miss Bingley offered her the carriage, and she only wanted a little pressing to accept it, when Jane testified such concern in parting with her, that Miss Bingley was obliged to convert the offer of the chaise into an invitation to remain at Netherfield for the present. Elizabeth most thankfully consented, and a servant was dispatched to Longbourn to acquaint the family with her stay, and bring back a supply of clothes.

CHAPTER VIII.

AT five o'clock the two ladies retired to dress, and at half past six Elizabeth was summoned to dinner. To the civil enquiries which then poured in, and amongst which she had the pleasure of distinguishing the much superior solicitude of Mr. Bingley's, she could not make a very favourable answer. Jane was by no

---

1   That is, of medicine. The apothecary is the Mr. Jones mentioned in Jane's letter home.

means better. The sisters, on hearing this, repeated three or four times how much they were grieved, how shocking it was to have a bad cold, and how excessively they disliked being ill themselves; and then thought no more of the matter: and their indifference towards Jane when not immediately before them, restored Elizabeth to the enjoyment of all her original dislike.

Their brother, indeed, was the only one of the party whom she could regard with any complacency. His anxiety for Jane was evident, and his attentions to herself most pleasing, and they prevented her feeling herself so much an intruder as she believed she was considered by the others. She had very little notice from any but him. Miss Bingley was engrossed by Mr. Darcy, her sister scarcely less so; and as for Mr. Hurst, by whom Elizabeth sat, he was an indolent man, who lived only to eat, drink, and play at cards, who when he found her prefer a plain dish to a ragout, had nothing to say to her.[1]

When dinner was over, she returned directly to Jane, and Miss Bingley began abusing her as soon as she was out of the room. Her manners were pronounced to be very bad indeed, a mixture of pride and impertinence; she had no conversation, no stile, no taste, no beauty. Mrs. Hurst thought the same, and added,

"She has nothing, in short, to recommend her, but being an excellent walker. I shall never forget her appearance this morning. She really looked almost wild."

"She did indeed, Louisa. I could hardly keep my countenance. Very nonsensical to come at all! Why must *she* be scampering about the country, because her sister had a cold? Her hair so untidy, so blowsy!"

"Yes, and her petticoat; I hope you saw her petticoat, six inches deep in mud, I am absolutely certain; and the gown which had been let down to hide it, not doing its office."[2]

---

1 A ragout is a highly-seasoned stew: shorthand for fashionable French cuisine as opposed to plain English fare.
2 The petticoat referred to here was an underskirt, designed to be seen (usually) through an opening in the front of a gown or overskirt: Elizabeth has tried to hide the former by closing this gap in the latter.

"Your picture may be very exact, Louisa," said Bingley; "but this was all lost upon me. I thought Miss Elizabeth Bennet looked remarkably well, when she came into the room this morning. Her dirty petticoat quite escaped my notice."

"*You* observed it, Mr. Darcy, I am sure," said Miss Bingley; "and I am inclined to think that you would not wish to see *your sister* make such an exhibition."

"Certainly not."

"To walk three miles, or four miles, or five miles, or whatever it is, above her ancles in dirt, and alone, quite alone! what could she mean by it? It seems to me to shew an abominable sort of conceited independence, a most country town indifference to decorum."

"It shews an affection for her sister that is very pleasing," said Bingley.

"I am afraid, Mr. Darcy," observed Miss Bingley in a half whisper, "that this adventure has rather affected your admiration of her fine eyes."

"Not at all," he replied; "they were brightened by the exercise." — A short pause followed this speech, and Mrs. Hurst began again.

"I have an excessive regard for Jane Bennet, she is really a very sweet girl, and I wish with all my heart she were well settled. But with such a father and mother, and such low connections, I am afraid there is no chance of it."

"I think I have heard you say, that their uncle is an attorney in Meryton."

"Yes; and they have another, who lives somewhere near Cheapside."[1]

"That is capital," added her sister, and they both laughed heartily.

"If they had uncles enough to fill *all* Cheapside," cried Bingley, "it would not make them one jot less agreeable."

"But it must very materially lessen their chance of marrying men of any consideration in the world," replied Darcy.

---

1 A district of the commercial City of London, rather than the fashionable West End.

To this speech Bingley made no answer; but his sisters gave it their hearty assent, and indulged their mirth for some time at the expense of their dear friend's vulgar relations.

With a renewal of tenderness, however, they repaired to her room on leaving the dining-parlour, and sat with her till summoned to coffee.[1] She was still very poorly, and Elizabeth would not quit her at all till late in the evening, when she had the comfort of seeing her asleep, and when it appeared to her rather right than pleasant that she should go down stairs herself. On entering the drawing-room she found the whole party at loo,[2] and was immediately invited to join them; but suspecting them to be playing high she declined it, and making her sister the excuse, said she would amuse herself for the short time she could stay below with a book. Mr. Hurst looked at her with astonishment.

"Do you prefer reading to cards?" said he; "that is rather singular."

"Miss Eliza Bennet," said Miss Bingley, "despises cards. She is a great reader and has no pleasure in any thing else."

"I deserve neither such praise nor such censure," cried Elizabeth; "I am *not* a great reader, and I have pleasure in many things."

"In nursing your sister I am sure you have pleasure," said Bingley; "and I hope it will soon be increased by seeing her quite well."

Elizabeth thanked him from her heart, and then walked towards a table where a few books were lying. He immediately offered to fetch her others; all that his library afforded.

"And I wish my collection were larger for your benefit and my own credit; but I am an idle fellow, and though I have not many, I have more than I ever look into."

Elizabeth assured him that she could suit herself perfectly with those in the room.

---

1 Women would normally have retired to the drawing room after dinner, allowing an interlude for single-sex conversation on both sides before the men joined them there for tea or coffee.

2 Loo is a card game. Gambling, often for very high stakes, was a characteristic vice of the eighteenth-century élite.

"I am astonished," said Miss Bingley, "that my father should have left so small a collection of books. — What a delightful library you have at Pemberley, Mr. Darcy!"

"It ought to be good," he replied, "it has been the work of many generations."

"And then you have added so much to it yourself, you are always buying books."

"I cannot comprehend the neglect of a family library in such days as these."

"Neglect! I am sure you neglect nothing that can add to the beauties of that noble place. Charles, when you build *your* house, I wish it may be half as delightful as Pemberley."

"I wish it may."

"But I would really advise you to make your purchase in that neighbourhood, and take Pemberley for a kind of model. There is not a finer county in England than Derbyshire."

"With all my heart; I will buy Pemberley itself if Darcy will sell it."

"I am talking of possibilities, Charles."

"Upon my word, Caroline, I should think it more possible to get Pemberley by purchase than by imitation."

Elizabeth was so much caught by what passed, as to leave her very little attention for her book; and soon laying it wholly aside, she drew near the card-table, and stationed herself between Mr. Bingley and his eldest sister, to observe the game.

"Is Miss Darcy much grown since the spring?" said Miss Bingley; "will she be as tall as I am?"

"I think she will. She is now about Miss Elizabeth Bennet's height, or rather taller."

"How I long to see her again! I never met with anybody who delighted me so much. Such a countenance, such manners! — and so extremely accomplished for her age! Her performance on the piano-forte is exquisite."

"It is amazing to me," said Bingley, "how young ladies can have patience to be so very accomplished, as they all are."

"All young ladies accomplished! My dear Charles, what do you mean?"

"Yes, all of them, I think. They all paint tables, cover skreens and net purses.[1] I scarcely know any one who cannot do all this, and I am sure I never heard a young lady spoken of for the first time, without being informed that she was very accomplished."

"Your list of the common extent of accomplishments," said Darcy, "has too much truth. The word is applied to many a woman who deserves it no otherwise than by netting a purse, or covering a skreen. But I am very far from agreeing with you in your estimation of ladies in general. I cannot boast of knowing more than half a dozen, in the whole range of my acquaintance, that are really accomplished."

"Nor I, I am sure," said Miss Bingley.

"Then," observed Elizabeth, "you must comprehend a great deal in your idea of an accomplished women."

"Yes; I do comprehend a great deal in it."[2]

"Oh! certainly," cried his faithful assistant, "no one can be really esteemed accomplished, who does not greatly surpass what is usually met with. A woman must have a thorough knowledge of music, singing, drawing, dancing, and the modern languages, to deserve the word; and besides all this, she must possess a certain something in her air and manner of walking, the tone of her voice, her address and expressions, or the word will be but half deserved."

"All this she must possess," added Darcy, "and to all this she must yet add something more substantial, in the improvement of her mind by extensive reading."

"I am no longer surprised at your knowing *only* six accomplished women. I rather wonder now at your knowing *any*."

"Are you so severe upon your own sex, as to doubt the possibility of all this?"

"*I* never saw such a woman. *I* never saw such capacity, and taste, and application, and elegance, as you describe, united."

---

1 Painting plain domestic items such as occasional tables or crockery (see chapter xvi in this volume) with decorative designs was a routine feminine "accomplishment." The latter two activities are types of embroidery: for "skreens" see note to p.188.

2 That is, include a great deal in it.

Mrs. Hurst and Miss Bingley both cried out against the injustice of her implied doubt, and were both protesting that they knew many women who answered this description, when Mr. Hurst called them to order, with bitter complaints of their inattention to what was going forward. As all conversation was thereby at an end, Elizabeth soon afterwards left the room.

"Eliza Bennet," said Miss Bingley, when the door was closed on her, "is one of those young ladies who seek to recommend themselves to the other sex, by undervaluing their own; and with many men, I dare say, it succeeds. But, in my opinion, it is a paltry device, a very mean art."

"Undoubtedly," replied Darcy, to whom this remark was chiefly addressed, "there is meanness in *all* the arts which ladies sometimes condescend to employ for captivation. Whatever bears affinity to cunning is despicable."

Miss Bingley was not so entirely satisfied with this reply as to continue the subject.

Elizabeth joined them again only to say that her sister was worse, and that she could not leave her. Bingley urged Mr. Jones's being sent for immediately; while his sisters, convinced that no country advice could be of any service, recommended an express[1] to town for one of the most eminent physicians. This, she would not hear of; but she was not so unwilling to comply with their brother's proposal; and it was settled that Mr. Jones should be sent for early in the morning, if Miss Bennet were not decidedly better. Bingley was quite uncomfortable; his sisters declared that they were miserable. They solaced their wretchedness, however, by duets after supper, while he could find no better relief to his feelings than by giving his house-keeper directions that every possible attention might be paid to the sick lady and her sister.

---

1 The term "express" could refer to either a specially-commissioned messenger, or the letter that he carried.

CHAPTER IX.

ELIZABETH passed the chief of the night in her sister's room, and in the morning had the pleasure of being able to send a tolerable answer to the enquiries which she very early received from Mr. Bingley by a house-maid, and some time afterwards from the two elegant ladies who waited on his sisters. In spite of this amendment, however, she requested to have a note sent to Longbourn, desiring her mother to visit Jane, and form her own judgment of her situation. The note was immediately dispatched, and its contents as quickly complied with. Mrs. Bennet, accompanied by her two youngest girls, reached Netherfield soon after the family breakfast.

Had she found Jane in any apparent danger, Mrs. Bennet would have been very miserable; but being satisfied on seeing her that her illness was not alarming, she had no wish of her recovering immediately, as her restoration to health would probably remove her from Netherfield. She would not listen therefore to her daughter's proposal of being carried home; neither did the apothecary, who arrived about the same time, think it at all advisable. After sitting a little while with Jane, on Miss Bingley's appearance and invitation, the mother and three daughters all attended her into the breakfast parlour. Bingley met them with hopes that Mrs. Bennet had not found Miss Bennet worse than she expected.

"Indeed I have, Sir," was her answer. "She is a great deal too ill to be moved. Mr. Jones says we must not think of moving her. We must trespass a little longer on your kindness."

"Removed!" cried Bingley. "It must not be thought of. My sister, I am sure, will not hear of her removal."

"You may depend upon it, Madam," said Miss Bingley, with cold civility, "that Miss Bennet shall receive every possible attention while she remains with us."

Mrs. Bennet was profuse in her acknowledgments.

"I am sure," she added, "if it was not for such good friends I do not know what would become of her, for she is very ill indeed, and suffers a vast deal, though with the greatest patience in the world, which is always the way with her, for she has, without exception, the sweetest temper I ever met with. I often tell my other girls they are nothing to *her*. You have a sweet room here, Mr. Bingley, and a charming prospect over that gravel walk. I do not know a place in the country that is equal to Netherfield. You will not think of quitting it in a hurry I hope, though you have but a short lease."

"Whatever I do is done in a hurry," replied he; "and therefore if I should resolve to quit Netherfield, I should probably be off in five minutes. At present, however, I consider myself as quite fixed here."

"That is exactly what I should have supposed of you," said Elizabeth.

"You begin to comprehend me, do you?" cried he, turning towards her.

"Oh! yes—I understand you perfectly."

"I wish I might take this for a compliment; but to be so easily seen through I am afraid is pitiful."

"That is as it happens. It does not necessarily follow that a deep, intricate character is more or less estimable than such a one as yours."

"Lizzy," cried her mother, "remember where you are, and do not run on in the wild manner that you are suffered to do at home."

"I did not know before," continued Bingley immediately, "that you were a studier of character. It must be an amusing study."

"Yes; but intricate characters are the *most* amusing. They have at least that advantage."

"The country," said Darcy, "can in general supply but few subjects for such a study. In a country neighbourhood you move in a very confined and unvarying society."

"But people themselves alter so much, that there is something new to be observed in them for ever."

"Yes, indeed," cried Mrs. Bennet, offended by his manner of mentioning a country neighbourhood. "I assure you there is quite as much of *that* going on in the country as in town."

Every body was surprised; and Darcy, after looking at her for a moment, turned silently away. Mrs. Bennet, who fancied she had gained a complete victory over him, continued her triumph.

"I cannot see that London has any great advantage over the country for my part, except the shops and public places. The country is a vast deal pleasanter, is not it, Mr. Bingley?"

"When I am in the country," he replied, "I never wish to leave it; and when I am in town it is pretty much the same. They have each their advantages, and I can be equally happy in either."

"Aye — that is because you have the right disposition. But that gentleman," looking at Darcy, "seemed to think the country was nothing at all."

"Indeed, Mama, you are mistaken," said Elizabeth, blushing for her mother. "You quite mistook Mr. Darcy. He only meant that there were not such a variety of people to be met with in the country as in town, which you must acknowledge to be true."

"Certainly, my dear, nobody said there were; but as to not meeting with many people in this neighbourhood, I believe there are few neighbourhoods larger. I know we dine with four and twenty families."

Nothing but concern for Elizabeth could enable Bingley to keep his countenance. His sister was less delicate, and directed her eye towards Mr. Darcy with a very expressive smile. Elizabeth, for the sake of saying something that might turn her mother's thoughts, now asked her if Charlotte Lucas had been at Longbourn since *her* coming away.

"Yes, she called yesterday with her father. What an agreeable man Sir William is, Mr. Bingley — is not he? so much the man of fashion! so genteel and so easy! — He has always something to say to every body. — *That* is my idea of good breeding; and those persons who fancy themselves very important and never open their mouths, quite mistake the matter."

"Did Charlotte dine with you?"

"No, she would go home. I fancy she was wanted about the mince pies. For my part, Mr. Bingley, *I* always keep servants that can do their own work; *my* daughters are brought up differently.[1] But every body is to judge for themselves, and the Lucases are very good sort of girls, I assure you. It is a pity they are not handsome! Not that *I* think Charlotte so *very* plain — but then she is our particular friend."

"She seems a very pleasant young woman," said Bingley.

"Oh! dear, yes; — but you must own she is very plain. Lady Lucas herself has often said so, and envied me Jane's beauty. I do not like to boast of my own child, but to be sure, Jane — one does not often see any body better looking. It is what every body says. I do not trust my own partiality. When she was only fifteen, there was a gentleman at my brother Gardiner's in town, so much in love with her, that my sister-in-law was sure he would make her an offer before we came away. But however er he did not. Perhaps he thought her too young. However, he wrote some verses on her, and very pretty they were."

"And so ended his affection," said Elizabeth impatiently. "There has been many a one, I fancy, overcome in the same way. I wonder who first discovered the efficacy of poetry in driving away love!"

"I have been used to consider poetry as the *food* of love," said Darcy.[2]

"Of a fine, stout, healthy love it may. Every thing nourishes what is strong already. But if it be only a slight, thin sort of inclination, I am convinced that one good sonnet will starve it entirely away."

Darcy only smiled; and the general pause which ensued made Elizabeth tremble lest her mother should be exposing herself again. She longed to speak, but could think of nothing to say; and after a short silence Mrs. Bennet began repeating her thanks to Mr. Bingley for his kindness to Jane, with an apology for troubling him also with Lizzy. Mr. Bingley was

---

1 That all her housekeeping is performed by servants, and none by her daughters, is an important signifier for Mrs. Bennet of her distance from her middle-class origins: she repeats it to Mr. Collins at the end of chapter xiii in this volume. We very rarely see those servants, however, and not until the start of that chapter are any of them referred to by name.

2 Darcy alludes to Duke Orsino's words in the opening line of Shakespeare's *Twelfth Night* ("If music be the food of love, play on").

unaffectedly civil in his answer, and forced his younger sister to be civil also, and say what the occasion required. She performed her part indeed without much graciousness, but Mrs. Bennet was satisfied, and soon afterwards ordered her carriage. Upon this signal, the youngest of her daughters put herself forward. The two girls had been whispering to each other during the whole visit, and the result of it was, that the youngest should tax Mr. Bingley with having promised on his first coming into the country to give a ball at Netherfield.

Lydia was a stout, well-grown girl of fifteen, with a fine complexion and good-humoured countenance; a favourite with her mother, whose affection had brought her into public at an early age.[1] She had high animal spirits, and a sort of natural self-consequence, which the attentions of the officers, to whom her uncle's good dinners and her own easy manners recommended her, had increased into assurance. She was very equal therefore to address Mr. Bingley on the subject of the ball, and abruptly reminded him of his promise; adding, that it would be the most shameful thing in the world if he did not keep it. His answer to this sudden attack was delightful to their mother's ear.

"I am perfectly ready, I assure you, to keep my engagement; and when your sister is recovered, you shall if you please name the very day of the ball. But you would not wish to be dancing while she is ill."

Lydia declared herself satisfied. "Oh! yes — it would be much better to wait till Jane was well, and by that time most likely Captain Carter would be at Meryton again. And when you have given *your* ball," she added, "I shall insist on their giving one also. I shall tell Colonel Forster it will be quite a shame if he does not."

Mrs. Bennet and her daughters then departed, and Elizabeth

---

1   A young woman's first appearance "in public" at assemblies and other social gatherings was something of a turning point in her life, marking as it did her entry into the marriage market. In higher metropolitan circles, this moment was formalised as "coming out" (which might include the ritual of being presented at court to the royal family at, for example, the celebration of a royal birthday), as the Lucas girls propose to themselves in chapter xxii of this volume.

returned instantly to Jane, leaving her own and her relations' behaviour to the remarks of the two ladies and Mr. Darcy; the latter of whom, however, could not be prevailed on to join in their censure of *her*, in spite of all Miss Bingley's witticisms on *fine eyes*.

CHAPTER X.

THE day passed much as the day before had done. Mrs. Hurst and Miss Bingley had spent some hours of the morning with the invalid, who continued, though slowly, to mend; and in the evening Elizabeth joined their party in the drawing-room. The loo table, however, did not appear. Mr. Darcy was writing, and Miss Bingley, seated near him, was watching the progress of his letter, and repeatedly calling off his attention by messages to his sister. Mr. Hurst and Mr. Bingley were at piquet,[1] and Mrs. Hurst was observing their game.

Elizabeth took up some needlework, and was sufficiently amused in attending to what passed between Darcy and his companion. The perpetual commendations of the lady either on his hand-writing, or on the evenness of his lines, or on the length of his letter, with the perfect unconcern with which her praises were received, formed a curious dialogue, and was exactly in unison with her opinion of each.

"How delighted Miss Darcy will be to receive such a letter!"

He made no answer.

"You write uncommonly fast."

"You are mistaken. I write rather slowly."

"How many letters you must have occasion to write in the course of the year! Letters of business too! How odious I should think them!"

"It is fortunate, then, that they fall to my lot instead of to yours."

"Pray tell your sister that I long to see her."

"I have already told her so once, by your desire."

---

1 Piquet is a card-game which unlike loo (see note on p.74) requires only two players.

"I am afraid you do not like your pen. Let me mend it for you. I mend pens remarkably well."

"Thank you—but I always mend my own."

"How can you contrive to write so even?"

He was silent.

"Tell your sister I am delighted to hear of her improvement on the harp, and pray let her know that I am quite in raptures with her beautiful little design for a table, and I think it infinitely superior to Miss Grantley's."

"Will you give me leave to defer your raptures till I write again?—At present I have not room to do them justice."

"Oh! it is of no consequence. I shall see her in January. But do you always write such charming long letters to her, Mr. Darcy?"

"They are generally long; but whether always charming, it is not for me to determine."

"It is a rule with me, that a person who can write a long letter, with ease, cannot write ill."

"That will not do for a compliment to Darcy, Caroline," cried her brother—"because he does *not* write with ease. He studies too much for words of four syllables.—Do not you, Darcy?"

"My stile of writing is very different from yours."

"Oh!" cried Miss Bingley, "Charles writes in the most careless way imaginable. He leaves out half his words, and blots the rest."

"My ideas flow so rapidly that I have not time to express them—by which means my letters sometimes convey no ideas at all to my correspondents."

"Your humility, Mr. Bingley," said Elizabeth, "must disarm reproof."

"Nothing is more deceitful," said Darcy, "than the appearance of humility. It is often only carelessness of opinion, and sometimes an indirect boast."

"And which of the two do you call *my* little recent piece of modesty?"

"The indirect boast;—for you are really proud of your defects in writing, because you consider them as proceeding from a rapidity of thought and carelessness of execution, which if not estimable, you think at least highly interesting. The power of doing any thing with quickness is always much prized by the possessor, and often without any attention to the imperfection of the performance. When you told Mrs. Bennet this morning that if you ever resolved on quitting Netherfield you should be gone in five minutes, you meant it to be a sort of panegyric, of compliment to yourself—and yet what is there so very laudable in a precipitance which must leave very necessary business undone, and can be of no real advantage to yourself or any one else?"

"Nay," cried Bingley, "this is too much, to remember at night all the foolish things that were said in the morning. And yet, upon my honour, I believed what I said of myself to be true, and I believe it at this moment. At least, therefore, I did not assume the character of needless precipitance merely to shew off before the ladies."

"I dare say you believed it; but I am by no means convinced that you would be gone with such celerity. Your conduct would be quite as dependant on chance as that of any man I know; and if, as you were mounting your horse, a friend were to say, 'Bingley, you had better stay till next week,' you would probably do it, you would probably not go—and, at another word, might stay a month."

"You have only proved by this," cried Elizabeth, "that Mr. Bingley did not do justice to his own disposition. You have shewn him off now much more than he did himself."

"I am exceedingly gratified," said Bingley, "by your converting what my friend says into a compliment on the sweetness of my temper. But I am afraid you are giving it a turn which that gentleman did by no means intend; for he would certainly think the better of me, if under such a circumstance I were to give a flat denial, and ride off as fast as I could."

"Would Mr. Darcy then consider the rashness of your original intention as atoned for by your obstinacy in adhering to it?"

"Upon my word I cannot exactly explain the matter; Darcy must speak for himself."

"You expect me to account for opinions which you chuse to call mine, but which I have never acknowledged. Allowing the case, however, to stand according to your representation, you must remember, Miss Bennet, that the friend who is supposed to desire his return to the house, and the delay of his plan, has merely desired it, asked it without offering one argument in favour of its propriety."

"To yield readily — easily — to the *persuasion* of a friend is no merit with you."

"To yield without conviction is no compliment to the understanding of either."

"You appear to me, Mr. Darcy, to allow nothing for the influence of friendship and affection. A regard for the requester would often make one readily yield to a request without waiting for arguments to reason one into it. I am not particularly speaking of such a case as you have supposed about Mr. Bingley. We may as well wait, perhaps, till the circumstance occurs, before we discuss the discretion of his behaviour thereupon. But in general and ordinary cases between friend and friend, where one of them is desired by the other to change a resolution of no very great moment, should you think ill of that person for complying with the desire, without waiting to be argued into it?"

"Will it not be advisable, before we proceed on this subject, to arrange with rather more precision the degree of importance which is to appertain to this request, as well as the degree of intimacy subsisting between the parties?"

"By all means," cried Bingley; "Let us hear all the particulars, not forgetting their comparative height and size; for that will have more weight in the argument, Miss Bennet, than you may be aware of. I assure you that if Darcy were not such a great tall fellow, in comparison with myself, I should not pay him half so much deference. I declare I do not know a more aweful object than Darcy, on particular occasions, and in particular places; at his own house especially, and of a Sunday evening when he has nothing to do."

Mr. Darcy smiled; but Elizabeth thought she could perceive that he was rather offended; and therefore checked her laugh.

Miss Bingley warmly resented the indignity he had received in an expostulation with her brother for talking such nonsense.

"I see your design, Bingley," said his friend. — "You dislike an argument, and want to silence this."

"Perhaps I do. Arguments are too much like disputes. If you and Miss Bennet will defer yours till I am out of the room, I shall be very thankful; and then you may say whatever you like of me."

"What you ask," said Elizabeth, "is no sacrifice on my side; and Mr. Darcy had much better finish his letter."

Mr. Darcy took her advice, and did finish his letter.

When that business was over, he applied to Miss Bingley and Elizabeth for the indulgence of some music. Miss Bingley moved with alacrity to the piano-forte, and after a polite request that Elizabeth would lead the way, which the other as politely and more earnestly negatived, she seated herself.

Mrs. Hurst sang with her sister, and while they were thus employed Elizabeth could not help observing as she turned over some music books that lay on the instrument, how frequently Mr. Darcy's eyes were fixed on her. She hardly knew how to suppose that she could be an object of admiration to so great a man; and yet that he should look at her because he disliked her, was still more strange. She could only imagine however at last, that she drew his notice because there was a something about her more wrong and reprehensible, according to his ideas of right, than in any other person present. The supposition did not pain her. She liked him too little to care for his approbation.

After playing some Italian songs, Miss Bingley varied the charm by a lively Scotch air; and soon afterwards Mr. Darcy, drawing near Elizabeth, said to her —

"Do not you feel a great inclination, Miss Bennet, to seize such an opportunity of dancing a reel?"

She smiled, but made no answer. He repeated the question, with some surprise at her silence.

"Oh!" said she, "I heard you before; but I could not immediately determine what to say in reply. You wanted me, I know, to say 'Yes,' that you might have the pleasure of despising my taste; but I always delight in overthrowing those kind of schemes, and cheating a person of their premeditated contempt. I have therefore made up my mind to tell you, that I do not want to dance a reel at all—and now despise me if you dare."

"Indeed I do not dare."

Elizabeth, having rather expected to affront him, was amazed at his gallantry; but there was a mixture of sweetness and archness in her manner which made it difficult for her to affront anybody; and Darcy had never been so bewitched by any woman as he was by her. He really believed, that were it not for the inferiority of her connections, he should be in some danger.

Miss Bingley saw, or suspected enough to be jealous; and her great anxiety for the recovery of her dear friend Jane, received some assistance from her desire of getting rid of Elizabeth.

She often tried to provoke Darcy into disliking her guest, by talking of their supposed marriage, and planning his happiness in such an alliance.

"I hope," said she, as they were walking together in the shrubbery the next day, "you will give your mother-in-law a few hints, when this desirable event takes place, as to the advantage of holding her tongue; and if you can compass it, do cure the younger girls of running after the officers. —And, if I may mention so delicate a subject, endeavour to check that little something, bordering on conceit and impertinence, which your lady possesses."

"Have you any thing else to propose for my domestic felicity?"

"Oh! yes. —Do let the portraits of your uncle and aunt Philips be placed in the gallery at Pemberley. Put them next to your great uncle the judge. They are in the same profession, you know; only in different lines. As for your Elizabeth's picture, you must not attempt to have it taken, for what painter could do justice to those beautiful eyes?"

"It would not be easy, indeed, to catch their expression, but their colour and shape, and the eye-lashes, so remarkably fine, might be copied."

At that moment they were met from another walk, by Mrs. Hurst and Elizabeth herself.

"I did not know that you intended to walk," said Miss Bingley, in some confusion, lest they had been overheard.

"You used us abominably ill," answered Mrs. Hurst, "in running away without telling us that you were coming out." Then taking the disengaged arm of Mr. Darcy, she left Elizabeth to walk by herself. The path just admitted three. Mr. Darcy felt their rudeness and immediately said,—

"This walk is not wide enough for our party. We had better go into the avenue."

But Elizabeth who had not the least inclination to remain with them, laughingly answered,

"No, no; stay where you are. — You are charmingly group'd, and appear to uncommon advantage. The picturesque would be spoilt by admitting a fourth.[1] Good bye."

She then ran gaily off, rejoicing as she rambled about, in the hope of being at home again in a day or two. Jane was already so much recovered as to intend leaving her room for a couple of hours that evening.

CHAPTER XI.

WHEN the ladies removed after dinner, Elizabeth ran up to her sister, and seeing her well guarded from cold, attended her into the drawing-room; where she was welcomed by her two friends with many professions of pleasure; and Elizabeth had never seen them so agreeable as they were during the hour which passed before the gentlemen appeared. Their powers of conversation were considerable. They could describe an entertainment with accuracy, relate an anecdote with humour, and laugh at their acquaintance with spirit.

But when the gentlemen entered, Jane was no longer the first object. Miss Bingley's eyes were instantly turned towards Darcy, and she had something to say to him before he had

---

1 Elizabeth uses the terminology of eighteenth-century aesthetics to imagine the group before her as assembled in a painting.

advanced many steps. He addressed himself directly to Miss Bennet, with a polite congratulation; Mr. Hurst also made her a slight bow, and said he was "very glad;" but diffuseness and warmth remained for Bingley's salutation. He was full of joy and attention. The first half hour was spent in piling up the fire, lest she should suffer from the change of room; and she removed at his desire to the other side of the fire-place, that she might be farther from the door. He then sat down by her, and talked scarcely to any one else. Elizabeth, at work in the opposite corner, saw it all with great delight.

When tea was over, Mr. Hurst reminded his sister-in-law of the card-table — but in vain. She had obtained private intelligence that Mr. Darcy did not wish for cards; and Mr. Hurst soon found even his open petition rejected. She assured him that no one intended to play, and the silence of the whole party on the subject, seemed to justify her. Mr. Hurst had therefore nothing to do, but to stretch himself on one of the sophas and go to sleep. Darcy took up a book; Miss Bingley did the same; and Mrs. Hurst, principally occupied in playing with her bracelets and rings, joined now and then in her brother's conversation with Miss Bennet.

Miss Bingley's attention was quite as much engaged in watching Mr. Darcy's progress through *his* book, as in reading her own; and she was perpetually either making some inquiry, or looking at his page. She could not win him, however, to any conversation; he merely answered her question, and read on. At length, quite exhausted by the attempt to be amused with her own book, which she had only chosen because it was the second volume of his, she gave a great yawn and said, "How pleasant it is to spend an evening in this way! I declare after all there is no enjoyment like reading! How much sooner one tires of any thing than of a book! — When I have a house of my own, I shall be miserable if I have not an excellent library."

No one made any reply. She then yawned again, threw aside her book, and cast her eyes round the room in quest of some amusement; when hearing her brother mentioning a ball to Miss Bennet, she turned suddenly towards him and said,

"By the bye, Charles, are you really serious in meditating a dance at Netherfield? — I would advise you, before you determine on it, to consult the wishes of the present party; I am much mistaken if there are not some among us to whom a ball would be rather a punishment than a pleasure."

"If you mean Darcy," cried her brother, "he may go to bed, if he chuses, before it begins—but as for the ball, it is quite a settled thing; and as soon as Nicholls has made white soup[1] enough I shall send round my cards."

"I should like balls infinitely better," she replied, "if they were carried on in a different manner; but there is something insufferably tedious in the usual process of such a meeting. It would surely be much more rational if conversation instead of dancing made the order of the day."

"Much more rational, my dear Caroline, I dare say, but it would not be near so much like a ball."

Miss Bingley made no answer; and soon afterwards got up and walked about the room. Her figure was elegant, and she walked well;—but Darcy, at whom it was all aimed, was still inflexibly studious. In the desperation of her feelings she resolved on one effort more; and turning to Elizabeth, said,

"Miss Eliza Bennet, let me persuade you to follow my example, and take a turn about the room.—I assure you it is very refreshing after sitting so long in one attitude."

Elizabeth was surprised, but agreed to it immediately. Miss Bingley succeeded no less in the real object of her civility; Mr. Darcy looked up. He was as much awake to the novelty of attention in that quarter as Elizabeth herself could be, and unconsciously closed his book. He was directly invited to join their party, but he declined it, observing, that he could imagine but two motives for their chusing to walk up and down the room together, with either of which motives his joining them would interfere. "What could he mean? she was dying to know what could be his meaning"—and asked Elizabeth whether she could at all understand him?

"Not at all," was her answer; "but depend upon it, he means to be severe on us, and our surest way of disappointing him, will be to ask nothing about it."

---

1   White soup, made with meat-stock, egg-yolks, ground almonds and cream, was the base for a sort of egg-nog made by adding hot wine and sugar, served at balls as a refreshment.

Miss Bingley, however, was incapable of disappointing Mr. Darcy in any thing, and persevered therefore in requiring an explanation of his two motives.

"I have not the smallest objection to explaining them," said he, as soon as she allowed him to speak. "You either chuse this method of passing the evening because you are in each other's confidence and have secret affairs to discuss, or because you are conscious that your figures appear to the greatest advantage in walking;—if the first, I should be completely in your way;—and if the second, I can admire you much better as I sit by the fire."

"Oh! shocking!" cried Miss Bingley. "I never heard any thing so abominable. How shall we punish him for such a speech?"

"Nothing so easy, if you have but the inclination," said Elizabeth. "We can all plague and punish one another. Teaze him—laugh at him. — Intimate as you are, you must know how it is to be done."

"But upon my honour I do *not*. I do assure you that my intimacy has not yet taught me *that*. Teaze calmness of temper and presence of mind! No, no — I feel he may defy us there. And as to laughter, we will not expose ourselves, if you please, by attempting to laugh without a subject. Mr. Darcy may hug himself."

"Mr. Darcy is not to be laughed at!" cried Elizabeth. "That is an uncommon advantage, and uncommon I hope it will continue, for it would be a great loss to *me* to have many such acquaintance. I dearly love a laugh."

"Miss Bingley," said he, "has given me credit for more than can be. The wisest and the best of men, nay, the wisest and best of their actions, may be rendered ridiculous by a person whose first object in life is a joke."

"Certainly," replied Elizabeth— "there are such people, but I hope I am not one of *them*. I hope I never ridicule what is wise or good. Follies and nonsense, whims and inconsistencies *do* divert me, I own, and I laugh at them whenever I can. — But these, I suppose, are precisely what you are without."

"Perhaps that is not possible for any one. But it has been the study of my life to avoid those weaknesses which often expose a strong understanding to ridicule."

"Such as vanity and pride."

"Yes, vanity is a weakness indeed. But pride—where there is a real superiority of mind, pride will be always under good regulation."

Elizabeth turned away to hide a smile.

"Your examination of Mr. Darcy is over, I presume," said Miss Bingley;—"and pray what is the result?"

"I am perfectly convinced by it that Mr. Darcy has no defect. He owns it himself without disguise."

"No"—said Darcy, "I have made no such pretension. I have faults enough, but they are not, I hope, of understanding. My temper I dare not vouch for.—It is I believe too little yielding—certainly too little for the convenience of the world. I cannot forget the follies and vices of others so soon as I ought, nor their offences against myself. My feelings are not puffed about with every attempt to move them. My temper would perhaps be called resentful.—My good opinion once lost is lost for ever."

"*That* is a failing indeed!"—cried Elizabeth. "Implacable resentment *is* a shade in a character. But you have chosen your fault well.—I really cannot *laugh* at it. You are safe from me."

"There is, I believe, in every disposition a tendency to some particular evil, a natural defect, which not even the best education can overcome."

"And *your* defect is a propensity to hate every body."

"And yours," he replied with a smile, "is wilfully to misunderstand them."

"Do let us have a little music,"—cried Miss Bingley, tired of a conversation in which she had no share.—"Louisa, you will not mind my waking Mr. Hurst."

Her sister made not the smallest objection, and the piano forte was opened, and Darcy, after a few moments recollection, was not sorry for it. He began to feel the danger of paying Elizabeth too much attention.

CHAPTER XII.

In consequence of an agreement between the sisters, Elizabeth wrote the next morning to her mother, to beg that the carriage might be sent for them in the course of the day. But Mrs. Bennet, who had calculated on her daughters remaining at Netherfield till the following Tuesday, which would exactly finish Jane's week, could not bring herself to receive them with pleasure before. Her answer, therefore, was not propitious, at least not to Elizabeth's wishes, for she was impatient to get home. Mrs. Bennet sent them word that they could not possibly have the carriage before Tuesday; and in her postscript it was added, that if Mr. Bingley and his sister pressed them to stay longer, she could spare them very well. — Against staying longer, however, Elizabeth was positively resolved—nor did she much expect it would be asked; and fearful, on the contrary, as being considered as intruding themselves needlessly long, she urged Jane to borrow Mr. Bingley's carriage immediately, and at length it was settled that their original design of leaving Netherfield that morning should be mentioned, and the request made.

The communication excited many professions of concern; and enough was said of wishing them to stay at least till the following day to work on Jane; and till the morrow, their going was deferred. Miss Bingley was then sorry that she had proposed the delay, for her jealousy and dislike of one sister much exceeded her affection for the other.

The master of the house heard with real sorrow that they were to go so soon, and repeatedly tried to persuade Miss Bennet that it would not be safe for her — that she was not enough recovered; but Jane was firm where she felt herself to be right.

To Mr. Darcy it was welcome intelligence—Elizabeth had been at Netherfield long enough. She attracted him more than he liked—and Miss Bingley was uncivil to *her*, and more teazing than usual to himself. He wisely resolved to be particularly careful that no sign of admiration should *now* escape him, nothing that could elevate her with the hope of influencing his felicity; sensible that if such an idea had been suggested, his behaviour during the last day must have material weight in confirming or crushing it. Steady to his purpose, he scarcely spoke ten words to her through the whole of Saturday, and though they were at one time left by themselves for half an hour, he adhered most conscientiously to his book, and would not even look at her.

On Sunday, after morning service, the separation, so agreeable to almost all, took place. Miss Bingley's civility to Elizabeth increased at last very rapidly, as well as her affection for Jane; and when they parted, after assuring the latter of the pleasure it would always give her to see her either at Longbourn or Netherfield, and embracing her most tenderly, she even shook hands with the former. — Elizabeth took leave of the whole party in the liveliest spirits.

They were not welcomed home very cordially by their mother. Mrs. Bennet wondered at their coming, and thought them very wrong to give so much trouble, and was sure Jane would have caught cold again. — But their father, though very laconic in his expressions of pleasure, was really glad to see them; he had felt their importance in the family circle. The evening conversation, when they were all assembled, had lost much of its animation, and almost all its sense, by the absence of Jane and Elizabeth.

They found Mary, as usual, deep in the study of thorough bass and human nature;[1] and had some new extracts to admire, and some new observations of thread-bare morality to listen to. Catherine and Lydia had information for them of a different sort. Much had been done, and much had been said in the regiment since the preceding Wednesday; several of the officers had dined lately with their uncle, a private had been flogged,[2] and it had actually been hinted that Colonel Forster was going to be married.

---

1 Thorough bass is a piano exercise which requires the player to improvise harmonies on top of a given bass line.
2 Army discipline was severe: the flogging to which Lydia refers could have consisted of as many as 1500 lashes. See Appendix E3 for an account of punishment in the militia.

CHAPTER XIII.

"I HOPE my dear," said Mr. Bennet to his wife, as they were at breakfast the next morning, "that you have ordered a good dinner to-day, because I have reason to expect an addition to our family party."

"Who do you mean, my dear? I know of nobody that is coming I am sure, unless Charlotte Lucas should happen to call in, and I hope *my* dinners are good enough for her. I do not believe she often sees such at home."

"The person of whom I speak, is a gentleman and a stranger." Mrs. Bennet's eyes sparkled. — "A gentleman and a stranger! It is Mr. Bingley, I am sure. Why Jane—you never dropt a word of this; you sly thing! Well, I am sure I shall be extremely glad to see Mr. Bingley. — But—good lord! how unlucky! there is not a bit of fish to be got to-day. Lydia, my love, ring the bell. I must speak to Hill, this moment."

"It is *not* Mr. Bingley," said her husband; "it is a person whom I never saw in the whole course of my life."

This roused a general astonishment; and he had the pleasure of being eagerly questioned by his wife and five daughters at once.

After amusing himself some time with their curiosity, he thus explained. "About a month ago I received this letter, and about a fortnight ago I answered it, for I thought it a case of some delicacy, and requiring early attention. It is from my cousin, Mr. Collins, who, when I am dead, may turn you all out of this house as soon as he pleases."

"Oh! my dear," cried his wife, "I cannot bear to hear that mentioned. Pray do not talk of that odious man. I do think it is the hardest thing in the world, that your estate should be entailed away from your own children; and I am sure if I had been you, I should have tried long ago to do something or other about it."

Jane and Elizabeth attempted to explain to her the nature of an entail. They had often attempted it before, but it was a subject on which Mrs. Bennet was beyond the reach of reason; and she continued to rail bitterly against the cruelty of settling an estate away from a family of five daughters, in favour of a man whom nobody cared anything about.

"It certainly is a most iniquitous affair," said Mr. Bennet, "and nothing can clear Mr. Collins from the guilt of inheriting Longbourn. But if you will listen to his letter, you may perhaps be a little softened by his manner of expressing himself."

"No, that I am sure I shall not; and I think it was very impertinent of him to write to you at all, and very hypocritical. I hate such false friends. Why could not he keep on quarrelling with you, as his father did before him?"

"Why, indeed, he does seem to have had some filial scruples on that head, as you will hear."

Hunsford, near Westerham, Kent,
15th October.

DEAR SIR,

THE disagreement subsisting between yourself and my late honoured father, always gave me much uneasiness, and since I have had the misfortune to lose him, I have frequently wished to heal the breach but for some time I was kept back by my own doubts, fearing lest it might seem disrespectful to his memory for me to be on good terms with any one, with whom it had always pleased him to be at variance. — "There, Mrs. Bennet." — "My mind however is now made up on the subject, for having received ordination at Easter, I have been so fortunate as to be distinguished by the patronage of the Right Honourable Lady Catherine de Bourgh, widow of Sir Lewis de Bourgh, whose bounty and beneficence has preferred me to the valuable rectory of this parish, where it shall be my earnest endeavour to demean myself with grateful respect towards her Ladyship, and be ever ready to perform those rites and cere-monies which are instituted by the Church of England.[1] As a clergyman, moreover, I feel it my duty to promote and establish

---

1   In the Church of England, positions as rector of a rural parish ("livings") were often in the gift of the landowner on whose estate the church was located. Austen's father, for example, gained the livings of Steventon and Deane from the landowner, his second cousin: one example of the patronage networks that also governed places in the army and government.

the blessing of peace in all families within the reach of my influence; and on these grounds I flatter myself that my present overtures of good-will are highly commendable, and that the circumstance of my being next in the entail of Longbourn estate, will be kindly overlooked on your side, and not lead you to reject the offered olive branch. I cannot be otherwise than concerned at being the means of injuring your amiable daughters, and beg leave to apologise for it, as well as to assure you of my readiness to make them every possible amends,—but of this hereafter. If you should have no objection to receive me into your house, I propose myself the satisfaction of waiting on you and your family, Monday, November 18th, by four o'clock, and shall probably trespass on your hospitality till the Saturday se'night following,[1] which I can do without any inconvenience, as Lady Catherine is far from objecting to my occasional absence on a Sunday, provided that some other clergyman is engaged to do the duty of the day. I remain, dear sir, with respectful compliments to your lady and daughters, your well-wisher and friend,

WILLIAM COLLINS.

"At four o'clock, therefore, we may expect this peace-making gentleman," said Mr. Bennet, as he folded up the letter. "He seems to be a most conscientious and polite young man, upon my word; and I doubt not will prove a valuable acquaintance, especially if Lady Catherine should be so indulgent as to let him come to us again."

"There is some sense in what he says about the girls however; and if he is disposed to make them any amends, I shall not be the person to discourage him."

"Though it is difficult," said Jane, "to guess in what way he can mean to make us the atonement he thinks our due, the wish is certainly to his credit."

Elizabeth was chiefly struck with his extraordinary deference for Lady Catherine, and his kind intention of christening, marrying, and burying his parishioners whenever it were required.

---

1 A "se'night" is one week.

"He must be an oddity, I think," said she. "I cannot make him out. — There is something very pompous in his stile. — And what can he mean by apologizing for being next in the entail? — We cannot suppose he would help it, if he could. — Can he be a sensible man, sir?"

"No, my dear; I think not. I have great hopes of finding him quite the reverse. There is a mixture of servility and self-importance in his letter, which promises well. I am impatient to see him."

"In point of composition," said Mary, "his letter does not seem defective. The idea of the olive branch perhaps is not wholly new, yet I think it is well expressed."

To Catherine and Lydia, neither the letter nor its writer were in any degree interesting. It was next to impossible that their cousin should come in a scarlet coat, and it was now some weeks since they had received pleasure from the society of a man in any other colour. As for their mother, Mr. Collins's letter had done away much of her ill-will, and she was preparing to see him with a degree of composure, which astonished her husband and daughters.

Mr. Collins was punctual to his time, and was received with great politeness by the whole family. Mr. Bennet indeed said little; but the ladies were ready enough to talk, and Mr. Collins seemed neither in need of encouragement, nor inclined to be silent himself. He was a tall, heavy looking young man of five and twenty. His air was grave and stately, and his manners were very formal. He had not been long seated before he complimented Mrs. Bennet on having so fine a family of daughters, said he had heard much of their beauty, but that, in this instance, fame had fallen short of the truth; and added, that he did not doubt her seeing them all in due time well disposed of in marriage. This gallantry was not much to the taste of some of his hearers, but Mrs. Bennet, who quarrelled with no compliments, answered most readily,

"You are very kind, sir, I am sure; and I wish with all my heart it may prove so; for else they will be destitute enough. Things are settled so oddly."

"You allude perhaps to the entail of this estate."

"Ah! sir, I do indeed. It is a grievous affair to my poor girls, you must confess. Not that I mean to find fault with *you*, for such things I know are all chance in this world. There is no knowing how estates will go when once they come to be entailed."

"I am very sensible, madam, of the hardship to my fair cousins,—and could say much on the subject, but that I am cautious of appearing forward and precipitate. But I can assure the young ladies that I come prepared to admire them. At present I will not say more, but perhaps when we are better acquainted—"

He was interrupted by a summons to dinner; and the girls smiled on each other. They were not the only objects of Mr. Collins's admiration. The hall, the dining-room, and all its furniture were examined and praised; and his commendation of every thing would have touched Mrs. Bennet's heart, but for the mortifying supposition of his viewing it all as his own future property. The dinner too in its turn was highly admired; and he begged to know to which of his fair cousins, the excellence of its cookery was owing. But here he was set right by Mrs. Bennet, who assured him with some asperity that they were very well able to keep a good cook, and that her daughters had nothing to do in the kitchen. He begged pardon for having displeased her. In a softened tone she declared herself not at all offended; but he continued to apologise for about a quarter of an hour.

CHAPTER XIV.

During dinner, Mr. Bennet scarcely spoke at all; but when the servants were withdrawn, he thought it time to have some conversation with his guest, and therefore started a subject in which he expected him to shine, by observing that he seemed very fortunate in his patroness. Lady Catherine de Bourgh's attention to his wishes, and consideration for his comfort, appeared very remarkable. Mr. Bennet could not have chosen better. Mr. Collins was eloquent in her praise. The subject elevated him to more than usual solemnity of manner, and with a most important aspect[1] he protested that he had never in his life witnessed such behaviour in a person of rank—such affability and condescension, as he had himself experienced from Lady Catherine. She had been graciously pleased to approve of both the discourses, which he had already had the honour of preaching before her. She had also asked him twice to dine at Rosings, and had sent for him only the Saturday before, to make up her pool of quadrille in the evening.[2] Lady Catherine was reckoned proud by many people he knew, but *he* had never seen any thing but affability in her. She had always spoken to him as she would to any other gentleman; she made not the smallest objection to his joining in the society of the neighbourhood, nor to his leaving his parish occasionally for a week or two, to visit his relations. She had even condescended to advise him to marry as soon as he could, provided he chose with discretion; and had once paid him a visit in his humble parsonage; where she had perfectly approved all the alterations he had been making, and had even vouchsafed to suggest some herself,—some shelves in the closets up stairs.

"That is all very proper and civil, I am sure," said Mrs. Bennet, "and I dare say she is a very agreeable woman. It is a pity that great ladies in general are not more like her. Does she live near you, sir?"

"The garden in which stands my humble abode, is separated only by a lane from Rosings Park, her ladyship's residence."

"I think you said she was a widow, sir? has she any family?"

"She has one only daughter, the heiress of Rosings, and of very extensive property."

"Ah!" cried Mrs. Bennet, shaking her head, "then she is better off than many girls. And what sort of young lady is she? is she handsome?"

"She is a most charming young lady indeed. Lady Catherine herself says that in point of true beauty, Miss De Bourgh is far superior to the handsomest of her sex; because there is that in her features which marks the young woman of distinguished

---

1 Aspect here means appearance or facial expression.
2 Another card-game, requiring four players.

birth. She is unfortunately of a sickly constitution, which has prevented her making that progress in many accomplishments, which she could not otherwise have failed of; as I am informed by the lady who superintended her education, and who still resides with them. But she is perfectly amiable, and often condescends to drive by my humble abode in her little phaeton and ponies."[1]

"Has she been presented? I do not remember her name among the ladies at court."[2]

"Her indifferent state of health unhappily prevents her being in town; and by that means, as I told Lady Catherine myself one day, has deprived the British court of its brightest ornament. Her ladyship seemed pleased with the idea, and you may imagine that I am happy on every occasion to offer those little delicate compliments which are always acceptable to ladies. I have more than once observed to Lady Catherine, that her charming daughter seemed born to be a duchess, and that the most elevated rank, instead of giving her consequence, would be adorned by her. — These are the kind of little things which please her ladyship, and it is a sort of attention which I conceive myself peculiarly bound to pay."

"You judge very properly," said Mr. Bennet, "and it is happy for you that you possess the talent of flattering with delicacy. May I ask whether these pleasing attentions proceed from the impulse of the moment, or are the result of previous study?"

"They arise chiefly from what is passing at the time, and though I sometimes amuse myself with suggesting and arranging such little elegant compliments as may be adapted to ordinary occasions, I always wish to give them as unstudied an air as possible."

Mr. Bennet's expectations were fully answered. His cousin was as absurd as he had hoped, and he listened to him with the keenest enjoyment, maintaining at the same time the most resolute composure of countenance, and except in an occasional glance at Elizabeth, requiring no partner in his pleasure.

By tea-time however the dose had been enough, and Mr.

---

1 A carriage for one person plus a driver.
2 See note to p.82.

Bennet was glad to take his guest into the drawing-room again, and when tea was over, glad to invite him to read aloud to the ladies. Mr. Collins readily assented, and a book was produced; but on beholding it, (for every thing announced it to be from a circulating library,) he started back, and begging pardon, protested that he never read novels. —Kitty stared at him, and Lydia exclaimed. —Other books were produced, and after some deliberation he chose Fordyce's Sermons.[1] Lydia gaped as he opened the volume, and before he had, with very monotonous solemnity, read three pages, she interrupted him with,

"Do you know, mama, that my uncle Philips talks of turning away Richard, and if he does, Colonel Forster will hire him. My aunt told me so herself on Saturday. I shall walk to Meryton to-morrow to hear more about it, and to ask when Mr. Denny comes back from town."

Lydia was bid by her two eldest sisters to hold her tongue; but Mr. Collins, much offended, laid aside his book, and said,

"I have often observed how little young ladies are interested by books of a serious stamp, though written solely for their benefit. It amazes me, I confess;—for certainly, there can be nothing so advantageous to them as instruction. But I will no longer importune my young cousin."

Then turning to Mr. Bennet, he offered himself as his antagonist at backgammon. Mr. Bennet accepted the challenge, observing that he acted very wisely in leaving the girls to their own trifling amusements. Mrs. Bennet and her daughters apologised most civilly for Lydia's interruption, and promised that it should not occur again, if he would resume his book; but Mr. Collins, after assuring them that he bore his young cousin no ill will, and should never resent her behaviour as any affront, seated himself at another table with Mr. Bennet, and prepared for backgammon.

---

1 See Appendix B.1.

CHAPTER XV.

MR. COLLINS was not a sensible man, and the deficiency of nature had been but little assisted by education or society; the greatest part of his life having been spent under the guidance of an illiterate and miserly father; and though he belonged to one of the universities, he had merely kept the necessary terms, without forming at it any useful acquaintance.[1] The subjection in which his father had brought him up, had given him originally great humility of manner, but it was now a good deal counteracted by the self-conceit of a weak head, living in retirement, and the consequential feelings of early and unexpected prosperity. A fortunate chance had recommended him to Lady Catherine de Bourgh when the living of Hunsford was vacant; and the respect which he felt for her high rank, and his veneration for her as his patroness, mingling with a very good opinion of himself, of his authority as a clergyman, and his rights as a rector, made him altogether a mixture of pride and obsequiousness, self-importance and humility.

Having now a good house and very sufficient income, he intended to marry; and in seeking a reconciliation with the Longbourn family he had a wife in view, as he meant to chuse one of the daughters, if he found them as handsome and amiable as they were represented by common report. This was his plan of amends — of atonement — for inheriting their father's estate; and he thought it an excellent one, full of eligibility and suitableness, and excessively generous and disinterested on his own part.

His plan did not vary on seeing them. — Miss Bennet's lovely face confirmed his views, and established all his strictest notions of what was due to seniority; and for the first evening *she* was his settled choice. The next morning, however, made an alteration; for in a quarter of an hour's tête-à-tête with Mrs. Bennet before breakfast, a conversation beginning with his par-

---

1 England's only universities in this period were Oxford and Cambridge. Austen implies, probably rightly, that for a man of Collins's modest background, attendance was of less use educationally (although a degree was a crucial step towards ordination) than as a way of meeting potential future patrons from the higher social ranks.

sonage-house, and leading naturally to the avowal of his hopes, that a mistress for it might be found at Longbourn, produced from her, amid very complaisant smiles and general encouragement, a caution against the very Jane he had fixed on. — "As to her *younger* daughters she could not take upon her to say — she could not positively answer — but she did not *know* of any prepossession;—her *eldest* daughter, she must just mention—she felt it incumbent on her to hint, was likely to be very soon engaged."

Mr. Collins had only to change from Jane to Elizabeth — and it was soon done—done while Mrs. Bennet was stirring the fire. Elizabeth, equally next to Jane in birth and beauty, succeeded her of course.

Mrs. Bennet treasured up the hint, and trusted that she might soon have two daughters married; and the man whom she could not bear to speak of the day before, was now high in her good graces.

Lydia's intention of walking to Meryton was not forgotten; every sister except Mary agreed to go with her; and Mr. Collins was to attend them, at the request of Mr. Bennet, who was most anxious to get rid of him, and have his library to himself; for thither Mr. Collins had followed him after breakfast, and there he would continue, nominally engaged with one of the largest folios[1] in the collection, but really talking to Mr. Bennet, with little cessation, of his house and garden at Hunsford. Such doings discomposed Mr. Bennet exceedingly. In his library he had been always sure of leisure and tranquillity; and though prepared, as he told Elizabeth, to meet with folly and conceit in every other room in the house, he was used to be free from them there; his civility, therefore, was most prompt in inviting Mr. Collins to join his daughters in their walk; and Mr. Collins, being in fact much better fitted for a walker than a reader, was extremely well pleased to close his large book, and go.

---

1 *Folio* pages are made by folding the printed sheet once to make two leaves (four pages) before binding; compare the standard *duodecimo* format of a novel, where the same-sized sheet is folded to make twelve leaves (24 pages). Large-format folio volumes of history, philosophy, or the classics might be expected to figure in a gentleman's library; novels were associated with women readers.

In pompous nothings on his side, and civil assents on that of his cousins, their time passed till they entered Meryton. The attention of the younger ones was then no longer to be gained by *him*. Their eyes were immediately wandering up in the street in quest of the officers, and nothing less than a very smart bonnet indeed, or a really new muslin in a shop window, could recal them.

But the attention of every lady was soon caught by a young man, whom they had never seen before, of most gentlemanlike appearance, walking with an officer on the other side of the way. The officer was the very Mr. Denny, concerning whose return from London Lydia came to inquire, and he bowed as they passed. All were struck with the stranger's air, all wondered who he could be, and Kitty and Lydia, determined if possible to find out, led the way across the street, under pretence of wanting something in an opposite shop, and fortunately had just gained the pavement when the two gentlemen turning back had reached the same spot. Mr. Denny addressed them directly, and entreated permission to introduce his friend, Mr. Wickham, who had returned with him the day before from town, and he was happy to say had accepted a commission in their corps. This was exactly as it should be; for the young man wanted only regimentals to make him completely charming. His appearance was greatly in his favour; he had all the best part of beauty, a fine countenance, a good figure, and very pleasing address. The introduction was followed up on his side by a happy readiness of conversation—a readiness at the same time perfectly correct and unassuming; and the whole party were still standing and talking together very agreeably, when the sound of horses drew their notice, and Darcy and Bingley were seen riding down the street. On distinguishing the ladies of the group, the two gentlemen came directly towards them, and began the usual civilities. Bingley was the principal spokesman, and Miss Bennet the principal object. He was then, he said, on his way to Longbourn on purpose to inquire after her. Mr. Darcy corroborated it with a bow, and was beginning to deter-mine not to fix his eyes on Elizabeth, when they were suddenly arrested by the sight of the stranger, and Elizabeth happening to see the countenance of both as they looked at each other, was all astonishment at the effect of the meeting. Both changed colour, one looked white, the other red. Mr. Wickham, after a few moments, touched his hat—a salutation which Mr. Darcy just deigned to return. What could be the meaning of it?—It was impossible to imagine; it was impossible not to long to know.

In another minute Mr. Bingley, but without seeming to have noticed what passed, took leave and rode on with his friend.

Mr. Denny and Mr. Wickham walked with the young ladies to the door of Mr. Philips's house, and then made their bows, in spite of Miss Lydia's pressing entreaties that they would come in, and even in spite of Mrs. Philips' throwing up the parlour window, and loudly seconding the invitation.

Mrs. Philips was always glad to see her nieces, and the two eldest, from their recent absence, were particularly welcome, and she was eagerly expressing her surprise at their sudden return home, which, as their own carriage had not fetched them, she should have known nothing about, if she had not happened to see Mr. Jones's shop boy in the street, who had told her that they were not to send any more draughts to Netherfield because the Miss Bennets were come away, when her civility was claimed towards Mr. Collins by Jane's introduction of him. She received him with her very best politeness, which he returned with as much more, apologising for his intrusion, without any previous acquaintance with her, which he could not help flattering himself however might be justified by his relationship to the young ladies who introduced him to her notice. Mrs. Philips was quite awed by such an excess of good breeding; but her contemplation of one stranger was soon put an end to by exclamations and inquiries about the other, of whom, however, she could only tell her nieces what they already knew, that Mr. Denny had brought him from London, and that he was to have a lieutenant's commission in the ——shire. She had been watching him the last hour, she said, as he walked up and down the street, and had Mr. Wickham appeared Kitty and Lydia would certainly have continued the occupation, but unluckily no one passed the windows now except a few of the officers, who in comparison with the stranger, were become "stupid, disagreeable fellows." Some of them were to dine with the Philipses the next day, and their aunt promised to make her husband call on Mr. Wickham, and give him an invitation also, if the family from Longbourn would come in the evening. This was agreed to, and Mrs. Philips protested that they would have a nice comfortable noisy game of lottery tickets,[1] and a little bit of hot supper afterwards. The prospect of such delights was very cheering, and they parted in mutual good spirits. Mr. Collins repeated his apologies in quitting the room, and was assured with unwearying civility that they were perfectly needless.

As they walked home, Elizabeth related to Jane what she had seen pass between the two gentlemen; but though Jane would have defended either or both, had they appeared to be wrong, she could no more explain such behaviour than her sister.

Mr. Collins on his return highly gratified Mrs. Bennet by admiring Mrs. Philips's manners and politeness. He protested that except Lady Catherine and her daughter, he had never seen a more elegant woman; for she had not only received him with the utmost civility, but had even pointedly included him in her invitation for the next evening, although utterly unknown to her before. Something he supposed might be attributed to his connection with them, but yet he had never met with so much attention in the whole course of his life.

---

1   A card game, in which receiving certain cards allowed the player to claim (noisily, apparently) corresponding prizes: a family amusement rather than an opportunity for serious gambling.

CHAPTER XVI.

As no objection was made to the young people's engagement with their aunt, and all Mr. Collins's scruples of leaving Mr. and Mrs. Bennet for a single evening during his visit were most steadily resisted, the coach conveyed him and his five cousins at a suitable hour to Meryton; and the girls had the pleasure of hearing, as they entered the drawing-room, that Mr. Wickham had accepted their uncle's invitation, and was then in the house.

When this information was given, and they had all taken their seats, Mr. Collins was at leisure to look around him and admire, and he was so much struck with the size and furniture of the apartment, that he declared he might almost have supposed himself in the small summer breakfast parlour at Rosings; a comparison that did not at first convey much gratification; but when Mrs. Philips understood from him what Rosings was, and who was its proprietor, when she had listened to the description of only one of Lady Catherine's drawing-rooms, and found that the chimney-piece alone had cost eight hundred pounds, she felt all the force of the compliment, and would hardly have resented a comparison with the housekeeper's room.

In describing to her all the grandeur of Lady Catherine and her mansion, with occasional digressions in praise of his own humble abode, and the improvements it was receiving, he was happily employed until the gentlemen joined them; and he found in Mrs. Philips a very attentive listener, whose opinion of his consequence increased with what she heard, and who was resolving to retail it all among her neighbours as soon as she could. To the girls, who could not listen to their cousin, and who had nothing to do but to wish for an instrument, and examine their own indifferent imitations of china on the mantlepiece,[1] the interval of waiting appeared very long. It was over at last however. The gentlemen did approach; and when Mr. Wickham walked into the room, Elizabeth felt that she had

---

1   That is, plain crockery painted in imitation of more expensive china: one of those feminine "accomplishments" at which Darcy sneers in chapter viii of this volume.

neither been seeing him before, nor thinking of him since, with the smallest degree of unreasonable admiration. The officers of the ——shire were in general a very creditable, gentlemanlike set, and the best of them were of the present party; but Mr. Wickham was as far beyond them all in person, countenance, air, and walk, as *they* were superior to the broad-faced stuffy uncle Philips, breathing port wine, who followed them into the room.

Mr. Wickham was the happy man towards whom almost every female eye was turned, and Elizabeth was the happy woman by whom he finally seated himself; and the agreeable manner in which he immediately fell into conversation, though it was only on its being a wet night, and on the probability of a rainy season, made her feel that the commonest, dullest, most threadbare topic might be rendered interesting by the skill of the speaker.

With such rivals for the notice of the fair, as Mr. Wickham and the officers, Mr. Collins seemed likely to sink into insignificance; to the young ladies he certainly was nothing; but he had still at intervals a kind listener in Mrs. Philips, and was, by her watchfulness, most abundantly supplied with coffee and muffin.

When the card tables were placed, he had an opportunity of obliging her in return, by sitting down to whist.

"I know little of the game, at present," said he, "but I shall be glad to improve myself, for in my situation of life" — Mrs. Philips was very thankful for his compliance, but could not wait for his reason.

Mr. Wickham did not play at whist, and with ready delight was he received at the other table between Elizabeth and Lydia. At first there seemed danger of Lydia's engrossing him entirely, for she was a most determined talker; but being likewise extremely fond of lottery tickets, she soon grew too much interested in the game, too eager in making bets and exclaiming after prizes, to have attention for any one in particular. Allowing for the common demands of the game, Mr. Wickham was therefore at leisure to talk to Elizabeth, and she was very willing to hear him, though what she chiefly wished to hear she could not hope to be told, the history of his acquaintance with Mr. Darcy. She dared not even mention that gentleman. Her curiosity however was unexpectedly relieved. Mr. Wickham began the subject himself. He inquired how far Netherfield was from Meryton; and, after receiving her answer, asked in an hesitating manner how long Mr. Darcy had been staying there.

"About a month," said Elizabeth; and then, unwilling to let the subject drop, added, "he is a man of very large property in Derbyshire, I understand."

"Yes," replied Wickham;— "his estate there is a noble one. A clear ten thousand per annum. You could not have met with a person more capable of giving you certain information on that head than myself— for I have been connected with his family in a particular manner from my infancy."

Elizabeth could not but look surprised.

"You may well be surprised, Miss Bennet, at such an assertion, after seeing, as you probably might, the very cold manner of our meeting yesterday.— Are you much acquainted with Mr. Darcy?"

"As much as I ever wish to be," cried Elizabeth warmly,— "I have spent four days in the same house with him, and I think him very disagreeable."

"I have no right to give *my* opinion," said Wickham, "as to his being agreeable or otherwise. I am not qualified to form one. I have known him too long and too well to be a fair judge. It is impossible for *me* to be impartial. But I believe your opinion of him would in general astonish—and perhaps you would not express it quite so strongly anywhere else. —Here you are in your own family."

"Upon my word I say no more *here* than I might say in any house in the neighbourhood, except Netherfield. He is not at all liked in Hertfordshire. Every body is disgusted with his pride. You will not find him more favourably spoken of by any one."

"I cannot pretend to be sorry," said Wickham, after a short interruption, "that he or that any man should not be estimated beyond their deserts; but with *him* I believe it does not often happen. The world is blinded by his fortune and consequence, or frightened by his high and imposing manners, and sees him only as he chuses to be seen."

"I should take him, even on *my* slight acquaintance, to be an ill-tempered man." Wickham only shook his head.

"I wonder," said he, at the next opportunity of speaking, "whether he is likely to be in this country much longer."

"I do not at all know; but I *heard* nothing of his going away when I was at Netherfield. I hope your plans in favour of the ——shire will not be affected by his being in the neighbourhood."

"Oh! no—it is not for *me* to be driven away by Mr. Darcy. If *he* wishes to avoid seeing *me*, he must go. We are not on friendly terms, and it always gives me pain to meet him, but I have no reason for avoiding *him* but what I might proclaim to all the world; a sense of very great ill-usage, and most painful regrets at his being what he is. His father, Miss Bennet, the late Mr. Darcy, was one of the best men that ever breathed, and the truest friend I ever had; and I can never be in company with this Mr. Darcy without being grieved to the soul by a thousand tender recollections. His behaviour to myself has been scandalous; but I verily believe I could forgive him any thing and every thing, rather than his disappointing the hopes and disgracing the memory of his father."

Elizabeth found the interest of the subject increase, and listened with all her heart; but the delicacy of it prevented farther inquiry.

Mr. Wickham began to speak on more general topics, Meryton, the neighbourhood, the society, appearing highly pleased with all that he had yet seen, and speaking of the latter especially, with gentle but very intelligible gallantry.

"It was the prospect of constant society, and good society," he added, "which was my chief inducement to enter the —— shire. I knew it to be a most respectable, agreeable corps, and my friend Denny tempted me farther by his account of their present quarters, and the very great attentions and excellent acquaintance Meryton had procured them. Society, I own, is necessary to me. I have been a disappointed man, and my spirits will not bear solitude. I *must* have employment and society. A military life is not what I was intended for, but circumstances have now made it eligible. The church *ought* to have been my profession — I was brought up for the church, and I should at this time have been in possession of a most valuable living, had it pleased the gentleman we were speaking of just now."

"Indeed!"

"Yes — the late Mr. Darcy bequeathed me the next presentation of the best living in his gift. He was my godfather, and excessively attached to me. I cannot do justice to his kindness. He meant to provide for me amply, and thought he had done it; but when the living fell, it was given elsewhere."

"Good heavens!" cried Elizabeth; "but how could *that* be? — How could his will be disregarded? — Why did not you seek legal redress?"

"There was just such an informality in the terms of the bequest as to give me no hope from law. A man of honour could not have doubted the intention, but Mr. Darcy chose to doubt it — or to treat it as a merely conditional recommendation, and to assert that I had forfeited all claim to it by extravagance, imprudence, in short any thing or nothing. Certain it is, that the living became vacant two years ago, exactly as I was of an age to hold it, and that it was given to another man; and no less certain is it, that I cannot accuse myself of having really done any thing to deserve to lose it. I have a warm, unguarded temper, and I may perhaps have sometimes spoken my opinion *of* him, and *to* him, too freely. I can recal nothing worse. But the fact is, that we are very different sort of men, and that he hates me."

"This is quite shocking! — He deserves to be publicly disgraced."

"Some time or other he *will* be — but it shall not be by *me*. Till I can forget his father, I can never defy or expose *him*."

Elizabeth honoured him for such feelings, and thought him handsomer than ever as he expressed them.

"But what," said she after a pause, "can have been his motive? — what can have induced him to behave so cruelly?"

"A thorough, determined dislike of me — a dislike which I

cannot but attribute in some measure to jealousy. Had the late Mr. Darcy liked me less, his son might have borne with me better; but his father's uncommon attachment to me, irritated him I believe very early in life. He had not a temper to bear the sort of competition in which we stood—the sort of preference which was often given me."

"I had not thought Mr. Darcy so bad as this—though I have never liked him, I had not thought so very ill of him—I had supposed him to be despising his fellow-creatures in general, but did not suspect him of descending to such malicious revenge, such injustice, such inhumanity as this!"

After a few minutes reflection, however, she continued, "I *do* remember his boasting one day, at Netherfield, of the implacability of his resentments, of his having an unforgiving temper. His disposition must be dreadful."

"I will not trust myself on the subject," replied Wickham, "*I* can hardly be just to him."

Elizabeth was again deep in thought, and after a time exclaimed, "To treat in such a manner, the godson, the friend, the favourite of his father!"—She could have added, "A young man too, like *you*, whose very countenance may vouch for your being amiable"—but she contented herself with "And one, too, who had probably been his own companion from childhood, connected together, as I think you said, in the closest manner!"

"We were born in the same parish, within the same park, the greatest part of our youth was passed together; inmates of the same house, sharing the same amusements, objects of the same parental care. *My* father began life in the profession which your uncle, Mr. Philips, appears to do so much credit to—but he gave up every thing to be of use to the late Mr. Darcy, and devoted all his time to the care of the Pemberley property. He was most highly esteemed by Mr. Darcy, a most intimate, confidential friend. Mr. Darcy often acknowledged himself to be under the greatest obligations to my father's active superintendance, and when immediately before my father's death, Mr. Darcy gave him a voluntary promise of providing for me, I am convinced that he felt it to be as much a debt of gratitude to *him*, as of affection to myself."

"How strange!" cried Elizabeth. "How abominable!—I wonder that the very pride of this Mr. Darcy has not made him just to you!—If from no better motive, that he should not have been too proud to be dishonest,—for dishonesty I must call it."

"It *is* wonderful,"—replied Wickham,—"for almost all his actions may be traced to pride;—and pride has often been his best friend. It has connected him nearer with virtue than any other feeling. But we are none of us consistent; and in his behaviour to me, there were stronger impulses even than pride."

"Can such abominable pride as his, have ever done him good?"

"Yes. It has often led him to be liberal and generous,—to give his money freely, to display hospitality, to assist his tenants, and relieve the poor. Family pride, and *filial* pride, for he is very proud of what his father was, have done this. Not to appear to disgrace his family, to degenerate from the popular qualities, or lose the influence of the Pemberley House, is a powerful motive. He has also *brotherly* pride, which with *some* brotherly affection, makes him a very kind and careful guardian of his sister; and you will hear him generally cried up as the most attentive and best of brothers."

"What sort of a girl is Miss Darcy,?"

He shook his head.—"I wish I could call her amiable. It gives me pain to speak ill of a Darcy. But she is too much like her brother,—very, very proud.—As a child, she was affectionate and pleasing, and extremely fond of me; and I have devoted hours and hours to her amusement. But she is nothing to me now. She is a handsome girl, about fifteen or sixteen, and I understand highly accomplished. Since her father's death, her home has been London, where a lady lives with her, and superintends her education."

After many pauses and many trials of other subjects, Elizabeth could not help reverting once more to the first, and saying,

"I am astonished at his intimacy with Mr. Bingley! How can Mr. Bingley, who seems good humour itself, and is, I really believe, truly amiable, be in friendship with such a man? How can they suit each other?—Do you know Mr. Bingley?"

"Not at all."

"He is a sweet tempered, amiable, charming man. He cannot know what Mr. Darcy is."

"Probably not;—but Mr. Darcy can please where he chuses. He does not want abilities. He can be a conversible companion if he thinks it worth his while. Among those who are at all his equals in consequence, he is a very different man from what he is to the less prosperous. His pride never deserts him; but with the rich, he is liberal-minded, just, sincere, rational, honourable, and perhaps agreeable,—allowing something for fortune and figure."

The whist party soon afterwards breaking up, the players gathered round the other table, and Mr. Collins took his station between his cousin Elizabeth and Mrs. Philips.—The usual inquiries as to his success were made by the latter. It had not been very great; he had lost every point; but when Mrs. Philips began to express her concern thereupon, he assured her with much earnest gravity that it was not of the least importance, that he considered the money as a mere trifle, and begged she would not make herself uneasy.

"I know very well, madam," said he, "that when persons sit down to a card table, they must take their chance of these things,—and happily I am not in such circumstances as to make five shillings any object. There are undoubtedly many who could not say the same, but thanks to Lady Catherine de Bourgh, I am removed far beyond the necessity of regarding little matters."[1]

Mr. Wickham's attention was caught; and after observing

---

1 Infatuated with aristocratic mores as he is, the only objection Mr. Collins can see to a churchman's gambling seems to be the practical one of being unable to afford it, and not the moral one mobilised by the Evangelical movement within the Anglican church in the early nineteenth century, to cards as to dancing (see following chapter), as part of their general drive towards a professional and vocational rather than a servitor clergy.

Mr. Collins for a few moments, he asked Elizabeth in a low voice whether her relation were very intimately acquainted with the family of de Bourgh.

"Lady Catherine de Bourgh," she replied, "has very lately given him a living. I hardly know how Mr. Collins was first introduced to her notice, but he certainly has not known her long."

"You know of course that Lady Catherine de Bourgh and Lady Anne Darcy were sisters; consequently that she is aunt to the present Mr. Darcy."

"No, indeed, I did not.—I knew nothing at all of Lady Catherine's connections. I never heard of her existence till the day before yesterday."

"Her daughter, Miss de Bourgh, will have a very large fortune, and it is believed that she and her cousin will unite the two estates."

This information made Elizabeth smile, as she thought of poor Miss Bingley. Vain indeed must be all her attentions, vain and useless her affection for his sister and her praise of himself, if he were already self-destined to another.

"Mr. Collins," said she, "speaks highly both of Lady Catherine and her daughter; but from some particulars that he has related of her ladyship, I suspect his gratitude misleads him, and that in spite of her being his patroness, she is an arrogant, conceited woman."

"I believe her to be both in a great degree," replied Wickham; "I have not seen her for many years, but I very well remember that I never liked her, and that her manners were dictatorial and insolent. She has the reputation of being remarkably sensible and clever; but I rather believe she derives part of her abilities from her rank and fortune, part from her authoritative manner, and the rest from the pride of her nephew, who chuses that every one connected with him should have an understanding of the first class."

Elizabeth allowed that he had given a very rational account of it, and they continued talking together with mutual satisfaction till supper put an end to cards; and gave the rest of the ladies their share of Mr. Wickham's attentions. There could be no conversation in the noise of Mrs. Philips's supper party, but his manners recommended him to every body. Whatever he said, was said well; and whatever he did, done gracefully. Elizabeth went away with her head full of him. She could think of nothing but of Mr. Wickham, and of what he had told her, all the way home; but there was not time for her even to mention his name as they went, for neither Lydia nor Mr. Collins were once silent. Lydia talked incessantly of lottery tickets, of the fish she had lost and the fish she had won,[1] and Mr. Collins, in describing the civility of Mr. and Mrs. Philips, protesting that he did not in the least regard his losses at whist, enumerating all the dishes at supper, and repeatedly fearing that he crouded his cousins, had more to say than he could well manage before the carriage stopped at Longbourn House.

CHAPTER XVII.

ELIZABETH related to Jane the next day, what had passed between Mr. Wickham and herself. Jane listened with astonishment and concern;—she knew not how to believe that Mr. Darcy could be so unworthy of Mr. Bingley's regard; and yet, it was not in her nature to question the veracity of a young man of such amiable appearance as Wickham. — The possibility of his having really endured such unkindness, was enough to interest all her tender feelings; and nothing therefore remained to be done, but to think well of them both, to defend the conduct of each, and throw into the account of accident or mistake, whatever could not be otherwise explained.

"They have both," said she, "been deceived, I dare say, in some way or other, of which we can form no idea. Interested people have perhaps misrepresented each to the other.[2] It is, in

---

1 "Fish" are the bone or ivory counters or chips (sometimes in the shape of fish) used instead of money in more serious card games such as quadrille and loo as well as lottery.
2 Interested here means biased in their opinions by some personal (usually financial) interest.

short, impossible for us to conjecture the causes or circumstances which may have alienated them, without actual blame on either side."

"Very true, indeed;—and now, my dear Jane, what have you got to say in behalf of the interested people who have probably been concerned in the business?—Do clear *them* too, or we shall be obliged to think ill of somebody."

"Laugh as much as you chuse, but you will not laugh me out of my opinion. My dearest Lizzy, do but consider in what a disgraceful light it places Mr. Darcy, to be treating his father's favourite in such a manner,—one, whom his father had promised to provide for.—It is impossible. No man of common humanity, no man who had any value for his character, could be capable of it. Can his most intimate friends be so excessively deceived in him? oh! no."

"I can much more easily believe Mr. Bingley's being imposed on, than that Mr. Wickham should invent such a history of himself as he gave me last night; names, facts, every thing mentioned without ceremony.—If it be not so, let Mr. Darcy contradict it. Besides, there was truth in his looks."

"It is difficult indeed—it is distressing.—One does not know what to think."

"I beg your pardon;—one knows exactly what to think."

But Jane could think with certainty on only one point,— that Mr. Bingley, if he *had been* imposed on, would have much to suffer when the affair became public.

The two young ladies were summoned from the shrubbery where this conversation passed, by the arrival of some of the very persons of whom they had been speaking; Mr. Bingley and his sisters came to give their personal invitation for the long expected ball at Netherfield, which was fixed for the following Tuesday. The two ladies were delighted to see their dear friend again, called it an age since they had met, and repeatedly asked what she had been doing with herself since their separation. To the rest of the family they paid little attention; avoiding Mrs. Bennet as much as possible, saying not much to Elizabeth, and nothing at all to the others. They were soon gone again, rising from their seats with an activity which took their brother by surprise, and hurrying off as if eager to escape from Mrs. Bennet's civilities.

The prospect of the Netherfield ball was extremely agreeable to every female of the family. Mrs. Bennet chose to consider it as given in compliment to her eldest daughter, and was particularly flattered by receiving the invitation from Mr. Bingley himself, instead of a ceremonious card. Jane pictured to herself a happy evening in the society of her two friends, and the attentions of their brother; and Elizabeth thought with pleasure of dancing a great deal with Mr. Wickham, and of seeing a confirmation of every thing in Mr. Darcy's looks and behaviour. The happiness anticipated by Catherine and Lydia, depended less on any single event, or any particular person, for though they each, like Elizabeth, meant to dance half the evening with Mr. Wickham, he was by no means the only partner who could satisfy them, and a ball was at any rate, a ball. And even Mary could assure her family that she had no disinclination for it.

"While I can have my mornings to myself," said she, "it is enough. — I think it no sacrifice to join occasionally in evening engagements. Society has claims on us all; and I profess myself one of those who consider intervals of recreation and amusement as desirable for every body."

Elizabeth's spirits were so high on the occasion that, though she did not often speak unnecessarily to Mr. Collins, she could not help asking him whether he intended to accept Mr. Bingley's invitation, and if he did, whether he would think it proper to join in the evening's amusement; and she was rather surprised to find that he entertained no scruple whatever on that head, and was very far from dreading a rebuke either from the Archbishop, or Lady Catherine de Bourgh, by venturing to dance.

"I am by no means of opinion, I assure you," said he, "that a ball of this kind, given by a young man of character, to respectable people, can have any evil tendency; and I am so far from objecting to dancing myself that I shall hope to be honoured with the hands of all my fair cousins in the course of the evening, and I take this opportunity of soliciting yours, Miss Elizabeth, for the two first dances especially, — a preference which I trust my cousin Jane will attribute to the right cause, and not to any disrespect for her."

Elizabeth felt herself completely taken in. She had fully proposed being engaged by Wickham for those very dances: — and to have Mr. Collins instead! — her liveliness had been never worse timed. There was no help for it however.[1] Mr. Wickham's happiness and her own was perforce delayed a little longer, and Mr. Collins's proposal accepted with as good a grace as she could. She was not the better pleased with his gallantry, from the idea it suggested of something more. — It now first struck her, that *she* was selected from among her sisters as worthy of being the mistress of Hunsford Parsonage, and of assisting to form a quadrille table at Rosings, in the absence of more eligible visitors. The idea soon reached to conviction, as she observed his increasing civilities toward herself, and heard his frequent attempt at a compliment on her wit and vivacity; and though more astonished than gratified herself, by this effect of her charms, it was not long before her mother gave her to understand that the probability of their marriage was exceedingly agreeable to *her*. Elizabeth however did not chuse to take the hint, being well aware that a serious dispute must be the consequence of any reply. Mr. Collins might never make the offer, and till he did, it was useless to quarrel about him.

If there had not been a Netherfield ball to prepare for and talk of, the younger Miss Bennets would have been in a pitiable state at this time, for from the day of the invitation, to the day of the ball, there was such a succession of rain as prevented their walking to Meryton once. No aunt, no officers, no news could be sought after;—the very shoe-roses[2] for Netherfield were got by proxy. Even Elizabeth might have found some trial of her patience in weather, which totally suspended the improvement of her acquaintance with Mr. Wickham; and nothing less than a dance on Tuesday, could have made such a Friday, Saturday, Sunday and Monday, endurable to Kitty and Lydia.

---

1 Note how rules of propriety prevent Elizabeth from simply saying no to Collins's solicitation.
2 Decorations for dancing shoes.

CHAPTER XVIII.

TILL Elizabeth entered the drawing-room at Netherfield and looked in vain for Mr. Wickham among the cluster of red coats there assembled, a doubt of his being present had never occurred to her. The certainty of meeting him had not been checked by any of those recollections that might not unreasonably have alarmed her. She had dressed with more than usual care, and prepared in the highest spirits for the conquest of all that remained unsubdued of his heart, trusting that it was not more than might be won in the course of the evening. But in an instant arose the dreadful suspicion of his being purposely omitted for Mr. Darcy's pleasure in the Bingleys' invitation to the officers; and though this was not exactly the case, the absolute fact of his absence was pronounced by his friend Mr. Denny, to whom Lydia eagerly applied, and who told them that Wickham had been obliged to go to town on business the day before, and was not yet returned; adding, with a significant smile,

"I do not imagine his business would have called him away just now, if he had not wished to avoid a certain gentleman here."

This part of his intelligence, though unheard by Lydia, was caught by Elizabeth, and as it assured her that Darcy was not less answerable for Wickham's absence than if her first surmise had been just, every feeling of displeasure against the former was so sharpened by immediate disappointment, that she could hardly reply with tolerable civility to the polite inquiries which he directly afterwards approached to make. — Attention, forbearance, patience with Darcy, was injury to Wickham. She was resolved against any sort of conversation with him, and turned away with a degree of ill humour, which she could not wholly surmount even in speaking to Mr. Bingley, whose blind partiality provoked her.

But Elizabeth was not formed for ill-humour; and though every prospect of her own was destroyed for the evening, it could not dwell long on her spirits; and having told all her griefs to Charlotte Lucas, whom she had not seen for a week, she was soon able to make a voluntary transition to the oddities of her cousin, and to point him out to her particular notice. The two first dances, however, brought a return of distress; they were dances of mortification. Mr. Collins, awkward and solemn, apologising instead of attending, and often moving wrong without being aware of it, gave her all the shame and misery which a disagreeable partner for a couple of dances can give. The moment of her release from him was exstacy.

She danced next with an officer, and had the refreshment of talking of Wickham, and of hearing that he was universally liked. When those dances were over she returned to Charlotte Lucas, and was in conversation with her, when she found herself suddenly addressed by Mr. Darcy, who took her so much by surprise in his application for her hand, that, without knowing what she did, she accepted him. He walked away again immediately, and she was left to fret over her own want of presence of mind; Charlotte tried to console her.

"I dare say you will find him very agreeable."

"Heaven forbid! — *That* would be the greatest misfortune of all! — To find a man agreeable whom one is determined to hate! — Do not wish me such an evil."

When the dancing recommenced, however, and Darcy approached to claim her hand, Charlotte could not help cautioning her in a whisper not to be a simpleton and allow her fancy for Wickham to make her appear unpleasant in the eyes of a man of ten times his consequence. Elizabeth made no answer, and took her place in the set, amazed at the dignity to which she was arrived in being allowed to stand opposite to Mr. Darcy, and reading in her neighbours' looks their equal amazement in beholding it. They stood for some time without speaking a word; and she began to imagine that their silence was to last through the two dances, and at first was resolved not to break it; till suddenly fancying that it would be the greater punishment to her partner to oblige him to talk, she made some slight observation on the dance. He replied, and was silent again. After a pause of some minutes she addressed him a second time with:

"It is *your* turn to say something now, Mr. Darcy. —*I* talked about the dance, and *you* ought to make some kind of remark on the size of the room, or the number of couples."

He smiled, and assured her that whatever she wished him to say should be said.

"Very well. — That reply will do for the present. — Perhaps by and by I may observe that private balls are much pleasanter than public ones. — But *now* we may be silent."

"Do you talk by rule then, while you are dancing?"

"Sometimes. One must speak a little, you know. It would look odd to be entirely silent for half an hour together, and yet for the advantage of *some*, conversation ought to be so arranged as that they may have the trouble of saying as little as possible."

"Are you consulting your own feelings in the present case, or do you imagine that you are gratifying mine?"

"Both," replied Elizabeth archly; "for I have always seen a great similarity in the turn of our minds. — We are each of an unsocial, taciturn disposition, unwilling to speak, unless we expect to say something that will amaze the whole room, and be handed down to posterity with all the eclat of a proverb."

"This is no very striking resemblance of your own character, I am sure," said he. "How near it may be to *mine*, I cannot pretend to say. — *You* think it a faithful portrait undoubtedly."

"I must not decide on my own performance."

He made no answer, and they were again silent till they had gone down the dance, when he asked her if she and her sisters did not very often walk to Meryton. She answered in the affirmative, and, unable to resist the temptation, added, "When you met us there the other day, we had just been forming a new acquaintance."

The effect was immediate. A deeper shade of hauteur overspread his features, but he said not a word, and Elizabeth, though blaming herself for her own weakness, could not go on. At length Darcy spoke, and in a constrained manner said,

"Mr. Wickham is blessed with such happy manners as may ensure his *making* friends — whether he may be equally capable of *retaining* them, is less certain."

"He has been so unlucky as to lose *your* friendship," replied Elizabeth with emphasis, "and in a manner which he is likely to suffer from all his life."

Darcy made no answer, and seemed desirous of changing the subject. At that moment Sir William Lucas appeared close to them, meaning to pass through the set to the other side of the room; but on perceiving Mr. Darcy he stopt with a bow of superior courtesy to compliment him on his dancing and his partner.

"I have been most highly gratified indeed, my dear Sir. Such very superior dancing is not often seen. It is evident that you belong to the first circles. Allow me to say, however, that your fair partner does not disgrace you, and that I must hope to have this pleasure often repeated, especially when a certain desirable event, my dear Miss Eliza, (glancing at her sister and Bingley,) shall take place. What congratulations will then flow in! I appeal to Mr. Darcy: — but let me not interrupt you, Sir. — You will not thank me for detaining you from the bewitching converse of that young lady, whose bright eyes are also upbraiding me."

The latter part of this address was scarcely heard by Darcy; but Sir William's allusion to his friend seemed to strike him forcibly, and his eyes were directed with a very serious expression towards Bingley and Jane, who were dancing together. Recovering himself, however, shortly, he turned to his partner, and said,

"Sir William's interruption has made me forget what we were talking of."

"I do not think we were speaking at all. Sir William could not have interrupted any two people in the room who had less to say for themselves. — We have tried two or three subjects already without success, and what we are to talk of next I cannot imagine."

"What think you of books?" said he, smiling.

"Books — Oh! no. — I am sure we never read the same, or not with the same feelings."

"I am sorry you think so; but if that be the case, there can at least be no want of subject. — We may compare our different opinions."

"No — I cannot talk of books in a ball-room; my head is always full of something else."

"The *present* always occupies you in such scenes — does it?" said he, with a look of doubt.

"Yes, always," she replied, without knowing what she said,

for her thoughts had wandered far from the subject, as soon afterwards appeared by her suddenly exclaiming, "I remember hearing you once say, Mr. Darcy, that you hardly ever forgave, that your resentment once created was unappeasable. You are very cautious, I suppose, as to its *being created*."

"I am," said he, with a firm voice.

"And never allow yourself to be blinded by prejudice?"

"I hope not."

"It is particularly incumbent on those who never change their opinion, to be secure of judging properly at first."

"May I ask to what these questions tend?"

"Merely to the illustration of *your* character," said she, endeavouring to shake off her gravity. "I am trying to make it out."

"And what is your success?"

She shook her head. "I do not get on at all. I hear such different accounts of you as puzzle me exceedingly."

"I can readily believe," answered he gravely, "that report may vary greatly with respect to me; and I could wish, Miss Bennet, that you were not to sketch my character at the present moment, as there is reason to fear that the performance would reflect no credit on either."

"But if I do not take your likeness now, I may never have another opportunity."

"I would by no means suspend any pleasure of yours," he coldly replied. She said no more, and they went down the other dance and parted in silence; on each side dissatisfied, though not to an equal degree, for in Darcy's breast there was a tolerable powerful feeling towards her, which soon procured her pardon, and directed all his anger against another.

They had not long separated when Miss Bingley came towards her, and with an expression of civil disdain thus accosted her,

"So, Miss Eliza, I hear you are quite delighted with George Wickham! — Your sister has been talking to me about him, and asking me a thousand questions; and I find that the young man forgot to tell you, among his other communications, that he was the son of old Wickham, the late Mr. Darcy's steward. Let me recommend you, however, as a friend, not to give implicit confidence to all his assertions; for as to Mr. Darcy's using him ill, it is perfectly false; for, on the contrary, he has been always remarkably kind to him, though George Wickham has treated Mr. Darcy in a most infamous manner. I do not know the particulars, but I know very well that Mr. Darcy is not in the least to blame, that he cannot bear to hear George Wickham mentioned, and that though my brother thought he could not well avoid including him in his invitation to the officers, he was excessively glad to find that he had taken himself out of the way. His coming into the country at all, is a most insolent thing indeed, and I wonder how he could presume to do it. I pity you, Miss Eliza, for this discovery of your favorite's guilt; but really considering his descent one could not expect much better."

"His guilt and his descent appear by your account to be the same," said Elizabeth angrily; "for I have heard you accuse him of nothing worse than of being the son of Mr. Darcy's steward, and of *that*, I can assure you, he informed me himself."

"I beg your pardon," replied Miss Bingley, turning away with a sneer. "Excuse my interference. — It was kindly meant."

"Insolent girl!" said Elizabeth to herself. — "You are much mistaken if you expect to influence me by such a paltry attack as this. I see nothing in it but your own wilful ignorance and the malice of Mr. Darcy." She then sought her eldest sister, who had undertaken to make inquiries on the same subject of Bingley. Jane met her with a smile of such sweet complacency, a glow of such happy expression, as sufficiently marked how well she was satisfied with the occurrences of the evening. — Elizabeth instantly read her feelings, and at that moment solicitude for Wickham, resentment against his enemies and every thing else gave way before the hope of Jane's being in the fairest way for happiness.

"I want to know," said she, with a countenance no less smiling than her sister's, "what you have learnt about Mr. Wickham. But perhaps you have been too pleasantly engaged to think of any third person; in which case you may be sure of my pardon."

"No," replied Jane, "I have not forgotten him; but I have nothing satisfactory to tell you. Mr. Bingley does not know the whole of his history, and is quite ignorant of the circumstances which have principally offended Mr. Darcy; but he will vouch for the good conduct, the probity and honour of his friend, and is perfectly convinced that Mr. Wickham has deserved much less attention from Mr. Darcy than he has received; and I am sorry to say that by his account as well as his sister's, Mr. Wickham is by no means a respectable young man. I am afraid he has been very imprudent, and has deserved to lose Mr. Darcy's regard."

"Mr. Bingley does not know Mr. Wickham himself?"

"No; he never saw him till the other morning at Meryton."

"This account then is what he has received from Mr. Darcy. I am perfectly satisfied. But what does he say of the living?"

"He does not exactly recollect the circumstances, though he has heard them from Mr. Darcy more than once, but he believes that it was left to him *conditionally* only."

"I have not a doubt of Mr. Bingley's sincerity," said Elizabeth warmly; "but you must excuse my not being convinced by assurances only. Mr. Bingley's defence of his friend was a very able one I dare say, but since he is unacquainted with several parts of the story, and has learnt the rest from that friend himself, I shall venture still to think of both gentlemen as I did before."

She then changed the discourse to one more gratifying to each, and on which there could be no difference of sentiment. Elizabeth listened with delight to the happy, though modest hopes which Jane entertained of Bingley's regard, and said all in her power to heighten her confidence in it. On their being joined by Mr. Bingley himself, Elizabeth withdrew to Miss Lucas; to whose inquiry after the pleasantness of her last partner she had scarcely replied, before Mr. Collins came up to them and told her with great exultation that he had just been so fortunate as to make a most important discovery.

"I have found out," said he, "by a singular accident, that there is now in the room a near relation of my patroness. I happened to overhear the gentleman himself mentioning to the young lady who does the honours of this house the names of his cousin Miss de Bourgh, and of her mother Lady Catherine. How wonderfully these sort of things occur! Who would have thought of my meeting with—perhaps—a nephew of Lady Catherine de Bourgh in this assembly!—I am most thankful that the discovery is made in time for me to pay my respects to him, which I am now going to do, and trust he will excuse my not having done it before. My total ignorance of the connection must plead my apology."

"You are not going to introduce yourself to Mr. Darcy?"

"Indeed I am. I shall intreat his pardon for not having done it earlier. I believe him to be Lady Catherine's *nephew*. It will be in my power to assure him that her ladyship was quite well yesterday se'nnight."

Elizabeth tried hard to dissuade him from such a scheme; assuring him that Mr. Darcy would consider his addressing him without introduction as an impertinent freedom, rather than a compliment to his aunt; that it was not in the least necessary there should be any notice on either side, and that if it were, it must belong to Mr. Darcy, the superior in consequence, to begin the acquaintance.—Mr. Collins listened to her with the determined air of following his own inclination, and when she ceased speaking, replied thus,

"My dear Miss Elizabeth, I have the highest opinion in the world of your excellent judgment in all matters within the scope of your understanding, but permit me to say that there must be a wide difference between the established forms of ceremony amongst the laity, and those which regulate the clergy; for give me leave to observe that I consider the clerical office as equal in point of dignity with the highest rank in the kingdom—provided that a proper humility of behaviour is at the same time maintained. You must therefore allow me to follow the dictates of my conscience on this occasion, which leads me to perform what I look on as a point of duty. Pardon me for neglecting to profit by your advice, which on every other subject shall be my constant guide, though in the case before us I consider myself more fitted by education and habitual study to decide on what is right than a young lady like yourself." And with a low bow he left her to attack Mr. Darcy, whose reception of his advances she eagerly watched, and whose astonishment at being so addressed was very evident. Her cousin prefaced his speech with a solemn bow, and though she could not hear a word of it, she felt as if hearing it all, and saw in the motion of his lips the words "apology," "Hunsford," and "Lady Catherine de Bourgh." — It vexed her to see him expose himself to such a man. Mr. Darcy was eyeing him with unrestrained wonder, and when at last Mr. Collins allowed him time to speak, replied with an air of distant civility. Mr. Collins, however, was not discouraged from speaking again, and Mr. Darcy's contempt seemed abundantly increasing with the length of his second speech, and at the end of it he only made him a slight bow, and moved another way. Mr. Collins then returned to Elizabeth.

"I have no reason, I assure you," said he, "to be dissatisfied with my reception. Mr. Darcy seemed much pleased with the attention. He answered me with the utmost civility, and even paid me the compliment of saying, that he was so well convinced of Lady Catherine's discernment as to be certain she could never bestow a favour unworthily. It was really a very handsome thought. Upon the whole, I am much pleased with him."

As Elizabeth had no longer any interest of her own to pursue, she turned her attention almost entirely on her sister and Mr. Bingley, and the train of agreeable reflections which her observations gave birth to, made her perhaps almost as happy as Jane. She saw her in idea settled in that very house in all the felicity which a marriage of true affection could bestow; and she felt capable under such circumstances, of endeavouring even to like Bingley's two sisters. Her mother's thoughts she plainly saw were bent the same way, and she determined not to venture near her, lest she might hear too much. When they sat down to supper, therefore, she considered it a most unlucky perverseness which placed them within one of each other; and deeply was she vexed to find that her mother was talking to that one person (Lady Lucas) freely, openly, and of nothing else but of her expectation that Jane would be soon married to Mr.

Bingley. — It was an animating subject, and Mrs. Bennet seemed incapable of fatigue while enumerating the advantages of the match. His being such a charming young man, and so rich, and living but three miles from them, were the first points of self-gratulation; and then it was such a comfort to think how fond the two sisters were of Jane, and to be certain that they must desire the connection as much as she could do. It was, moreover, such a promising thing for her younger daughters, as Jane's marrying so greatly must throw them in the way of other rich men; and lastly, it was so pleasant at her time of life to be able to consign her single daughters to the care of their sister, that she might not be obliged to go into company more than she liked. It was necessary to make this circumstance a matter of pleasure, because on such occasions it is the etiquette; but no one was less likely than Mrs. Bennet to find comfort in staying at home at any period of her life. She concluded with many good wishes that Lady Lucas might soon be equally fortunate, though evidently and triumphantly believing there was no chance of it.

In vain did Elizabeth endeavour to check the rapidity of her mother's words, or persuade her to describe her felicity in a less audible whisper; for to her inexpressible vexation, she could perceive that the chief of it was overheard by Mr. Darcy, who sat opposite to them. Her mother only scolded her for being nonsensical.

"What is Mr. Darcy to me, pray, that I should be afraid of him? I am sure we owe him no such particular civility as to be obliged to say nothing *he* may not like to hear."

"For heaven's sake, madam, speak lower. — What advantage can it be to you to offend Mr. Darcy? — You will never recommend yourself to his friend by so doing."

Nothing that she could say, however, had any influence. Her mother would talk of her views in the same intelligible tone. Elizabeth blushed and blushed again with shame and vexation. She could not help frequently glancing her eye at Mr. Darcy, though every glance convinced her of what she dreaded; for though he was not always looking at her mother, she was convinced that his attention was invariably fixed by her. The expression of his face changed gradually from indignant contempt to a composed and steady gravity.

At length however Mrs. Bennet had no more to say; and Lady Lucas, who had been long yawning at the repetition of delights which she saw no likelihood of sharing, was left to the comforts of cold ham and chicken. Elizabeth now began to revive. But not long was the interval of tranquillity; for when supper was over, singing was talked of, and she had the mortification of seeing Mary, after very little entreaty, preparing to oblige the company. By many significant looks and silent entreaties, did she endeavour to prevent such a proof of complaisance,—but in vain; Mary would not understand them; such an opportunity of exhibiting was delightful to her, and she began her song. Elizabeth's eyes were fixed on her with most painful sensations; and she watched her progress through the several stanzas with an impatience which was very ill rewarded at their close; for Mary, on receiving amongst the thanks of the table, the hint of a hope that she might be prevailed on to favour them again, after the pause of half a minute began another. Mary's powers were by no means fitted for such a display; her voice was weak, and her manner affected. — Elizabeth was in agonies. She looked at Jane, to see how she bore it; but Jane was very composedly talking to Bingley. She looked at his two sisters, and saw them making signs of derision at each other, and at Darcy, who continued however impenetrably grave. She looked at her father to entreat his interference, lest Mary should be singing all night. He took the hint, and when Mary had finished her second song, said aloud,

"That will do extremely well, child. You have delighted us long enough. Let the other young ladies have time to exhibit."

Mary, though pretending not to hear, was somewhat disconcerted; and Elizabeth sorry for her, and sorry for her father's speech, was afraid her anxiety had done no good. — Others of the party were now applied to.

"If I," said Mr. Collins, "were so fortunate as to be able to sing, I should have great pleasure, I am sure, in obliging the company with an air; for I consider music as a very innocent diversion, and perfectly compatible with the profession of a clergyman. —I do not mean however to assert that we can be justified in devoting too much of our time to music, for there are certainly other things to be attended to. The rector of a parish has much to do. — In the first place, he must make such an agreement for tithes[1] as may be beneficial to himself and not offensive to his patron. He must write his own sermons;[2] and the time that remains will not be too much for his parish duties, and the care and improvement of his dwelling, which he cannot be excused from making as comfortable as possible. And I do not think it of light importance that he should have attentive and conciliatory manners towards every body, especially towards those to whom he owes his preferment. I cannot acquit him of that duty; nor could I think well of the man who should omit an occasion of testifying his respect towards any body connected with the family." And with a bow to Mr. Darcy, he concluded his speech, which had been spoken so loud as to be heard by half the room. —Many stared. —Many smiled; but no one looked more amused than Mr. Bennet himself, while his wife seriously commended Mr. Collins for having spoken so sensibly, and observed in a half-whisper to Lady Lucas, that he was a remarkably clever, good kind of young man.

To Elizabeth it appeared, that had her family made an agreement to expose themselves as much as they could during the evening, it would have been impossible for them to play their parts with more spirit, or finer success; and happy did she think it for Bingley and her sister that some of the exhibition had escaped his notice, and that his feelings were not of a sort to be much distressed by the folly which he must have witnessed. That his two sisters and Mr. Darcy, however, should have such an opportunity of ridiculing her relations was bad enough, and she could not determine whether the silent contempt of the gentleman, or the insolent smiles of the ladies, were more intolerable.

---

1   Tythes or tithes were the ten per cent share in income from an estate to which a clergyman was entitled.

2   It was by no means unheard-of for Anglican clergy to preach from volumes of ready-made sermons rather than composing their own.

The rest of the evening brought her little amusement. She was teazed by Mr. Collins, who continued most perseveringly by her side, and though he could not prevail with her to dance with him again, put it out of her power to dance with others. In vain did she entreat him to stand up with somebody else, and offer to introduce him to any young lady in the room. He assured her that as to dancing, he was perfectly indifferent to it; that his chief object was by delicate attentions to recommend himself to her, and that he should therefore make a point of remaining close to her the whole evening. There was no arguing upon such a project. She owed her greatest relief to her friend Miss Lucas, who often joined them, and goodnaturedly engaged Mr. Collins's conversation to herself.

She was at least free from the offence of Mr. Darcy's farther notice; though often standing within a very short distance of her, quite disengaged, he never came near enough to speak. She felt it to be the probable consequence of her allusions to Mr. Wickham, and rejoiced in it.

The Longbourn party were the last of all the company to depart; and by a manoeuvre of Mrs. Bennet, had to wait for their carriages a quarter of an hour after every body else was gone,[1] which gave them time to see how heartily they were wished away by some of the family. Mrs. Hurst and her sister scarcely opened their mouths except to complain of fatigue, and were evidently impatient to have the house to themselves. They repulsed every attempt of Mrs. Bennet at conversation, and by so doing, threw a languor over the whole party, which was very little relieved by the long speeches of Mr. Collins, who was complimenting Mr. Bingley and his sisters on the elegance of their entertainment, and the hospitality and politeness which had marked their behaviour to their guests. Darcy said nothing at all. Mr. Bennet, in equal silence, was enjoying the scene. Mr. Bingley and Jane were standing together, a little detached from the rest, and talked only to each other. Elizabeth preserved as steady a silence as either Mrs. Hurst or Miss Bing-

---

1   As Chapman notes (p.392), the Bennets' own vehicle carries six in chapter xvi of this volume; here, a full family party of eight (including Mr. Collins) has required a second carriage to be hired for the occasion.

ley; and even Lydia was too much fatigued to utter more than the occasional exclamation of "Lord, how tired I am!" accompanied by a violent yawn.

When at length they arose to take leave, Mrs. Bennet was most pressingly civil in her hope of seeing the whole family soon at Longbourn; and addressed herself particularly to Mr. Bingley, to assure him how happy he would make them, by eating a family dinner with them at any time, without the ceremony of a formal invitation. Bingley was all grateful pleasure, and he readily engaged for taking the earliest opportunity of waiting on her, after his return from London, whither he was obliged to go the next day for a short time.

Mrs. Bennet was perfectly satisfied; and quitted the house under the delightful persuasion that, allowing for the necessary preparations of settlements, new carriages and wedding clothes, she should undoubtedly see her daughter settled at Netherfield in the course of three or four months. Of having another daughter married to Mr. Collins, she thought with equal certainty, and with considerable, though not equal, pleasure. Elizabeth was the least dear to her of all her children; and though the man and the match were quite good enough for *her*, the worth of each was eclipsed by Mr. Bingley and Netherfield.

CHAPTER XIX.

THE next day opened a new scene at Longbourn. Mr. Collins made his declaration in form. Having resolved to do it without loss of time, as his leave of absence extended only to the following Saturday, and having no feelings of diffidence to make it distressing to himself even at the moment, he set about it in a very orderly manner, with all the observances which he supposed a regular part of the business. On finding Mrs. Bennet, Elizabeth, and one of the younger girls together, soon after breakfast, he addressed the mother in these words,

"May I hope, Madam, for your interest with your fair daughter Elizabeth, when I solicit for the honour of a private audience with her in the course of this morning?"

Before Elizabeth had time for any thing but a blush of surprise, Mrs. Bennet instantly answered,

"Oh dear! — Yes — certainly. — I am sure Lizzy will be very happy — I am sure she can have no objection. — Come, Kitty, I want you up stairs." And gathering her work together, she was hastening away, when Elizabeth called out,

"Dear Ma'am, do not go. — I beg you will not go. — Mr. Collins must excuse me. — He can have nothing to say to me that any body need not hear. I am going away myself."

"No, no, nonsense, Lizzy. — I desire you will stay where you are." — And upon Elizabeth's seeming really, with vexed and embarrassed looks, about to escape, she added, "Lizzy, I *insist* upon your staying and hearing Mr. Collins."

Elizabeth would not oppose such an injunction — and a moment's consideration making her also sensible that it would be wisest to get it over as soon and as quietly as possible, she sat down again, and tried to conceal by incessant employment the feelings which were divided between distress and diversion. Mrs. Bennet and Kitty walked off, and as soon as they were gone Mr. Collins began.

"Believe me, my dear Miss Elizabeth, that your modesty, so far from doing you any disservice, rather adds to your other perfections. You would have been less amiable in my eyes had there *not* been this little unwillingness; but allow me to assure you that I have your respected mother's permission for this address. You can hardly doubt the purport of my discourse, however your natural delicacy may lead you to dissemble; my attentions have been too marked to be mistaken. Almost as soon as I entered the house I singled you out as the companion of my future life. But before I am run away with by my feelings on this subject, perhaps it will be advisable for me to state my reasons for marrying — and moreover for coming into Hertfordshire with the design of selecting a wife, as I certainly did."

The idea of Mr. Collins, with all his solemn composure, being run away with by his feelings, made Elizabeth so near laughing that she could not use the short pause he allowed in any attempt to stop him farther, and he continued:

"My reasons for marrying are, first, that I think it a right thing for every clergyman in easy circumstances (like myself) to set the example of matrimony in his parish. Secondly, that I am convinced it will add very greatly to my happiness; and thirdly — which perhaps I ought to have mentioned earlier, that it is the particular advice and recommendation of the very noble lady whom I have the honour of calling patroness. Twice has she condescended to give me her opinion (unasked too!) on this subject; and it was but the very Saturday night before I left Hunsford — between our pools at quadrille, while Mrs. Jenkinson was arranging Miss de Bourgh's foot-stool, that she said, 'Mr. Collins, you must marry. A clergyman like you must marry. — Chuse properly, chuse a gentlewoman for *my* sake; and for your *own*, let her be an active, useful sort of person, not brought up high, but able to make a small income go a good way. This is my advice. Find such a woman as soon as you can, bring her to Hunsford, and I will visit her.' Allow me, by the way, to observe, my fair cousin, that I do not reckon the notice and kindness of Lady Catherine de Bourgh as among the least of the advantages in my power to offer. You will find her manners beyond any thing I can describe; and your wit and vivacity I think must be acceptable to her, especially when tempered with the silence and respect which her rank will inevitably excite. Thus much for my general intention in favour of matrimony; it remains to be told why my views were directed to Longbourn instead of my own neighbourhood, where I assure you there are many amiable young women. But the fact is, that being, as I am, to inherit this estate after the death of your honoured father, (who, however, may live many years longer,) I could not satisfy myself without resolving to chuse a wife from among his daughters, that the loss to them might be as little as possible, when the melancholy event takes place — which, however, as I have already said, may not be for several years. This has been my motive, my fair cousin, and I flatter myself it will not sink me in your esteem. And now nothing remains for me but to assure you in the most animated language of the violence of my affection. To fortune I am perfectly indifferent, and shall make no demand of that nature on your father, since I am well aware that it could not be complied with; and that one thousand pounds in the 4 per cents. which will not be yours till after your mother's decease, is all that you may ever be entitled to.[1] On that head, therefore, I shall be uniformly silent; and you may assure yourself that no ungenerous reproach shall ever pass my lips when we are married."

not exactly a proposal

It was absolutely necessary to interrupt him now.

"You are too hasty, Sir," she cried. "You forget that I have made no answer. Let me do it without farther loss of time. Accept my thanks for the compliment you are paying me. I am very sensible of the honour of your proposals, but it is impossible for me to do otherwise than decline them."

"I am not now to learn," replied Mr. Collins, with a formal wave of the hand, "that it is usual with young ladies to reject the addresses of the man whom they secretly mean to accept, when he first applies for their favour; and that sometimes the refusal is repeated a second or even a third time. I am therefore by no means discouraged by what you have just said, and shall hope to lead you to the altar ere long."

"Upon my word, Sir," cried Elizabeth, "your hope is rather an extraordinary one after my declaration. I do assure you that I am not one of those young ladies (if such young ladies there are) who are so daring as to risk their happiness on the chance of being asked a second time. I am perfectly serious in my refusal. — You could not make *me* happy, and I am convinced that I am the last woman in the world who would make *you* so. — Nay, were your friend Lady Catherine to know me, I am persuaded she would find me in every respect ill qualified for the situation."

"Were it certain that Lady Catherine would think so," said Mr. Collins very gravely — "but I cannot imagine that her ladyship would at all disapprove of you. And you may be certain that when I have the honour of seeing her again I shall speak in the highest terms of your modesty, economy, and other amiable qualifications."

"Indeed, Mr. Collins, all praise of me will be unnecessary.

---

1 The "four per cents" are government stocks yielding annual interest at this rate. Collins is ostentatiously disavowing a dowry, the money given by a father with his daughter to her husband at marriage. Compare Mr. Bennet's comment in Volume III, chapter vii, regarding the sum a suitor might demand.

You must give me leave to judge for myself, and pay me the compliment of believing what I say. I wish you very happy and very rich, and by refusing your hand, do all in my power to prevent your being otherwise. In making me the offer, you must have satisfied the delicacy of your feelings with regard to my family, and may take possession of Longbourn estate whenever it falls, without any self-reproach. This matter may be considered, therefore, as finally settled." And rising as she thus spoke, she would have quitted the room, had not Mr. Collins thus addressed her,

"When I do myself the honour of speaking to you next on this subject I shall hope to receive a more favourable answer than you have now given me; though I am far from accusing you of cruelty at present, because I know it to be the established custom of your sex to reject a man on the first application, and perhaps you have even now said as much to encourage my suit as would be consistent with the true delicacy of the female character."

"Really, Mr. Collins," cried Elizabeth with some warmth, "you puzzle me exceedingly. If what I have hitherto said can appear to you in the form of encouragement, I know not how to express my refusal in such a way as may convince you of its being one."

"You must give me leave to flatter myself, my dear cousin, that your refusal of my addresses are merely words of course. My reasons for believing it are briefly these: — It does not appear to me that my hand is unworthy your acceptance, or that at the establishment I can offer would be any other than highly desirable. My situation in life, my connections with the family of De Bourgh, and my relationship to your own, are circumstances highly in my favour; and you should take it into farther consideration that in spite of your manifold attractions, it is by no means certain that another offer of marriage may ever be made you. Your portion is unhappily so small that it will in all likelihood undo the effects of your loveliness and amiable qualifications.[1] As I must therefore conclude that you

---

1   Given the disavowal noted above, by "portion" Mr. Collins must mean the small amount Elizabeth will inherit on her mother's death, although the word could also refer to a dowry.

are not serious in your rejection of me, I shall chuse to attribute it to your wish of increasing my love by suspense, according to the usual practice of elegant females."

"I do assure you, Sir, that I have no pretension whatever to that kind of elegance which consists in tormenting a respectable man. I would rather be paid the compliment of being believed sincere. I thank you again and again for the honour you have done me in your proposals, but to accept them is absolutely impossible. My feelings in every respect forbid it. Can I speak plainer? Do not consider me now as an elegant female intending to plague you, but as a rational creature speaking the truth from her heart."

"You are uniformly charming!" cried he, with an air of awkward gallantry; "and I am persuaded that when sanctioned by the express authority of both your excellent parents, my proposals will not fail of being acceptable."

To such perseverance in wilful self-deception Elizabeth would make no reply, and immediately and in silence withdrew; determined, that if he persisted in considering her repeated refusals as flattering encouragement, to apply to her father, whose negative might be uttered in such a manner as must be decisive, and whose behaviour at least could not be mistaken for the affectation and coquetry of an elegant female.

CHAPTER XX.

MR. COLLINS was not left long to the silent contemplation of his successful love; for Mrs. Bennet, having dawdled about in the vestibule to watch for the end of the conference, no sooner saw Elizabeth open the door and with quick step pass her towards the staircase, than she entered the breakfast-room, and congratulated both him and herself in warm terms on the happy prospect of their nearer connection. Mr. Collins received and returned these felicitations with equal pleasure, and then proceeded to relate the particulars of their interview, with the result of which he trusted he had every reason to be satisfied, since the refusal which his cousin had stedfastly given him would naturally flow from her bashful modesty and the genuine delicacy of her character.

This information, however, startled Mrs. Bennet;—she would have been glad to be equally satisfied that her daughter had meant to encourage him by protesting against his proposals, but she dared not to believe it, and could not help saying so.

"But depend upon it, Mr. Collins," she added, "that Lizzy shall be brought to reason. I will speak to her about it myself directly. She is a very headstrong foolish girl, and does not know her own interest; but I will *make* her know it."

"Pardon me for interrupting you, Madam," cried Mr. Collins; "but if she is really headstrong and foolish, I know not whether she would altogether be a very desirable wife to a man in my situation, who naturally looks for happiness in the marriage state. If therefore she actually persists in rejecting my suit, perhaps it were better not to force her into accepting me, because if liable to such defects of temper, she could not contribute much to my felicity."

"Sir, you quite misunderstand me," said Mrs. Bennet, alarmed. "Lizzy is only headstrong in such matters as these. In every thing else she is as good natured a girl as ever lived. I will go directly to Mr. Bennet, and we shall very soon settle it with her, I am sure."

She would not give him time to reply, but hurrying instantly to her husband, called out as she entered the library,

"Oh! Mr. Bennet, you are wanted immediately; we are all in an uproar. You must come and make Lizzy marry Mr. Collins, for she vows she will not have him, and if you do not make haste he will change his mind and not have *her*."

Mr. Bennet raised his eyes from his book as she entered, and fixed them on her face with a calm unconcern which was not in the least altered by her communication.

"I have not the pleasure of understanding you," said he, when she had finished her speech. "Of what are you talking?"

"Of Mr. Collins and Lizzy. Lizzy declares she will not have

Mr. Collins, and Mr. Collins begins to say that he will not have Lizzy."

"And what am I to do on the occasion?—It seems an hopeless business."

"Speak to Lizzy about it yourself. Tell her that you insist upon her marrying him."

"Let her be called down. She shall hear my opinion."

Mrs. Bennet rang the bell, and Miss Elizabeth was summoned to the library.

"Come here, child," cried her father as she appeared. "I have sent for you on an affair of importance. I understand that Mr. Collins has made you an offer of marriage. Is it true?" Elizabeth replied that it was. "Very well—and this offer of marriage you have refused?"

"I have, Sir."

"Very well. We now come to the point. Your mother insists upon your accepting it. Is not it so, Mrs. Bennet?"

"Yes, or I will never see her again."

"An unhappy alternative is before you, Elizabeth. From this day you must be a stranger to one of your parents. — Your mother will never see you again if you do *not* marry Mr. Collins, and I will never see you again if you *do*."

Elizabeth could not but smile at such a conclusion of such a beginning; but Mrs. Bennet, who had persuaded herself that her husband regarded the affair as she wished, was excessively disappointed.

"What do you mean, Mr. Bennet, by talking in this way? You promised me to *insist* upon her marrying him."

"My dear," replied her husband, "I have two small favours to request. First, that you will allow me the free use of my understanding on the present occasion; and secondly, of my room. I shall be glad to have the library to myself as soon as may be."

Not yet, however, in spite of her disappointment in her husband, did Mrs. Bennet give up the point. She talked to Elizabeth again and again; coaxed and threatened her by turns. She endeavoured to secure Jane in her interest, but Jane with all possible mildness declined interfering;—and Elizabeth sometimes with real earnestness and sometimes with playful gaiety replied to her attacks. Though her manner varied however, her determination never did.

Mr. Collins, meanwhile, was meditating in solitude on what had passed. He thought too well of himself to comprehend on what motive his cousin could refuse him; and though his pride was hurt, he suffered in no other way. His regard for her was quite imaginary; and the possibility of her deserving her mother's reproach prevented his feeling any regret.

While the family were in this confusion, Charlotte Lucas came to spend the day with them. She was met in the vestibule by Lydia, who, flying to her, cried in a half whisper, "I am glad you are come, for there is such fun here! — What do you think has happened this morning? — Mr. Collins has made an offer to Lizzy, and she will not have him."

Charlotte had hardly time to answer, before they were joined by Kitty, who came to tell the same news, and no sooner had they entered the breakfast-room, where Mrs. Bennet was alone, than she likewise began on the subject, calling on Miss Lucas for her compassion, and entreating her to persuade her friend Lizzy to comply with the wishes of all her family. "Pray do, my dear Miss Lucas," she added in a melancholy tone, "for nobody is on my side, nobody takes part with me, I am cruelly used, nobody feels for my poor nerves."

Charlotte's reply was spared by the entrance of Jane and Elizabeth.

"Aye, there she comes," continued Mrs. Bennet, "looking as unconcerned as may be, and caring no more for us than if we were at York, provided she can have her own way. — But I tell you what, Miss Lizzy, if you take it into your head to go on refusing every offer of marriage in this way, you will never get a husband at all — and I am sure I do not know who is to maintain you when your father is dead. — *I* shall not be able to keep you — and so I warn you. — I have done with you from this very day. — I told you in the library, you know, that I should never speak to you again, and you will find me as good as my word. I have no pleasure in talking to undutiful children. —

Not that I have much pleasure indeed in talking to any body. People who suffer as I do from nervous complaints can have no great inclination for talking. Nobody can tell what I suffer! — But it is always so. Those who do not complain are never pitied."

Her daughters listened in silence to this effusion, sensible that any attempt to reason with or sooth her would only increase the irritation. She talked on, therefore, without interruption from any of them till they were joined by Mr. Collins, who entered with an air more stately than usual, and on perceiving whom, she said to the girls,

"Now, I do insist upon it, that you, all of you, hold your tongues, and let Mr. Collins and me have a little conversation together."

Elizabeth passed quietly out of the room, Jane and Kitty followed, but Lydia stood her ground, determined to hear all she could; and Charlotte, detained first by the civility of Mr. Collins, whose inquiries after herself and all her family were very minute, and then by a little curiosity, satisfied herself with walking to the window and pretending not to hear. In a doleful voice Mrs. Bennet thus began the projected conversation. — "Oh! Mr. Collins!" —

"My dear Madam," replied he, "let us be for ever silent on this point. Far be it from me," he presently continued in a voice that marked his displeasure, "to resent the behaviour of your daughter. Resignation to inevitable evils is the duty of us all; the peculiar duty of a young man who has been so fortunate as I have been in early preferment; and I trust I am resigned. Perhaps not the less so from feeling a doubt of my positive happiness had my fair cousin honoured me with her hand; for I have often observed that resignation is never so perfect as when the blessing denied begins to lose somewhat of its value in our estimation. You will not, I hope, consider me as shewing any disrespect to your family, my dear Madam, by thus withdrawing my pretensions to your daughter's favour, without having paid yourself and Mr. Bennet the compliment of requesting you to interpose your authority in my behalf. My conduct may I fear be objectionable in having accepted my dismission from your daughter's lips instead of your own. But we are all liable to error. I have certainly meant well through the whole affair. My object has been to secure an amiable companion for myself, with due consideration for the advantage of all your family, and if my *manner* has been at all reprehensible, I here beg leave to apologise."

CHAPTER XXI.

THE discussion of Mr. Collins's offer was now nearly at an end, and Elizabeth had only to suffer from the uncomfortable feelings necessarily attending it, and occasionally from some peevish allusion of her mother. As for the gentleman himself, *his* feelings were chiefly expressed, not by embarrassment or dejection, or by trying to avoid her, but by stiffness of manner and resentful silence. He scarcely ever spoke to her, and the assiduous attentions which he had been so sensible of himself, were transferred for the rest of the day to Miss Lucas, whose civility in listening to him, was a seasonable relief to them all, and especially to her friend.

The morrow produced no abatement of Mrs. Bennet's ill humour or ill health. Mr. Collins was also in the same state of angry pride. Elizabeth had hoped that his resentment might shorten his visit, but his plan did not appear in the least affected by it. He was always to have gone on Saturday, and to Saturday he still meant to stay.

After breakfast the girls walked to Meryton to inquire if Mr. Wickham were returned, and to lament over his absence from the Netherfield ball. He joined them on their entering the town and attended them to their aunt's, where his regret and vexation, and the concern of every body was well talked over. — To Elizabeth, however, he voluntarily acknowledged that the necessity of his absence *had* been self imposed.

"I found," said he, "as the time drew near, that I had better not meet Mr. Darcy;—that to be in the same room, the same party with him for so many hours together, might be more than I could bear, and that scenes might arise unpleasant to more than myself."

She highly approved his forbearance, and they had leisure for a full discussion of it, and for all the commendation which they civilly bestowed on each other, as Wickham and another officer walked back with them to Longbourn, and during the walk, he particularly attended to her. His accompanying them was a double advantage; she felt all the compliment it offered to herself, and it was most acceptable as an occasion of introducing him to her father and mother.

Soon after their return, a letter was delivered to Miss Bennet; it came from Netherfield, and was opened immediately. The envelope contained a sheet of elegant, little, hot pressed paper,[1] well covered with a lady's fair, flowing hand; and Elizabeth saw her sister's countenance change as she read it, and saw her dwelling intently on some particular passages. Jane recollected herself soon, and putting the letter away, tried to join with her usual cheerfulness in the general conversation; but Elizabeth felt an anxiety on the subject which drew off her attention even from Wickham; and no sooner had he and his companion taken leave, than a glance from Jane invited her to follow her upstairs. When they had gained their own room, Jane taking out the letter, said,

"This is from Caroline Bingley; what it contains, has surprised me a good deal. The whole party have left Netherfield by this time, and are on their way to town; and without any intention of coming back again. You shall hear what she says."

She then read the first sentence aloud, which comprised the information of their having just resolved to follow their brother to town directly, and of their meaning to dine that day in Grosvenor street, where Mr. Hurst had a house.[2] The next was in these words. "I do not pretend to regret any thing I shall leave in Hertfordshire, except your society, my dearest friend; but we will hope at some future period, to enjoy many returns of the delightful intercourse we have known, and in the mean

---

1   Hot-pressed paper was smoother and thus more expensive than ordinary.
2   Grosvenor Street is in London's expensive Mayfair district.

while may lessen the pain of separation by a very frequent and most unreserved correspondence. I depend on you for that." To these high flown expressions, Elizabeth listened with all the insensibility of distrust; and though the suddenness of their removal surprised her, she saw nothing in it really to lament; it was not to be supposed that their absence from Netherfield would prevent Mr. Bingley's being there; and as to the loss of their society, she was persuaded that Jane must soon cease to regard it, in the enjoyment of his.

"It is unlucky," said she, after a short pause, "that you should not be able to see your friends before they leave the country. But may we not hope that the period of future happiness to which Miss Bingley looks forward, may arrive earlier than she is aware, and that the delightful intercourse you have known as friends, will be renewed with yet greater satisfaction as sisters? — Mr. Bingley will not be detained in London by them."

"Caroline decidedly says that none of the party will return into Hertfordshire this winter. I will read it to you —

"When my brother left us yesterday, he imagined that the business which took him to London, might be concluded in three or four days, but as we are certain it cannot be so, and at the same time convinced that when Charles gets to town, he will be in no hurry to leave it again, we have determined on following him thither, that he may not be obliged to spend his vacant hours in a comfortless hotel. Many of my acquaintance are already there for the winter; I wish I could hear that you, my dearest friend, had any intention of making one in the croud, but of that I despair. I sincerely hope your Christmas in Hertfordshire may abound in the gaieties which that season generally brings, and that your beaux will be so numerous as to prevent your feeling the loss of the three, of whom we shall deprive you."

"It is evident by this," added Jane, "that he comes back no more this winter."

"It is only evident that Miss Bingley does not mean he *should*."

"Why will you think so? It must be his own doing. — He is his own master. But you do not know *all*. I *will* read you the passage which particularly hurts me. I will have no reserves from *you*." "Mr. Darcy is impatient to see his sister, and to confess the truth, *we* are scarcely less eager to meet her again. I really do not think Georgiana Darcy has her equal for beauty, elegance, and accomplishments; and the affection she inspires in Louisa and myself is heightened into something still more interesting, from the hope we dare to entertain of her being hereafter our sister. I do not know whether I ever before mentioned to you my feelings on this subject, but I will not leave the country without confiding them, and I trust you will not esteem them unreasonable. My brother admires her greatly already, he will have frequent opportunity now of seeing her on the most intimate footing, her relations all wish the connection as much as his own, and a sister's partiality is not misleading me, I think, when I call Charles most capable of engaging any woman's heart. With all these circumstances to favour an attachment and nothing to prevent it, am I wrong, my dearest Jane, in indulging the hope of an event which will secure the happiness of so many?" "What think you of *this* sentence, my dear Lizzy?" — said Jane as she finished it. "Is it not clear enough? — Does it not expressly declare that Caroline neither expects nor wishes me to be her sister; that she is perfectly convinced of her brother's indifference, and that if she suspects the nature of my feelings for him, she means (most kindly!) to put me on my guard? Can there be any other opinion on the subject?"

"Yes, there can; for mine is totally different. — Will you hear it?"

"Most willingly."

"You shall have it in few words. Miss Bingley sees that her brother is in love with you, and wants him to marry Miss Darcy. She follows him to town in the hope of keeping him there, and tries to persuade you that he does not care about you."

Jane shook her head.

"Indeed, Jane, you ought to believe me. — No one who has ever seen you together, can doubt his affection. Miss Bingley I am sure cannot. She is not such a simpleton. Could she have seen half as much love in Mr. Darcy for herself, she would have ordered her wedding clothes. But the case is this. We are not rich enough, or grand enough for them; and she is the more anxious to get Miss Darcy for her brother, from the notion that when there has been *one* intermarriage, she may have less trouble in achieving a second; in which there is certainly some ingenuity, and I dare say it would succeed, if Miss de Bourgh were out of the way. But, my dearest Jane, you cannot seriously imagine that because Miss Bingley tells you her brother greatly admires Miss Darcy, he is in the smallest degree less sensible of *your* merit than when he took leave of you on Tuesday, or that it will be in her power to persuade him that instead of being in love with you, he is very much in love with her friend."

"If we thought alike of Miss Bingley," replied Jane, "your representation of all this, might make me quite easy. But I know the foundation is unjust. Caroline is incapable of wilfully deceiving any one; and all that I can hope in this case is, that she is deceived herself."

"That is right. — You could not have started a more happy idea, since you will not take comfort in mine. Believe her to be deceived by all means. You have now done your duty by her, and must fret no longer."

"But, my dear sister, can I be happy, even supposing the best, in accepting a man whose sisters and friends are all wishing him to marry elsewhere?"

"You must decide for yourself," said Elizabeth, "and if upon mature deliberation, you find that the misery of disobliging his two sisters is more than equivalent to the happiness of being his wife, I advise you by all means to refuse him."

"How can you talk so?" — said Jane faintly smiling, — "You must know that though I should be exceedingly grieved at their disapprobation, I could not hesitate."

"I did not think you would; — and that being the case, I cannot consider your situation with much compassion."

"But if he returns no more this winter, my choice will never be required. A thousand things may arise in six months!"

The idea of his returning no more Elizabeth treated with the utmost contempt. It appeared to her merely the suggestion of Caroline's interested wishes, and she could not for a moment suppose that those wishes, however openly or artfully spoken, could influence a young man so totally independent of every one.

She represented to her sister as forcibly as possible what she felt on the subject, and had soon the pleasure of seeing its happy effect. Jane's temper was not desponding, and she was gradually led to hope, though the diffidence of affection some-times overcame the hope, that Bingley would return to Netherfield and answer every wish of her heart.

They agreed that Mrs. Bennet should only hear of the departure of the family, without being alarmed on the score of the gentleman's conduct; but even this partial communication gave her a great deal of concern, and she bewailed it as exceed-ingly unlucky that the ladies should happen to go away, just as they were all getting so intimate together. After lamenting it however at some length, she had the consolation of thinking that Mr. Bingley would be soon down again and soon dining at Longbourn, and the conclusion of all was the comfortable dec-laration that, though he had been invited only to a family din-ner, she would take care to have two full courses.[1]

CHAPTER XXII.

THE Bennets were engaged to dine with the Lucases, and again during the chief of the day, was Miss Lucas so kind as to listen to Mr. Collins. Elizabeth took an opportunity of thanking her. "It keeps him in good humour," said she, "and I am more oblig-ed to you than I can express." Charlotte assured her friend of her satisfaction in being useful, and that it amply repaid her for the little sacrifice of her time. This was very amiable, but Char-lotte's kindness extended farther than Elizabeth had any con-ception of;—its object was nothing less, than to secure her from any return of Mr. Collins's addresses, by engaging them

---

1 That is, two main *meat* courses: when Mr. Bingley finally gets his dinner at Long-bourn in Volume III, chapter xii, it consists of venison *and* partridge as well as soup and (presumably) dessert.

towards herself. Such was Miss Lucas's scheme; and appearances were so favourable that when they parted at night, she would have felt almost sure of success if he had not been to leave Hertfordshire so very soon. But here, she did injustice to the fire and independence of his character, for it led him to escape out of Longbourn House the next morning with admirable slyness, and hasten to Lucas Lodge to throw himself at her feet. He was anxious to avoid the notice of his cousins, from a conviction that if they saw him depart, they could not fail to conjecture his design, and he was not willing to have the attempt known till its success could be known likewise; for though feeling almost secure, and with reason, for Charlotte had been tolerably encouraging, he was comparatively diffident since the adventure of Wednesday. His reception however was of the most flattering kind. Miss Lucas perceived him from an upper window as he walked towards the house, and instantly set out to meet him accidentally in the lane. But little had she dared to hope that so much love and eloquence awaited her there.

In as short a time as Mr. Collins's long speeches would allow, every thing was settled between them to the satisfaction of both; and as they entered the house, he earnestly entreated her to name the day that was to make him the happiest of men; and though such a solicitation must be waved for the present, the lady felt no inclination to trifle with his happiness. The stupidity with which he was favoured by nature, must guard his courtship from any charm that could make a woman wish for its continuance; and Miss Lucas, who accepted him solely from the pure and disinterested desire of an establishment, cared not how soon that establishment were gained.[1]

Sir William and Lady Lucas were speedily applied to for their consent; and it was bestowed with a most joyful alacrity. Mr. Collins's present circumstances made it a most eligible match for their daughter, to whom they could give little fortune; and his prospects of future wealth were exceedingly fair. Lady Lucas began directly to calculate with more interest than the matter had ever excited before, how many years longer Mr.

---

1 An establishment: simply, a household of her own.

Bennet was likely to live; and Sir William gave it as his decided opinion, that whenever Mr. Collins should be in possession of the Longbourn estate, it would be highly expedient that both he and his wife should make their appearance at St. James's.[1] The whole family in short were properly overjoyed on the occasion. The younger girls formed hopes of *coming out* a year or two sooner than they might otherwise have done; and the boys were relieved from their apprehension of Charlotte's dying an old maid.[2] Charlotte herself was tolerably composed. She had gained her point, and had time to consider of it. Her reflections were in general satisfactory. Mr. Collins to be sure was neither sensible nor agreeable; his society was irksome, and his attachment to her must be imaginary. But still he would be her husband. — Without thinking highly either of men or of matrimony, marriage had always been her object; it was the only honourable provision for well-educated young women of small fortune, and however uncertain of giving happiness, must be their pleasantest preservative from want. This preservative she had now obtained; and at the age of twenty-seven, without having ever been handsome, she felt all the good luck of it. The least agreeable circumstance in the business, was the surprise it must occasion to Elizabeth Bennet, whose friendship she valued beyond that of any other person. Elizabeth would wonder, and probably would blame her; and though her resolution was not to be shaken, her feelings must be hurt by such disapprobation. She resolved to give her the information herself, and therefore charged Mr. Collins when he returned to Longbourn to dinner, to drop no hint of what had passed before any of the family. A promise of secrecy was of course very dutifully given, but it could not be kept without difficulty; for the curiosity excited by his long absence, burst forth in such very direct questions on his return, as required some ingenuity to evade,

---

1 That is, at court; although why this should follow from their daughter's establishment at Longbourn is perhaps clear only to Sir William.

2 There was some expectation that an older sister would be married off before a younger, and so Charlotte's marriage will remove one objection to her younger sisters entering the marriage market. An unmarried sister would become the financial responsibility of her brothers on the death of their father.

and he was at the same time exercising great self-denial, for he was longing to publish his prosperous love.

As he was to begin his journey too early on the morrow to see any of the family, the ceremony of leavetaking was performed when the ladies moved for the night; and Mrs. Bennet with great politeness and cordiality said how happy they should be to see him at Longbourn again, whenever his other engagements might allow him to visit them.

"My dear Madam," he replied, "this invitation is particularly gratifying, because it is what I have been hoping to receive; and you may be very certain that I shall avail myself of it as soon as possible."

They were all astonished; and Mr. Bennet, who could by no means wish for so speedy a return, immediately said,

"But is there not danger of Lady Catherine's disapprobation here, my good sir? — You had better neglect your relations, than run the risk of offending your patroness."

"My dear sir," replied Mr. Collins, "I am particularly obliged to you for this friendly caution, and you may depend upon my not taking so material a step without her ladyship's concurrence."

"You cannot be too much on your guard. Risk any thing rather than her displeasure; and if you find it likely to be raised by your coming to us again, which I should think exceedingly probable, stay quietly at home, and be satisfied that *we* shall take no offence."

"Believe me, my dear sir, my gratitude is warmly excited by such affectionate attention; and depend upon it, you will speedily receive from me a letter of thanks for this, as well as for every other mark of your regard during my stay in Hertfordshire. As for my fair cousins, though my absence may not be long enough to render it necessary, I shall now take the liberty of wishing them health and happiness, not excepting my cousin Elizabeth."

With proper civilities the ladies then withdrew; all of them equally surprised to find that he meditated a quick return. Mrs. Bennet wished to understand by it that he thought of paying his addresses to one of her younger girls, and Mary might have been prevailed on to accept him. She rated his abilities much higher than any of the others; there was a solidity in his reflections which often struck her, and though by no means so clever as herself, she thought that if encouraged to read and improve himself by such an example as her's, he might become a very agreeable companion. But on the following morning, every hope of this kind was done away. Miss Lucas called soon after breakfast, and in a private conference with Elizabeth related the event of the day before.

The possibility of Mr. Collins's fancying himself in love with her friend had once occurred to Elizabeth within the last day or two; but that Charlotte could encourage him, seemed almost as far from possibility as that she could encourage him herself, and her astonishment was consequently so great as to overcome at first the bounds of decorum, and she could not help crying out,

"Engaged to Mr. Collins! my dear Charlotte,—impossible!"

The steady countenance which Miss Lucas had commanded in telling her story, gave way to a momentary confusion here on receiving so direct a reproach; though, as it was no more than she expected, she soon regained her composure, and calmly replied,

"Why should you be surprised, my dear Eliza?—Do you think it incredible that Mr. Collins should be able to procure any woman's good opinion, because he was not so happy as to succeed with you?"

But Elizabeth had now recollected herself, and making a strong effort for it, was able to assure her with tolerable firmness that the prospect of their relationship was highly grateful to her, and that she wished her all imaginable happiness.

"I see what you are feeling,"—replied Charlotte,—"you must be surprised, very much surprised,—so lately as Mr. Collins was wishing to marry you. But when you have had time to think it all over, I hope you will be satisfied with what I have done. I am not romantic you know. I never was. I ask only a comfortable home; and considering Mr. Collins's character, connections, and situation in life, I am convinced that my chance of happiness with him is as fair, as most people can boast on entering the marriage state."[1]

Elizabeth quietly answered "Undoubtedly;" — and after an awkward pause, they returned to the rest of the family. Charlotte did not stay much longer, and Elizabeth was then left to reflect on what she had heard. It was a long time before she became at all reconciled to the idea of so unsuitable a match. The strangeness of Mr. Collins's making two offers of marriage within three days, was nothing in comparison of his being now accepted. She had always felt that Charlotte's opinion of matrimony was not exactly like her own, but she could not have supposed it possible that, when called into action, she would have sacrificed every better feeling to worldly advantage. Charlotte the wife of Mr. Collins, was a most humiliating picture! — And to the pang of a friend disgracing herself and sunk in her esteem, was added the distressing conviction that it was impossible for that friend to be tolerably happy in the lot she had chosen.

CHAPTER XXIII.

ELIZABETH was sitting with her mother and sisters, reflecting on what she had heard, and doubting whether she were authorised to mention it, when Sir William Lucas himself appeared, sent by his daughter to announce her engagement to the family. With many compliments to them, and much self-gratulation on the prospect of a connection between the houses,[2] he unfolded the matter, — to an audience not merely wondering, but incredulous; for Mrs. Bennet, with more perseverance than politeness, protested he must be entirely mistaken, and Lydia, always unguarded and often uncivil, boisterously exclaimed,

---

1 Charlotte's pragmatism is very close to that counselled by Gregory in his chapter on "Friendship, Love, Marriage": see Appendix B.2.
2 In referring to the families as "houses" Sir William is once again aping the aristocracy: Lady Catherine talks of the respective "houses" of Darcy and her daughter in Volume III, chapter xiv.

"Good Lord! Sir William, how can you tell such a story? — Do not you know that Mr. Collins wants to marry Lizzy?"

Nothing less than the complaisance of a courtier could have borne without anger such treatment; but Sir William's good breeding carried him through it all; and though he begged leave to be positive as to the truth of his information, he listened to all their impertinence with the most forbearing courtesy.

Elizabeth, feeling it incumbent on her to relieve him from so unpleasant a situation, now put herself forward to confirm his account, by mentioning her prior knowledge of it from Charlotte herself; and endeavoured to put a stop to the exclamations of her mother and sisters, by the earnestness of her congratulations to Sir William, in which she was readily joined by Jane, and by making a variety of remarks on the happiness that might be expected from the match, the excellent character of Mr. Collins, and the convenient distance of Hunsford from London.

Mrs. Bennet was in fact too much overpowered to say a great deal while Sir William remained; but no sooner had he left them than her feelings found a rapid vent. In the first place, she persisted in disbelieving the whole of the matter; secondly, she was very sure that Mr. Collins had been taken in; thirdly, she trusted that they would never be happy together; and fourthly, that the match might be broken off. Two inferences, however, were plainly deduced from the whole; one, that Elizabeth was the real cause of all the mischief; and the other, that she herself had been barbarously used by them all; and on these two points she principally dwelt during the rest of the day. Nothing could console and nothing appease her. — Nor did that day wear out her resentment. A week elapsed before she could see Elizabeth without scolding her, a month passed away before she could speak to Sir William or Lady Lucas without being rude, and many months were gone before she could at all forgive their daughter.

Mr. Bennet's emotions were much more tranquil on the occasion, and such as he did experience he pronounced to be of a most agreeable sort; for it gratified him, he said, to discover that Charlotte Lucas, whom he had been used to think tolerably sensible, was as foolish as his wife, and more foolish than his daughter!

Jane confessed herself a little surprised at the match; but she said less of her astonishment than of her earnest desire for their happiness; nor could Elizabeth persuade her to consider it as improbable. Kitty and Lydia were far from envying Miss Lucas, for Mr. Collins was only a clergyman; and it affected them in no other way than as a piece of news to spread at Meryton.

Lady Lucas could not be insensible of triumph on being able to retort on Mrs. Bennet the comfort of having a daughter well married; and she called at Longbourn rather oftener than usual to say how happy she was, though Mrs. Bennet's sour looks and ill-natured remarks might have been enough to drive happiness away.

Between Elizabeth and Charlotte there was a restraint which kept them mutually silent on the subject; and Elizabeth felt persuaded that no real confidence could ever subsist between them again. Her disappointment in Charlotte made her turn with fonder regard to her sister, of whose rectitude and delicacy she was sure her opinion could never be shaken, and for whose happiness she grew daily more anxious, as Bingley had now been gone a week, and nothing was heard of his return.

Jane had sent Caroline an early answer to her letter, and was counting the days till she might reasonably hope to hear again. The promised letter of thanks from Mr. Collins arrived on Tuesday, addressed to their father, and written with all the solemnity of gratitude which a twelvemonth's abode in the family might have prompted. After discharging his conscience on that head, he proceeded to inform them, with many rapturous expressions, of his happiness in having obtained the affection of their amiable neighbour, Miss Lucas, and then explained that it was merely with the view of enjoying her society that he had been so ready to close with their kind wish of seeing him again at Longbourn, whither he hoped to be able to return on Monday fortnight; for Lady Catherine, he added, so heartily approved his marriage, that she wished it to take place as soon as possible, which he trusted would be an unanswerable argument with his amiable Charlotte to name an early day for making him the happiest of men.

Mr. Collins's return into Hertfordshire was no longer a matter of pleasure to Mrs. Bennet. On the contrary she was as much disposed to complain of it as her husband. — It was very strange that he should come to Longbourn instead of to Lucas Lodge; it was also very inconvenient and exceedingly troublesome. — She hated having visitors in the house while her health was so indifferent, and lovers were of all people the most disagreeable. Such were the gentle murmurs of Mrs. Bennet, and they gave way only to the greater distress of Mr. Bingley's continued absence.

Neither Jane nor Elizabeth were comfortable on this subject. Day after day passed away without bringing any other tidings of him than the report which shortly prevailed in Meryton of his coming no more to Netherfield the whole winter; a report which highly incensed Mrs. Bennet, and which she never failed to contradict as a most scandalous falsehood.

Even Elizabeth began to fear — not that Bingley was indifferent — but that his sisters would be successful in keeping him away. Unwilling as she was to admit an idea so destructive of Jane's happiness, and so dishonourable to the stability of her lover, she could not prevent its frequently recurring. The united efforts of his two unfeeling sisters and of his overpowering friend, assisted by the attractions of Miss Darcy and the amusements of London, might be too much, she feared, for the strength of his attachment.

As for Jane, *her* anxiety under this suspence was, of course, more painful than Elizabeth's; but whatever she felt she was desirous of concealing, and between herself and Elizabeth, therefore, the subject was never alluded to. But as no such delicacy restrained her mother, an hour seldom passed in which she did not talk of Bingley, express her impatience for his arrival, or even require Jane to confess that if he did not come back, she should think herself very ill used. It needed all Jane's steady mildness to bear these attacks with tolerable tranquillity.

Mr. Collins returned most punctually on the Monday fortnight, but his reception at Longbourn was not quite so gracious
as it had been on his first introduction. He was too happy,
however, to need much attention; and luckily for the others,
the business of love-making relieved them from a great deal of
his company. The chief of every day was spent by him at Lucas
Lodge, and he sometimes returned to Longbourn only in time
to make an apology for his absence before the family went to
bed.

Mrs. Bennet was really in a most pitiable state. The very
mention of any thing concerning the match threw her into an
agony of ill humour, and wherever she went she was sure of
hearing it talked of. The sight of Miss Lucas was odious to her.
As her successor in that house, she regarded her with jealous
abhorrence. Whenever Charlotte came to see them she concluded her to be anticipating the hour of possession; and
whenever she spoke in a low voice to Mr. Collins, was convinced that they were talking of the Longbourn estate, and
resolving to turn herself and her daughters out of the house, as
soon as Mr. Bennet were dead. She complained bitterly of all
this to her husband.

"Indeed, Mr. Bennet," said she, "it is very hard to think that
Charlotte Lucas should ever be mistress of this house, that *I*
should be forced to make way for *her*, and live to see her take
my place in it!"

"My dear, do not give way to such gloomy thoughts. Let us
hope for better things. Let us flatter ourselves that *I* may be the
survivor."

This was not very consoling to Mrs. Bennet, and, therefore,
instead of making any answer, she went on as before,

"I cannot bear to think that they should have all this estate.
If it was not for the entail I should not mind it."

"What should not you mind?"

"I should not mind any thing at all."

"Let us be thankful that you are preserved from a state of
such insensibility."

"I never can be thankful, Mr. Bennet, for any thing about the entail. How any one could have the conscience to entail away an estate from one's own daughters I cannot understand; and all for the sake of Mr. Collins too! — Why should *he* have it more than anybody else?"

"I leave it to yourself to determine," said Mr. Bennet.

END OF VOL. I.

VOLUME II

barons start to speak

education plot

CHAPTER I.

Miss Bingley's letter arrived, and put an end to doubt. The very first sentence conveyed the assurance of their being all settled in London for the winter, and concluded with her brother's regret at not having had time to pay his respects to his friends in Hertfordshire before he left the country.

Hope was over, entirely over; and when Jane could attend to the rest of the letter, she found little, except the professed affection of the writer, that could give her any comfort. Miss Darcy's praise occupied the chief of it. Her many attractions were again dwelt on, and Caroline boasted joyfully of their increasing intimacy, and ventured to predict the accomplishment of the wishes which had been unfolded in her former letter. She wrote also with great pleasure of her brother's being an inmate of Mr. Darcy's house, and mentioned with raptures, some plans of the latter with regard to new furniture.

Elizabeth, to whom Jane very soon communicated the chief of all this, heard it in silent indignation. Her heart was divided between concern for her sister, and resentment against all the others. To Caroline's assertion of her brother's being partial to Miss Darcy she paid no credit. That he was really fond of Jane, she doubted no more than she had ever done; and much as she had always been disposed to like him, she could not think without anger, hardly without contempt, on that easiness of temper, that want of proper resolution which now made him the slave of his designing friends,[1] and led him to sacrifice his own happiness to the caprice of their inclinations. Had his own happiness, however, been the only sacrifice, he might have been allowed to sport with it in what ever manner he thought best; but her sister's was involved in it, as she thought he must be sensible himself. It was a subject, in short, on which reflection would be long indulged, and must be unavailing. She could think of nothing else, and yet whether Bingley's regard had really died away, or were suppressed by his friends' interference; whether he had been aware of Jane's attachment, or whether it

---

1   The term "friends" in this period can encompass family relations as well.

had escaped his observation; whichever were the case, though her opinion of him must be materially affected by the difference, her sister's situation remained the same, her peace equally wounded.

A day or two passed before Jane had courage to speak of her feelings to Elizabeth; but at last on Mrs. Bennet's leaving them together, after a longer irritation than usual about Netherfield and its master, she could not help saying,

"Oh! that my dear mother had more command over herself; she can have no idea of the pain she gives me by her continual reflections on him. But I will not repine. It cannot last long. He will be forgot, and we shall all be as we were before."

Elizabeth looked at her sister with incredulous solicitude, but said nothing.

"You doubt me," cried Jane slightly colouring; "indeed you have no reason. He may live in my memory as the most amiable man of my acquaintance, but that is all. I have nothing either to hope or fear, and nothing to reproach him with. Thank God! I have not *that* pain. A little time therefore. — I shall certainly try to get the better."

With a stronger voice she soon added, "I have this comfort immediately, that it has not been more than an error of fancy on my side, and that it has done no harm to any one but myself."

"My dear Jane!" exclaimed Elizabeth, "you are too good. Your sweetness and disinterestedness are really angelic; I do not know what to say to you. I feel as if I had never done you justice, or loved you as you deserve."

Miss Bennet eagerly disclaimed all extraordinary merit, and threw back the praise on her sister's warm affection.

"Nay," said Elizabeth, "this is not fair. *You* wish to think all the world respectable, and are hurt if I speak ill of any body. *I* only want to think *you* perfect, and you set yourself against it. Do not be afraid of my running into any excess, of my encroaching on your privilege of universal good will. You need not. There are few people whom I really love, and still fewer of whom I think well. The more I see of the world, the more am

I dissatisfied with it; and every day confirms my belief of the inconsistency of all human characters, and of the little dependence that can be placed on the appearance of either merit or sense. I have met with two instances lately; one I will not mention; the other is Charlotte's marriage. It is unaccountable! in every view it is unaccountable!"

"My dear Lizzy, do not give way to such feelings as these. They will ruin your happiness. You do not make allowance enough for difference of situation and temper. Consider Mr. Collins's respectability, and Charlotte's prudent, steady character. Remember that she is one of a large family; that as to fortune, it is a most eligible match; and be ready to believe, for every body's sake, that she may feel something like regard and esteem for our cousin."

"To oblige you, I would try to believe almost any thing, but no one else could be benefited by such a belief as this; for were I persuaded that Charlotte had any regard for him, I should only think worse of her understanding, than I now do of her heart. My dear Jane, Mr. Collins is a conceited, pompous, narrowminded, silly man; you know he is, as well as I do; and you must feel, as well as I do, that the woman who marries him, cannot have a proper way of thinking. You shall not defend her, though it is Charlotte Lucas. You shall not, for the sake of one individual, change the meaning of principle and integrity, nor endeavour to persuade yourself or me, that selfishness is prudence, and insensibility of danger, security for happiness."

"I must think your language too strong in speaking of both," replied Jane, "and I hope you will be convinced of it, by seeing them happy together. But enough of this. You alluded to something else. You mentioned two instances. I cannot misunderstand you, but I intreat you, dear Lizzy, not to pain me by thinking *that person* to blame, and saying your opinion of him is sunk. We must not be so ready to fancy ourselves intentionally injured. We must not expect a lively young man to be always so guarded and circumspect. It is very often nothing but our own vanity that deceives us. Women fancy admiration means more than it does."

"And men take care that they should."

"If it is designedly done, they cannot be justified; but I have no idea of there being so much design in the world as some persons imagine."

"I am far from attributing any part of Mr. Bingley's conduct to design," said Elizabeth; "but without scheming to do wrong, or to make others unhappy, there may be error, and there may be misery. Thoughtlessness, want of attention to other people's feelings, and want of resolution, will do the business."

"And do you impute it to either of those?"

"Yes; to the last. But if I go on, I shall displease you by saying what I think of persons you esteem. Stop me whilst you can."

"You persist, then, in supposing his sisters influence him."

"Yes, in conjunction with his friend."

"I cannot believe it. Why should they try to influence him? They can only wish his happiness, and if he is attached to me, no other woman can secure it."

"Your first position is false. They may wish many things besides his happiness; they may wish his increase of wealth and consequence; they may wish him to marry a girl who has all the importance of money, great connections, and pride."

"Beyond a doubt, they *do* wish him to chuse Miss Darcy," replied Jane; "but this may be from better feelings than you are supposing. They have known her much longer than they have known me; no wonder if they love her better. But, whatever may be their own wishes, it is very unlikely they should have opposed their brother's. What sister would think herself at liberty to do it, unless there were something very objectionable? If they believed him attached to me, they would not try to part us; if he were so, they could not succeed. By supposing such an affection, you make every body acting unnaturally and wrong, and me most unhappy. Do not distress me by the idea. I am not ashamed of having been mistaken—or, at least, it is slight, it is nothing in comparison of what I should feel in thinking ill of him or his sisters. Let me take it in the best light, in the light in which it may be understood."

Elizabeth could not oppose such a wish; and from this time

Mr. Bingley's name was scarcely ever mentioned between them.

Mrs. Bennet still continued to wonder and repine at his returning no more, and though a day seldom passed in which Elizabeth did not account for it clearly, there seemed little chance of her ever considering it with less perplexity. Her daughter endeavoured to convince her of what she did not believe herself, that his attentions to Jane had been merely the effect of a common and transient liking, which ceased when he saw her no more; but though the probability of the statement was admitted at the time, she had the same story to repeat every day. Mrs. Bennet's best comfort was, that Mr. Bingley must be down again in the summer.

Mr. Bennet treated the matter differently. "So, Lizzy," said he one day, "your sister is crossed in love I find. I congratulate her. Next to being married, a girl likes to be crossed in love a little now and then. It is something to think of, and gives her a sort of distinction among her companions. When is your turn to come? You will hardly bear to be long outdone by Jane. Now is your time. Here are officers enough at Meryton to disappoint all the young ladies in the country. Let Wickham be *your* man. He is a pleasant fellow, and would jilt you creditably."

"Thank you, Sir, but a less agreeable man would satisfy me. We must not all expect Jane's good fortune."

"True," said Mr. Bennet, "but it is a comfort to think that, whatever of that kind may befall you, you have an affectionate mother who will always make the most of it."

Mr. Wickham's society was of material service in dispelling the gloom, which the late perverse occurrences had thrown on many of the Longbourn family. They saw him often, and to his other recommendations was now added that of general unreserve. The whole of what Elizabeth had already heard, his claims on Mr. Darcy, and all that he had suffered from him, was now openly acknowledged and publicly canvassed; and every body was pleased to think how much they had always disliked Mr. Darcy before they had known any thing of the matter.

Miss Bennet was the only creature who could suppose there

might be any extenuating circumstances in the case, unknown to the society of Hertfordshire; her mild and steady candour always pleaded for allowances, and urged the possibility of mistakes — but by everybody else Mr. Darcy was condemned as the worst of men.

CHAPTER II.

AFTER a week spent in professions of love and schemes of felicity, Mr. Collins was called from his amiable Charlotte by the arrival of Saturday. The pain of separation, however, might be alleviated on his side, by preparations for the reception of his bride, as he had reason to hope, that shortly after his next return into Hertfordshire, the day would be fixed that was to make him the happiest of men. He took leave of his relations at Longbourn with as much solemnity as before; wished his fair cousins health and happiness again, and promised their father another letter of thanks.

On the following Monday, Mrs. Bennet had the pleasure of receiving her brother and his wife, who came as usual to spend the Christmas at Longbourn. Mr. Gardiner was a sensible, gentlemanlike man, greatly superior to his sister as well by nature as education. The Netherfield ladies would have had difficulty in believing that a man who lived by trade, and within view of his own warehouses, could have been so well bred and agreeable. Mrs. Gardiner, who was several years younger than Mrs. Bennet and Mrs. Philips, was an amiable, intelligent, elegant woman, and a great favourite with all her Longbourn nieces. Between the two eldest and herself especially, there subsisted a very particular regard. They had frequently been staying with her in town.

The first part of Mrs. Gardiner's business on her arrival, was to distribute her presents and describe the newest fashions. When this was done, she had a less active part to play. It became her turn to listen. Mrs. Bennet had many grievances to relate, and much to complain of. They had all been very ill-used since she last saw her sister. Two of her girls had been on the point of marriage, and after all there was nothing in it.

"I do not blame Jane," she continued, "for Jane would have got Mr. Bingley, if she could. But, Lizzy! Oh, sister! it is very hard to think that she might have been Mr. Collins's wife by this time, had not it been for her own perverseness. He made her an offer in this very room, and she refused him. The consequence of it is, that Lady Lucas will have a daughter married before I have, and that Longbourn estate is just as much entailed as ever. The Lucases are very artful people indeed, sister. They are all for what they can get. I am sorry to say it of them, but so it is. It makes me very nervous and poorly, to be thwarted so in my own family, and to have neighbours who think of themselves before anybody else. However, your coming just at this time is the greatest of comforts, and I am very glad to hear what you tell us, of long sleeves."

Mrs. Gardiner, to whom the chief of this news had been given before, in the course of Jane and Elizabeth's correspondence with her, made her sister a slight answer, and in compassion to her nieces turned the conversation.

When alone with Elizabeth afterwards, she spoke more on the subject. "It seems likely to have been a desirable match for Jane," said she. "I am sorry it went off. But these things happen so often! A young man, such as you describe Mr. Bingley, so easily falls in love with a pretty girl for a few weeks, and when accident separates them, so easily forgets her, that these sort of inconstancies are very frequent."

"An excellent consolation in its way," said Elizabeth, "but it will not do for *us*. We do not suffer by *accident*. It does not often happen that the interference of friends will persuade a young man of independent fortune to think no more of a girl, whom he was violently in love with only a few days before."

"But that expression of 'violently in love' is so hackneyed, so doubtful, so indefinite, that it gives me very little idea. It is as often applied to feelings which arise from an half-hour's acquaintance, as to a real, strong attachment. Pray, how *violent was* Mr. Bingley's love?"

"I never saw a more promising inclination. He was growing quite inattentive to other people, and wholly engrossed by her. Every time they met, it was more decided and remarkable. At his own ball he offended two or three young ladies, by not asking them to dance, and I spoke to him twice myself, without receiving an answer. Could there be finer symptoms? Is not general incivility the very essence of love?"

"Oh, yes! — of that kind of love which I suppose him to have felt. Poor Jane! I am sorry for her, because, with her disposition, she may not get over it immediately. It had better have happened to *you*, Lizzy; you would have laughed yourself out of it sooner. But do you think she would be prevailed on to go back with us? Change of scene might be of service — and perhaps a little relief from home, may be as useful as anything."

Elizabeth was exceedingly pleased with this proposal, and felt persuaded of her sister's ready acquiescence.

"I hope," added Mrs. Gardiner, "that no consideration with regard to this young man will influence her. We live in so different a part of town, all our connections are so different, and, as you well know, we go out so little, that it is very improbable they should meet at all, unless he really comes to see her."

"And *that* is quite impossible; for he is now in the custody of his friend, and Mr. Darcy would no more suffer him to call on Jane in such a part of London! My dear aunt, how could you think of it? Mr. Darcy may perhaps have *heard* of such a place as Gracechurch Street, but he would hardly think a month's ablution enough to cleanse him from its impurities, were he once to enter it;[1] and depend upon it, Mr. Bingley never stirs without him."

"So much the better. I hope they will not meet at all. But does not Jane correspond with the sister? *She* will not be able to help calling."

"She will drop the acquaintance entirely."

But in spite of the certainty in which Elizabeth affected to place this point, as well as the still more interesting one of Bingley's being withheld from seeing Jane, she felt a solicitude on

---

1 Gracechurch Street is in the City of London, the capital's commercial district.

the subject which convinced her, on examination, that she did not consider it entirely hopeless. It was possible, and sometimes she thought it probable, that his affection might be re-animated, and the influence of his friends successfully combated by the more natural influence of Jane's attractions.

Miss Bennet accepted her aunt's invitation with pleasure; and the Bingleys were no otherwise in her thoughts at the time, than as she hoped that, by Caroline's not living in the same house with her brother, she might occasionally spend a morning with her, without any danger of seeing him.

The Gardiners staid a week at Longbourn; and what with the Philipses, the Lucases, and the officers, there was not a day without its engagement. Mrs. Bennet had so carefully provided for the entertainment of her brother and sister, that they did not once sit down to a family dinner. When the engagement was for home, some of the officers always made part of it, of which officers Mr. Wickham was sure to be one; and on these occasions, Mrs. Gardiner, rendered suspicious by Elizabeth's warm commendation of him, narrowly observed them both. Without supposing them, from what she saw, to be very seriously in love, their preference of each other was plain enough to make her a little uneasy; and she resolved to speak to Elizabeth on the subject before she left Hertfordshire, and represent to her the imprudence of encouraging such an attachment.

To Mrs. Gardiner, Wickham had one means of affording pleasure, unconnected with his general powers. About ten or a dozen years ago, before her marriage, she had spent a considerable time in that very part of Derbyshire to which he belonged. They had, therefore, many acquaintance in common; and, though Wickham had been little there since the death of Darcy's father, five years before, it was yet in his power to give her fresher intelligence of her former friends, than she had been in the way of procuring.

Mrs. Gardiner had seen Pemberley, and known the late Mr. Darcy by character perfectly well. Here consequently was an inexhaustible subject of discourse. In comparing her recollection of Pemberley, with the minute description which Wickham could give, and in bestowing her tribute of praise on the character of its late possessor, she was delighting both him and herself. On being made acquainted with the present Mr. Darcy's treatment of him, she tried to remember something of that gentleman's reputed disposition when quite a lad, which might agree with it, and was confident at last, that she recollected having heard Mr. Fitzwilliam Darcy formerly spoken of as a very proud, ill-natured boy.

CHAPTER III.

MRS. GARDINER'S caution to Elizabeth was punctually and kindly given on the first favourable opportunity of speaking to her alone; after honestly telling her what she thought, she thus went on:

"You are too sensible a girl, Lizzy, to fall in love merely because you are warned against it; and, therefore, I am not afraid of speaking openly. Seriously, I would have you be on your guard. Do not involve yourself, or endeavour to involve him in an affection which the want of fortune would make so very imprudent. I have nothing to say against *him*; he is a most interesting young man; and if he had the fortune he ought to have, I should think you could not do better. But as it is — you must not let your fancy run away with you. You have sense, and we all expect you to use it. Your father would depend on *your* resolution and good conduct, I am sure. You must not disappoint your father."

"My dear aunt, this is being serious indeed."

"Yes, and I hope to engage you to be serious likewise."

"Well, then, you need not be under any alarm. I will take care of myself, and of Mr. Wickham too. He shall not be in love with me, if I can prevent it."

"Elizabeth, you are not serious now."

"I beg your pardon. I will try again. At present I am not in love with Mr. Wickham; no, I certainly am not. But he is, beyond all comparison, the most agreeable man I ever saw — and if he becomes really attached to me — I believe it will be better that he should not. I see the imprudence of it. —Oh! *that* abominable Mr. Darcy! —My father's opinion of me does me the greatest honor; and I should be miserable to forfeit it. My father, however, is partial to Mr. Wickham. In short, my dear aunt, I should be very sorry to be the means of making any of you unhappy; but since we see every day that where there is affection, young people are seldom withheld by immediate want of fortune, from entering into engagements with each other, how can I promise to be wiser than so many of my fellow-creatures if I am tempted, or how am I even to know that it would be wisdom to resist? All that I can promise you, therefore, is not to be in a hurry. I will not be in a hurry to believe myself his first object. When I am in company with him, I will not be wishing. In short, I will do my best."

"Perhaps it will be as well, if you discourage his coming here so very often. At least, you should not *remind* your Mother of inviting him."

"As I did the other day," said Elizabeth, with a conscious smile; "very true, it will be wise in me to refrain from *that*. But do not imagine that he is always here so often. It is on your account that he has been so frequently invited this week. You know my mother's ideas as to the necessity of constant company for her friends. But really, and upon my honour, I will try to do what I think to be wisest; and now, I hope you are satisfied."

Her aunt assured her that she was; and Elizabeth having thanked her for the kindness of her hints, they parted; a wonderful instance of advice being given on such a point, without being resented.

Mr. Collins returned into Hertfordshire soon after it had been quitted by the Gardiners and Jane; but as he took up his abode with the Lucases, his arrival was no great inconvenience to Mrs. Bennet. His marriage was now fast approaching, and she was at length so far resigned as to think it inevitable, and even repeatedly to say in an ill-natured tone that she "*wished* they might be happy." Thursday was to be the wedding day, and on Wednesday Miss Lucas paid her farewell visit; and when she rose to take leave, Elizabeth, ashamed of her mother's ungracious and reluctant good wishes, and sincerely affected herself, accompanied her out of the room. As they went down stairs together, Charlotte said,

"I shall depend on hearing from you very often, Eliza."

"*That* you certainly shall."

"And I have another favour to ask. Will you come and see me?"

"We shall often meet, I hope, in Hertfordshire."

"I am not likely to leave Kent for some time. Promise me, therefore, to come to Hunsford."

Elizabeth could not refuse, though she foresaw little pleasure in the visit.

"My father and Maria are to come to me in March," added Charlotte, "and I hope you will consent to be of the party. Indeed, Eliza, you will be as welcome to me as either of them."

The wedding took place; the bride and bridegroom set off for Kent from the church door, and every body had as much to say or to hear on the subject as usual. Elizabeth soon heard from her friend; and their correspondence was as regular and frequent as it had ever been; that it should be equally unreserved was impossible. Elizabeth could never address her without feeling that all the comfort of intimacy was over, and, though determined not to slacken as a correspondent, it was for the sake of what had been, rather than what was. Charlotte's first letters were received with a good deal of eagerness; there could not but be curiosity to know how she would speak of her new home, how she would like Lady Catherine, and how happy she would dare pronounce herself to be; though, when the letters were read, Elizabeth felt that Charlotte expressed herself on every point exactly as she might have foreseen. She wrote cheerfully, seemed surrounded with comforts, and mentioned nothing which she could not praise. The house, furniture, neighbourhood, and roads, were all to her taste, and Lady Catherine's behaviour was most friendly and obliging. It was Mr. Collins's picture of Hunsford and Rosings rationally softened; and Elizabeth perceived that she must wait for her own visit there, to know the rest.

Jane had already written a few lines to her sister to announce their safe arrival in London; and when she wrote again, Elizabeth hoped it would be in her power to say something of the Bingleys.

Her impatience for this second letter was as well rewarded as impatience generally is. Jane had been a week in town, without either seeing or hearing from Caroline. She accounted for it, however, by supposing that her last letter to her friend from Longbourn, had by some accident been lost.

"My aunt," she continued, "is going to-morrow into that part of the town, and I shall take the opportunity of calling in Grosvenor-street."

She wrote again when the visit was paid, and she had seen Miss Bingley. "I did not think Caroline in spirits," were her words, "but she was very glad to see me, and reproached me for giving her no notice of my coming to London. I was right, therefore; my last letter had never reached her. I enquired after their brother, of course. He was well, but so much engaged with Mr. Darcy, that they scarcely ever saw him. I found that Miss Darcy was expected to dinner. I wish I could see her. My visit was not long, as Caroline and Mrs. Hurst were going out. I dare say I shall soon see them here."

Elizabeth shook her head over this letter. It convinced her that accident only could discover to Mr. Bingley her sister's being in town.

Four weeks passed away, and Jane saw nothing of him. She endeavoured to persuade herself that she did not regret it; but she could no longer be blind to Miss Bingley's inattention. After waiting at home every morning for a fortnight, and inventing every evening a fresh excuse for her, the visitor did at last appear;[1] but the shortness of her stay, and yet more, the alteration of her manner, would allow Jane to deceive herself no longer. The letter which she wrote on this occasion to her sister, will prove what she felt.

"My dearest Lizzy will, I am sure, be incapable of triumphing in her better judgment, at my expence, when I confess

---

1 Politeness would demand that a visit such as Jane's to Miss Bingley would be returned.

myself to have been entirely deceived in Miss Bingley's regard for me. But, my dear sister, though the event has proved you right, do not think me obstinate if I still assert, that, considering what her behaviour was, my confidence was as natural as your suspicion. I do not at all comprehend her reason for wishing to be intimate with me, but if the same circumstances were to happen again, I am sure I should be deceived again. Caroline did not return my visit till yesterday; and not a note, not a line, did I receive in the mean time. When she did come, it was very evident that she had no pleasure in it; she made a slight, formal, apology, for not calling before, said not a word of wishing to see me again, and was in every respect so altered a creature, that when she went away, I was perfectly resolved to continue the acquaintance no longer. I pity, though I cannot help blaming her. She was very wrong in singling me out as she did; I can safely say, that every advance to intimacy began on her side. But I pity her, because she must feel that she has been acting wrong, and because I am very sure that anxiety for her brother is the cause of it. I need not explain myself farther; and though *we* know this anxiety to be quite needless, yet if she feels it, it will easily account for her behaviour to me; and so deservedly dear as he is to his sister, whatever anxiety she may feel on his behalf, is natural and amiable. I cannot but wonder, however, at her having any such fears now, because, if he had at all cared about me, we must have met long, long ago. He knows of my being in town, I am certain, from something she said herself; and yet it should seem by her manner of talking, as if she wanted to persuade herself that he is really partial to Miss Darcy. I cannot understand it. If I were not afraid of judging harshly, I should be almost tempted to say, that there is a strong appearance of duplicity in all this. But I will endeavour to banish every painful thought, and think only of what will make me happy: your affection, and the invariable kindness of my dear uncle and aunt. Let me hear from you very soon. Miss Bingley said something of his never returning to Netherfield again, of giving up the house, but not with any certainty. We had better not mention it. I am extremely glad that you have such pleasant accounts from our friends at Hunsford. Pray go to see them, with Sir William and Maria. I am sure you will be very comfortable there.

"Your's, &c."

This letter gave Elizabeth some pain; but her spirits returned as she considered that Jane would no longer be duped, by the sister at least. All expectation from the brother was now absolutely over. She would not even wish for any renewal of his attentions. His character sunk on every review of it; and as a punishment for him, as well as a possible advantage to Jane, she seriously hoped he might really soon marry Mr. Darcy's sister, as, by Wickham's account, she would make him abundantly regret what he had thrown away.

Mrs. Gardiner about this time reminded Elizabeth of her promise concerning that gentleman, and required information; and Elizabeth had such to send as might rather give contentment to her aunt than to herself. His apparent partiality had subsided, his attentions were over, he was the admirer of some one else. Elizabeth was watchful enough to see it all, but she could see it and write of it without material pain. Her heart had been but slightly touched, and her vanity was satisfied with believing that *she* would have been his only choice, had fortune permitted it. The sudden acquisition of ten thousand pounds was the most remarkable charm of the young lady, to whom he was now rendering himself agreeable; but Elizabeth, less clear sighted perhaps in his case than in Charlotte's, did not quarrel with him for his wish of independence. Nothing, on the contrary, could be more natural; and while able to suppose that it cost him a few struggles to relinquish her, she was ready to allow it a wise and desirable measure for both, and could very sincerely wish him happy.

All this was acknowledged to Mrs. Gardiner; and after relating the circumstances, she thus went on: — "I am now convinced, my dear aunt, that I have never been much in love; for had I really experienced that pure and elevating passion, I should at present detest his very name, and wish him all manner of evil. But my feelings are not only cordial towards *him*; they are even impartial towards Miss King. I cannot find out that I hate her at all, or that I am in the least unwilling to think her a very good sort of girl. There can be no love in all this. My watchfulness has been effectual; and though I should certainly be a more interesting object to all my acquaintance, were I distractedly in love with him, I cannot say that I regret my comparative insignificance. Importance may sometimes be purchased too dearly. Kitty and Lydia take his defection much' more to heart than I do. They are young in the ways of the world, and not yet open to the mortifying conviction that handsome young men must have something to live on, as well as the plain."

CHAPTER IV.

WITH no greater events than these in the Longbourn family, and otherwise diversified by little beyond the walks to Meryton, sometimes dirty and sometimes cold, did January and February pass away. March was to take Elizabeth to Hunsford. She had not at first thought very seriously of going thither; but Charlotte, she soon found, was depending on the plan, and she gradually learned to consider it herself with greater pleasure as well as greater certainty. Absence had increased her desire of seeing Charlotte again, and weakened her disgust of Mr. Collins. There was novelty in the scheme, and as, with such a mother and such uncompanionable sisters, home could not be faultless, a little change was not unwelcome for its own sake. The journey would moreover give her a peep at Jane; and, in short, as the time drew near, she would have been very sorry for any delay. Every thing, however, went on smoothly, and was finally settled according to Charlotte's first sketch. She was to accompany Sir William and his second daughter. The improvement of spending a night in London was added in time, and the plan became perfect as plan could be.

The only pain was in leaving her father, who would certainly miss her, and who, when it came to the point, so little liked her going, that he told her to write to him, and almost promised to answer her letter.

The farewell between herself and Mr. Wickham was perfectly friendly; on his side even more. His present pursuit could not make him forget that Elizabeth had been the first to excite and to deserve his attention, the first to listen and to pity, the first to be admired; and in his manner of bidding her adieu, wishing her every enjoyment, reminding her of what she was to expect in Lady Catherine de Bourgh, and trusting their opinion of her — their opinion of every body — would always coincide, there was a solicitude, an interest which she felt must ever attach her to him with a most sincere regard; and she parted from him convinced, that whether married or single, he must always be her model of the amiable and pleasing.

Her fellow-travellers the next day, were not of a kind to make her think him less agreeable. Sir William Lucas, and his daughter Maria, a good humoured girl, but as empty-headed as himself, had nothing to say that could be worth hearing, and were listened to with about as much delight as the rattle of the chaise. Elizabeth loved absurdities, but she had known Sir William's too long. He could tell her nothing new of the wonders of his presentation and knighthood; and his civilities were worn out like his information.

It was a journey of only twenty-four miles, and they began it so early as to be in Gracechurch-street by noon. As they drove to Mr. Gardiner's door, Jane was at a drawing-room window watching their arrival; when they entered the passage she was there to welcome them, and Elizabeth, looking earnestly in her face, was pleased to see it healthful and lovely as ever. On the stairs were a troop of little boys and girls, whose eagerness for their cousin's appearance would not allow them to wait in the drawing-room, and whose shyness, as they had not seen her for a twelvemonth, prevented their coming lower. All was joy and kindness. The day passed most pleasantly away; the morning in bustle and shopping, and the evening at one of the theatres.

Elizabeth then contrived to sit by her aunt. Their first subject was her sister; and she was more grieved than astonished to hear, in reply to her minute enquiries, that though Jane always struggled to support her spirits, there were periods of dejection. It was reasonable, however, to hope, that they would not continue long. Mrs. Gardiner gave her the particulars also of

Miss Bingley's visit in Gracechurch-street, and repeated conversations occurring at different times between Jane and herself, which proved that the former had, from her heart, given up the acquaintance.

Mrs. Gardiner then rallied her niece on Wickham's desertion, and complimented her on bearing it so well.

"But, my dear Elizabeth," she added, "what sort of girl is Miss King? I should be sorry to think our friend mercenary."

"Pray, my dear aunt, what is the difference in matrimonial affairs, between the mercenary and the prudent motive? Where does discretion end, and avarice begin? Last Christmas you were afraid of his marrying me, because it would be imprudent; and now, because he is trying to get a girl with only ten thousand pounds, you want to find out that he is mercenary."

"If you will only tell me what sort of girl Miss King is, I shall know what to think."

"She is a very good kind of girl, I believe. I know no harm of her."

"But he paid her not the smallest attention, till her grandfather's death made her mistress of this fortune."

"No—why should he? If it was not allowable for him to gain *my* affections, because I had no money, what occasion could there be for making love to a girl whom he did not care about, and who was equally poor?"

"But there seems indelicacy in directing his attentions towards her, so soon after this event."

"A man in distressed circumstances has not time for all those elegant decorums which other people may observe. If *she* does not object to it, why should *we*?"

"*Her* not objecting, does not justify *him*. It only shews her being deficient in something herself—sense or feeling."

"Well," cried Elizabeth, "have it as you choose. *He* shall be mercenary, and *she* shall be foolish."

"No, Lizzy, that is what I do *not* choose. I should be sorry, you know, to think ill of a young man who has lived so long in Derbyshire."

"Oh! if that is all, I have a very poor opinion of young men who live in Derbyshire; and their intimate friends who live in Hertfordshire are not much better. I am sick of them all. Thank Heaven! I am going tomorrow where I shall find a man who has not one agreeable quality, who has neither manner nor sense to recommend him. Stupid men are the only ones worth knowing, after all."

"Take care, Lizzy; that speech savours strongly of disappointment."

Before they were separated by the conclusion of the play, she had the unexpected happiness of an invitation to accompany her uncle and aunt in a tour of pleasure which they proposed taking in the summer.

"We have not quite determined how far it shall carry us," said Mrs. Gardiner, "but perhaps to the Lakes."

No scheme could have been more agreeable to Elizabeth, and her acceptance of the invitation was most ready and grateful. "My dear, dear aunt," she rapturously cried, "what delight! what felicity! You give me fresh life and vigour. Adieu to disappointment and spleen. What are men to rocks and mountains? Oh! what hours of transport we shall spend![1] And when we *do* return, it shall not be like other travellers, without being able to give one accurate idea of any thing. We *will* know where we have gone — we *will* recollect what we have seen. Lakes, mountains, and rivers, shall not be jumbled together in our imaginations; nor, when we attempt to describe any particular scene, will we begin quarrelling about its relative situation. Let *our* first effusions be less insupportable than those of the generality of travellers."

---

1   "Transport" here meaning "ecstasy." The mountainous Lake District in the northwest corner of England was popular with tourists seeking picturesque landscape, and Elizabeth's genuine delight at the Gardiners' plan topples over into satire of their conventional responses.

CHAPTER V.

EVERY object in the next day's journey was new and interesting to Elizabeth; and her spirits were in a state for enjoyment; for she had seen her sister looking so well as to banish all fear for her health, and the prospect of her northern tour was a constant source of delight.

When they left the high-road for the lane to Hunsford, every eye was in search of the Parsonage, and every turning expected to bring it in view. The paling of Rosings park was their boundary on one side. Elizabeth smiled at the recollection of all that she had heard of its inhabitants.

At length the Parsonage was discernable. The garden sloping to the road, the house standing in it, the green pales and the laurel hedge, everything declared that they were arriving. Mr. Collins and Charlotte appeared at the door, and the carriage stopped at a small gate, which led by a short gravel walk to the house, amidst the nods and smiles of the whole party. In a moment they were all out of the chaise, rejoicing at the sight of each other. Mrs. Collins welcomed her friend with the liveliest pleasure, and Elizabeth was more and more satisfied with coming, when she found herself so affectionately received. She saw instantly that her cousin's manners were not altered by his marriage; his formal civility was just what it had been, and he detained her some minutes at the gate to hear and satisfy his enquiries after all her family. They were then, with no other delay than his pointing out the neatness of the entrance, taken into the house; and as soon as they were in the parlour, he welcomed them a second time with ostentatious formality to his humble abode, and punctually repeated all his wife's offers of refreshment.

Elizabeth was prepared to see him in his glory; and she could not help fancying that in displaying the good proportion of the room, its aspect and its furniture, he addressed himself particularly to her, as if wishing to make her feel what she had lost in refusing him. But though every thing seemed neat and comfortable, she was not able to gratify him by any sigh of repentance; and rather looked with wonder at her friend that she

could have so cheerful an air, with such a companion. When
Mr. Collins said any thing of which his wife might reasonably
be ashamed, which certainly was not unseldom, she involuntarily turned her eye on Charlotte. Once or twice she could discern a faint blush; but in general Charlotte wisely did not hear.
After sitting long enough to admire every article of furniture in
the room, from the sideboard to the fender, to give an account
of their journey and of all that had happened in London, Mr.
Collins invited them to take a stroll in the garden, which was
large and well laid out, and to the cultivation of which he
attended himself. To work in his garden was one of his most
respectable pleasures; and Elizabeth admired the command of
countenance with which Charlotte talked of the healthfulness
of the exercise, and owned she encouraged it as much as possible. Here, leading the way through every walk and cross walk,
and scarcely allowing them an interval to utter the praises he
asked for, every view was pointed out with a minuteness which
left beauty entirely behind. He could number the fields in
every direction, and could tell how many trees there were in
the most distant clump. But of all the views which his garden,
or which the country, or the kingdom could boast, none were
to be compared with the prospect of Rosings, afforded by an
opening in the trees that bordered the park nearly opposite the
front of his house. It was a handsome modern building, well
situated on rising ground.

From his garden, Mr. Collins would have led them round his
two meadows, but the ladies not having shoes to encounter the
remains of a white frost, turned back; and while Sir William
accompanied him, Charlotte took her sister and friend over the
house, extremely well pleased, probably, to have the opportunity of shewing it without her husband's help. It was rather small,
but well built and convenient; and everything was fitted up and
arranged with a neatness and consistency of which Elizabeth
gave Charlotte all the credit. When Mr. Collins could be forgotten, there was really a great air of comfort throughout, and
by Charlotte's evident enjoyment of it, Elizabeth supposed he
must be often forgotten.

She had already learnt that Lady Catherine was still in the

country. It was spoken of again while they were at dinner, when Mr. Collins joining in, observed,

"Yes, Miss Elizabeth, you will have the honour of seeing Lady Catherine de Bourgh on the ensuing Sunday at church, and I need not say you will be delighted with her. She is all affability and condescension, and I doubt not but you will be honoured with some portion of her notice when service is over. I have scarcely any hesitation in saying that she will include you and my sister Maria in every invitation with which she honours us during your stay here. Her behaviour to my dear Charlotte is charming. We dine at Rosings twice every week, and are never allowed to walk home. Her ladyship's carriage is regularly ordered for us. I *should* say, one of her ladyship's carriages, for she has several."

"Lady Catherine is a very respectable, sensible woman indeed," added Charlotte, "and a most attentive neighbour."

"Very true, my dear, that is exactly what I say. She is the sort of woman whom one cannot regard with too much deference."

The evening was spent chiefly in talking over Hertfordshire news, and telling again what had been already written; and when it closed, Elizabeth in the solitude of her chamber had to meditate upon Charlotte's degree of contentment, to understand her address in guiding, and composure in bearing with her husband, and to acknowledge that it was all done very well. She had also to anticipate how her visit would pass, the quiet tenor of their usual employments, the vexatious interruptions of Mr. Collins, and the gaieties of their intercourse with Rosings. A lively imagination soon settled it all.

About the middle of the next day, as she was in her room getting ready for a walk, a sudden noise below seemed to speak the whole house in confusion; and after listening a moment, she heard somebody running up stairs in a violent hurry, and calling loudly after her. She opened the door, and met Maria in the landing place, who, breathless with agitation, cried out,

"Oh, my dear Eliza! pray make haste and come into the dining-room, for there is such a sight to be seen! I will not tell you what it is. Make haste, and come down this moment."

Elizabeth asked questions in vain; Maria would tell her nothing more, and down they ran into the diningroom, which fronted the lane, in quest of this wonder; it was two ladies stopping in a low phaeton at the garden gate.

"And is this all?" cried Elizabeth. "I expected at least that the pigs were got into the garden, and here is nothing but Lady Catherine and her daughter!"

"La! my dear," said Maria quite shocked at the mistake, "it is not Lady Catherine. The old lady is Mrs. Jenkinson, who lives with them. The other is Miss De Bourgh. Only look at her. She is quite a little creature. Who would have thought she could be so thin and small!"

"She is abominably rude to keep Charlotte out of doors in all this wind. Why does she not come in?"

"Oh! Charlotte says, she hardly ever does. It is the greatest of favours when Miss De Bourgh comes in."

"I like her appearance," said Elizabeth, struck with other ideas. "She looks sickly and cross. — Yes, she will do for him very well. She will make him a very proper wife."

Mr. Collins and Charlotte were both standing at the gate in conversation with the ladies; and Sir William, to Elizabeth's high diversion, was stationed in the door-way, in earnest contemplation of the greatness before him, and constantly bowing whenever Miss De Bourgh looked that way.

At length there was nothing more to be said; the ladies drove on, and the others returned into the house. Mr. Collins no sooner saw the two girls than he began to congratulate them on their good fortune, which Charlotte explained by letting them know that the whole party was asked to dine at Rosings the next day.

CHAPTER VI.

Mr. Collins's triumph in consequence of this invitation was complete. The power of displaying the grandeur of his patroness to his wondering visitors, and of letting them see her civility towards himself and his wife, was exactly what he had wished for; and that an opportunity of doing it should be given so soon, was such an instance of Lady Catherine's condescension as he knew not how to admire enough.

"I confess," said he, "that I should not have been at all surprised by her Ladyship's asking us on Sunday to drink tea and spend the evening at Rosings. I rather expected, from my knowledge of her affability, that it would happen. But who could have foreseen such an attention as this? Who could have imagined that we should receive an invitation to dine there (an invitation moreover including the whole party) so immediately after your arrival!"

"I am the less surprised at what has happened," replied Sir William, "from that knowledge of what the manners of the great really are, which my situation in life has allowed me to acquire. About the Court, such instances of elegant breeding are not uncommon."

Scarcely any thing was talked of the whole day or next morning, but their visit to Rosings. Mr. Collins was carefully instructing them in what they were to expect, that the sight of such rooms, so many servants, and so splendid a dinner might not wholly overpower them.

When the ladies were separating for the toilette,[1] he said to Elizabeth,

"Do not make yourself uneasy, my dear cousin, about your apparel. Lady Catherine is far from requiring that elegance of dress in us, which becomes herself and daughter. I would advise you merely to put on whatever of your clothes is superior to the rest, there is no occasion for any thing more. Lady Catherine will not think the worse of you for being simply dressed. She likes to have the distinction of rank preserved."

1   That is, to wash and dress for dinner.

While they were dressing, he came two or three times to their different doors, to recommend their being quick, as Lady Catherine very much objected to be kept waiting for her dinner. — Such formidable accounts of her Ladyship, and her manner of living, quite frightened Maria Lucas, who had been little used to company, and she looked forward to her introduction at Rosings, with as much apprehension, as her father had done to his presentation at St. James's.

As the weather was fine, they had a pleasant walk of about half a mile across the park. — Every park has its beauty and its prospects; and Elizabeth saw much to be pleased with, though she could not be in such raptures as Mr. Collins expected the scene to inspire, and was but slightly affected by his enumeration of the windows in front of the house, and his relation of what the glazing altogether had originally cost Sir Lewis De Bourgh.

When they ascended the steps to the hall, Maria's alarm was every moment increasing, and even Sir William did not look perfectly calm. — Elizabeth's courage did not fail her. She had heard nothing of Lady Catherine that spoke her awful from any extraordinary talents or miraculous virtue, and the mere stateliness of money and rank, she thought she could witness without trepidation.

From the entrance hall, of which Mr. Collins pointed out, with a rapturous air, the fine proportion and finished ornaments, they followed the servants through an antichamber, to the room where Lady Catherine, her daughter, and Mrs. Jenkinson were sitting. — Her Ladyship, with great condescension, arose to receive them; and as Mrs. Collins had settled it with her husband that the office of introduction should be her's, it was performed in a proper manner, without any of those apologies and thanks which he would have thought necessary.

In spite of having been at St. James's, Sir William was so completely awed, by the grandeur surrounding him, that he had but just courage enough to make a very low bow, and take his seat without saying a word; and his daughter, frightened almost out of her senses, sat on the edge of her chair, not knowing which way to look. Elizabeth found herself quite equal to the scene, and could observe the three ladies before her composedly. — Lady Catherine was a tall, large woman, with strongly-marked features, which might once have been handsome. Her air was not conciliating, nor was her manner of receiving them, such as to make her visitors forget their inferior rank. She was not rendered formidable by silence; but whatever she said, was spoken in so authoritative a tone, as marked her self-importance, and brought Mr. Wickham immediately to Elizabeth's mind; and from the observation of the day altogether, she believed Lady Catherine to be exactly what he had represented.

When, after examining the mother, in whose countenance and deportment she soon found some resemblance of Mr. Darcy, she turned her eyes on the daughter, she could almost have joined in Maria's astonishment, at her being so thin, and so small. There was neither in figure nor face, any likeness between the ladies. Miss De Bourgh was pale and sickly; her features, though not plain, were insignificant; and she spoke very little, except in a low voice, to Mrs. Jenkinson, in whose appearance there was nothing remarkable, and who was entirely engaged in listening to what she said, and placing a screen in the proper direction before her eyes.[1]

After sitting a few minutes, they were all sent to one of the windows, to admire the view, Mr. Collins attending them to point out its beauties, and Lady Catherine kindly informing them that it was much better worth looking at in the summer.

The dinner was exceedingly handsome, and there were all the servants, and all the articles of plate which Mr. Collins had promised; and, as he had likewise foretold, he took his seat at the bottom of the table, by her ladyship's desire, and looked as if he felt that life could furnish nothing greater. — He carved, and ate, and praised with delighted alacrity; and every dish was commended, first by him, and then by Sir William, who was now enough recovered to echo whatever his son in law said, in a manner which Elizabeth wondered Lady Catherine could bear. But Lady Catherine seemed gratified by their excessive

---

1   Screens were used to protect women's complexions from the heat of a fire.

confines of community   s+s   no talk or incorrigible talk

admiration, and gave most gracious smiles, especially when any dish on the table proved a novelty to them. The party did not supply much conversation. Elizabeth was ready to speak whenever there was an opening, but she was seated between Charlotte and Miss De Bourgh—the former of whom was engaged in listening to Lady Catherine, and the latter said not a word to her all dinner time. Mrs. Jenkinson was chiefly employed in watching how little Miss De Bourgh ate, pressing her to try some other dish, and fearing she were indisposed. Maria thought speaking out of the question, and the gentlemen did nothing but eat and admire.

When the ladies returned to the drawing room, there was little to be done but to hear Lady Catherine talk, which she did without any intermission till coffee came in, delivering her opinion on every subject in so decisive a manner as proved that she was not used to have her judgment controverted. She enquired into Charlotte's domestic concerns familiarly and minutely, and gave her a great deal of advice as to the management of them all; told her how every thing ought to be regulated in so small a family as her's, and instructed her as to the care of her cows and her poultry. Elizabeth found that nothing was beneath this great Lady's attention, which could furnish her with an occasion of dictating to others. In the intervals of her discourse with Mrs. Collins, she addressed a variety of questions to Maria and Elizabeth, but especially to the latter, of whose connections she knew the least, and who she observed to Mrs. Collins, was a very genteel, pretty kind of girl. She asked her at different times, how many sisters she had, whether they were older or younger than herself, whether any of them were likely to be married, whether they were handsome, where they had been educated, what carriage her father kept, and what had been her mother's maiden name?— Elizabeth felt all the impertinence of her questions, but answered them very composedly.—Lady Catherine then observed,

"Your father's estate is entailed on Mr. Collins, I think. For your sake," turning to Charlotte, "I am glad of it; but otherwise I see no occasion for entailing estates from the female line.—It was not thought necessary in Sir Lewis de Bourgh's family. — Do you play and sing, Miss Bennet?"

"A little."

"Oh! then — some time or other we shall be happy to hear you. Our instrument is a capital one, probably superior to — You shall try it some day. — Do your sisters play and sing?"

"One of them does."

"Why did not you all learn? — You ought all to have learned. The Miss Webbs all play, and their father has not so good an income as your's. — Do you draw?"

"No, not at all."

"What, none of you?"

"Not one."

"That is very strange. But I suppose you had no opportunity. Your mother should have taken you to town every spring for the benefit of masters."

"My mother would have had no objection, but my father hates London."

"Has your governess left you?"

"We never had any governess."

"No governess! How was that possible? Five daughters brought up at home without a governess! — I never heard of such a thing.[1] Your mother must have been quite a slave to your education."

Elizabeth could hardly help smiling, as she assured her that had not been the case.

"Then, who taught you? who attended to you? — Without a governess you must have been neglected."

"Compared with some families, I believe we were; but such of us as wished to learn, never wanted the means. We were always encouraged to read, and had all the masters that were necessary. Those who chose to be idle, certainly might."

"Aye, no doubt; but that is what a governess will prevent, and if I had known your mother, I should have advised her

---

[1] A governess might be employed to care for and educate children at home, as an alternative to sending them to a boarding school. Being "placed out" (as Lady Catherine goes on to call it) with a family in this capacity was the last resort for educated but unmarried women with no other income.

most strenuously to engage one. I always say that nothing is to be done in education without steady and regular instruction, and nobody but a governess can give it. It is wonderful how many families I have been the means of supplying in that way. I am always glad to get a young person well placed out. Four nieces of Mrs. Jenkinson are most delightfully situated through my means; and it was but the other day, that I recommended another young person, who was merely accidentally mentioned to me, and the family are quite delighted with her. Mrs. Collins, did I tell you of Lady Metcalfe's calling yesterday to thank me? She finds Miss Pope a treasure. 'Lady Catherine,' said she, 'you have given me a treasure.' Are any of your younger sisters out, Miss Bennet?"

"Yes, Ma'am, all."

"All! — What, all five out at once? Very odd! — And you only the second. — The younger ones out before the elder are married! — Your younger sisters must be very young?"

"Yes, my youngest is not sixteen. Perhaps *she* is full young to be much in company. But really, Ma'am, I think it would be very hard upon younger sisters, that they should not have their share of society and amusement because the elder may not have the means or inclination to marry early. — The last born has as good a right to the pleasures of youth, as the first. And to be kept back on *such* a motive! — I think it would not be very likely to promote sisterly affection or delicacy of mind."

"Upon my word," said her Ladyship, "you give your opinion very decidedly for so young a person. — Pray, what is your age?"

"With three younger sisters grown up," replied Elizabeth smiling, "your Ladyship can hardly expect me to own it."

Lady Catherine seemed quite astonished at not receiving a direct answer; and Elizabeth suspected herself to be the first creature who had ever dared to trifle with so much dignified impertinence!

"You cannot be more than twenty, I am sure, — therefore you need not conceal your age."

"I am not one and twenty."

When the gentlemen had joined them, and tea was over, the

card tables were placed. Lady Catherine, Sir William, and Mr. and Mrs. Collins sat down to quadrille; and as Miss De Bourgh chose to play at cassino,[1] the two girls had the honour of assisting Mrs. Jenkinson to make up her party. Their table was superlatively stupid. Scarcely a syllable was uttered that did not relate to the game, except when Mrs. Jenkinson expressed her fears of Miss De Bourgh's being too hot or too cold, or having too much or too little light. A great deal more passed at the other table. Lady Catherine was generally speaking—stating the mistakes of the three others, or relating some anecdote of herself. Mr. Collins was employed in agreeing to every thing her Ladyship said, thanking her for every fish he won, and apologising if he thought he won too many. Sir William did not say much. He was storing his memory with anecdotes and noble names.

When Lady Catherine and her daughter had played as long as they chose, the tables were broke up, the carriage was offered to Mrs. Collins, gratefully accepted, and immediately ordered. The party then gathered round the fire to hear Lady Catherine determine what weather they were to have on the morrow. From these instructions they were summoned by the arrival of the coach, and with many speeches of thankfulness on Mr. Collins's side, and as many bows on Sir William's, they departed. As soon as they had driven from the door, Elizabeth was called on by her cousin, to give her opinion of all that she had seen at Rosings, which, for Charlotte's sake, she made more favourable than it really was. But her commendation, though costing her some trouble, could by no means satisfy Mr. Collins, and he was very soon obliged to take her Ladyship's praise into his own hands.

---

1 Cassino is yet another card game.

CHAPTER VII.

SIR WILLIAM staid only a week at Hunsford; but his visit was long enough to convince him of his daughter's being most comfortably settled, and of her possessing such a husband and such a neighbour as were not often met with. While Sir William was with them, Mr. Collins devoted his mornings to driving him out in his gig,[1] and shewing him the country; but when he went away, the whole family returned to their usual employments, and Elizabeth was thankful to find that they did not see more of her cousin by the alteration, for the chief of the time between breakfast and dinner was now passed by him either at work in the garden, or in reading and writing, and looking out of window in his own book room, which fronted the road. The room in which the ladies sat was backwards.[2] Elizabeth at first had rather wondered that Charlotte should not prefer the dining parlour for common use; it was a better sized room, and had a pleasanter aspect; but she soon saw that her friend had an excellent reason for what she did, for Mr. Collins would undoubtedly have been much less in his own apartment, had they sat in one equally lively; and she gave Charlotte credit for the arrangement.

From the drawing room they could distinguish nothing in the lane, and were indebted to Mr. Collins for the knowledge of what carriages went along, and how often especially Miss De Bourgh drove by in her phaeton, which he never failed coming to inform them of, though it happened almost every day. She not unfrequently stopped at the Parsonage, and had a few minutes' conversation with Charlotte, but was scarcely ever prevailed on to get out.

Very few days passed in which Mr. Collins did not walk to Rosings, and not many in which his wife did not think it necessary to go likewise; and till Elizabeth recollected that there might be other family livings to be disposed of, she could not understand the sacrifice of so many hours. Now and then, they were honoured with a call from her Ladyship, and nothing

---

1 A gig is a light two-wheeled, two-person carriage.
2 That is, facing to the rear of the house.

escaped her observation that was passing in the room during these visits. She examined into their employments, looked at their work, and advised them to do it differently; found fault with the arrangement of the furniture, or detected the house-maid in negligence; and if she accepted any refreshment, seemed to do it only for the sake of finding out that Mrs. Collins's joints of meat were too large for her family.

Elizabeth soon perceived that though this great lady was not in the commission of the peace for the county, she was a most active magistrate in her own parish, the minutest concerns of which were carried to her by Mr. Collins;[1] and whenever any of the cottagers were disposed to be quarrelsome, discontented or too poor, she sallied forth into the village to settle their differences, silence their complaints, and scold them into harmony and plenty.

The entertainment of dining at Rosings was repeated about twice a week; and, allowing for the loss of Sir William, and there being only one card table in the evening, every such entertainment was the counterpart of the first. Their other engagements were few; as the style of living of the neighbour-hood in general, was beyond the Collinses' reach. This however was no evil to Elizabeth, and upon the whole she spent her time comfortably enough; there were half hours of pleasant conversation with Charlotte, and the weather was so fine for the time of year, that she had often great enjoyment out of doors. Her favourite walk, and where she frequently went while the others were calling on Lady Catherine, was along the open grove which edged that side of the park, where there was a nice sheltered path, which no one seemed to value but her-self, and where she felt beyond the reach of Lady Catherine's curiosity.

In this quiet way, the first fortnight of her visit soon passed away. Easter was approaching, and the week preceding it, was to bring an addition to the family at Rosings, which in so small a

---

1   Women, of however high a rank, could not of course exercise the *legal* authority that male landowners could wield as local magistrates: Elizabeth observes the displacement of this assumption of power into the *domestic* sphere in the case of Lady Catherine.

circle must be important. Elizabeth had heard soon after her arrival, that Mr. Darcy was expected there in the course of a few weeks, and though there were not many of her acquaintance whom she did not prefer, his coming would furnish one comparatively new to look at in their Rosings parties, and she might be amused in seeing how hopeless Miss Bingley's designs on him were, by his behaviour to his cousin, for whom he was evidently destined by Lady Catherine; who talked of his coming with the greatest satisfaction, spoke of him in terms of the highest admiration, and seemed almost angry to find that he had already been frequently seen by Miss Lucas and herself.

His arrival was soon known at the Parsonage, for Mr. Collins was walking the whole morning within view of the lodges opening into Hunsford Lane, in order to have the earliest assurance of it; and after making his bow as the carriage turned into the Park, hurried home with the great intelligence. On the following morning he hastened to Rosings to pay his respects. There were two nephews of Lady Catherine to require them, for Mr. Darcy had brought with him a Colonel Fitzwilliam, the younger son of his uncle, Lord—— and to the great surprise of all the party, when Mr. Collins returned the gentlemen accompanied him. Charlotte had seen them, from her husband's room, crossing the road, and immediately running into the other, told the girls what an honour they might expect, adding,

"I may thank you, Eliza, for this piece of civility. Mr. Darcy would never have come so soon to wait upon me."

Elizabeth had scarcely time to disclaim all right to the compliment, before their approach was announced by the door-bell, and shortly afterwards the three gentlemen entered the room. Colonel Fitzwilliam, who led the way, was about thirty, not handsome, but in person and address most truly the gentleman. Mr. Darcy looked just as he had been used to look in Hertfordshire, paid his compliments, with his usual reserve, to Mrs. Collins; and whatever might be his feelings towards her friend, met her with every appearance of composure. Elizabeth merely curtseyed to him, without saying a word.

Colonel Fitzwilliam entered into conversation directly with

the readiness and ease of a well-bred man, and talked very pleasantly; but his cousin, after having addressed a slight observation on the house and garden to Mrs. Collins, sat for some time without speaking to any body. At length, however, his civility was so far awakened as to enquire of Elizabeth after the health of her family. She answered him in the usual way, and after a moment's pause, added,

"My eldest sister has been in town these three months. Have you never happened to see her there?"

She was perfectly sensible that he never had; but she wished to see whether he would betray any consciousness of what had passed between the Bingleys and Jane; and she thought he looked a little confused as he answered that he had never been so fortunate as to meet Miss Bennet. The subject was pursued no farther, and the gentlemen soon afterwards went away.

CHAPTER VIII.

COLONEL FITZWILLIAM'S manners were very much admired at the parsonage, and the ladies all felt that he must add considerably to the pleasure of their engagements at Rosings. It was some days, however, before they received any invitation thither, for while there were visitors in the house, they could not be necessary; and it was not till Easter-day, almost a week after the gentlemen's arrival, that they were honoured by such an attention, and then they were merely asked on leaving church to come there in the evening. For the last week they had seen very little of either Lady Catherine or her daughter. Colonel Fitzwilliam had called at the parsonage more than once during the time, but Mr. Darcy they had only seen at church.

The invitation was accepted of course, and at a proper hour they joined the party in Lady Catherine's drawing room. Her ladyship received them civilly, but it was plain that their company was by no means so acceptable as when she could get nobody else; and she was, in fact, almost engrossed by her nephews, speaking to them, especially to Darcy, much more than to any other person in the room.

Colonel Fitzwilliam seemed really glad to see them; any thing was a welcome relief to him at Rosings; and Mrs. Collins's pretty friend had moreover caught his fancy very much. He now seated himself by her, and talked so agreeably of Kent and Hertfordshire, of travelling and staying at home, of new books and music, that Elizabeth had never been half so well entertained in that room before; and they conversed with so much spirit and flow, as to draw the attention of Lady Catherine herself, as well as of Mr. Darcy. *His* eyes had been soon and repeatedly turned towards them with a look of curiosity; and that her ladyship after a while shared the feeling, was more openly acknowledged, for she did not scruple to call out,

"What is that you are saying, Fitzwilliam? What is it you are talking of? What are you telling Miss Bennet? Let me hear what it is."

"We are speaking of music, Madam," said he, when no longer able to avoid a reply.

"Of music! Then pray speak aloud. It is of all subjects my delight. I must have my share in the conversation, if you are speaking of music. There are few people in England, I suppose, who have more true enjoyment of music than myself, or a better natural taste. If I had ever learnt, I should have been a great proficient. And so would Anne, if her health had allowed her to apply. I am confident that she would have performed delightfully. How does Georgiana get on, Darcy?"

Mr. Darcy spoke with affectionate praise of his sister's proficiency.

"I am very glad to hear such a good account of her," said Lady Catherine; "and pray tell her from me, that she cannot expect to excel, if she does not practise a great deal."

"I assure you, Madam," he replied, "that she does not need such advice. She practises very constantly."

"So much the better. It cannot be done too much; and when I next write to her, I shall charge her not to neglect it on any account. I often tell young ladies, that no excellence in music is to be acquired, without constant practice. I have told Miss Bennet several times, that she will never play really well, unless she practises more; and though Mrs. Collins has no instrument, she is very welcome, as I have often told her, to come to Rosings every day, and play on the piano forte in Mrs. Jenkinson's room. She would be in nobody's way, you know, in that part of the house."

Mr. Darcy looked a little ashamed of his aunt's ill breeding, and made no answer.

When coffee was over, Colonel Fitzwilliam reminded Elizabeth of having promised to play to him; and she sat down directly to the instrument. He drew a chair near her. Lady Catherine listened to half a song, and then talked, as before, to her other nephew; till the latter walked away from her, and moving with his usual deliberation towards the piano forte, stationed himself so as to command a full view of the fair performer's countenance. Elizabeth saw what he was doing, and at the first convenient pause, turned to him with an arch smile, and said,

"You mean to frighten me, Mr. Darcy, by coming in all this state to hear me? But I will not be alarmed though your sister *does* play so well. There is a stubbornness about me that never can bear to be frightened at the will of others. My courage always rises with every attempt to intimidate me."

"I shall not say that you are mistaken," he replied, "because you could not really believe me to entertain any design of alarming you; and I have had the pleasure of your acquaintance long enough to know, that you find great enjoyment in occasionally professing opinions which in fact are not your own."

Elizabeth laughed heartily at this picture of herself, and said to Colonel Fitzwilliam, "Your cousin will give you a very pretty notion of me, and teach you not to believe a word I say. I am particularly unlucky in meeting with a person so well able to expose my real character, in a part of the world where I had hoped to pass myself off with some degree of credit. Indeed, Mr. Darcy, it is very ungenerous in you to mention all that you knew to my disadvantage in Hertfordshire — and, give me leave to say, very impolitic too — for it is provoking me to retaliate, and such things may come out, as will shock your relations to hear."

shame

"I am not afraid of you," said he, smilingly.

"Pray let me hear what you have to accuse him of," cried Colonel Fitzwilliam. "I should like to know how he behaves among strangers."

"You shall hear then—but prepare yourself for something very dreadful. The first time of my ever seeing him in Hertfordshire, you must know, was at a ball—and at this ball, what do you think he did? He danced only four dances! I am sorry to pain you—but so it was. He danced only four dances, though gentlemen were scarce; and, to my certain knowledge, more than one young lady was sitting down in want of a partner. Mr. Darcy, you cannot deny the fact."

"I had not at that time the honour of knowing any lady in the assembly beyond my own party."

"True; and nobody can ever be introduced in a ball room. Well, Colonel Fitzwilliam, what do I play next? My fingers wait your orders."

"Perhaps," said Darcy, "I should have judged better, had I sought an introduction, but I am ill qualified to recommend myself to strangers."

"Shall we ask your cousin the reason of this?" said Elizabeth, still addressing Colonel Fitzwilliam. "Shall we ask him why a man of sense and education, and who has lived in the world, is ill-qualified to recommend himself to strangers?"

"I can answer your question," said Fitzwilliam, "without applying to him. It is because he will not give himself the trouble."

"I certainly have not the talent which some people possess," said Darcy, "of conversing easily with those I have never seen before. I cannot catch their tone of conversation, or appear interested in their concerns, as I often see done."

"My fingers," said Elizabeth, "do not move over this instrument in the masterly manner which I see so many women's do. They have not the same force or rapidity, and do not produce the same expression. But then I have always supposed it to be my own fault—because I would not take the trouble of practising. It is not that I do not believe *my* fingers as capable as any other woman's of superior execution."

perform
to each other
instead

Darcy smiled, and said, "You are perfectly right. You have employed your time much better. No one admitted to the privilege of hearing you, can think any thing wanting. We neither of us perform to strangers."

Here they were interrupted by Lady Catherine, who called out to know what they were talking of. Elizabeth immediately began playing again. Lady Catherine approached, and, after listening for a few minutes, said to Darcy,

"Miss Bennet would not play at all amiss, if she practised more, and could have the advantage of a London master. She has a very good notion of fingering, though her taste is not equal to Anne's. Anne would have been a delightful performer, had her health allowed her to learn."

Elizabeth looked at Darcy to see how cordially he assented to his cousin's praise; but neither at that moment nor at any other could she discern any symptom of love; and from the whole of his behaviour to Miss De Bourgh she derived this comfort for Miss Bingley, that he might have been just as likely to marry *her*, had she been his relation.

Lady Catherine continued her remarks on Elizabeth's performance, mixing with them many instructions on execution and taste. Elizabeth received them with all the forbearance of civility; and at the request of the gentlemen remained at the instrument till her ladyship's carriage was ready to take them all home.

CHAPTER IX.

ELIZABETH was sitting by herself the next morning, and writing to Jane, while Mrs. Collins and Maria were gone on business into the village, when she was startled by a ring at the door, the certain signal of a visitor. As she had heard no carriage, she thought it not unlikely to be Lady Catherine, and under that apprehension was putting away her half-finished letter that she might escape all impertinent questions, when the door opened, and to her very great surprise, Mr. Darcy, and Mr. Darcy only, entered the room.

He seemed astonished too on finding her alone, and apologised for his intrusion, by letting her know that he had understood all the ladies to be within.

They then sat down, and when her enquiries after Rosings were made, seemed in danger of sinking into total silence. It was absolutely necessary, therefore, to think of something, and in this emergence recollecting *when* she had seen him last in Hertfordshire, and feeling curious to know what he would say on the subject of their hasty departure, she observed,

"How very suddenly you all quitted Netherfield last November, Mr. Darcy! It must have been a most agreeable surprise to Mr. Bingley to see you all after him so soon; for, if I recollect right, he went but the day before. He and his sisters were well, I hope, when you left London."

"Perfectly so — I thank you."

She found that she was to receive no other answer — and, after a short pause, added,

"I think I have understood that Mr. Bingley has not much idea of ever returning to Netherfield again?"

"I have never heard him say so; but it is probable that he may spend very little of his time there in future. He has many friends, and he is at a time of life when friends and engagements are continually increasing."

"If he means to be but little at Netherfield, it would be better for the neighbourhood that he should give up the place entirely, for then we might possibly get a settled family there. But perhaps Mr. Bingley did not take the house so much for the convenience of the neighbourhood as for his own, and we must expect him to keep or quit it on the same principle."

"I should not be surprised," said Darcy, "if he were to give it up, as soon as any eligible purchase offers."

Elizabeth made no answer. She was afraid of talking longer of his friend; and, having nothing else to say, was now determined to leave the trouble of finding a subject to him.

He took the hint, and soon began with, "This seems a very comfortable house. Lady Catherine, I believe, did a great deal to it when Mr. Collins first came to Hunsford."

"I believe she did — and I am sure she could not have bestowed her kindness on a more grateful object."

"Mr. Collins appears very fortunate in his choice of a wife."

"Yes, indeed; his friends may well rejoice in his having met with one of the very few sensible women who would have accepted him, or have made him happy if they had. My friend has an excellent understanding—though I am not certain that I consider her marrying Mr. Collins as the wisest thing she ever did. She seems perfectly happy, however, and in a prudential light, it is certainly a very good match for her."

"It must be very agreeable to her to be settled within so easy a distance of her own family and friends."

"An easy distance do you call it? It is nearly fifty miles."

"And what is fifty miles of good road? Little more than half a day's journey. Yes, I call it a *very* easy distance."

"I should never have considered the distance as one of the *advantages* of the match," cried Elizabeth. "I should never have said Mrs. Collins was settled *near* her family."

"It is a proof of your own attachment to Hertfordshire. Any thing beyond the very neighbourhood of Longbourn, I suppose, would appear far."

As he spoke there was a sort of smile, which Elizabeth fancied she understood; he must be supposing her to be thinking of Jane and Netherfield, and she blushed as she answered,

"I do not mean to say that a woman may not be settled too near her family. The far and the near must be relative, and depend on many varying circumstances. Where there is fortune to make the expence of travelling unimportant, distance becomes no evil. But that is not the case *here*. Mr. and Mrs. Collins have a comfortable income, but not such a one as will allow of frequent journeys—and I am persuaded my friend would not call herself *near* her family under less than *half* the present distance."

Mr. Darcy drew his chair a little towards her, and said, "*You* cannot have a right to such very strong local attachment. *You* cannot have been always at Longbourn."

Elizabeth looked surprised. The gentleman experienced some change of feeling; he drew back his chair, took a newspaper from the table, and, glancing over it, said, in a colder voice,

"Are you pleased with Kent?"

A short dialogue on the subject of the country ensued, on

either side calm and concise—and soon put an end to by the entrance of Charlotte and her sister, just returned from their walk. The tête a tête surprised them. Mr. Darcy related the mistake which had occasioned his intruding on Miss Bennet, and after sitting a few minutes longer without saying much to any body, went away.

"What can be the meaning of this!" said Charlotte, as soon as he was gone. "My dear Eliza he must be in love with you, or he would never have called on us in this familiar way."

But when Elizabeth told of his silence, it did not seem very likely, even to Charlotte's wishes, to be the case; and after various conjectures, they could at last only suppose his visit to proceed from the difficulty of finding any thing to do, which was the more probable from the time of year. All field sports were over.[1] Within doors there was Lady Catherine, books, and a billiard table, but gentlemen cannot be always within doors; and in the nearness of the Parsonage, or the pleasantness of the walk to it, or of the people who lived in it, the two cousins found a temptation from this period of walking thither almost every day. They called at various times of the morning, sometimes separately, sometimes together, and now and then accompanied by their aunt. It was plain to them all that Colonel Fitzwilliam came because he had pleasure in their society, a persuasion which of course recommended him still more; and Elizabeth was reminded by her own satisfaction in being with him, as well as by his evident admiration of her, of her former favourite George Wickham; and though, in comparing them, she saw there was less captivating softness in Colonel Fitzwilliam's manners, she believed he might have the best informed mind.

But why Mr. Darcy came so often to the Parsonage, it was more difficult to understand. It could not be for society, as he frequently sat there ten minutes together without opening his lips; and when he did speak, it seemed the effect of necessity rather than of choice—a sacrifice to propriety, not a pleasure to himself. He seldom appeared really animated. Mrs. Collins knew not what to make of him. Colonel Fitzwilliam's occa-

---

1 "Field sports" here means game-bird shooting: the close-season for grouse began on December 10, for partridge on February 1, and for bustard on March 1.

sionally laughing at his stupidity, proved that he was generally different, which her own knowledge of him could not have told her; and as she would have liked to believe this change the effect of love, and the object of that love, her friend Eliza, she sat herself seriously to work to find it out. —She watched him whenever they were at Rosings, and whenever he came to Hunsford; but without much success. He certainly looked at her friend a great deal, but the expression of that look was disputable. It was an earnest, steadfast gaze, but she often doubted whether there were much admiration in it, and sometimes it seemed nothing but absence of mind.

She had once or twice suggested to Elizabeth the possibility of his being partial to her, but Elizabeth always laughed at the idea; and Mrs. Collins did not think it right to press the subject, from the danger of raising expectations which might only end in disappointment; for in her opinion it admitted not of a doubt, that all her friend's dislike would vanish, if she could suppose him to be in her power.

In her kind schemes for Elizabeth, she sometimes planned her marrying Colonel Fitzwilliam. He was beyond comparison the pleasantest man; he certainly admired her, and his situation in life was most eligible; but, to counterbalance these advantages, Mr. Darcy had considerable patronage in the church, and his cousin could have none at all.

CHAPTER X.

MORE than once did Elizabeth in her ramble within the Park, unexpectedly meet Mr. Darcy. —She felt all the perverseness of the mischance that should bring him where no one else was brought; and to prevent its ever happening again, took care to inform him at first, that it was a favourite haunt of hers.— How it could occur a second time therefore was very odd!— Yet it did, and even a third. It seemed like wilful ill-nature, or a voluntary penance, for on these occasions it was not merely a few formal enquiries and an awkward pause and then away, but he actually thought it necessary to turn back and walk with her. He never said a great deal, nor did she give herself the trouble of talking or of listening much; but it struck her in the course of their third rencontre that he was asking some odd unconnected questions — about her pleasure in being at Hunsford, her love of solitary walks, and her opinion of Mr. and Mrs. Collins's happiness; and that in speaking of Rosings and her not perfectly understanding the house, he seemed to expect that whenever she came into Kent again she would be staying *there* too. His words seemed to imply it. Could he have Colonel Fitzwilliam in his thoughts? She supposed, if he meant any thing, he must mean an allusion to what might arise in that quarter. It distressed her a little, and she was quite glad to find herself at the gate in the pales opposite the Parsonage.

She was engaged one day as she walked, in re-perusing Jane's last letter, and dwelling on some passages which proved that Jane had not written in spirits, when, instead of being again surprised by Mr. Darcy, she saw on looking up that Colonel Fitzwilliam was meeting her. Putting away the letter immediately and forcing a smile, she said,

"I did not know before that you ever walked this way."

"I have been making the tour of the Park," he replied, "as I generally do every year, and intend to close it with a call at the Parsonage. Are you going much farther?"

"No, I should have turned in a moment."

And accordingly she did turn, and they walked towards the Parsonage together.

"Do you certainly leave Kent on Saturday?" said she.

"Yes — if Darcy does not put it off again. But I am at his disposal. He arranges the business just as he pleases."

"And if not able to please himself in the arrangement, he has at least great pleasure in the power of choice. I do not know any body who seems more to enjoy the power of doing what he likes than Mr. Darcy."

"He likes to have his own way very well," replied Colonel Fitzwilliam. "But so we all do. It is only that he has better means of having it than many others, because he is rich, and many others are poor. I speak feelingly. A younger son, you know, must be inured to self-denial and dependence."

& + mobility freedom

"In my opinion, the younger son of an Earl can know very little of either. Now, seriously, what have you ever known of self-denial and dependence? When have you been prevented by want of money from going wherever you chose, or procuring any thing you had a fancy for?"

"These are home questions—and perhaps I cannot say that I have experienced many hardships of that nature. But in matters of greater weight, I may suffer from the want of money. Younger sons cannot marry where they like."

"Unless where they like women of fortune, which I think they very often do."

"Our habits of expence make us too dependant, and there are not many in my rank of life who can afford to marry without some attention to money."

men dependant & too

"Is this," thought Elizabeth, "meant for me?" and she coloured at the idea; but, recovering herself, said in a lively tone, "and pray, what is the usual price of an Earl's younger son? Unless the elder brother is very sickly, I suppose you would not ask above fifty thousand pounds."[1]

He answered her in the same style, and the subject dropped. To interrupt a silence which might make him fancy her affected with what had passed, she soon afterwards said,

"I imagine your cousin brought you down with him chiefly for the sake of having somebody at his disposal. I wonder he does not marry, to secure a lasting convenience of that kind. But, perhaps his sister does as well for the present, and, as she is under his sole care, he may do what he likes with her."

"No," said Colonel Fitzwilliam, "that is an advantage which he must divide with me. I am joined with him in the guardianship of Miss Darcy."

"Are you, indeed? And pray what sort of guardians do you make? Does your charge give you much trouble? Young ladies of her age, are sometimes a little difficult to manage, and if she has the true Darcy spirit, she may like to have her own way."

As she spoke, she observed him looking at her earnestly, and the manner in which he immediately asked her why she sup-

---

1 Once again the talk is of dowries: see note to p.138.

posed Miss Darcy likely to give them any uneasiness, convinced her that she had somehow or other got pretty near the truth. She directly replied,

"You need not be frightened. I never heard any harm of her; and I dare say she is one of the most tractable creatures in the world. She is a very great favourite with some ladies of my acquaintance, Mrs. Hurst and Miss Bingley. I think I have heard you say that you know them."

"I know them a little. Their brother is a pleasant gentleman-like man — he is a great friend of Darcy's."

"Oh! yes," said Elizabeth drily — "Mr. Darcy is uncommon-ly kind to Mr. Bingley, and takes a prodigious deal of care of him."

"Care of him! — Yes, I really believe Darcy *does* take care of him in those points where he most wants care. From something that he told me in our journey hither, I have reason to think Bingley very much indebted to him. But I ought to beg his pardon, for I have no right to suppose that Bingley was the person meant. It was all conjecture."

"What is it you mean?"

"It is a circumstance which Darcy of course would not wish to be generally known, because if it were to get round to the lady's family, it would be an unpleasant thing."

"You may depend upon my not mentioning it."

"And remember that I have not much reason for supposing it to be Bingley. What he told me was merely this; that he congratulated himself on having lately saved a friend from the inconveniences of a most imprudent marriage, but without mentioning names or any other particulars, and I only suspected it to be Bingley from believing him the kind of young man to get into a scrape of that sort, and from knowing them to have been together the whole of last summer."

"Did Mr. Darcy give you his reasons for this interference?"

"I understood that there were some very strong objections against the lady."

"And what arts did he use to separate them?"

"He did not talk to me of his own arts," said Fitzwilliam smiling. "He only told me what I have now told you."

Elizabeth made no answer, and walked on, her heart swelling with indignation. After watching her a little, Fitzwilliam asked her why she was so thoughtful.

"I am thinking of what you have been telling me," said she. "Your cousin's conduct does not suit my feelings. Why was he to be the judge?"

"You are rather disposed to call his interference officious?"

"I do not see what right Mr. Darcy had to decide on the propriety of his friend's inclination, or why, upon his own judgment alone, he was to determine and direct in what manner that friend was to be happy." "But," she continued, recollecting herself, "as we know none of the particulars, it is not fair to condemn him. It is not to be supposed that there was much affection in the case."

"That is not an unnatural surmise," said Fitzwilliam, "but it is lessening the honour of my cousin's triumph very sadly."

This was spoken jestingly, but it appeared to her so just a picture of Mr. Darcy that she would not trust herself with an answer; and, therefore, abruptly changing the conversation, talked on indifferent matters till they reached the parsonage. There, shut into her own room, as soon as their visitor left them, she could think without interruption of all that she had heard. It was not to be supposed that any other people could be meant than those with whom she was connected. There could not exist in the world *two* men, over whom Mr. Darcy could have such boundless influence. That he had been concerned in the measures taken to separate Mr. Bingley and Jane, she had never doubted; but she had always attributed to Miss Bingley the principal design and arrangement of them. If his own vanity, however, did not mislead him, *he* was the cause, his pride and caprice were the cause of all that Jane had suffered, and still continued to suffer. He had ruined for a while every hope of happiness for the most affectionate, generous heart in the world; and no one could say how lasting an evil he might have inflicted.

"There were some very strong objections against the lady," were Colonel Fitzwilliam's words, and these strong objections probably were, her having one uncle who was a country attorney, and another who was in business in London. "To Jane herself," she exclaimed, "there could be no possibility of objection. All loveliness and goodness as she is! Her understanding excellent, her mind improved, and her manners captivating. Neither could any thing be urged against my father, who, though with some peculiarities, has abilities which Mr. Darcy himself need not disdain, and respectability which he will probably never reach." When she thought of her mother indeed, her confidence gave way a little, but she would not allow that any objections *there* had material weight with Mr. Darcy, whose pride, she was convinced, would receive a deeper wound from the want of importance in his friend's connections, than from their want of sense; and she was quite decided at last, that he had been partly governed by this worst kind of pride, and partly by the wish of retaining Mr. Bingley for his sister.

The agitation and tears which the subject occasioned, brought on a headache; and it grew so much worse towards the evening that, added to her unwillingness to see Mr. Darcy, it determined her not to attend her cousins to Rosings, where they were engaged to drink tea. Mrs. Collins, seeing that she was really unwell, did not press her to go, and as much as possible prevented her husband from pressing her, but Mr. Collins could not conceal his apprehension of Lady Catherine's being rather displeased by her staying at home.

CHAPTER XI.

WHEN they were gone, Elizabeth, as if intending to exasperate herself as much as possible against Mr. Darcy, chose for her employment the examination of all the letters which Jane had written to her since her being in Kent. They contained no actual complaint, nor was there any revival of past occurrences, or any communication of present suffering. But in all, and in almost every line of each, there was a want of that cheerfulness which had been used to characterize her style, and which, proceeding from the serenity of a mind at ease with itself, and kindly disposed towards every one, had been scarcely ever clouded. Elizabeth noticed every sentence conveying the idea of uneasiness, with an attention which it had hardly received on the first perusal. Mr. Darcy's shameful boast of what misery he had been able to inflict, gave her a keener sense of her sister's sufferings. It was some consolation to think that his visit to Rosings was to end on the day after the next, and a still greater, that in less than a fortnight she should herself be with Jane again, and enabled to contribute to the recovery of her spirits, by all that affection could do.

She could not think of Darcy's leaving Kent, without remembering that his cousin was to go with him; but Colonel Fitzwilliam had made it clear that he had no intentions at all, and agreeable as he was, she did not mean to be unhappy about him.

While settling this point, she was suddenly roused by the sound of the door bell, and her spirits were a little fluttered by the idea of its being Colonel Fitzwilliam himself, who had once before called late in the evening, and might now come to enquire particularly after her. But this idea was soon banished, and her spirits were very differently affected, when, to her utter amazement, she saw Mr. Darcy walk into the room. In an hurried manner he immediately began an enquiry after her health, imputing his visit to a wish of hearing that she were better. She answered him with cold civility. He sat down for a few moments, and then getting up walked about the room. Elizabeth was surprised, but said not a word. After a silence of several minutes he came towards her in an agitated manner, and thus began,

"In vain have I struggled. It will not do. My feelings will not be repressed. You must allow me to tell you how ardently I admire and love you."

Elizabeth's astonishment was beyond expression. She stared, coloured, doubted, and was silent. This he considered sufficient encouragement, and the avowal of all that he felt and had long felt for her, immediately followed. He spoke well, but there were feelings besides those of the heart to be detailed, and he was not more eloquent on the subject of tenderness than of pride. His sense of her inferiority—of its being a degradation—of the family obstacles which judgment had always opposed to inclination, were dwelt on with a warmth which seemed due to the consequence he was wounding, but was very unlikely to recommend his suit.

In spite of her deeply-rooted dislike, she could not be insensible to the compliment of such a man's affection, and though her intentions did not vary for an instant, she was at first sorry for the pain he was to receive; till, roused to resentment by his subsequent language, she lost all compassion in anger. She tried, however, to compose herself to answer him with patience, when he should have done. He concluded with representing to her the strength of that attachment which, in spite of all his endeavours, he had found impossible to conquer; and with expressing his hope that it would now be rewarded by her acceptance of his hand. As he said this, she could easily see that he had no doubt of a favourable answer. He *spoke* of apprehension and anxiety, but his countenance expressed real security. Such a circumstance could only exasperate farther, and when he ceased, the colour rose into her cheeks, and she said,

again, not really a proposal

"In such cases as this, it is, I believe, the established mode to express a sense of obligation for the sentiments avowed, however unequally they may be returned. It is natural that obligation should be felt, and if I could *feel* gratitude, I would now thank you. But I cannot—I have never desired your good opinion, and you have certainly bestowed it most unwillingly. I am sorry to have occasioned pain to any one. It has been most unconsciously done, however, and I hope will be of short duration. The feelings which, you tell me, have long prevented the acknowledgment of your regard, can have little difficulty in overcoming it after this explanation."

Mr. Darcy, who was leaning against the mantle-piece with his eyes fixed on her face, seemed to catch her words with no less resentment than surprise. His complexion became pale with anger, and the disturbance of his mind was visible in every feature. He was struggling for the appearance of composure, and would not open his lips, till he believed himself to have attained it. The pause was to Elizabeth's feelings dreadful. At length, in a voice of forced calmness, he said,

"And this is all the reply which I am to have the honour of expecting! I might, perhaps, wish to be informed why, with so little *endeavour* at civility, I am thus rejected. But it is of small importance."

"I might as well enquire," replied she, "why with so evident a design of offending and insulting me, you chose to tell me that you liked me against your will, against your reason, and even against your character? Was not this some excuse for incivility, if I *was* uncivil? But I have other provocations. You know I have. Had not my own feelings decided against you, had they been indifferent, or had they even been favourable, do you think that any consideration would tempt me to accept the man, who has been the means of ruining, perhaps for ever, the happiness of a most beloved sister?"

As she pronounced these words, Mr. Darcy changed colour; but the emotion was short, and he listened without attempting to interrupt her while she continued.

"I have every reason in the world to think ill of you. No motive can excuse the unjust and ungenerous part you acted *there*. You dare not, you cannot deny that you have been the principal, if not the only means of dividing them from each other, of exposing one to the censure of the world for caprice and instability, the other to its derision for disappointed hopes, and involving them both in misery of the acutest kind."

She paused, and saw with no slight indignation that he was listening with an air which proved him wholly unmoved by any feeling of remorse. He even looked at her with a smile of affected incredulity.

"Can you deny that you have done it?" she repeated.

With assumed tranquillity he then replied, "I have no wish of denying that I did every thing in my power to separate my friend from your sister, or that I rejoice in my success. Towards *him* I have been kinder than towards myself."

Elizabeth disdained the appearance of noticing this civil reflection, but its meaning did not escape, nor was it likely to conciliate, her.

"But it is not merely this affair," she continued, "on which my dislike is founded. Long before it had taken place, my opinion of you was decided. Your character was unfolded in the recital which I received many months ago from Mr. Wickham. On this subject, what can you have to say? In what imaginary act of friendship can you here defend yourself? or under what misrepresentation, can you here impose upon others?"

"You take an eager interest in that gentleman's concerns," said Darcy in a less tranquil tone, and with a heightened colour.

"Who that knows what his misfortunes have been, can help feeling an interest in him?"

"His misfortunes!" repeated Darcy contemptuously; "yes, his misfortunes have been great indeed."

"And of your infliction," cried Elizabeth with energy. "You have reduced him to his present state of poverty, comparative poverty. You have withheld the advantages, which you must know to have been designed for him. You have deprived the best years of his life, of that independence which was no less his due than his desert. You have done all this! and yet you can treat the mention of his misfortunes with contempt and ridicule."

"And this," cried Darcy, as he walked with quick steps across the room, "is your opinion of me! This is the estimation in which you hold me! I thank you for explaining it so fully. My faults, according to this calculation, are heavy indeed! But perhaps," added he, stopping in his walk, and turning towards her, "these offences might have been overlooked, had not your pride been hurt by my honest confession of the scruples that had long prevented my forming any serious design. These bitter accusations might have been suppressed, had I with greater policy concealed my struggles, and flattered you into the belief of my being impelled by unqualified, unalloyed inclination; by reason, by reflection, by every thing. But disguise of every sort is my abhorrence. Nor am I ashamed of the feelings I related. They were natural and just. Could you expect me to rejoice in the inferiority of your connections? To congratulate myself on the hope of relations, whose condition in life is so decidedly beneath my own?"

Elizabeth felt herself growing more angry every moment; yet she tried to the utmost to speak with composure when she said,

"You are mistaken, Mr. Darcy, if you suppose that the mode

of your declaration affected me in any other way, than as it spared me the concern which I might have felt in refusing you, had you behaved in a more gentleman-like manner."

She saw him start at this, but he said nothing, and she continued,

"You could not have made me the offer of your hand in any possible way that would have tempted me to accept it."

Again his astonishment was obvious; and he looked at her with an expression of mingled incredulity and mortification. She went on.

"From the very beginning, from the first moment I may almost say, of my acquaintance with you, your manners impressing me with the fullest belief of your arrogance, your conceit, and your selfish disdain of the feelings of others, were such as to form that ground-work of disapprobation, on which succeeding events have built so immoveable a dislike; and I had not known you a month before I felt that you were the last man in the world whom I could ever be prevailed on to marry."

"You have said quite enough, madam. I perfectly comprehend your feelings, and have now only to be ashamed of what my own have been. Forgive me for having taken up so much of your time, and accept my best wishes for your health and happiness."

And with these words he hastily left the room, and Elizabeth heard him the next moment open the front door and quit the house.

The tumult of her mind was now painfully great. She knew not how to support herself, and from actual weakness sat down and cried for half an hour. Her astonishment, as she reflected on what had passed, was increased by every review of it. That she should receive an offer of marriage from Mr. Darcy! that he should have been in love with her for so many months! so much in love as to wish to marry her in spite of all the objections which had made him prevent his friend's marrying her sister, and which must appear at least with equal force in his own case, was almost incredible! it was gratifying to have inspired unconsciously so strong an affection. But his pride, his abominable pride, his shameless avowal of what he had done with respect to Jane, his unpardonable assurance in acknowledging, though he could not justify it, and the unfeeling manner in which he had mentioned Mr. Wickham, his cruelty towards whom he had not attempted to deny, soon overcame the pity which the consideration of his attachment had for a moment excited.

She continued in very agitating reflections till the sound of Lady Catherine's carriage made her feel how unequal she was to encounter Charlotte's observation, and hurried her away to her room.

CHAPTER XII.

ELIZABETH awoke the next morning to the same thoughts and meditations which had at length closed her eyes. She could not yet recover from the surprise of what had happened; it was impossible to think of any thing else, and totally indisposed for employment, she resolved soon after breakfast to indulge herself in air and exercise. She was proceeding directly to her favourite walk, when the recollection of Mr. Darcy's sometimes coming there stopped her, and instead of entering the park, she turned up the lane, which led her farther from the turnpike road. The park paling was still the boundary on one side, and she soon passed one of the gates into the ground.

After walking two or three times along that part of the lane, she was tempted, by the pleasantness of the morning, to stop at the gates and look into the park. The five weeks which she had now passed in Kent, had made a great difference in the country, and every day was adding to the verdure of the early trees. She was on the point of continuing her walk, when she caught a glimpse of a gentleman within the sort of grove which edged the park; he was moving that way; and fearful of its being Mr. Darcy, she was directly retreating. But the person who advanced, was now near enough to see her, and stepping forward with eagerness, pronounced her name. She had turned away, but on hearing herself called, though in a voice which proved it to be Mr. Darcy, she moved again towards the gate. He had by that time reached it also, and holding out a letter, which she instinctively took, said with a look of haughty composure, "I have been walking in the grove some time in the hope of meeting you. Will you do me the honour of reading that letter?"—And then, with a slight bow, turned again into the plantation, and was soon out of sight.

With no expectation of pleasure, but with the strongest curiosity, Elizabeth opened the letter, and, to her still increasing wonder, perceived an envelope containing two sheets of letter paper, written quite through, in a very close hand.—The envelope itself was likewise full.[1]—Pursuing her way along the lane, she then began it. It was dated from Rosings, at eight o'clock in the morning, and was as follows:—

"Be not alarmed, Madam, on receiving this letter, by the apprehension of its containing any repetition of those sentiments, or renewal of those offers, which were last night so disgusting to you. I write without any intention of paining you, or humbling myself, by dwelling on wishes, which, for the happiness of both, cannot be too soon forgotten; and the effort which the formation, and the perusal of this letter must occasion, should have been spared, had not my character required it to be written and read. You must, therefore, pardon the freedom with which I demand your attention; your feelings, I know, will bestow it unwillingly, but I demand it of your justice.

"Two offences of a very different nature, and by no means of equal magnitude, you last night laid to my charge. The first mentioned was, that, regardless of the sentiments of either, I had detached Mr. Bingley from your sister,—and the other, that I had, in defiance of various claims, in defiance of honour and humanity, ruined the immediate prosperity, and blasted the prospects of Mr. Wickham.—Wilfully and wantonly to have thrown off the companion of my youth, the acknowledged favourite of my father, a young man who had scarcely any

---

1 The envelope of a letter was simply the outermost of its sheets, when they were folded together and sealed with wax; its inner surface was therefore available for writing.

other dependence than on our patronage, and who had been brought up to expect its exertion, would be a depravity, to which the separation of two young persons, whose affection could be the growth of only a few weeks, could bear no comparison. — But from the severity of that blame which was last night so liberally bestowed, respecting each circumstance, I shall hope to be in future secured, when the following account of my actions and their motives has been read. — If, in the explanation of them which is due to myself, I am under the necessity of relating feelings which may be offensive to your's, I can only say that I am sorry. — The necessity must be obeyed — and farther apology would be absurd. — I had not been long in Hertfordshire, before I saw, in common with others, that Bingley preferred your eldest sister, to any other young woman in the country. — But it was not till the evening of the dance at Netherfield that I had any apprehension of his feeling a serious attachment. — I had often seen him in love before. — At that ball, while I had the honour of dancing with you, I was first made acquainted, by Sir William Lucas's accidental information, that Bingley's attentions to your sister had given rise to a general expectation of their marriage. He spoke of it as a certain event, of which the time alone could be undecided. From that moment I observed my friend's behaviour attentively; and I could then perceive that his partiality for Miss Bennet was beyond what I had ever witnessed in him. Your sister I also watched. — Her look and manners were open, cheerful and engaging as ever, but without any symptom of peculiar regard, and I remained convinced from the evening's scrutiny, that though she received his attentions with pleasure, she did not invite them by any participation of sentiment. — If *you* have not been mistaken here, *I* must have been in an error. Your superior knowledge of your sister must make the latter probable. — If it be so, if I have been misled by such error, to inflict pain on her, your resentment has not been unreasonable. But I shall not scruple to assert, that the serenity of your sister's countenance and air was such, as might have given the most acute observer, a conviction that, however amiable her temper, her heart was not likely to be easily touched. —That I was desirous of believing her indifferent is certain,—but I will venture to say that my investigations and decisions are not usually influenced by my hopes or fears. —I did not believe her to be indifferent because I wished it;—I believed it on impartial conviction, as truly as I wished it in reason. —My objections to the marriage were not merely those, which I last night acknowledged to have required the utmost force of passion to put aside, in my own case; the want of connection could not be so great an evil to my friend as to me. —But there were other causes of repugnance;—causes which, though still existing, and existing to an equal degree in both instances, I had myself endeavoured to forget, because they were not immediately before me. —These causes must be stated, though briefly. —The situation of your mother's family, though objectionable, was nothing in comparison of that total want of propriety so frequently, so almost uniformly betrayed by herself, by your three younger sisters, and occasionally even by your father. —Pardon me. —It pains me to offend you. But amidst your concern for the defects of your nearest relations, and your displeasure at this representation of them, let it give you consolation to consider that, to have conducted yourselves so as to avoid any share of the like censure, is praise no less generally bestowed on you and your eldest sister, than it is honourable to the sense and disposition of both. —I will only say farther, that from what passed that evening, my opinion of all parties was confirmed, and every inducement heightened, which could have led me before, to preserve my friend from what I esteemed a most unhappy connection. —He left Netherfield for London, on the day following, as you, I am certain, remember, with the design of soon returning. —The part which I acted, is now to be explained. —His sisters' uneasiness had been equally excited with my own; our coincidence of feeling was soon discovered; and, alike sensible that no time was to be lost in detaching their brother, we shortly resolved on joining him directly in London. —We accordingly went—and there I readily engaged in the office of pointing out to my friend, the certain evils of such a choice. —I described, and enforced them earnestly. —But, however this remonstrance might have staggered or delayed his determination, I do not suppose that it would ultimately have prevented the marriage, had it not been seconded by the assurance which I hesitated not in giving, of your sister's indifference. He had before believed her to return his affection with sincere, if not with equal regard. — But Bingley has great natural modesty, with a stronger dependence on my judgment than on his own. — To convince him, therefore, that he had deceived himself, was no very difficult point. To persuade him against returning into Hertfordshire, when that conviction had been given, was scarcely the work of a moment. — I cannot blame myself for having done thus much. There is but one part of my conduct in the whole affair, on which I do not reflect with satisfaction; it is that I condescended to adopt the measures of art so far as to conceal from him your sister's being in town. I knew it myself, as it was known to Miss Bingley, but her brother is even yet ignorant of it. — That they might have met without ill consequence, is perhaps probable;—but his regard did not appear to me enough extinguished for him to see her without some danger. — Perhaps this concealment, this disguise, was beneath me. — It is done, however, and it was done for the best. — On this subject I have nothing more to say, no other apology to offer. If I have wounded your sister's feelings, it was unknowingly done; and though the motives which governed me may to you very naturally appear insufficient, I have not yet learnt to condemn them. — With respect to that other, more weighty accusation, of having injured Mr. Wickham, I can only refute it by laying before you the whole of his connection with my family. Of what he has *particularly* accused me I am ignorant; but of the truth of what I shall relate, I can summon more than one witness of undoubted veracity. Mr. Wickham is the son of a very respectable man, who had for many years the management of all the Pemberley estates; and whose good conduct in the discharge of his trust, naturally inclined my father to be of service to him, and on George Wickham, who was his god-son, his kindness was therefore liberally bestowed. My father supported him at school, and afterwards at Cambridge;—most important assistance, as his own father, always poor from the extravagance of his wife, would have been unable to give him a gentleman's education. My father was not only fond of this young man's society, whose manners were always engaging; he had also the highest opinion of him, and hoping the church would be his profession, intended to provide for him in it. As for myself, it is many, many years since I first began to think of him in a very different manner. The vicious propensities—the want of principle which he was careful to guard from the knowledge of his best friend, could not escape the observation of a young man of nearly the same age with himself, and who had opportunities of seeing him in unguarded moments, which Mr. Darcy could not have. Here again I shall give you pain—to what degree you only can tell. But whatever may be the sentiments which Mr. Wickham has created, a suspicion of their nature shall not prevent me from unfolding his real character. It adds even another motive. My excellent father died about five years ago; and his attachment to Mr. Wickham was to the last so steady, that in his will he particularly recommended it to me, to promote his advancement in the best manner that his profession might allow, and if he took orders, desired that a valuable family living might be his as soon as it became vacant. There was also a legacy of one thousand pounds. His own father did not long survive mine, and within half a year from these events, Mr. Wickham wrote to inform me that, having finally resolved against taking orders, he hoped I should not think it unreasonable for him to expect some more immediate pecuniary advantage, in lieu of the preferment, by which he could not be benefited. He had some intention, he added, of studying the law, and I must be aware that the interest of one thousand pounds would be a very insufficient support therein. I rather wished, than believed him to be sincere; but at any rate, was perfectly ready to accede to his proposal. I knew that Mr. Wickham ought not to be a clergyman. The business was therefore soon settled. He resigned all claim to assistance in the church, were it possible that he could ever be in a situation to receive it, and accepted in return three thousand pounds. All connection between us seemed now dissolved. I thought too ill of him, to invite him to

Pemberley, or admit his society in town. In town I believe he chiefly lived, but his studying the law was a mere pretence, and being now free from all restraint, his life was a life of idleness and dissipation. For about three years I heard little of him; but on the decease of the incumbent of the living which had been designed for him, he applied to me again by letter for the presentation. His circumstances, he assured me, and I had no difficulty in believing it, were exceedingly bad. He had found the law a most unprofitable study, and was now absolutely resolved on being ordained, if I would present him to the living in question — of which he trusted there could be little doubt, as he was well assured that I had no other person to provide for, and I could not have forgotten my revered father's intentions. You will hardly blame me for refusing to comply with this entreaty, or for resisting every repetition of it. His resentment was in proportion to the distress of his circumstances — and he was doubtless as violent in his abuse of me to others, as in his reproaches to myself. After this period, every appearance of acquaintance was dropt. How he lived I know not. But last summer he was again most painfully obtruded on my notice. I must now mention a circumstance which I would wish to forget myself, and which no obligation less than the present should induce me to unfold to any human being. Having said thus much, I feel no doubt of your secrecy. My sister, who is more than ten years my junior, was left to the guardianship of my mother's nephew, Colonel Fitzwilliam, and myself. About a year ago, she was taken from school, and an establishment formed for her in London; and last summer she went with the lady who presided over it, to Ramsgate;[1] and thither also went Mr. Wickham, undoubtedly by design; for there proved to have been a prior acquaintance between him and Mrs. Younge, in whose character we were most unhappily deceived; and by her connivance and aid, he so far recommended himself to Georgiana, whose affectionate heart retained a strong impression of his kindness to her as a child, that she was persuaded to believe herself in love, and to consent to an elopement. She was then

---

1 A fashionable resort on the south-east coast.

but fifteen, which must be her excuse; and after stating her imprudence, I am happy to add, that I owed the knowledge of it to herself. I joined them unexpectedly a day or two before the intended elopement, and then Georgiana, unable to support the idea of grieving and offending a brother whom she almost looked up to as a father, acknowledged the whole to me. You may imagine what I felt and how I acted. Regard for my sister's credit and feelings prevented any public exposure, but I wrote to Mr. Wickham, who left the place immediately, and Mrs. Younge was of course removed from her charge. Mr. Wickham's chief object was unquestionably my sister's fortune, which is thirty thousand pounds; but I cannot help supposing that the hope of revenging himself on me, was a strong inducement. His revenge would have been complete indeed. This, madam, is a faithful narrative of every event in which we have been concerned together; and if you do not absolutely reject it as false, you will, I hope, acquit me henceforth of cruelty towards Mr. Wickham. I know not in what manner, under what form of falsehood he has imposed on you; but his success is not perhaps to be wondered at, ignorant as you previously were of every thing concerning either. Detection could not be in your power, and suspicion certainly not in your inclination. You may possibly wonder why all this was not told you last night. But I was not then master enough of myself to know what could or ought to be revealed. For the truth of every thing here related, I can appeal more particularly to the testimony of Colonel Fitzwilliam, who from our near relationship and constant intimacy, and still more as one of the executors of my father's will, has been unavoidably acquainted with every particular of these transactions. If your abhorrence of *me* should make *my* assertions valueless, you cannot be prevented by the same cause from confiding in my cousin; and that there may be the possibility of consulting him, I shall endeavour to find some opportunity of putting this letter in your hands in the course of the morning. I will only add, God bless you.

"FITZWILLIAM DARCY."

CHAPTER XIII.

IF Elizabeth, when Mr. Darcy gave her the letter, did not expect it to contain a renewal of his offers, she had formed no expectation at all of its contents. But such as they were, it may be well supposed how eagerly she went through them, and what a contrariety of emotion they excited. Her feelings as she read were scarcely to be defined. With amazement did she first understand that he believed any apology to be in his power; and stedfastly was she persuaded that he could have no explanation to give, which a just sense of shame would not conceal. With a strong prejudice against every thing he might say, she began his account of what had happened at Netherfield. She read, with an eagerness which hardly left her power of comprehension, and from impatience of knowing what the next sentence might bring, was incapable of attending to the sense of the one before her eyes. His belief of her sister's insensibility, she instantly resolved to be false, and his account of the real, the worst objections to the match, made her too angry to have any wish of doing him justice. He expressed no regret for what he had done which satisfied her; his style was not penitent, but haughty. It was all pride and insolence.

But when this subject was succeeded by his account of Mr. Wickham, when she read with somewhat clearer attention, a relation of events, which, if true, must overthrow every cherished opinion of his worth, and which bore so alarming an affinity to his own history of himself, her feelings were yet more acutely painful and more difficult of definition. Astonishment, apprehension, and even horror, oppressed her. She wished to discredit it entirely, repeatedly exclaiming, "This must be false! This cannot be! This must be the grossest falsehood!"—and when she had gone through the whole letter, though scarcely knowing any thing of the last page or two, put it hastily away, protesting that she would not regard it, that she would never look in it again.

In this perturbed state of mind, with thoughts that could rest on nothing, she walked on; but it would not do; in half a minute the letter was unfolded again, and collecting herself as well as she could, she again began the mortifying perusal of all that related to Wickham, and commanded herself so far as to examine the meaning of every sentence. The account of his connection with the Pemberley family was exactly what he had related himself; and the kindness of the late Mr. Darcy, though she had not before known its extent, agreed equally well with his own words. So far each recital confirmed the other: but when she came to the will, the difference was great. What Wickham had said of the living was fresh in her memory, and as she recalled his very words, it was impossible not to feel that there was gross duplicity on one side or the other; and, for a few moments, she flattered herself that her wishes did not err. But when she read, and re-read with the closest attention, the particulars immediately following of Wickham's resigning all pretensions to the living, of his receiving in lieu, so considerable a sum as three thousand pounds, again was she forced to hesitate. She put down the letter, weighed every circumstance with what she meant to be impartiality—deliberated on the probability of each statement—but with little success. On both sides it was only assertion. Again she read on. But every line proved more clearly that the affair, which she had believed it impossible that any contrivance could so represent, as to render Mr. Darcy's conduct in it less than infamous, was capable of a turn which must make him entirely blameless throughout the whole.

The extravagance and general profligacy which he scrupled not to lay to Mr. Wickham's charge, exceedingly shocked her; the more so, as she could bring no proof of its injustice. She had never heard of him before his entrance into the ——shire Militia, in which he had engaged at the persuasion of the young man, who, on meeting him accidentally in town, had there renewed a slight acquaintance. Of his former way of life, nothing had been known in Hertfordshire but what he told himself. As to his real character, had information been in her power, she had never felt a wish of enquiring. His countenance, voice, and manner, had established him at once in the possession of every virtue. She tried to recollect some instance of goodness, some distinguished trait of integrity or benevolence, that might rescue him from the attacks of Mr. Darcy; or at least, by the predominance of virtue, atone for those casual errors, under which she would endeavour to class, what Mr. Darcy had described as the idleness and vice of many years continuance. But no such recollection befriended her. She could see him instantly before her, in every charm of air and address; but she could remember no more substantial good than the general approbation of the neighbourhood, and the regard which his social powers had gained him in the mess.[1] After pausing on this point a considerable while, she once more continued to read. But, alas! the story which followed of his designs on Miss Darcy, received some confirmation from what had passed between Colonel Fitzwilliam and herself only the morning before; and at last she was referred for the truth of every particular to Colonel Fitzwilliam himself—from whom she had previously received the information of his near concern in all his cousin's affairs, and whose character she had no reason to question. At one time she had almost resolved on applying to him, but the idea was checked by the awkwardness of the application, and at length wholly banished by the conviction that Mr. Darcy would never have hazarded such a proposal, if he had not been well assured of his cousin's corroboration.

She perfectly remembered every thing that had passed in conversation between Wickham and herself, in their first evening at Mr. Philips's. Many of his expressions were still fresh in her memory. She was *now* struck with the impropriety of such communications to a stranger, and wondered it had escaped her before. She saw the indelicacy of putting himself forward as he had done, and the inconsistency of his professions with his conduct. She remembered that he had boasted of having no fear of seeing Mr. Darcy—that Mr. Darcy might leave the country, but that *he* should stand his ground; yet he had avoided the Netherfield ball the very next week. She remembered also, that till the Netherfield family had quitted the country, he had told his story to no one but herself; but that after their removal, it had been every where discussed; that he

---

1   That is, among his fellow officers: the mess is their common-room and dining-space in barracks.

had then no reserves, no scruples in sinking Mr. Darcy's character, though he had assured her that respect for the father, would always prevent his exposing the son.

How differently did every thing now appear in which he was concerned! His attentions to Miss King were now the consequence of views solely and hatefully mercenary; and the mediocrity of her fortune proved no longer the moderation of his wishes, but his eagerness to grasp at any thing. His behaviour to herself could now have had no tolerable motive; he had either been deceived with regard to her fortune, or had been gratifying his vanity by encouraging the preference which she believed she had most incautiously shewn. Every lingering struggle in his favour grew fainter and fainter; and in farther justification of Mr. Darcy, she could not but allow that Mr. Bingley, when questioned by Jane, had long ago asserted his blamelessness in the affair; that proud and repulsive as were his manners, she had never, in the whole course of their acquaintance, an acquaintance which had latterly brought them much together, and given her a sort of intimacy with his ways, seen any thing that betrayed him to be unprincipled or unjust — any thing that spoke him of irreligious or immoral habits. That among his own connections he was esteemed and valued — that even Wickham had allowed him merit as a brother, and that she had often heard him speak so affectionately of his sister as to prove him capable of *some* amiable feeling. That had his actions been what Wickham represented them, so gross a violation of every thing right could hardly have been concealed from the world; and that friendship between a person capable of it, and such an amiable man as Mr. Bingley, was incomprehensible.

She grew absolutely ashamed of herself. —Of neither Darcy nor Wickham could she think, without feeling that she had been blind, partial, prejudiced, absurd.

"How despicably have I acted!" she cried. — "I, who have prided myself on my discernment! — I, who have valued myself on my abilities! who have often disdained the generous candour of my sister, and gratified my vanity, in useless or blameable distrust. — How humiliating is this discovery! — Yet, how just a humiliation! — Had I been in love, I could not have been more wretchedly blind. But vanity, not love, has been my folly. — Pleased with the preference of one, and offended by the neglect of the other, on the very beginning of our acquaintance, I have courted prepossession and ignorance, and driven reason away, where either were concerned. Till this moment, I never knew myself."

From herself to Jane — from Jane to Bingley, her thoughts were in a line which soon brought to her recollection that Mr. Darcy's explanation *there* had appeared very insufficient; and she read it again. Widely different was the effect of a second perusal. — How could she deny that credit to his assertions, in one instance, which she had been obliged to give in the other? — He declared himself to have been totally unsuspicious of her sister's attachment;— and she could not help remembering what Charlotte's opinion had always been. — Neither could she deny the justice of his description of Jane. — She felt that Jane's feelings, though fervent, were little displayed, and that there was a constant complacency[1] in her air and manner, not often united with great sensibility.

When she came to that part of the letter, in which her family were mentioned, in terms of such mortifying, yet merited reproach, her sense of shame was severe. The justice of the charge struck her too forcibly for denial, and the circumstances to which he particularly alluded, as having passed at the Netherfield ball, and as confirming all his first disapprobation, could not have made a stronger impression on his mind than on hers.

The compliment to herself and her sister, was not unfelt. It soothed, but it could not console her for the contempt which had been thus self-attracted by the rest of her family;— and as she considered that Jane's disappointment had in fact been the work of her nearest relations, and reflected how materially the credit of both must be hurt by such impropriety of conduct, she felt depressed beyond any thing she had ever known before.

After wandering along the lane for two hours, giving way to

---

1 Another inflection of the word "complacency," which seems here to mean equanimity, or even-temperedness.

every variety of thought; re-considering events, determining probabilities, and reconciling herself as well as she could, to a change so sudden and so important, fatigue, and a recollection of her long absence, made her at length return home; and she entered the house with the wish of appearing cheerful as usual, and the resolution of repressing such reflections as must make her unfit for conversation.

She was immediately told, that the two gentlemen from Rosings had each called during her absence; Mr. Darcy, only for a few minutes to take leave, but that Colonel Fitzwilliam had been sitting with them at least an hour, hoping for her return, and almost resolving to walk after her till she could be found. — Elizabeth could but just *affect* concern in missing him; she really rejoiced at it. Colonel Fitzwilliam was no longer an object. She could think only of her letter.

CHAPTER XIV.

THE two gentlemen left Rosings the next morning; and Mr. Collins having been in waiting near the lodges, to make them his parting obeisance, was able to bring home the pleasing intelligence, of their appearing in very good health, and in as tolerable spirits as could be expected, after the melancholy scene so lately gone through at Rosings. To Rosings he then hastened to console Lady Catherine, and her daughter; and on his return, brought back, with great satisfaction, a message from her Ladyship, importing that she felt herself so dull as to make her very desirous of having them all to dine with her.

Elizabeth could not see Lady Catherine without recollecting, that had she chosen it, she might by this time have been presented to her, as her future niece; nor could she think, without a smile, of what her ladyship's indignation would have been. "What would she have said? — how would she have behaved?" were questions with which she amused herself.

Their first subject was the diminution of the Rosings party. — "I assure you, I feel it exceedingly," said Lady Catherine; "I believe nobody feels the loss of friends so much as I do.

But I am particularly attached to these young men; and know them to be so much attached to me! — They were excessively sorry to go! But so they always are. The dear colonel rallied his spirits tolerably till just at last; but Darcy seemed to feel it most acutely, more I think than last year. His attachment to Rosings, certainly increases."

Mr. Collins had a compliment, and an allusion to throw in here, which were kindly smiled on by the mother and daughter.

Lady Catherine observed, after dinner, that Miss Bennet seemed out of spirits, and immediately accounting for it herself, by supposing that she did not like to go home again so soon, she added,

"But if that is the case, you must write to your mother to beg that you may stay a little longer. Mrs. Collins will be very glad of your company, I am sure."

"I am much obliged to your ladyship for your kind invitation," replied Elizabeth, "but it is not in my power to accept it. — I must be in town next Saturday."

"Why, at that rate, you will have been here only six weeks. I expected you to stay two months. I told Mrs. Collins so before you came. There can be no occasion for your going so soon. Mrs. Bennet could certainly spare you for another fortnight."

"But my father cannot. — He wrote last week to hurry my return."

"Oh! your father of course may spare you, if your mother can. — Daughters are never of so much consequence to a father. And if you will stay another *month* complete, it will be in my power to take one of you as far as London, for I am going there early in June, for a week; and as Dawson does not object to the Barouche box, [1] there will be very good room for one of you — and indeed, if the weather should happen to be cool, I should not object to taking you both, as you are neither of you large."

"You are all kindness, Madam; but I believe we must abide by our original plan."

---

1   A barouche was a four-wheeled, four-seater carriage, pulled by four or six horses: the box is the driver's seat, with room, apparently, for a passenger.

Lady Catherine seemed resigned. —

"Mrs. Collins, you must send a servant with them. You know I always speak my mind, and I cannot bear the idea of two young women travelling post by themselves.[1] It is highly improper. You must contrive to send somebody. I have the greatest dislike in the world to that sort of thing. — Young women should always be properly guarded and attended, according to their situation in life. When my niece Georgiana went to Ramsgate last summer, I made a point of her having two men servants go with her. — Miss Darcy, the daughter of Mr. Darcy, of Pemberley, and Lady Anne, could not have appeared with propriety in a different manner. — I am excessively attentive to all those things. You must send John with the young ladies, Mrs. Collins. I am glad it occurred to me to mention it; for it would really be discreditable to *you* to let them go alone."

"My uncle is to send a servant for us."

"Oh! — Your uncle! — He keeps a man-servant, does he? — I am very glad you have somebody who thinks of those things. Where shall you change horses? — Oh! Bromley, of course. — If you mention my name at the Bell, you will be attended to."

Lady Catherine had many other questions to ask respecting their journey, and as she did not answer them all herself, attention was necessary, which Elizabeth believed to be lucky for her; or, with a mind so occupied, she might have forgotten where she was. Reflection must be reserved for solitary hours; whenever she was alone, she gave way to it as the greatest relief; and not a day went by without a solitary walk, in which she might indulge in all the delight of unpleasant recollections.

Mr. Darcy's letter, she was in a fair way of soon knowing by heart. She studied every sentence: and her feelings towards its writer were at times widely different. When she remembered the style of his address, she was still full of indignation; but when she considered how unjustly she had condemned and upbraided him, her anger was turned against herself; and his disappointed feelings became the object of compassion. His

---

1   That is, on the mail-carriages, which also functioned as a public transport network.

attachment excited gratitude, his general character respect; but she could not approve him; nor could she for a moment repent her refusal, or feel the slightest inclination ever to see him again. In her own past behaviour, there was a constant source of vexation and regret; and in the unhappy defects of her family a subject of yet heavier chagrin. They were hopeless of remedy. Her father, contented with laughing at them, would never exert himself to restrain the wild giddiness of his youngest daughters; and her mother, with manners so far from right herself, was entirely insensible of the evil. Elizabeth had frequently united with Jane in an endeavour to check the imprudence of Catherine and Lydia; but while they were supported by their mother's indulgence, what chance could there be of improvement? Catherine, weak-spirited, irritable, and completely under Lydia's guidance, had been always affronted by their advice; and Lydia, self-willed and careless, would scarcely give them a hearing. They were ignorant, idle, and vain. While there was an officer in Meryton, they would flirt with him; and while Meryton was within a walk of Longbourn, they would be going there for ever.

Anxiety on Jane's behalf, was another prevailing concern, and Mr. Darcy's explanation, by restoring Bingley to all her former good opinion, heightened the sense of what Jane had lost. His affection was proved to have been sincere, and his conduct cleared of all blame, unless any could attach to the implicitness of his confidence in his friend. How grievous then was the thought that, of a situation so desirable in every respect, so replete with advantage, so promising for happiness, Jane had been deprived, by the folly and indecorum of her own family!

When to these recollections was added the developement of Wickham's character, it may be easily believed that the happy spirits which had seldom been depressed before, were now so much affected as to make it almost impossible for her to appear tolerably cheerful.

Their engagements at Rosings were as frequent during the last week of her stay as they had been at first. The very last evening was spent there; and her Ladyship again enquired minutely into the particulars of their journey, gave them directions as to the best method of packing, and was so urgent on the necessity of placing gowns in the only right way, that Maria thought herself obliged, on her return, to undo all the work of the morning, and pack her trunk afresh.

When they parted, Lady Catherine, with great condescension, wished them a good journey, and invited them to come to Hunsford again next year; and Miss De Bourgh exerted herself so far as to curtsey and hold out her hand to both.

CHAPTER XV.

ON Saturday morning Elizabeth and Mr. Collins met for breakfast a few minutes before the others appeared; and he took the opportunity of paying the parting civilities which he deemed indispensably necessary.

"I know not, Miss Elizabeth," said he, "whether Mrs. Collins has yet expressed her sense of your kindness in coming to us, but I am very certain you will not leave the house without receiving her thanks for it. The favour of your company has been much felt, I assure you. We know how little there is to tempt any one to our humble abode. Our plain manner of living, our small rooms, and few domestics, and the little we see of the world, must make Hunsford extremely dull to a young lady like yourself; but I hope you will believe us grateful for the condescension, and that we have done every thing in our power to prevent your spending your time unpleasantly."

Elizabeth was eager with her thanks and assurances of happiness. She had spent six weeks with great enjoyment; and the pleasure of being with Charlotte, and the kind attentions she had received, must make *her* feel the obliged. Mr. Collins was gratified; and with a more smiling solemnity replied,

"It gives me the greatest pleasure to hear that you have passed your time not disagreeably. We have certainly done our best; and most fortunately having it in our power to introduce you to very superior society, and from our connection with Rosings, the frequent means of varying the humble home scene, I think we may flatter ourselves that your Hunsford visit cannot have been entirely irksome. Our situation with regard to Lady Catherine's family is indeed the sort of extraordinary advantage and blessing which few can boast. You see on what a footing we are. You see how continually we are engaged there. In truth I must acknowledge that, with all the disadvantages of this humble parsonage, I should not think any one abiding in it an object of compassion, while they are sharers of our intimacy at Rosings."

Words were insufficient for the elevation of his feelings; and he was obliged to walk about the room, while Elizabeth tried to unite civility and truth in a few short sentences.

"You may, in fact, carry a very favourable report of us into Hertfordshire, my dear cousin. I flatter myself at least that you will be able to do so. Lady Catherine's great attentions to Mrs. Collins you have been a daily witness of; and altogether I trust it does not appear that your friend has drawn an unfortunate — but on this point it will be as well to be silent. Only let me assure you, my dear Miss Elizabeth, that I can from my heart most cordially wish you equal felicity in marriage. My dear Charlotte and I have but one mind and one way of thinking. There is in every thing a most remarkable resemblance of character and ideas between us. We seem to have been designed for each other."

Elizabeth could safely say that it was a great happiness where that was the case, and with equal sincerity could add that she firmly believed and rejoiced in his domestic comforts. She was not sorry, however, to have the recital of them interrupted by the entrance of the lady from whom they sprung. Poor Charlotte! — it was melancholy to leave her to such society! — But she had chosen it with her eyes open; and though evidently regretting that her visitors were to go, she did not seem to ask for compassion. Her home and her housekeeping, her parish and her poultry, and all their dependent concerns, had not yet lost their charms.

At length the chaise arrived, the trunks were fastened on, the parcels placed within, and it was pronounced to be ready. After an affectionate parting between the friends, Elizabeth was attended to the carriage by Mr. Collins, and as they walked down the garden, he was commissioning her with his best respects to all her family, not forgetting his thanks for the kindness he had received at Longbourn in the winter, and his compliments to Mr. and Mrs. Gardiner, though unknown. He then handed her in, Maria followed, and the door was on the point of being closed, when he suddenly reminded them, with some consternation, that they had hitherto forgotten to leave any message for the ladies at Rosings.

"But," he added, "you will of course wish to have your humble respects delivered to them, with your grateful thanks for their kindness to you while you have been here."

Elizabeth made no objection;— the door was then allowed to be shut, and the carriage drove off.

"Good gracious!" cried Maria, after a few minutes silence, "it seems but a day or two since we first came!— and yet how many things have happened!"

"A great many indeed," said her companion with a sigh.

"We have dined nine times at Rosings, besides drinking tea there twice!— How much I shall have to tell!"

Elizabeth privately added, "and how much I shall have to conceal."

Their journey was performed without much conversation, or any alarm; and within four hours of their leaving Hunsford, they reached Mr. Gardiner's house, where they were to remain a few days.

Jane looked well, and Elizabeth had little opportunity of studying her spirits, amidst the various engagements which the kindness of her aunt had reserved for them. But Jane was to go home with her, and at Longbourn there would be leisure enough for observation.

It was not without an effort meanwhile that she could wait even for Longbourn, before she told her sister of Mr. Darcy's proposals. To know that she had the power of revealing what would so exceedingly astonish Jane, and must, at the same time, so highly gratify whatever of her own vanity she had not yet been able to reason away, was such a temptation to openness as nothing could have conquered, but the state of indecision in which she remained, as to the extent of what she should communicate; and her fear, if she once entered on the subject, of being hurried into repeating something of Bingley, which might only grieve her sister farther.

CHAPTER XVI.

It was the second week in May, in which the three young ladies set out together from Gracechurch-street for the town of —— in Hertfordshire; and, as they drew near the appointed inn where Mr. Bennet's carriage was to meet them, they quickly perceived, in token of the coachman's punctuality, both Kitty and Lydia looking out of a dining room up stairs. These two girls had been above an hour in the place, happily employed in visiting an opposite milliner, watching the sentinel on guard, and dressing a sallad and cucumber.

After welcoming their sisters, they triumphantly displayed a table set out with such cold meat as an inn larder usually affords, exclaiming, "Is not this nice? is not this an agreeable surprise?"

"And we mean to treat you all," added Lydia; "but you must lend us the money, for we have just spent ours at the shop out there." Then shewing her purchases: "Look here, I have bought this bonnet. I do not think it is very pretty; but I thought I might as well buy it as not. I shall pull it to pieces as soon as I get home, and see if I can make it up any better."

And when her sisters abused it as ugly, she added, with perfect unconcern, "Oh! but there were two or three much uglier in the shop; and when I have bought some prettier-coloured satin to trim it with fresh, I think it will be very tolerable. Besides, it will not much signify what one wears this summer, after the ——shire have left Meryton, and they are going in a fortnight."

"Are they indeed?" cried Elizabeth, with the greatest satisfaction.

"They are going to be encamped near Brighton; and I do so want papa to take us all there for the summer! It would be such a delicious scheme, and I dare say would hardly cost any thing at all. Mamma would like to go too of all things! Only think what a miserable summer else we shall have!"

"Yes," thought Elizabeth, "*that* would be a delightful scheme, indeed, and completely do for us at once. Good Heaven! Brighton,[1] and a whole campful of soldiers, to us, who have been overset already by one poor regiment of militia, and the monthly balls of Meryton."

"Now I have got some news for you," said Lydia, as they sat down to table. "What do you think? It is excellent news, capital news, and about a certain person that we all like."

Jane and Elizabeth looked at each other, and the waiter was told that he need not stay. Lydia laughed, and said, "Aye, that is just like your formality and discretion. You thought the waiter must not hear, as if he cared! I dare say he often hears worse things said than I am going to say. But he is an ugly fellow! I am glad he is gone. I never saw such a long chin in my life. Well, but now for my news: it is about dear Wickham; too good for the waiter, is not it? There is no danger of Wickham's marrying Mary King. There's for you! She is gone down to her uncle at Liverpool; gone to stay. Wickham is safe."

"And Mary King is safe!" added Elizabeth; "safe from a connection imprudent as to fortune."

"She is a great fool for going away, if she liked him."

"But I hope there is no strong attachment on either side," said Jane.

"I am sure there is not on *his*. I will answer for it he never cared three straws about her. Who *could* about such a nasty little freckled thing?"

Elizabeth was shocked to think that, however incapable of such coarseness of *expression* herself, the coarseness of the *sentiment* was little other than her own breast had formerly harboured and fancied liberal!

As soon as all had ate, and the elder ones paid, the carriage was ordered; and after some contrivance, the whole party, with

---

1   For the grounds of Elizabeth's anxieties about Brighton, see introduction to and section 1 of Appendix F.

all their boxes, workbags, and parcels, and the unwelcome addition of Kitty's and Lydia's purchases, were seated in it.

"How nicely we are crammed in!" cried Lydia. "I am glad I bought my bonnet, if it is only for the fun of having another bandbox! Well, now let us be quite comfortable and snug, and talk and laugh all the way home. And in the first place, let us hear what has happened to you all, since you went away. Have you seen any pleasant men? Have you had any flirting? I was in great hopes that one of you would have got a husband before you came back. Jane will be quite an old maid soon, I declare. She is almost three and twenty! Lord, how ashamed I should be of not being married before three and twenty! My aunt Philips wants you so to get husbands, you can't think. She says Lizzy had better have taken Mr. Collins; but *I* do not think there would have been any fun in it. Lord! how I should like to be married before any of you; and then I would chaperon you about to all the balls. Dear me! we had such a good piece of fun the other day at Colonel Foster's! Kitty and me were to spend the day there, and Mrs. Forster promised to have a little dance in the evening; (by the bye, Mrs. Forster and me are *such* friends!) and so she asked the two Harringtons to come, but Harriet was ill, and so Pen was forced to come by herself; and then, what do you think we did? We dressed up Chamberlayne in woman's clothes, on purpose to pass for a lady,—only think what fun! Not a soul knew of it but Col. and Mrs. Forster, and Kitty and me, except my aunt, for we were forced to borrow one of her gowns; and you cannot imagine how well he looked! When Denny, and Wickham, and Pratt, and two or three more of the men came in, they did not know him in the least. Lord! how I laughed! and so did Mrs. Forster. I thought I should have died. And *that* made the men suspect something, and then they soon found out what was the matter."

With such kind of histories of their parties and good jokes, did Lydia, assisted by Kitty's hints and additions, endeavour to amuse her companions all the way to Longbourn. Elizabeth listened as little as she could, but there was no escaping the frequent mention of Wickham's name.

Their reception at home was most kind. Mrs. Bennet rejoiced to see Jane in undiminished beauty; and more than once during dinner did Mr. Bennet say voluntarily to Elizabeth,

"I am glad you are come back, Lizzy."

Their party in the dining-room was large, for almost all the Lucases came to meet Maria and hear the news: and various were the subjects which occupied them; lady Lucas was enquiring of Maria across the table, after the welfare and poultry of her eldest daughter; Mrs. Bennet was doubly engaged, on one hand collecting an account of the present fashions from Jane, who sat some way below her, and on the other, retailing them all to the younger Miss Lucasses; and Lydia, in a voice rather louder than any other person's, was enumerating the various pleasures of the morning to any body who would hear her.

"Oh! Mary," said she, "I wish you had gone with us, for we had such fun! as we went along Kitty and me drew up all the blinds, and pretended there was nobody in the coach; and I should have gone so all the way, if Kitty had not been sick; and when we got to the George, I do think we behaved very handsomely, for we treated the other three with the nicest cold luncheon in the world, and if you would have gone, we would have treated you too. And then when we came away it was such fun! I thought we never should have got into the coach. I was ready to die of laughter. And then we were so merry all the way home! we talked and laughed so loud, that any body might have heard us ten miles off!"

To this, Mary very gravely replied, "Far be it from me, my dear sister, to depreciate such pleasures. They would doubtless be congenial with the generality of female minds. But I confess they would have no charms for *me*. I should infinitely prefer a book."

But of this answer Lydia heard not a word. She seldom listened to any body for more than half a minute, and never attended to Mary at all.

In the afternoon Lydia was urgent with the rest of the girls to walk to Meryton, and see how every body went on; but Elizabeth steadily opposed the scheme. It should not be said, that the Miss Bennets could not be at home half a day before they were in pursuit of the officers. There was another reason too for her opposition. She dreaded seeing Wickham again, and was resolved to avoid it as long as possible. The comfort to *her*, of the regiment's approaching removal, was indeed beyond expression. In a fortnight they were to go, and once gone, she hoped there could be nothing more to plague her on his account.

She had not been many hours at home, before she found that the Brighton scheme, of which Lydia had given them a hint at the inn, was under frequent discussion between her parents. Elizabeth saw directly that her father had not the smallest intention of yielding; but his answers were at the same time so vague and equivocal, that her mother, though often disheartened, had never yet despaired of succeeding at last.

CHAPTER XVII.

ELIZABETH'S impatience to acquaint Jane with what had happened could no longer be overcome; and at length resolving to suppress every particular in which her sister was concerned, and preparing her to be surprised, she related to her the next morning the chief of the scene between Mr. Darcy and herself.

Miss Bennet's astonishment was soon lessened by the strong sisterly partiality which made any admiration of Elizabeth appear perfectly natural; and all surprise was shortly lost in other feelings. She was sorry that Mr. Darcy should have delivered his sentiments in a manner so little suited to recommend them; but still more was she grieved for the unhappiness which her sister's refusal must have given him.

"His being so sure of succeeding, was wrong," said she; "and certainly ought not to have appeared; but consider how much it must increase his disappointment."

"Indeed," replied Elizabeth, "I am heartily sorry for him; but he has other feelings which will probably soon drive away his regard for me. You do not blame me, however, for refusing him?"

"Blame you! Oh, no."

"But you blame me for having spoken so warmly of Wickham."

"No—I do not know that you were wrong in saying what you did."

"But you *will* know it, when I have told you what happened the very next day."

She then spoke of the letter, repeating the whole of its contents as far as they concerned George Wickham. What a stroke was this for poor Jane! who would willingly have gone through the world without believing that so much wickedness existed in the whole race of mankind, as was here collected in one individual. Nor was Darcy's vindication, though grateful to her feelings, capable of consoling her for such discovery. Most earnestly did she labour to prove the probability of error, and seek to clear one, without involving the other.

"This will not do," said Elizabeth. "You never will be able to make both of them good for any thing. Take your choice, but you must be satisfied with only one. There is but such a quantity of merit between them; just enough to make one good sort of man; and of late it has been shifting about pretty much. For my part, I am inclined to believe it all Mr. Darcy's, but you shall do as you chuse."

It was some time, however, before a smile could be extorted from Jane.

"I do not know when I have been more shocked," said she. "Wickham so very bad! It is almost past belief. And poor Mr. Darcy! dear Lizzy, only consider what he must have suffered. Such a disappointment! and with the knowledge of your ill opinion too! and having to relate such a thing of his sister! It is really too distressing. I am sure you must feel it so."

"Oh! no, my regret and compassion are all done away by seeing you so full of both. I know you will do him such ample justice, that I am growing every moment more unconcerned and indifferent. Your profusion makes me saving; and if you lament over him much longer, my heart will be as light as a feather."

"Poor Wickham; there is such an expression of goodness in his countenance! such an openness and gentleness in his manner."

"There certainly was some great mismanagement in the education of those two young men. One has got all the goodness, and the other all the appearance of it."

"I never thought Mr. Darcy so deficient in the *appearance* of it as you used to do."

"And yet I meant to be uncommonly clever in taking so decided a dislike to him, without any reason. It is such a spur to one's genius, such an opening for wit to have a dislike of that kind. One may be continually abusive without saying any thing just; but one cannot be always laughing at a man without now and then stumbling on something witty."

"Lizzy, when you first read that letter, I am sure you could not treat the matter as you do now."

"Indeed I could not. I was uncomfortable enough. I was very uncomfortable, I may say unhappy. And with no one to speak to, of what I felt, no Jane to comfort me and say that I had not been so very weak and vain and nonsensical as I knew I had! Oh! how I wanted you!"

"How unfortunate that you should have used such very strong expressions in speaking of Wickham to Mr. Darcy, for now they *do* appear wholly undeserved."

"Certainly. But the misfortune of speaking with bitterness, is a most natural consequence of the prejudices I had been encouraging. There is one point, on which I want your advice. I want to be told whether I ought, or ought not to make our acquaintance in general understand Wickham's character."

Miss Bennet paused a little and then replied, "Surely there can be no occasion for exposing him so dreadfully. What is your own opinion?"

"That it ought not to be attempted. Mr. Darcy has not authorised me to make his communication public. On the contrary every particular relative to his sister, was meant to be kept as much as possible to myself; and if I endeavour to undeceive people as to the rest of his conduct, who will believe me?

The general prejudice against Mr. Darcy is so violent, that it would be the death of half the good people in Meryton, to attempt to place him in an amiable light. I am not equal to it. Wickham will soon be gone; and therefore it will not signify to anybody here, what he really is. Sometime hence it will be all found out, and then we may laugh at their stupidity in not knowing it before. At present I will say nothing about it."

"You are quite right. To have his errors made public might ruin him for ever. He is now perhaps sorry for what he has done, and anxious to re-establish a character. We must not make him desperate."

The tumult of Elizabeth's mind was allayed by this conversation. She had got rid of two of the secrets which had weighed on her for a fortnight, and was certain of a willing listener in Jane, whenever she might wish to talk again of either. But there was still something lurking behind, of which prudence forbad the disclosure. She dared not relate the other half of Mr. Darcy's letter, nor explain to her sister how sincerely she had been valued by his friend. Here was knowledge in which no one could partake; and she was sensible that nothing less than a perfect understanding between the parties could justify her in throwing off this last incumbrance of mystery. "And then," said she, "if that very improbable event should ever take place, I shall merely be able to tell what Bingley may tell in a much more agreeable manner himself. The liberty of communication cannot be mine till it has lost all its value!"

She was now, on being settled at home, at leisure to observe the real state of her sister's spirits. Jane was not happy. She still cherished a very tender affection for Bingley. Having never even fancied herself in love before, her regard had all the warmth of first attachment, and from her age and disposition, greater steadiness than first attachments often boast; and so fervently did she value his remembrance, and prefer him to every other man, that all her good sense, and all her attention to the feelings of her friends, were requisite to check the indulgence of those regrets, which must have been injurious to her own health and their tranquillity.

"Well, Lizzy," said Mrs. Bennet one day, "what is your opinion *now* of this sad business of Jane's? For my part, I am determined never to speak of it again to anybody. I told my sister Philips so the other day. But I cannot find out that Jane saw any thing of him in London. Well, he is a very undeserving young man—and I do not suppose there is the least chance in the world of her ever getting him now. There is no talk of his coming to Netherfield again in the summer; and I have enquired of every body too, who is likely to know."

"I do not believe that he will ever live at Netherfield any more."

"Oh, well! it is just as he chooses. Nobody wants him to come. Though I shall always say that he used my daughter extremely ill; and if I was her, I would not have put up with it. Well, my comfort is, I am sure Jane will die of a broken heart, and then he will be sorry for what he has done."

But as Elizabeth could not receive comfort from any such expectation, she made no answer.

"Well, Lizzy," continued her mother soon afterwards, "and so the Collinses live very comfortable, do they? Well, well, I only hope it will last. And what sort of table do they keep? Charlotte is an excellent manager, I dare say. If she is half as sharp as her mother, she is saving enough. There is nothing extravagant in *their* housekeeping, I dare say."

"No, nothing at all."

"A great deal of good management, depend upon it. Yes, yes. *They* will take care not to outrun their income. *They* will never be distressed for money. Well, much good may it do them! And so, I suppose, they often talk of having Longbourn when your father is dead. They look upon it quite as their own, I dare say, whenever that happens."

"It was a subject which they could not mention before me."

"No. It would have been strange if they had. But I make no doubt, they often talk of it between themselves. Well, if they can be easy with an estate that is not lawfully their own, so much the better. *I* should be ashamed of having one that was only entailed on me."

CHAPTER XVIII.

THE first week of their return was soon gone. The second began. It was the last of the regiment's stay in Meryton, and all the young ladies in the neighbourhood were drooping apace. The dejection was almost universal. The elder Miss Bennets alone were still able to eat, drink, and sleep, and pursue the usual course of their employments. Very frequently were they reproached for this insensibility by Kitty and Lydia, whose own misery was extreme, and who could not comprehend such hard-heartedness in any of the family.

"Good Heaven! What is to become of us! What are we to do!" would they often exclaim in the bitterness of woe. "How can you be smiling so, Lizzy?" Their affectionate mother shared all their grief; she remembered what she had herself endured on a similar occasion, five and twenty years ago.

"I am sure," said she, "I cried for two days together when Colonel Millar's regiment went away. I thought I should have broke my heart."

"I am sure I shall break *mine*," said Lydia.

"If one could but go to Brighton!" observed Mrs. Bennet.

"Oh, yes!—if one could but go to Brighton! But papa is so disagreeable."

"A little sea-bathing would set me up for ever."

"And my aunt Philips is sure it would do *me* a great deal of good," added Kitty.

Such were the kind of lamentations resounding perpetually through Longbourn-house. Elizabeth tried to be diverted by them; but all sense of pleasure was lost in shame. She felt anew the justice of Mr. Darcy's objections; and never had she before been so much disposed to pardon his interference in the views of his friend.

But the gloom of Lydia's prospect was shortly cleared away; for she received an invitation from Mrs. Forster, the wife of the Colonel of the regiment, to accompany her to Brighton. This invaluable friend was a very young woman, and very lately married. A resemblance in good humour and good spirits had recommended her and Lydia to each other, and out of their *three* months' acquaintance they had been intimate *two*.

The rapture of Lydia on this occasion, her adoration of Mrs. Forster, the delight of Mrs. Bennet, and the mortification of Kitty, are scarcely to be described. Wholly inattentive to her sister's feelings, Lydia flew about the house in restless ecstacy, calling for every one's congratulations, and laughing and talking with more violence than ever; whilst the luckless Kitty continued in the parlour repining at her fate in terms as unreasonable as her accent was peevish.

"I cannot see why Mrs. Forster should not ask *me* as well as Lydia," said she, "though I am *not* her particular friend. I have just as much right to be asked as she has, and more too, for I am two years older."

In vain did Elizabeth attempt to make her reasonable, and Jane to make her resigned. As for Elizabeth herself, this invitation was so far from exciting in her the same feelings as in her mother and Lydia, that she considered it as the death-warrant of all possibility of common sense for the latter; and detestable as such a step must make her were it known, she could not help secretly advising her father not to let her go. She represented to him all the improprieties of Lydia's general behaviour, the little advantage she could derive from the friendship of such a woman as Mrs. Forster, and the probability of her being yet more imprudent with such a companion at Brighton, where the temptations must be greater than at home. He heard her attentively, and then said,

"Lydia will never be easy till she has exposed herself in some public place or other, and we can never expect her to do it with so little expense or inconvenience to her family as under the present circumstances."

"If you were aware," said Elizabeth, "of the very great disadvantage to us all, which must arise from the public notice of Lydia's unguarded and imprudent manner; nay, which has already arisen from it, I am sure you would judge differently in the affair."

"Already arisen!" repeated Mr. Bennet. "What, has she

frightened away some of your lovers? Poor little Lizzy! But do not be cast down. Such squeamish youths as cannot bear to be connected with a little absurdity, are not worth a regret. Come, let me see the list of the pitiful fellows who have been kept aloof by Lydia's folly."

"Indeed you are mistaken. I have no such injuries to resent. It is not of peculiar, but of general evils, which I am now complaining. Our importance, our respectability in the world, must be affected by the wild volatility, the assurance and disdain of all restraint which mark Lydia's character. Excuse me—for I must speak plainly. If you, my dear father, will not take the trouble of checking her exuberant spirits, and of teaching her that her present pursuits are not to be the business of her life, she will soon be beyond the reach of amendment. Her character will be fixed, and she will, at sixteen, be the most determined flirt that ever made herself and her family ridiculous. A flirt too, in the worst and meanest degree of flirtation; without any attraction beyond youth and a tolerable person; and from the ignorance and emptiness of her mind, wholly unable to ward off any portion of that universal contempt which her rage for admiration will excite. In this danger Kitty is also comprehended. She will follow wherever Lydia leads. Vain, ignorant, idle, and absolutely uncontrouled! Oh! my dear father, can you suppose it possible that they will not be censured and despised wherever they are known, and that their sisters will not be often involved in the disgrace?"

Mr. Bennet saw that her whole heart was in the subject; and affectionately taking her hand, said in reply,

"Do not make yourself uneasy, my love. Wherever you and Jane are known, you must be respected and valued; and you will not appear to less advantage for having a couple of—or I may say, three very silly sisters. We shall have no peace at Longbourn if Lydia does not go to Brighton. Let her go then. Colonel Forster is a sensible man, and will keep her out of any real mischief; and she is luckily too poor to be an object of prey to any body.[1] At Brighton she will be of less importance even as a

---

1   That is, to be lured into marriage by a fortune hunter.

common flirt than she has been here. The officers will find women better worth their notice. Let us hope, therefore, that her being there may teach her her own insignificance. At any rate, she cannot grow many degrees worse, without authorizing us to lock her up for the rest of her life."

With this answer Elizabeth was forced to be content; but her own opinion continued the same, and she left him disappointed and sorry. It was not in her nature, however, to increase her vexations by dwelling on them. She was confident of having performed her duty, and to fret over unavoidable evils, or augment them by anxiety, was no part of her disposition.

Had Lydia and her mother known the substance of her conference with her father, their indignation would hardly have found expression in their united volubility. In Lydia's imagination, a visit to Brighton comprised every possibility of earthly happiness. She saw with the creative eye of fancy, the streets of that gay bathing place covered with officers. She saw herself the object of attention, to tens and to scores of them at present unknown. She saw all the glories of the camp; its tents stretched forth in beauteous uniformity of lines, crowded with the young and the gay, and dazzling with scarlet; and to complete the view, she saw herself seated beneath a tent, tenderly flirting with at least six officers at once.[1]

Had she known that her sister sought to tear her from such prospects and such realities as these, what would have been her sensations? They could have been understood only by her mother, who might have felt nearly the same. Lydia's going to Brighton was all that consoled her for the melancholy conviction of her husband's never intending to go there himself.

But they were entirely ignorant of what had passed; and their raptures continued with little intermission to the very day of Lydia's leaving home.

Elizabeth was now to see Mr. Wickham for the last time. Having been frequently in company with him since her return, agitation was pretty well over; the agitations of former partiality entirely so. She had even learnt to detect, in the very gentle-

---

1   Compare this day-dream, and Mr. Bennet's prediction of Lydia's "exposing" herself, with the Brighton song-lyrics and verse reproduced in Appendix F.1.

ness which had first delighted her, an affectation and a sameness to disgust and weary. In his present behaviour to herself, moreover, she had a fresh source of displeasure, for the inclination he soon testified of renewing those attentions which had marked the early part of their acquaintance, could only serve, after what had since passed, to provoke her. She lost all concern for him in finding herself thus selected as the object of such idle and frivolous gallantry; and while she steadily repressed it, could not but feel the reproof contained in his believing, that however long, and for whatever cause, his attentions had been withdrawn, her vanity would be gratified and her preference secured at any time by their renewal.

On the very last day of the regiment's remaining in Meryton, he dined with others of the officers at Longbourn; and so little was Elizabeth disposed to part from him in good humour, that on his making some enquiry as to the manner in which her time had passed at Hunsford, she mentioned Colonel Fitzwilliam's and Mr. Darcy's having both spent three weeks at Rosings, and asked him if he were acquainted with the former.

He looked surprised, displeased, alarmed; but with a moment's recollection and a returning smile, replied, that he had formerly seen him often; and after observing that he was a very gentlemanlike man, asked her how she had liked him. Her answer was warmly in his favour. With an air of indifference he soon afterwards added, "How long did you say that he was at Rosings?"

"Nearly three weeks."

"And you saw him frequently?"

"Yes, almost every day."

"His manners are very different from his cousin's."

"Yes, very different. But I think Mr. Darcy improves on acquaintance."

"Indeed!" cried Wickham with a look which did not escape her. "And pray may I ask?" but checking himself, he added in a gayer tone, "Is it in address that he improves? Has he deigned to add ought of civility to his ordinary style? for I dare not hope," he continued in a lower and more serious tone, "that he is improved in essentials."

"Oh, no!" said Elizabeth. "In essentials, I believe, he is very much what he ever was."

While she spoke, Wickham looked as if scarcely knowing whether to rejoice over her words, or to distrust their meaning. There was a something in her countenance which made him listen with an apprehensive and anxious attention, while she added,

"When I said that he improved on acquaintance, I did not mean that either his mind or manners were in a state of improvement, but that from knowing him better, his disposition was better understood."

Wickham's alarm now appeared in a heightened complexion and agitated look; for a few minutes he was silent; till, shaking off his embarrassment, he turned to her again, and said in the gentlest of accents,

"You, who so well know my feelings towards Mr. Darcy, will readily comprehend how sincerely I must rejoice that he is wise enough to assume even the *appearance* of what is right. His pride, in that direction, may be of service, if not to himself, to many others, for it must deter him from such foul misconduct as I have suffered by. I only fear that the sort of cautiousness, to which you, I imagine, have been alluding, is merely adopted on his visits to his aunt, of whose good opinion and judgment he stands much in awe. His fear of her, has always operated, I know, when they were together; and a good deal is to be imputed to his wish of forwarding the match with Miss De Bourgh, which I am certain he has very much at heart."

Elizabeth could not repress a smile at this, but she answered only by a slight inclination of the head. She saw that he wanted to engage her on the old subject of his grievances, and she was in no humour to indulge him. The rest of the evening passed with the *appearance*, on his side, of usual cheerfulness, but with no farther attempt to distinguish Elizabeth; and they parted at last with mutual civility, and possibly a mutual desire of never meeting again.

When the party broke up, Lydia returned with Mrs. Forster to Meryton, from whence they were to set out early the next morning. The separation between her and her family was rather noisy than pathetic. Kitty was the only one who shed tears; but she did weep from vexation and envy. Mrs. Bennet was diffuse in her good wishes for the felicity of her daughter, and impressive in her injunctions that she would not miss the opportunity of enjoying herself as much as possible; advice, which there was every reason to believe would be attended to; and in the clamorous happiness of Lydia herself in bidding farewell, the more gentle adieus of her sisters were uttered without being heard.

CHAPTER XIX.

HAD Elizabeth's opinion been all drawn from her own family, she could not have formed a very pleasing picture of conjugal felicity or domestic comfort. Her father captivated by youth and beauty, and that appearance of good humour, which youth and beauty generally give, had married a woman whose weak understanding and illiberal mind, had very early in their marriage put an end to all real affection for her. Respect, esteem, and confidence, had vanished for ever; and all his views of domestic happiness were overthrown. But Mr. Bennet was not of a disposition to seek comfort for the disappointment which his own imprudence had brought on, in any of those pleasures which too often console the unfortunate for their folly or their vice. He was fond of the country and of books; and from these tastes had arisen his principal enjoyments. To his wife he was very little otherwise indebted, than as her ignorance and folly had contributed to his amusement. This is not the sort of happiness which a man would in general wish to owe to his wife; but where other powers of entertainment are wanting, the true philosopher will derive benefit from such as are given.

Elizabeth, however, had never been blind to the impropriety of her father's behaviour as a husband. She had always seen it with pain; but respecting his abilities, and grateful for his affectionate treatment of herself, she endeavoured to forget what she could not overlook, and to banish from her thoughts that continual breach of conjugal obligation and decorum which, in exposing his wife to the contempt of her own children, was so highly reprehensible. But she had never felt so strongly as now, the disadvantages which must attend the children of so unsuitable a marriage, nor ever been so fully aware of the evils arising from so ill-judged a direction of talents; talents which rightly used, might at least have preserved the respectability of his daughters, even if incapable of enlarging the mind of his wife.

When Elizabeth had rejoiced over Wickham's departure, she found little other cause for satisfaction in the loss of the regiment. Their parties abroad were less varied than before; and at home she had a mother and sister whose constant repinings at the dulness of every thing around them, threw a real gloom over their domestic circle; and, though Kitty might in time regain her natural degree of sense, since the disturbers of her brain were removed, her other sister, from whose disposition greater evil might be apprehended, was likely to be hardened in all her folly and assurance, by a situation of such double danger as a watering place and a camp. Upon the whole, therefore, she found, what has been sometimes found before, that an event to which she had looked forward with impatient desire, did not in taking place, bring all the satisfaction she had promised herself. It was consequently necessary to name some other period for the commencement of actual felicity; to have some other point on which her wishes and hopes might be fixed, and by again enjoying the pleasure of anticipation, console herself for the present, and prepare for another disappointment. Her tour to the Lakes was now the object of her happiest thoughts; it was her best consolation for all the uncomfortable hours, which the discontentedness of her mother and Kitty made inevitable; and could she have included Jane in the scheme, every part of it would have been perfect.

"But it is fortunate," thought she, "that I have something to wish for. Were the whole arrangement complete, my disappointment would be certain. But here, by carrying with me one ceaseless source of regret in my sister's absence, I may reasonably hope to have all my expectations of pleasure realized. A scheme of which every part promises delight, can never be successful; and general disappointment is only warded off by the defence of some little peculiar vexation."

When Lydia went away, she promised to write very often and very minutely to her mother and Kitty; but her letters were always long expected, and always very short. Those to her mother, contained little else, than that they were just returned from the library, where such and such officers had attended them, and where she had seen such beautiful ornaments as made her quite wild; that she had a new gown, or a new parasol, which she would have described more fully, but was obliged to leave off in a violent hurry, as Mrs. Forster called her, and they were going to the camp;—and from her correspondence with her sister, there was still less to be learnt—for her letters to Kitty, though rather longer, were much too full of lines under the words to be made public.

After the first fortnight or three weeks of her absence, health, good humour and cheerfulness began to reappear at Longbourn. Everything wore a happier aspect. The families who had been in town for the winter came back again, and summer finery and summer engagements arose. Mrs. Bennet was restored to her usual querulous serenity, and by the middle of June Kitty was so much recovered as to be able to enter Meryton without tears; an event of such happy promise as to make Elizabeth hope, that by the following Christmas, she might be so tolerably reasonable as not to mention an officer above once a day, unless by some cruel and malicious arrangement at the war-office, another regiment should be quartered in Meryton.

The time fixed for the beginning of their Northern tour was now fast approaching; and a fortnight only was wanting of it, when a letter arrived from Mrs. Gardiner, which at once delayed its commencement and curtailed its extent. Mr. Gardiner would be prevented by business from setting out till a fortnight later in July, and must be in London again within a month; and as that left too short a period for them to go so far, and see so much as they had proposed, or at least to see it with the leisure and comfort they had built on, they were obliged to give up the Lakes, and substitute a more contracted tour; and, according to the present plan, were to go no farther northward than Derbyshire. In that county, there was enough to be seen to occupy the chief of their three weeks; and to Mrs. Gardiner it had a peculiarly strong attraction. The town where she had formerly passed some years of her life, and where they were now to spend a few days, was probably as great an object of her curiosity, as all the celebrated beauties of Matlock, Chatsworth, Dovedale, or the Peak.[1]

Elizabeth was excessively disappointed; she had set her heart on seeing the Lakes; and still thought there might have been time enough. But it was her business to be satisfied — and certainly her temper to be happy; and all was soon right again.

With the mention of Derbyshire, there were many ideas connected. It was impossible for her to see the word without thinking of Pemberley and its owner. "But surely," said she, "I may enter his county with impunity, and rob it of a few petrified spars without his perceiving me."[2]

The period of expectation was now doubled. Four weeks were to pass away before her uncle and aunt's arrival. But they did pass away, and Mr. and Mrs. Gardiner, with their four children, did at length appear at Longbourn. The children, two girls of six and eight years old, and two younger boys, were to be left under the particular care of their cousin Jane, who was the general favourite, and whose steady sense and sweetness of temper exactly adapted her for attending to them in every way — teaching them, playing with them, and loving them.

The Gardiners staid only one night at Longbourn, and set off the next morning with Elizabeth in pursuit of novelty and amusement. One enjoyment was certain — that of suitableness as companions; a suitableness which comprehended health and temper to bear inconveniences — cheerfulness to enhance every pleasure — and affection and intelligence, which might

---

1 Matlock, Dovedale and the Peak are areas of scenic beauty, though none of them quite so grand as the Lake District. Chatsworth was the Duke of Devonshire's very grand country house: see appendix E.2.

2 Fluor-spar, a beautiful mineral known as Derbyshire Spar or Blue John Stone, is still mined from caves at Castleton in that county; or Elizabeth may have in mind the petrified objects produced by the hot mineral-springs at Matlock.

supply it among themselves if there were disappointments abroad.

It is not the object of this work to give a description of Derbyshire, nor of any of the remarkable places through which their route thither lay; Oxford, Blenheim, Warwick, Kenelworth, Birmingham, &c. are sufficiently known.[1] A small part of Derbyshire is all the present concern. To the little town of Lambton, the scene of Mrs. Gardiner's former residence, and where she had lately learned that some acquaintance still remained, they bent their steps, after having seen all the principal wonders of the country; and within five miles of Lambton, Elizabeth found from her aunt, that Pemberley was situated. It was not in their direct road, nor more than a mile or two out of it. In talking over their route the evening before, Mrs. Gardiner expressed an inclination to see the place again. Mr. Gardiner declared his willingness, and Elizabeth was applied to for her approbation.

"My love, should not you like to see a place of which you have heard so much?" said her aunt. "A place too, with which so many of your acquaintance are connected. Wickham passed all his youth there, you know."

Elizabeth was distressed. She felt that she had no business at Pemberley, and was obliged to assume a disinclination for seeing it. She must own that she was tired of great houses; after going over so many, she really had no pleasure in fine carpets or satin curtains.

Mrs. Gardiner abused her stupidity. "If it were merely a fine house richly furnished," said she, "I should not care about it myself; but the grounds are delightful. They have some of the finest woods in the country."

Elizabeth said no more — but her mind could not acquiesce. The possibility of meeting Mr. Darcy, while viewing the place, instantly occurred. It would be dreadful! She blushed at the

---

1   Oxford and Warwick are of course ancient towns popular with tourists, but Birmingham was in this period just beginning its rise to industrial greatness. Blenheim Palace, in Oxfordshire, is the seat of the Dukes of Marlborough; Kenilworth, near Warwick, a major fortress in medieval times, was abandoned after the civil war to become, then as now, an imposing ruin.

very idea; and thought it would be better to speak openly to her aunt, than to run such a risk. But against this there were objections; and she finally resolved that it could be the last resource, if her private enquiries as to the absence of the family, were unfavourably answered.

Accordingly, when she retired at night, she asked the chambermaid whether Pemberley were not a very fine place, what was the name of its proprietor, and with no little alarm, whether the family were down for the summer. A most welcome negative followed the last question—and her alarms being now removed, she was at leisure to feel a great deal of curiosity to see the house herself; and when the subject was revived the next morning, and she was again applied to, could readily answer, and with a proper air of indifference, that she had not really any dislike to the scheme.

To Pemberley, therefore, they were to go.

END OF THE SECOND VOLUME

VOLUME III

Pemberly looking after
the community.

homeowner
metonomy:
House stands in for
the owner.

CHAPTER I.

ELIZABETH, as they drove along, watched for the first appearance of Pemberley Woods with some perturbation; and when at length they turned in at the lodge, her spirits were in a high flutter.

The park was very large, and contained great variety of ground. They entered it in one of its lowest points, and drove for some time through a beautiful wood, stretching over a wide extent.

Elizabeth's mind was too full for conversation, but she saw and admired every remarkable spot and point of view. They gradually ascended for half a mile, and then found themselves at the top of a considerable eminence, where the wood ceased, and the eye was instantly caught by Pemberley House, situated on the opposite side of a valley, into which the road with some abruptness wound. It was a large, handsome, stone building, standing well on rising ground, and backed by a ridge of high woody hills;—and in front, a stream of some natural importance was swelled into greater, but without any artificial appearance. Its banks were neither formal, nor falsely adorned. Elizabeth was delighted. She had never seen a place for which nature had done more, or where natural beauty had been so little counteracted by an awkward taste. They were all of them warm in their admiration; and at that moment she felt, that to be mistress of Pemberley might be something!

beautiful improvements

They descended the hill, crossed the bridge, and drove to the door; and, while examining the nearer aspect of the house, all her apprehensions of meeting its owner returned. She dreaded lest the chambermaid had been mistaken. On applying to see the place, they were admitted into the hall; and Elizabeth, as they waited for the housekeeper, had leisure to wonder at her being where she was.

The housekeeper came; a respectable-looking, elderly woman, much less fine, and more civil, than she had any notion of finding her. They followed her into the dining-parlour. It was a large, well-proportioned room, handsomely fitted up.

Elizabeth, after slightly surveying it, went to a window to enjoy its prospect. The hill, crowned with wood, from which they had descended, receiving increased abruptness from the distance, was a beautiful object. Every disposition of the ground was good; and she looked on the whole scene, the river, the trees scattered on its banks, and the winding of the valley, as far as she could trace it, with delight. As they passed into other rooms, these objects were taking different positions; but from every window there were beauties to be seen. The rooms were lofty and handsome, and their furniture suitable to the fortune of their proprietor; but Elizabeth saw, with admiration of his taste, that it was neither gaudy nor uselessly fine; with less of splendor, and more real elegance, than the furniture of Rosings.

"And of this place," thought she, "I might have been mistress! With these rooms I might now have been familiarly acquainted! Instead of viewing them as a stranger, I might have rejoiced in them as my own, and welcomed to them as visitors my uncle and aunt. — But no," — recollecting herself, — "that could never be: my uncle and aunt would have been lost to me: I should not have been allowed to invite them."

This was a lucky recollection — it saved her from something like regret.

She longed to enquire of the housekeeper, whether her master were really absent, but had not courage for it. At length, however, the question was asked by her uncle; and she turned away with alarm, while Mrs. Reynolds replied, that he was, adding, "but we expect him to morrow, with a large party of friends." How rejoiced was Elizabeth that their own journey had not by any circumstance been delayed a day!

Her aunt now called her to look at a picture. She approached, and saw the likeness of Mr. Wickham suspended, amongst several other miniatures, over the mantle-piece. Her aunt asked her, smilingly, how she liked it. The housekeeper came forward, and told them it was the picture of a young gentleman, the son of her late master's steward, who had been brought up by him at his own expence. — "He is now gone into the army," she added, "but I am afraid he has turned out very wild."

Mrs. Gardiner looked at her niece with a smile, but Elizabeth could not return it.

"And that," said Mrs. Reynolds, pointing to another of the miniatures, "is my master—and very like him. It was drawn at the same time as the other—about eight years ago."

"I have heard much of your master's fine person," said Mrs. Gardiner, looking at the picture; "it is a handsome face. But, Lizzy, you can tell us whether it is like or not."

Mrs. Reynolds's respect for Elizabeth seemed to increase on this intimation of her knowing her master.

"Does that young lady know Mr. Darcy?"

Elizabeth coloured, and said—"A little."

"And do not you think him a very handsome gentleman, Ma'am?"

"Yes, very handsome."

"I am sure *I* know none so handsome; but in the gallery up stairs you will see a finer, larger picture of him than this. This room was my late master's favourite room, and these miniatures are just as they used to be then. He was very fond of them."

This accounted to Elizabeth for Mr. Wickham's being among them.

Mrs. Reynolds then directed their attention to one of Miss Darcy, drawn when she was only eight years old.

"And is Miss Darcy as handsome as her brother?" said Mr. Gardiner.

"Oh! yes—the handsomest young lady that ever was seen; and so accomplished!—She plays and sings all day long. In the next room is a new instrument just come down for her—a present from my master; she comes here to-morrow with him."

Mr. Gardiner, whose manners were easy and pleasant, encouraged her communicativeness by his questions and remarks; Mrs. Reynolds, either from pride or attachment, had evidently great pleasure in talking of her master and his sister.

"Is your master much at Pemberley in the course of the year?"

"Not so much as I could wish, Sir; but I dare say he may spend half his time here; and Miss Darcy is always down for the summer months."

wordsworth
"the child is
father to the
man"

"Except," thought Elizabeth, "when she goes to Ramsgate."

"If your master would marry, you might see more of him."

"Yes, Sir; but I do not know when *that* will be. I do not know who is good enough for him."

Mr. and Mrs. Gardiner smiled. Elizabeth could not help saying, "It is very much to his credit, I am sure, that you should think so."

"I say no more than the truth, and what every body will say that knows him," replied the other. Elizabeth thought this was going pretty far; and she listened with increasing astonishment as the housekeeper added, "I have never had a cross word from him in my life, and I have known him ever since he was four years old."

This was praise, of all others most extraordinary, most opposite to her ideas. That he was not a good tempered man, had been her firmest opinion. Her keenest attention was awakened; she longed to hear more, and was grateful to her uncle for saying,

"There are very few people of whom so much can be said. You are lucky in having such a master."

"Yes, Sir, I know I am. If I was to go through the world, I could not meet with a better. But I have always observed, that they who are good-natured when children, are good-natured when they grow up; and he was always the sweetest-tempered, most generous-hearted, boy in the world."

Elizabeth almost stared at her. — "Can this be Mr. Darcy!" thought she.

"His father was an excellent man," said Mrs. Gardiner.

"Yes, Ma'am, that he was indeed; and his son will be just like him — just as affable to the poor."

Elizabeth listened, wondered, doubted, and was impatient for more. Mrs. Reynolds could interest her on no other point. She related the subject of the pictures, the dimensions of the rooms, and the price of the furniture, in vain. Mr. Gardiner, highly amused by the kind of family prejudice, to which he attributed her excessive commendation of her master, soon led again to the subject; and she dwelt with energy on his many merits, as they proceeded together up the great staircase.

"He is the best landlord, and the best master," said she, "that ever lived. Not like the wild young men now-a-days, who think of nothing but themselves. There is not one of his tenants or servants but what will give him a good name. Some people call him proud; but I am sure I never saw any thing of it. To my fancy, it is only because he does not rattle away like other young men."

"In what an amiable light does this place him!" thought Elizabeth.

"This fine account of him," whispered her aunt, as they walked, "is not quite consistent with his behaviour to our poor friend."

"Perhaps we might be deceived."

"That is not very likely; our authority was too good."

On reaching the spacious lobby above, they were shewn into a very pretty sitting-room, lately fitted up with greater elegance and lightness than the apartments below; and were informed that it was but just done, to give pleasure to Miss Darcy, who had taken a liking to the room, when last at Pemberley.

"He is certainly a good brother," said Elizabeth, as she walked towards one of the windows.

Mrs. Reynolds anticipated Miss Darcy's delight, when she should enter the room. "And this is always the way with him," she added. — "Whatever can give his sister any pleasure, is sure to be done in a moment. There is nothing he would not do for her."

The picture-gallery, and two or three of the principal bedrooms, were all that remained to be shewn. In the former were many good paintings; but Elizabeth knew nothing of the art; and from such as had been already visible below, she had willingly turned to look at some drawings of Miss Darcy's, in crayons, whose subjects were usually more interesting, and also more intelligible.

In the gallery there were many family portraits, but they could have little to fix the attention of a stranger. Elizabeth walked on in quest of the only face whose features would be known to her. At last it arrested her — and she beheld a striking resemblance of Mr. Darcy, with such a smile over the face, as she remembered to have sometimes seen, when he looked at her. She stood several minutes before the picture in earnest contemplation, and returned to it again before they quitted the gallery. Mrs. Reynolds informed them, that it had been taken in his father's life time.

There was certainly at this moment, in Elizabeth's mind, a more gentle sensation towards the original, than she had ever felt in the height of their acquaintance. The commendation bestowed on him by Mrs. Reynolds was of no trifling nature. What praise is more valuable than the praise of an intelligent servant? As a brother, a landlord, a master, she considered how many people's happiness were in his guardianship! — How much of pleasure or pain it was in his power to bestow! — How much of good or evil must be done by him! Every idea that had been brought forward by the housekeeper was favourable to his character, and as she stood before the canvas, on which he was represented, and fixed his eyes upon herself, she thought of his regard with a deeper sentiment of gratitude than it had ever raised before; she remembered its warmth, and softened its impropriety of expression.

When all of the house that was open to general inspection had been seen, they returned down stairs, and taking leave of the housekeeper, were consigned over to the gardener, who met them at the hall door.

As they walked across the lawn towards the river, Elizabeth turned back to look again; her uncle and aunt stopped also, and while the former was conjecturing as to the date of the building, the owner of it himself suddenly came forward from the road, which led behind it to the stables.

They were within twenty yards of each other, and so abrupt was his appearance, that it was impossible to avoid his sight. Their eyes instantly met, and the cheeks of each were overspread with the deepest blush. He absolutely started, and for a moment seemed immoveable from surprise; but shortly recovering himself, advanced towards the party, and spoke to Elizabeth, if not in terms of perfect composure, at least of perfect civility.

She had instinctively turned away; but, stopping on his

approach, received his compliments with an embarrassment impossible to be overcome. Had his first appearance, or his resemblance to the picture they had just been examining, been insufficient to assure the other two that they now saw Mr. Darcy, the gardener's expression of surprise, on beholding his master, must immediately have told it. They stood a little aloof while he was talking to their niece, who, astonished and confused, scarcely dared lift her eyes to his face, and knew not what answer she returned to his civil enquiries after her family. Amazed at the alteration in his manner since they last parted, every sentence that he uttered was increasing her embarrassment; and every idea of the impropriety of her being found there, recurring to her mind, the few minutes in which they continued together, were some of the most uncomfortable of her life. Nor did he seem much more at ease; when he spoke, his accent had none of its usual sedateness; and he repeated his enquiries as to the time of her having left Longbourn, and of her stay in Derbyshire, so often, and in so hurried a way, as plainly spoke the distraction of his thoughts.

At length, every idea seemed to fail him; and, after standing a few moments without saying a word, he suddenly recollected himself, and took leave.

The others then joined her, and expressed their admiration of his figure; but Elizabeth heard not a word, and, wholly engrossed by her own feelings, followed them in silence. She was overpowered by shame and vexation. Her coming there was the most unfortunate, the most ill-judged thing in the world! How strange must it appear to him! In what a disgraceful light might it not strike so vain a man! It might seem as if she had purposely thrown herself in his way again! Oh! why did she come? or, why did he thus come a day before he was expected? Had they been only ten minutes sooner, they should have been beyond the reach of his discrimination, for it was plain that he was that moment arrived, that moment alighted from his horse or his carriage. She blushed again and again over the perverseness of the meeting. And his behaviour, so strikingly altered,— what could it mean? That he should even speak to her was amazing!—but to speak with such civility, to enquire after her family! Never in her life had she seen his manners so little dignified, never had he spoken with such gentleness as on this unexpected meeting. What a contrast did it offer to his last address in Rosing's Park, when he put his letter into her hand! She knew not what to think, nor how to account for it.

They had now entered a beautiful walk by the side of the water, and every step was bringing forward a nobler fall of ground, or a finer reach of the woods to which they were approaching; but it was some time before Elizabeth was sensible of any of it; and, though she answered mechanically to the repeated appeals of her uncle and aunt, and seemed to direct her eyes to such objects as they pointed out, she distinguished no part of the scene. Her thoughts were all fixed on that one spot of Pemberley House, whichever it might be, where Mr. Darcy then was. She longed to know what at that moment was passing in his mind; in what manner he thought of her, and whether, in defiance of every thing, she was still dear to him. Perhaps he had been civil, only because he felt himself at ease; yet there had been *that* in his voice, which was not like ease. Whether he had felt more of pain or of pleasure in seeing her, she could not tell, but he certainly had not seen her with composure.

At length, however, the remarks of her companions on her absence of mind roused her, and she felt the necessity of appearing more like herself.

They entered the woods, and bidding adieu to the river for a while, ascended some of the higher grounds; whence, in spots where the opening of the trees gave the eye power to wander, were many charming views of the valley, the opposite hills, with the long range of woods overspreading many, and occasionally part of the stream. Mr. Gardiner expressed a wish of going round the whole Park, but feared it might be beyond a walk. With a triumphant smile, they were told that it was ten miles round. It settled the matter; and they pursued the accustomed circuit; which brought them again, after some time, in a descent among hanging woods, to the edge of the water, in one of its narrowest parts. They crossed it by a simple bridge, in character with the general air of the scene; it was a spot less adorned than any they had yet visited; and the valley, here contracted into a glen, allowed room only for the stream, and a narrow walk amidst the rough coppice-wood which bordered it. Elizabeth longed to explore its windings; but when they had crossed the bridge, and perceived their distance from the house, Mrs. Gardiner, who was not a great walker, could go no farther, and thought only of returning to the carriage as quickly as possible. Her niece was, therefore, obliged to submit, and they took their way towards the house on the opposite side of the river, in the nearest direction; but their progress was slow, for Mr. Gardiner, though seldom able to indulge the taste, was very fond of fishing, and was so much engaged in watching the occasional appearance of some trout in the water, and talking to the man about them, that he advanced but little. Whilst wandering on in this slow manner, they were again surprised, and Elizabeth's astonishment was quite equal to what it had been at first, by the sight of Mr. Darcy approaching them, and at no great distance. The walk being here less sheltered than on the other side, allowed them to see him before they met. Elizabeth, however astonished, was at least more prepared for an interview than before, and resolved to appear and to speak with calmness, if he really intended to meet them. For a few moments, indeed, she felt that he would probably strike into some other path. This idea lasted while a turning in the walk concealed him from their view; the turning past, he was immediately before them. With a glance she saw, that he had lost none of his recent civility; and, to imitate his politeness, she began, as they met, to admire the beauty of the place; but she had not got beyond the words "delightful," and "charming," when some unlucky recollections obtruded, and she fancied that praise of Pemberley from her, might be mischievously construed. Her colour changed, and she said no more.

Mrs. Gardiner was standing a little behind; and on her pausing, he asked her, if she would do him the honour of introducing him to her friends. This was a stroke of civility for which she was quite unprepared; and she could hardly suppress a smile, at his being now seeking the acquaintance of some of those very people, against whom his pride had revolted, in his offer to herself. "What will be his surprise," thought she, "when he knows who they are! He takes them now for people of fashion."

The introduction, however, was immediately made; and as she named their relationship to herself, she stole a sly look at him, to see how he bore it; and was not without the expectation of his decamping as fast as he could from such disgraceful companions. That he was *surprised* by the connexion was evident; he sustained it however with fortitude, and so far from going away, turned back with them, and entered into conversation with Mr. Gardiner. Elizabeth could not but be pleased, could not but triumph. It was consoling, that he should know she had some relations for whom there was no need to blush. She listened most attentively to all that passed between them, and gloried in every expression, every sentence of her uncle, which marked his intelligence, his taste, or his good manners.

The conversation soon turned upon fishing, and she heard Mr. Darcy invite him, with the greatest civility, to fish there as often as he chose, while he continued in the neighbourhood, offering at the same time to supply him with fishing tackle, and pointing out those parts of the stream where there was usually most sport. Mrs. Gardiner, who was walking arm in arm with Elizabeth, gave her a look expressive of her wonder. Elizabeth said nothing, but it gratified her exceedingly; the compliment must be all for herself. Her astonishment, however, was extreme; and continually was she repeating, "Why is he so altered? From what can it proceed? It cannot be for *me*, it cannot be for *my* sake that his manners are thus softened. My reproofs at Hunsford could not work such a change as this. It is impossible that he should still love me."

After walking some time in this way, the two ladies in front, the two gentlemen behind, on resuming their places, after descending to the brink of the river for the better inspection of some curious water-plant, there chanced to be a little alteration. It originated in Mrs. Gardiner, who, fatigued by the exercise of the morning, found Elizabeth's arm inadequate to her support, and consequently preferred her husband's. Mr.

Darcy took her place by her niece, and they walked on together. After a short silence, the lady first spoke. She wished him to know that she had been assured of his absence before she came to the place, and accordingly began by observing, that his arrival had been very unexpected—"for your housekeeper," she added, "informed us that you would certainly not be here till tomorrow; and indeed, before we left Bakewell, we understood that you were not immediately expected in the country." He acknowledged the truth of it all; and said that business with his steward had occasioned his coming forward a few hours before the rest of the party with whom he had been travelling. "They will join me early to-morrow," he continued, "and among them are some who will claim an acquaintance with you,—Mr. Bingley and his sisters."

Elizabeth answered only by a slight bow. Her thoughts were instantly driven back to the time when Mr. Bingley's name had been last mentioned between them; and if she might judge from his complexion, *his* mind was not very differently engaged.

"There is also one other person in the party," he continued after a pause, "who more particularly wishes to be known to you,—Will you allow me, or do I ask too much, to introduce my sister to your acquaintance during your stay at Lambton?"

The surprise of such an application was great indeed; it was too great for her to know in what manner she acceded to it. She immediately felt that whatever desire Miss Darcy might have of being acquainted with her, must be the work of her brother, and without looking farther, it was satisfactory; it was gratifying to know that his resentment had not made him think really ill of her.

They now walked on in silence; each of them deep in thought. Elizabeth was not comfortable; that was impossible; but she was flattered and pleased. His wish of introducing his sister to her, was a compliment of the highest kind. They soon outstripped the others, and when they had reached the carriage, Mr. and Mrs. Gardiner were half a quarter of a mile behind.

He then asked her to walk into the house—but she declared

herself not tired, and they stood together on the lawn. At such a time, much might have been said, and silence was very awkward. She wanted to talk, but there seemed an embargo on every subject. At last she recollected that she had been travelling, and they talked of Matlock and Dove Dale with great perseverance. Yet time and her aunt moved slowly — and her patience and her ideas were nearly worn out before the tete-a-tete was over. On Mr. and Mrs. Gardiner's coming up, they were all pressed to go into the house and take some refreshment; but this was declined, and they parted on each side with the utmost politeness. Mr. Darcy handed the ladies into the carriage, and when it drove off, Elizabeth saw him walking slowly towards the house.

The observations of her uncle and aunt now began; and each of them pronounced him to be infinitely superior to any thing they had expected. "He is perfectly well behaved, polite, and unassuming," said her uncle.

"There *is* something a little stately in him to be sure," replied her aunt, "but it is confined to his air, and is not unbecoming. I can now say with the housekeeper, that though some people may call him proud, *I* have seen nothing of it."

"I was never more surprised than by his behaviour to us. It was more than civil; it was really attentive; and there was no necessity for such attention. His acquaintance with Elizabeth was very trifling."

"To be sure, Lizzy," said her aunt, "he is not so handsome as Wickham; or rather he has not Wickham's countenance, for his features are perfectly good. But how came you to tell us that he was so disagreeable?"

Elizabeth excused herself as well as she could; said that she had liked him better when they met in Kent than before, and that she had never seen him so pleasant as this morning.

"But perhaps he may be a little whimsical in his civilities," replied her uncle. "Your great men often are; and therefore I shall not take him at his word about fishing, as he might change his mind another day, and warn me off his grounds."

Elizabeth felt that they had entirely mistaken his character, but said nothing.

"From what we have seen of him," continued Mrs. Gardiner, "I really should not have thought that he could have behaved in so cruel a way by any body, as he has done by poor Wickham. He has not an ill-natured look. On the contrary, there is something pleasing about his mouth when he speaks. And there is something of dignity in his countenance, that would not give one an unfavourable idea of his heart. But to be sure, the good lady who shewed us the house did give him a most flaming character! I could hardly help laughing aloud sometimes. But he is a liberal master, I suppose, and *that* in the eye of a servant comprehends every virtue."

Elizabeth here felt herself called on to say something in vindication of his behaviour to Wickham; and therefore gave them to understand, in as guarded a manner as she could, that by what she had heard from his relations in Kent, his actions were capable of a very different construction; and that his character was by no means so faulty, nor Wickham's so amiable, as they had been considered in Hertfordshire. In confirmation of this, she related the particulars of all the pecuniary transactions in which they had been connected, without actually naming her authority, but stating it to be such as might be relied on.

Mrs. Gardiner was surprised and concerned; but as they were now approaching the scene of her former pleasures, every idea gave way to the charm of recollection; and she was too much engaged in pointing out to her husband all the interesting spots in its environs, to think of any thing else. Fatigued as she had been by the morning's walk, they had no sooner dined than she set off again in quest of her former acquaintance, and the evening was spent in the satisfactions of an intercourse renewed after many years discontinuance.

The occurrences of the day were too full of interest to leave Elizabeth much attention for any of these new friends; and she could do nothing but think, and think with wonder, of Mr. Darcy's civility, and above all, of his wishing her to be acquainted with his sister.

CHAPTER II.

ELIZABETH had settled it that Mr. Darcy would bring his sister to visit her, the very day after her reaching Pemberley; and was consequently resolved not to be out of sight of the inn the whole of that morning. But her conclusion was false; for on the very morning after their own arrival at Lambton, these visitors came. They had been walking about the place with some of their new friends, and were just returned to the inn to dress themselves for dining with the same family, when the sound of a carriage drew them to a window, and they saw a gentleman and lady in a curricle, driving up the street. Elizabeth immediately recognising the livery,[1] guessed what it meant, and imparted no small degree of surprise to her relations, by acquainting them with the honour which she expected. Her uncle and aunt were all amazement; and the embarrassment of her manner as she spoke, joined to the circumstance itself, and many of the circumstances of the preceding day, opened to them a new idea on the business. Nothing had ever suggested it before, but they now felt that there was no other way of accounting for such attentions from such a quarter, than by supposing a partiality for their niece. While these newly-born notions were passing in their heads, the perturbation of Elizabeth's feelings was every moment increasing. She was quite amazed at her own discomposure; but amongst other causes of disquiet, she dreaded lest the partiality of the brother should have said too much in her favour; and more than commonly anxious to please, she naturally suspected that every power of pleasing would fail her.

She retreated from the window, fearful of being seen; and as she walked up and down the room, endeavouring to compose herself, saw such looks of enquiring surprise in her uncle and aunt, as made every thing worse.

Miss Darcy and her brother appeared, and this formidable introduction took place. With astonishment did Elizabeth see,

---

1 A curricle is a small carriage similar to a gig; its livery is the colour-scheme of its paintwork, upholstery and other fittings, which would denote its owner, as the livery of a servant, a sort of uniform, denoted their master.

that her new acquaintance was at least as much embarrassed as herself. Since her being at Lambton, she had heard that Miss Darcy was exceedingly proud; but the observation of a very few minutes convinced her that she was only exceedingly shy. She found it difficult to obtain even a word from her beyond a monosyllable.

Miss Darcy was tall, and on a larger scale than Elizabeth; and, though little more than sixteen, her figure was formed, and her appearance womanly and graceful. She was less handsome than her brother, but there was sense and good humour in her face, and her manners were perfectly unassuming and gentle. Elizabeth, who had expected to find in her as acute and unembarrassed an observer as ever Mr. Darcy had been, was much relieved by discerning such different feelings.

They had not been long together, before Darcy told her that Bingley was also coming to wait on her; and she had barely time to express her satisfaction, and prepare for such a visitor, when Bingley's quick step was heard on the stairs, and in a moment he entered the room. All Elizabeth's anger against him had been long done away; but, had she still felt any, it could hardly have stood its ground against the unaffected cordiality with which he expressed himself, on seeing her again. He enquired in a friendly, though general way, after her family, and looked and spoke with the same good-humoured ease that he had ever done.

To Mr. and Mrs. Gardiner he was scarcely a less interesting personage than to herself. They had long wished to see him. The whole party before them, indeed, excited a lively attention. The suspicions which had just arisen of Mr. Darcy and their niece, directed their observation towards each with an earnest, though guarded, enquiry; and they soon drew from those enquiries the full conviction that one of them at least knew what it was to love. Of the lady's sensations they remained a little in doubt; but that the gentleman was overflowing with admiration was evident enough.

Elizabeth, on her side, had much to do. She wanted to ascertain the feelings of each of her visitors, she wanted to compose her own, and to make herself agreeable to all; and in the latter object, where she feared most to fail, she was most sure of success, for those to whom she endeavoured to give pleasure were prepossessed in her favour. Bingley was ready, Georgiana was eager, and Darcy determined to be pleased.

In seeing Bingley, her thoughts naturally flew to her sister; and oh! how ardently did she long to know, whether any of his were directed in a like manner. Sometimes she could fancy, that he talked less than on former occasions, and once or twice pleased herself with the notion that as he looked at her, he was trying to trace a resemblance. But, though this might be imaginary, she could not be deceived as to his behaviour to Miss Darcy, who had been set up as a rival of Jane. No look appeared on either side that spoke particular regard. Nothing occurred between them that could justify the hopes of his sister. On this point she was soon satisfied; and two or three little circumstances occurred ere they parted, which, in her anxious interpretation, denoted a recollection of Jane, not untinctured by tenderness, and a wish of saying more that might lead to the mention of her, had he dared. He observed to her, at a moment when the others were talking together, and in a tone which had something of real regret, that it "was a very long time since he had had the pleasure of seeing her;" and, before she could reply, he added, "It is above eight months. We have not met since the 26th of November, when we were all dancing together at Netherfield."

Elizabeth was pleased to find his memory so exact; and he afterwards took occasion to ask her, when unattended to by any of the rest, whether *all* her sisters were at Longbourn. There was not much in the question, nor in the preceding remark, but there was a look and a manner which gave them meaning.

It was not often that she could turn her eyes on Mr. Darcy himself; but, whenever she did catch a glimpse, she saw an expression of general complaisance, and in all that he said, she heard an accent so far removed from hauteur or disdain of his companions, as convinced her that the improvement of manners which she had yesterday witnessed, however temporary its existence might prove, had at least outlived one day. When she saw him thus seeking the acquaintance, and courting the good opinion of people, with whom any intercourse a few months ago would have been a disgrace; when she saw him thus civil, not only to herself, but to the very relations whom he had openly disdained, and recollected their last lively scene in Hunsford Parsonage, the difference, the change was so great, and struck so forcibly on her mind, that she could hardly restrain her astonishment from being visible. Never, even in the company of his dear friends at Netherfield, or his dignified relations at Rosings, had she seen him so desirous to please, so free from self-consequence or unbending reserve as now, when no importance could result from the success of his endeavours, and when even the acquaintance of those to whom his attentions were addressed, would draw down the ridicule and censure of the ladies both of Netherfield and Rosings.

Their visitors staid with them above half an hour, and when they arose to depart, Mr. Darcy called on his sister to join him in expressing their wish of seeing Mr. and Mrs. Gardiner, and Miss Bennet, to dinner at Pemberley, before they left the country. Miss Darcy, though with a diffidence which marked her little in the habit of giving invitations, readily obeyed. Mrs. Gardiner looked at her niece, desirous of knowing how *she*, whom the invitation most concerned, felt disposed as to its acceptance, but Elizabeth had turned away her head. Presuming, however, that this studied avoidance spoke rather a momentary embarrassment, than any dislike of the proposal, and seeing in her husband, who was fond of society, a perfect willingness to accept it, she ventured to engage for her attendance, and the day after the next was fixed on.

Bingley expressed great pleasure in the certainty of seeing Elizabeth again, having still a great deal to say to her, and many enquiries to make after all their Hertfordshire friends. Elizabeth, construing all this into a wish of hearing her speak of her sister, was pleased; and on this account, as well as some others, found herself, when their visitors left them, capable of considering the last half hour with some satisfaction, though while it was passing, the enjoyment of it had been little. Eager to be alone, and fearful of enquiries or hints from her uncle and aunt, she staid with them only long enough to hear their favourable opinion of Bingley, and then hurried away to dress.

But she had no reason to fear Mr. and Mrs. Gardiner's curiosity; it was not their wish to force her communication. It was evident that she was much better acquainted with Mr. Darcy than they had before any idea of; it was evident that he was very much in love with her. They saw much to interest, but nothing to justify enquiry.

Of Mr. Darcy it was now a matter of anxiety to think well; and, as far as their acquaintance reached, there was no fault to find. They could not be untouched by his politeness, and had they drawn his character from their own feelings, and his servant's report, without any reference to any other account, the circle in Hertfordshire to which he was known, would not have recognised it for Mr. Darcy. There was now an interest, however, in believing the housekeeper; and they soon became sensible, that the authority of a servant who had known him since he was four years old, and whose own manners indicated respectability, was not to be hastily rejected. Neither had any thing occurred in the intelligence of their Lambton friends, that could materially lessen its weight. They had nothing to accuse him of but pride; pride he probably had, and if not, it would certainly be imputed by the inhabitants of a small market-town, where the family did not visit. It was acknowledged, however, that he was a liberal man, and did much good among the poor.

With respect to Wickham, the travellers soon found that he was not held there in much estimation; for though the chief of his concerns, with the son of his patron, were imperfectly understood, it was yet a well known fact that, on his quitting Derbyshire, he had left many debts behind him, which Mr. Darcy afterwards discharged.

As for Elizabeth, her thoughts were at Pemberley this evening more than the last; and the evening, though as it passed it seemed long, was not long enough to determine her feelings towards *one* in that mansion; and she lay awake two whole hours, endeavouring to make them out. She certainly did not hate him. No; hatred had vanished long ago, and she had almost as long been ashamed of ever feeling a dislike against him, that could be so called. The respect created by the conviction of his valuable qualities, though at first unwillingly admitted, had for some time ceased to be repugnant to her feelings; and it was now heightened into somewhat of a friendlier nature, by the testimony so highly in his favour, and bringing forward his disposition in so amiable a light, which yesterday had produced. But above all, above respect and esteem, there was a motive within her of good will which could not be overlooked. It was gratitude. — Gratitude, not merely for having once loved her, but for loving her still well enough, to forgive all the petulance and acrimony of her manner in rejecting him, and all the unjust accusations accompanying her rejection. He who, she had been persuaded, would avoid her as his greatest enemy, seemed, on this accidental meeting, most eager to preserve the acquaintance, and without any indelicate display of regard, or any peculiarity of manner, where their two selves only were concerned, was soliciting the good opinion of her friends, and bent on making her known to his sister. Such a change in a man of so much pride, excited not only astonishment but gratitude — for to love, ardent love, it must be attributed; and as such its impression on her was of a sort to be encouraged, as by no means unpleasing, though it could not be exactly defined. She respected, she esteemed, she was grateful to him, she felt a real interest in his welfare; and she only wanted to know how far she wished that welfare to depend upon herself, and how far it would be for the happiness of both that she should employ the power, which her fancy told her she still possessed, of bringing on the renewal of his addresses.

It had been settled in the evening, between the aunt and niece, that such a striking civility as Miss Darcy's, in coming to them on the very day of her arrival at Pemberley, for she had reached it only to a late breakfast, ought to be imitated, though it could not be equalled, by some exertion of politeness on their side; and, consequently, that it would be highly expedient to wait on her at Pemberley the following morning. They were, therefore, to go. — Elizabeth was pleased, though, when she asked herself the reason, she had very little to say in reply.

Mr. Gardiner left them soon after breakfast. The fishing scheme had been renewed the day before, and a positive engagement made of his meeting some of the gentlemen at Pemberley by noon.

CHAPTER III.

CONVINCED as Elizabeth now was that Miss Bingley's dislike of her had originated in jealousy, she could not help feeling how very unwelcome her appearance at Pemberley must be to her, and was curious to know with how much civility on that lady's side, the acquaintance would now be renewed.

On reaching the house, they were shewn through the hall into the saloon, whose northern aspect rendered it delightful for summer. Its windows opening to the ground, admitted a most refreshing view of the high woody hills behind the house, and of the beautiful oaks and Spanish chesnuts which were scattered over the intermediate lawn.

In this room they were received by Miss Darcy, who was sitting there with Mrs. Hurst and Miss Bingley, and the lady with whom she lived in London. Georgiana's reception of them was very civil; but attended with all that embarrassment which, though proceeding from shyness and the fear of doing wrong, would easily give to those who felt themselves inferior, the belief of her being proud and reserved. Mrs. Gardiner and her niece, however, did her justice, and pitied her.

By Mrs. Hurst and Miss Bingley, they were noticed only by a curtsey; and on their being seated, a pause, awkward as such pauses must always be, succeeded for a few moments. It was first broken by Mrs. Annesley, a genteel, agreeable-looking woman, whose endeavour to introduce some kind of discourse, proved her to be more truly well bred than either of the others; and between her and Mrs. Gardiner, with occasional help from Elizabeth, the conversation was carried on. Miss Darcy looked as if she wished for courage enough to join in it; and some-times did venture a short sentence, when there was least danger of its being heard.

Elizabeth soon saw that she was herself closely watched by Miss Bingley, and that she could not speak a word, especially to Miss Darcy, without calling her attention. This observation would not have prevented her from trying to talk to the latter, had they not been seated at an inconvenient distance; but she was not sorry to be spared the necessity of saying much. Her own thoughts were employing her. She expected every moment that some of the gentlemen would enter the room. She wished, she feared that the master of the house might be amongst them; and whether she wished or feared it most, she could scarcely determine. After sitting in this manner a quarter of an hour, without hearing Miss Bingley's voice, Elizabeth was roused by receiving from her a cold enquiry after the health of her family. She answered with equal indifference and brevity, and the other said no more.

The next variation which their visit afforded was produced by the entrance of servants with cold meat, cake, and a variety of all the finest fruits in season; but this did not take place till after many a significant look and smile from Mrs. Annesley to Miss Darcy had been given, to remind her of her post. There was now employment for the whole party; for though they could not all talk, they could all eat; and the beautiful pyramids of grapes, nectarines, and peaches, soon collected them round the table.

While thus engaged, Elizabeth had a fair opportunity of deciding whether she most feared or wished for the appearance of Mr. Darcy, by the feelings which prevailed on his entering the room; and then, though but a moment before she had believed her wishes to predominate, she began to regret that he came.

He had been some time with Mr. Gardiner, who, with two or three other gentlemen from the house, was engaged by the river, and had left him only on learning that the ladies of the family intended a visit to Georgiana that morning. No sooner did he appear, than Elizabeth wisely resolved to be perfectly easy and unembarrassed;—a resolution the more necessary to be made, but perhaps not the more easily kept, because she saw that the suspicions of the whole party were awakened against them, and that there was scarcely an eye which did not watch his behaviour when he first came into the room. In no countenance was attentive curiosity so strongly marked as in Miss Bingley's, in spite of the smiles which overspread her face whenever she spoke to one of its objects; for jealousy had not yet made her desperate, and her attentions to Mr. Darcy were by no means over. Miss Darcy, on her brother's entrance, exerted herself much more to talk; and Elizabeth saw that he was anxious for his sister and herself to get acquainted, and forwarded, as much as possible, every attempt at conversation on either side. Miss Bingley saw all this likewise; and, in the imprudence of anger, took the first opportunity of saying, with sneering civility,

"Pray, Miss Eliza, are not the ——shire militia removed from Meryton? They must be a great loss to *your* family."

In Darcy's presence she dared not mention Wickham's name; but Elizabeth instantly comprehended that he was uppermost in her thoughts; and the various recollections connected with him gave her a moment's distress; but, exerting herself vigorously to repel the ill-natured attack, she presently answered the question in a tolerably disengaged tone. While she spoke, an involuntary glance shewed her Darcy with an heightened complexion, earnestly looking at her, and his sister overcome with confusion, and unable to lift up her eyes. Had Miss Bingley known what pain she was then giving her beloved friend, she undoubtedly would have refrained from the hint; but she had merely intended to discompose Elizabeth, by bringing forward the idea of a man to whom she believed her partial, to make her betray a sensibility which might injure her in Darcy's opinion, and perhaps to remind the latter of all the follies and absurdities, by which some part of her family were connected with that corps. Not a syllable had ever reached her of Miss Darcy's meditated elopement. To no creature had it been revealed, where secrecy was possible, except to Elizabeth; and from all Bingley's connections her brother was particularly anxious to conceal it, from that very wish which Elizabeth had long ago attributed to him, of their becoming hereafter her own. He had certainly formed such a plan, and without meaning that it should affect his endeavour to separate him from Miss Bennet, it is probable that it might add something to his lively concern for the welfare of his friend.

Elizabeth's collected behaviour, however, soon quieted his emotion; and as Miss Bingley, vexed and disappointed, dared not approach nearer to Wickham, Georgiana also recovered in time, though not enough to be able to speak any more. Her brother, whose eye she feared to meet, scarcely recollected her interest in the affair, and the very circumstance which had been designed to turn his thoughts from Elizabeth, seemed to have fixed them on her more, and more cheerfully.

Their visit did not continue long after the question and answer above-mentioned; and while Mr. Darcy was attending them to their carriage, Miss Bingley was venting her feelings in criticisms on Elizabeth's person, behaviour, and dress. But Georgiana would not join her. Her brother's recommendation was enough to ensure her favour: his judgment could not err, and he had spoken in such terms of Elizabeth, as to leave Georgiana without the power of finding her otherwise than lovely and amiable. When Darcy returned to the saloon, Miss Bingley could not help repeating to him some part of what she had been saying to his sister.

"How very ill Eliza Bennet looks this morning, Mr. Darcy," she cried; "I never in my life saw any one so much altered as she is since the winter. She is grown so brown and coarse! Louisa and I were agreeing that we should not have known her again."

However little Mr. Darcy might have liked such an address, he contented himself with coolly replying, that he perceived no other alteration than her being rather tanned,—no miraculous consequence of travelling in the summer.

"For my own part," she rejoined, "I must confess that I never could see any beauty in her. Her face is too thin; her complexion has no brilliancy; and her features are not at all handsome. Her nose wants character; there is nothing marked in its lines.

Her teeth are tolerable, but not out of the common way; and as for her eyes, which have sometimes been called so fine, I never could perceive any thing extraordinary in them. They have a sharp, shrewish look, which I do not like at all; and in her air altogether, there is a self-sufficiency without fashion, which is intolerable."

Persuaded as Miss Bingley was that Darcy admired Elizabeth, this was not the best method of recommending herself; but angry people are not always wise; and in seeing him at last look somewhat nettled, she had all the success she expected. He was resolutely silent however; and, from a determination of making him speak, she continued,

"I remember, when we first knew her in Hertfordshire, how amazed we all were to find that she was a reputed beauty; and I particularly recollect your saying one night, after they had been dining at Netherfield, '*She* a beauty!—I should as soon call her mother a wit.' But afterwards she seemed to improve on you, and I believe you thought her rather pretty at one time."

"Yes," replied Darcy, who could contain himself no longer, "but *that* was only when I first knew her, for it is many months since I have considered her as one of the handsomest women of my acquaintance."

He then went away, and Miss Bingley was left to all the satisfaction of having forced him to say what gave no one any pain but herself.

Mrs. Gardiner and Elizabeth talked of all that had occurred, during their visit, as they returned except what had particularly interested them both. The looks and behaviour of every body they had seen were discussed, except of the person who had mostly engaged their attention. They talked of his sister, his friends, his house, his fruit, of every thing but himself; yet Elizabeth was longing to know what Mrs. Gardiner thought of him, and Mrs. Gardiner would have been highly gratified by her niece's beginning the subject.

CHAPTER IV.

ELIZABETH had been a good deal disappointed in not finding a letter from Jane, on their first arrival at Lambton; and this disappointment had been renewed on each of the mornings that had now been spent there; but on the third, her repining was over, and her sister justified by the receipt of two letters from her at once, on one of which was marked that it had been mis-sent elsewhere. Elizabeth was not surprised at it, as Jane had written the direction remarkably ill.

They had just been preparing to walk as the letters came in; and her uncle and aunt, leaving her to enjoy them in quiet, set off by themselves. The one missent must be first attended to; it had been written five days ago. The beginning contained an account of all their little parties and engagements, with such news as the country afforded; but the latter half, which was dated a day later, and written in evident agitation, gave more important intelligence. It was to this effect:

"Since writing the above, dearest Lizzy, something has occurred of a most unexpected and serious nature; but I am afraid of alarming you — be assured that we are all well. What I have to say relates to poor Lydia. An express came at twelve last night, just as we were all gone to bed, from Colonel Forster, to inform us that she was gone off to Scotland with one of his officers;[1] to own the truth, with Wickham! — Imagine our surprise. To Kitty, however, it does not seem so wholly unexpected. I am very, very sorry. So imprudent a match on both sides! — But I am willing to hope the best, and that his character has been misunderstood. Thoughtless and indiscreet I can easily believe him, but this step (and let us rejoice over it) marks nothing bad at heart. His choice is disinterested at least, for he must know my father can give her nothing. Our poor mother is sadly grieved. My father bears it better. How thankful am I, that we never let them know what has been said against him;

---

1   This implies that they intend to marry there, probably at Gretna Green, as Lydia, a minor, could not marry in England and Wales without her father's consent: see introduction to Appendix A.

we must forget it ourselves. They were off Saturday night about twelve, as is conjectured, but were not missed till yesterday morning at eight. The express was sent off directly. My dear Lizzy, they must have passed within ten miles of us. Colonel Forster gives us reason to expect him here soon. Lydia left a few lines for his wife, informing her of their intention. I must conclude, for I cannot be long from my poor mother. I am afraid you will not be able to make it out, but I hardly know what I have written."

Without allowing herself time for consideration, and scarcely knowing what she felt, Elizabeth on finishing this letter, instantly seized the other, and opening it with the utmost impatience, read as follows: it had been written a day later than the conclusion of the first.

"By this time, my dearest sister, you have received my hurried letter; I wish this may be more intelligible, but though not confined for time, my head is so bewildered that I cannot answer for being coherent. Dearest Lizzy, I hardly know what I would write, but I have bad news for you, and it cannot be delayed. Imprudent as a marriage between Mr. Wickham and our poor Lydia would be, we are now anxious to be assured it has taken place, for there is but too much reason to fear they are not gone to Scotland. Colonel Forster came yesterday, having left Brighton the day before, not many hours after the express. Though Lydia's short letter to Mrs. F. gave them to understand that they were going to Gretna Green, something was dropped by Denny expressing his belief that W. never intended to go there, or to marry Lydia at all, which was repeated to Colonel F. who instantly taking the alarm, set off from B. intending to trace their route. He did trace them easily to Clapham, but no farther; for on entering that place they removed into a hackney-coach and dismissed the chaise that brought them from Epsom. All that is known after this is, that they were seen to continue the London road. I know not what to think. After making every possible enquiry on that side London, Colonel F. came on into Hertfordshire, anxiously renewing them at all the turnpikes, and at the inns in Barnet and Hatfield, but without any success, no such people had been seen to pass through.[1] With the kindest concern he came on to Longbourn, and broke his apprehensions to us in a manner most creditable to his heart. I am sincerely grieved for him and Mrs. F. but no one can throw any blame on them. Our distress, my dear Lizzy, is very great. My father and mother believe the worst, but I cannot think so ill of him. Many circumstances might make it more eligible for them to be married privately in town than to pursue their first plan; and even if *he* could form such a design against a young woman of Lydia's connections, which is not likely, can I suppose her so lost to every thing? — Impossible. I grieve to find, however, that Colonel F. is not disposed to depend upon their marriage; he shook his head when I expressed my hopes, and said he feared W. was not a man to be trusted. My poor mother is really ill and keeps her room. Could she exert herself it would be better, but this is not to be expected; and as to my father, I never in my life saw him so affected. Poor Kitty has anger for having concealed their attachment; but as it was a matter of confidence one cannot wonder. I am truly glad, dearest Lizzy, that you have been spared something of these distressing scenes; but now as the first shock is over, shall I own that I long for your return? I am not so selfish, however, as to press for it, if inconvenient. Adieu. I take up my pen again to do, what I have just told you I would not, but circumstances are such, that I cannot help earnestly begging you all to come here, as soon as possible. I know my dear uncle and aunt so well, that I am not afraid of requesting it, though I have still something more to ask of the former. My father is going to London with Colonel Forster instantly, to try to discover her. What he means to do, I am sure I know not;

---

1   The "turnpikes" referred to are the toll-gates and toll-houses where travellers made a contribution to an independent Turnpike Trust for the maintenance of the road: such arrangements facilitated the considerable improvements in the road network by the end of the eighteenth century, improvements that make possible the characters' mobility that is so central to this novel. Now a district of London, Clapham was then a village to its south, and Epsom a town further south again, on the way from Brighton. Barnet and Hatfield lie on the main road from the capital towards Scotland, Barnet just before it crosses into Hertfordshire, Hatfield further north.

but his excessive distress will not allow him to pursue any measure in the best and safest way, and Colonel Forster is obliged to be at Brighton again to-morrow evening. In such an exigence my uncle's advice and assistance would be every thing in the world; he will immediately comprehend what I must feel, and I rely upon his goodness."

"Oh! where, where is my uncle?" cried Elizabeth, darting from her seat as she finished the letter, in eagerness to follow him, without losing a moment of the time so precious; but as she reached the door, it was opened by a servant, and Mr. Darcy appeared. Her pale face and impetuous manner made him start, and before he could recover himself enough to speak, she, in whose mind every idea was superseded by Lydia's situation, hastily exclaimed, "I beg your pardon, but I must leave you. I must find Mr. Gardiner this moment, on business that cannot be delayed; I have not a moment to lose."

"Good God! what is the matter?" cried he, with more feeling than politeness; then recollecting himself, "I will not detain you a minute, but let me, or let the servant, go after Mr. and Mrs. Gardiner. You are not well enough;— you cannot go yourself."

Elizabeth hesitated, but her knees trembled under her, and she felt how little would be gained by her attempting to pursue them. Calling back the servant, therefore, she commissioned him, though in so breathless an accent as made her almost unintelligible, to fetch his master and mistress home, instantly.

On his quitting the room, she sat down, unable to support herself, and looking so miserably ill, that it was impossible for Darcy to leave her, or to refrain from saying, in a tone of gentleness and commiseration, "Let me call your maid. Is there nothing you could take, to give you present relief? — A glass of wine;— shall I get you one? — You are very ill."

"No, I thank you;" she replied, endeavouring to recover herself. "There is nothing the matter with me. I am quite well. I am only distressed by some dreadful news which I have just received from Longbourn."

She burst into tears as she alluded to it, and for a few minutes could not speak another word. Darcy, in wretched suspense, could only say something indistinctly of his concern, and observe her in compassionate silence. At length, she spoke again. "I have just had a letter from Jane, with such dreadful news. It cannot be concealed from any one. My youngest sister has left all her friends—has eloped;—has thrown herself into the power of—of Mr. Wickham. They are gone off together from Brighton. *You* know him too well to doubt the rest. She has no money, no connections, nothing that can tempt him to—she is lost for ever."

Darcy was fixed in astonishment. "When I consider," she added, in a yet more agitated voice, "that *I* might have prevented it!—*I* who knew what he was. Had I but explained some part of it only—some part of what I learnt—to my own family! Had his character been known, this could not have happened. But it is all, all too late now."

"I am grieved, indeed," cried Darcy; "grieved—shocked. But is it certain, absolutely certain?"

"Oh yes!—They left Brighton together on Sunday night, and were traced almost to London, but not beyond; they are certainly not gone to Scotland."

"And what has been done, what has been attempted, to recover her?"

"My father is gone to London, and Jane has written to beg my uncle's immediate assistance, and we shall be off, I hope, in half an hour. But nothing can be done; I know very well that nothing can be done. How is such a man to be worked on? How are they even to be discovered? I have not the smallest hope. It is every way horrible!"

Darcy shook his head in silent acquiescence.

"When *my* eyes were opened to his real character.—Oh! had I known what I ought, what I dared, to do! But I knew not—I was afraid of doing too much. Wretched, wretched, mistake!"

Darcy made no answer. He seemed scarcely to hear her, and was walking up and down the room in earnest meditation; his brow contracted, his air gloomy. Elizabeth soon observed, and instantly understood it. Her power was sinking; every thing *must* sink under such a proof of family weakness, such an assurance of the deepest disgrace. She could neither wonder nor condemn, but the belief of his self-conquest brought nothing consolatory to her bosom, afforded no palliation of her distress. It was, on the contrary, exactly calculated to make her understand her own wishes; and never had she so honestly felt that she could have loved him, as now, when all love must be vain.

But self, though it would intrude, could not engross her. Lydia — the humiliation, the misery, she was bringing on them all, soon swallowed up every private care; and covering her face with her handkerchief, Elizabeth was soon lost to every thing else; and, after a pause of several minutes, was only recalled to a sense of her situation by the voice of her companion, who, in a manner, which though it spoke compassion, spoke likewise restraint, said, "I am afraid you have been long desiring my absence, nor have I any thing to plead in excuse of my stay, but real, though unavailing, concern. Would to heaven that any thing could be either said or done on my part, that might offer consolation to such distress. — But I will not torment you with vain wishes, which may seem purposely to ask for your thanks. This unfortunate affair will, I fear, prevent my sister's having the pleasure of seeing you at Pemberley to-day."

"Oh, yes. Be so kind as to apologize for us to Miss Darcy. Say that urgent business calls us home immediately. Conceal the unhappy truth as long as it is possible. — I know it cannot be long."

He readily assured her of his secrecy — again expressed his sorrow for her distress, wished it a happier conclusion than there was at present reason to hope, and leaving his compliments for her relations, with only one serious, parting, look, went away.

As he quitted the room, Elizabeth felt how improbable it was that they should ever see each other again on such terms of cordiality as had marked their several meetings in Derbyshire; and as she threw a retrospective glance over the whole of their acquaintance, so full of contradictions and varieties, sighed at the perverseness of those feelings which would now have promoted its continuance, and would formerly have rejoiced in its termination.

If gratitude and esteem are good foundations of affection,

Elizabeth's change of sentiment will be neither improbable nor faulty. But if otherwise, if the regard springing from such sources is unreasonable or unnatural, in comparison of what is so often described as arising on a first interview with its object, and even before two words have been exchanged, nothing can be said in her defence, except that she had given somewhat of a trial to the latter method, in her partiality for Wickham, and that its ill-success might perhaps authorise her to seek the other less interesting mode of attachment. Be that as it may, she saw him go with regret; and in this early example of what Lydia's infamy must produce, found additional anguish as she reflected on that wretched business. Never, since reading Jane's second letter, had she entertained a hope of Wickham's meaning to marry her. No one but Jane, she thought, could flatter herself with such an expectation. Surprise was the least of her feelings on this developement. While the contents of the first letter remained on her mind, she was all surprise—all astonishment that Wickham should marry a girl, whom it was impossible he could marry for money; and how Lydia could ever have attached him, had appeared incomprehensible. But now it was all too natural. For such an attachment as this, she might have sufficient charms; and though she did not suppose Lydia to be deliberately engaging in an elopement, without the intention of marriage, she had no difficulty in believing that neither her virtue nor her understanding would preserve her from falling an easy prey.

She had never perceived, while the regiment was in Hertfordshire, that Lydia had any partiality for him, but she was convinced that Lydia had wanted only encouragement to attach herself to any body. Sometimes one officer, sometimes another had been her favourite, as their attentions raised them in her opinion. Her affections had been continually fluctuating, but never without an object. The mischief of neglect and mistaken indulgence towards such a girl. —Oh! how acutely did she now feel it.

She was wild to be at home—to hear, to see, to be upon the spot, to share with Jane in the cares that must now fall wholly upon her, in a family so deranged; a father absent, a mother incapable of exertion, and requiring constant attendance; and though almost persuaded that nothing could be done for Lydia, her uncle's interference seemed of the utmost importance, and till he entered the room, the misery of her impatience was severe. Mr. and Mrs. Gardiner had hurried back in alarm, supposing, by the servant's account, that their niece was taken suddenly ill;—but satisfying them instantly on that head, she eagerly communicated the cause of their summons, reading the two letters aloud, and dwelling on the postscript of the last, with trembling energy. — Though Lydia had never been a favourite with them, Mr. and Mrs. Gardiner could not but be deeply affected. Not Lydia only, but all were concerned in it; and after the first exclamations of surprise and horror, Mr. Gardiner readily promised every assistance in his power. — Elizabeth, though expecting no less, thanked him with tears of gratitude; and all three being actuated by one spirit, every thing relating to their journey was speedily settled. They were to be off as soon as possible. "But what is to be done about Pemberley?" cried Mrs. Gardiner. "John told us Mr. Darcy was here when you sent for us;— was it so?"

"Yes; and I told him we should not be able to keep our engagement. *That* is all settled."

"That is all settled;" repeated the other, as she ran into her room to prepare. "And are they upon such terms as for her to disclose the real truth! Oh, that I knew how it was!"

But wishes were vain; or at best could serve only to amuse her in the hurry and confusion of the following hour. Had Elizabeth been at leisure to be idle, she would have remained certain that all employment was impossible to one so wretched as herself; but she had her share of business as well as her aunt, and amongst the rest there were notes to be written to all their friends in Lambton, with false excuses for their sudden departure. An hour, however, saw the whole completed; and Mr. Gardiner meanwhile having settled his account at the inn, nothing remained to be done but to go; and Elizabeth, after all the misery of the morning, found herself, in a shorter space of time than she could have supposed, seated in the carriage, and on the road to Longbourn.

CHAPTER V.

"I HAVE been thinking it over again, Elizabeth," said her uncle as they drove from the town; "and really, upon serious consideration, I am much more inclined than I was to judge as your eldest sister does of the matter. It appears to me so very unlikely, that any young man should form such a design against a girl who is by no means unprotected or friendless, and who was actually staying in his colonel's family, that I am strongly inclined to hope the best. Could he expect that her friends would not step forward? Could he expect to be noticed again by the regiment, after such an affront to Colonel Forster? His temptation is not adequate to the risk."

"Do you really think so?" cried Elizabeth, brightening up for a moment.

"Upon my word," said Mrs. Gardiner, "I begin to be of your uncle's opinion. It is really too great a violation of decency, honour, and interest, for him to be guilty of it. I cannot think so very ill of Wickham. Can you, yourself, Lizzy, so wholly give him up as to believe him capable of it?"

"Not perhaps of neglecting his own interest. But of every other neglect I can believe him capable. If, indeed, it should be so! But I dare not hope it. Why should they not go on to Scotland, if that had been the case?"

"In the first place," replied Mr. Gardiner, "there is no absolute proof that they are not gone to Scotland."

"Oh! but their removing from the chaise into an hackney coach is such a presumption![1] And, besides, no traces of them were to be found on the Barnet road."

"Well, then—supposing them to be in London. They may be there, though for the purpose of concealment, for no more exceptionable purpose. It is not likely that money should be very abundant on either side; and it might strike them that they could be more economically, though less expeditiously, married in London, than in Scotland."

---

1   A hackney coach is the equivalent of a modern taxi, an urban form of public transport, and this move thus suggests that the couple did not intend to proceed beyond London.

"But why all this secrecy? Why any fear of detection? Why must their marriage be private? Oh! no, no, this is not likely. His most particular friend, you see by Jane's account, was persuaded of his never intending to marry her. Wickham will never marry a woman without some money. He cannot afford it. And what claims has Lydia, what attractions has she beyond youth, health, and good humour, that could make him for her sake, forgo every chance of benefiting himself by marrying well. As to what restraint the apprehension of disgrace in the corps might throw on a dishonourable elopement with her, I am not able to judge; for I know nothing of the effects that such a step might produce. But as to your other objection, I am afraid it will hardly hold good. Lydia has no brothers to step forward; and he might imagine, from my father's behaviour, from his indolence and the little attention he has ever seemed to give to what was going forward in his family, that *he* would do as little, and think as little about it, as any father could do in such a matter."

"But can you think that Lydia is so lost to every thing but love of him, as to consent to live with him on any other terms than marriage?"

"It does seem, and it is most shocking indeed," replied Elizabeth, with tears in her eyes, "that a sister's sense of decency and virtue in such a point should admit of doubt. But, really, I know not what to say. Perhaps I am not doing her justice. But she is very young; she has never been taught to think on serious subjects; and for the last half year, nay, for a twelvemonth, she has been given up to nothing but amusement and vanity. She has been allowed to dispose of her time in the most idle and frivolous manner, and to adopt any opinions that came in her way. Since the ——shire were first quartered in Meryton, nothing but love, flirtation, and officers, have been in her head. She has been doing every thing in her power, by thinking and talking on the subject, to give greater — what shall I call it? susceptibility to her feelings; which are naturally lively enough. And we all know that Wickham has every charm of person and address that can captivate a woman."

"But you see that Jane," said her aunt, "does not think so ill of Wickham, as to believe him capable of the attempt."

"Of whom does Jane ever think ill? And who is there, whatever might be their former conduct, that she would believe capable of such an attempt, till it were proved against them? But Jane knows, as well as I do, what Wickham really is. We both know that he has been profligate in every sense of the word. That he has neither integrity nor honour. That he is as false and deceitful, as he is insinuating."

"And do you really know all this?" cried Mrs. Gardiner, whose curiosity as to the mode of her intelligence was all alive.

"I do, indeed," replied Elizabeth, colouring. "I told you the other day, of his infamous behaviour to Mr. Darcy; and you, yourself, when last at Longbourn, heard in what manner he spoke of the man, who had behaved with such forbearance and liberality towards him. And there are other circumstances which I am not at liberty —— which it is not worth while to relate; but his lies about the whole Pemberley family are endless. From what he said of Miss Darcy, I was thoroughly prepared to see a proud, reserved, disagreeable girl. Yet he knew to the contrary himself. He must know that she was as amiable and unpretending as we have found her."

"But does Lydia know nothing of this? Can she be ignorant of what you and Jane seem so well to understand?"

"Oh, yes! — that, that is the worst of all. Till I was in Kent, and saw so much both of Mr. Darcy and his relation, Colonel Fitzwilliam, I was ignorant of the truth myself. And when I returned home, the ——shire was to leave Meryton in a week or fortnight's time. As that was the case, neither Jane, to whom I related the whole, nor I, thought it necessary to make our knowledge public; for of what use could it apparently be to any one, that the good opinion which all the neighbourhood had of him, should then be overthrown? And even when it was settled that Lydia should go with Mrs. Forster, the necessity of opening her eyes to his character never occurred to me. That *she* could be in any danger from the deception never entered my head. That such a consequence as *this* should ensue, you may easily believe was far enough from my thoughts."

"When they all removed to Brighton, therefore, you had no reason, I suppose, to believe them fond of each other."

"Not the slightest. I can remember no symptom of affection on either side; and had any thing of the kind been perceptible, you must be aware that ours is not a family, on which it could be thrown away. When first he entered the corps, she was ready enough to admire him; but so we all were. Every girl in, or near Meryton, was out of her senses about him for the first two months; but he never distinguished *her* by any particular attention, and, consequently, after a moderate period of extravagant and wild admiration, her fancy for him gave way, and others of the regiment, who treated her with more distinction, again became her favourites."

———————

It may be easily believed, that however little of novelty could be added to their fears, hopes, and conjectures, on this interesting subject, by its repeated discussion, no other could detain them from it long, during the whole of the journey. From Elizabeth's thoughts it was never absent. Fixed there by the keenest of all anguish, self reproach, she could find no interval of ease or forgetfulness.

They travelled as expeditiously as possible; and sleeping one night on the road, reached Longbourn by dinner-time the next day. It was a comfort to Elizabeth to consider that Jane could not have been wearied by long expectations.

The little Gardiners, attracted by the sight of a chaise, were standing on the steps of the house, as they entered the paddock; and when the carriage drove up to the door, the joyful surprise that lighted up their faces, and displayed itself over their whole bodies, in a variety of capers and frisks, was the first pleasing earnest of their welcome.

Elizabeth jumped out; and, after giving each of them an hasty kiss, hurried into the vestibule, where Jane, who came running down stairs from her mother's apartment, immediately met her.

Elizabeth, as she affectionately embraced her, whilst tears filled the eyes of both, lost not a moment in asking whether any thing had been heard of the fugitives.

"Not yet," replied Jane. "But now that my dear uncle is come, I hope every thing will be well."

"Is my father in town?"

"Yes, he went on Tuesday, as I wrote you word."

"And have you heard from him often?"

"We have heard only once. He wrote me a few lines on Wednesday, to say that he had arrived in safety, and to give me his directions, which I particularly begged him to do. He merely added, that he should not write again, till he had something of importance to mention."

"And my mother—How is she? How are you all?"

"My mother is tolerably well, I trust; though her spirits are greatly shaken. She is up stairs, and will have great satisfaction in seeing you all. She does not yet leave her dressing-room. Mary and Kitty, thank Heaven! are quite well."

"But you—How are you?" cried Elizabeth. "You look pale. How much you must have gone through!"

Her sister, however, assured her, of her being perfectly well; and their conversation, which had been passing while Mr. and Mrs. Gardiner were engaged with their children, was now put an end to, by the approach of the whole party. Jane ran to her uncle and aunt, and welcomed and thanked them both, with alternate smiles and tears.

When they were all in the drawing room, the questions which Elizabeth had already asked, were of course repeated by the others, and they soon found that Jane had no intelligence to give. The sanguine hope of good, however, which the benevolence of her heart suggested, had not yet deserted her; she still expected that it would all end well, and that every morning would bring some letter, either from Lydia or her father, to explain their proceedings, and perhaps announce the marriage.

Mrs. Bennet, to whose apartment they all repaired, after a few minutes conversation together, received them exactly as might be expected; with tears and lamentations of regret, invectives against the villainous conduct of Wickham, and complaints of her own sufferings and ill usage; blaming every body but the person to whose ill judging indulgence the errors of her daughter must be principally owing.

"If I had been able," said she, "to carry my point of going to Brighton, with all my family *this* would not have happened; but poor dear Lydia had nobody to take care of her. Why did the Forsters ever let her go out of their sight? I am sure there was some great neglect or other on their side, for she is not the kind of girl to do such a thing, if she had been well looked after. I always thought they were very unfit to have the charge of her; but I was over-ruled, as I always am. Poor dear child! And now here's Mr. Bennet gone away, and I know he will fight Wickham, wherever he meets him, and then he will be killed, and what is to become of us all? The Collinses will turn us out, before he is cold in his grave; and if you are not kind to us, brother, I do not know what we shall do."

They all exclaimed against such terrific ideas;[1] and Mr. Gardiner, after general assurances of his affection for her and all her family, told her that he meant to be in London the very next day, and would assist Mr. Bennet in every endeavour for recovering Lydia.

"Do not give way to useless alarm," added he, "though it is right to be prepared for the worst, there is no occasion to look on it as certain. It is not quite a week since they left Brighton. In a few days more, we may gain some news of them, and till we know that they are not married, and have no design of marrying, do not let us give the matter over as lost. As soon as I get to town, I shall go to my brother, and make him come home with me to Gracechurch Street, and then we may consult together as to what is to be done."

---

1   The "terrific" (that is, terrifying) notion that her husband might challenge Wickham to a duel reveals only Mrs. Bennet's slender grasp on reality: the sort of honour that could be recovered by violence was a strictly aristocratic one, and duelling in any case was both disreputable and illegal.

"Oh! my dear brother," replied Mrs. Bennet, "that is exactly what I could most wish for. And now do, when you get to town, find them out, wherever they may be; and if they are not married already, *make* them marry. And as for wedding clothes, do not let them wait for that, but tell Lydia she shall have as much money as she chuses, to buy them, after they are married. And, above all things, keep Mr. Bennet from fighting. Tell him what a dreadful state I am in,—that I am frightened out of my wits; and have such tremblings, such flutterings, all over me, such spasms in my side, and pains in my head, and such beatings at heart, that I can get no rest by night nor by day. And tell my dear Lydia, not to give any directions about her clothes, till she has seen me, for she does not know which are the best warehouses. Oh, brother, how kind you are! I know you will contrive it all."

But Mr. Gardiner, though he assured her again of his earnest endeavours in the cause, could not avoid recommending moderation to her, as well in her hopes as her fears; and, after talking with her in this manner till dinner was on table, they left her to vent all her feelings on the housekeeper, who attended in the absence of her daughters.

Though her brother and sister were persuaded that there was no real occasion for such a seclusion from the family, they did not attempt to oppose it, for they knew that she had not prudence enough to hold her tongue before the servants, while they waited at table, and judged it better that *one* only of the household, and the one whom they could most trust, should comprehend all her fears and solicitude on the subject.[1]

In the dining-room they were soon joined by Mary and Kitty, who had been too busily engaged in their separate apartments, to make their appearance before. One came from her books, and the other from her toilette. The faces of both, however, were tolerably calm; and no change was visible in either, except that the loss of her favourite sister, or the anger which she had herself incurred in the business, had given something

---

1 The servants of the Bennet household have so far figured only as signs of its claim to gentility; now, they constitute its permeability, as channels through which its private affairs can reach the wider community.

more of fretfulness than usual, to the accents of Kitty. As for Mary, she was mistress enough of herself to whisper to Elizabeth with a countenance of grave reflection, soon after they were seated at table,

"This is a most unfortunate affair; and will probably be much talked of. But we must stem the tide of malice, and pour into the wounded bosoms of each other, the balm of sisterly consolation."

Then, perceiving in Elizabeth no inclination of replying, she added, "Unhappy as the event must be for Lydia, we may draw from it this useful lesson: that loss of virtue in a female is irretrievable—that one false step involves her in endless ruin— that her reputation is no less brittle than it is beautiful,—and that she cannot be too much guarded in her behaviour towards the undeserving of the other sex."[1]

Elizabeth lifted up her eyes in amazement, but was too much oppressed to make any reply. Mary, however, continued to console herself with such kind of moral extractions from the evil before them.

In the afternoon, the two elder Miss Bennets were able to be for half an hour by themselves; and Elizabeth instantly availed herself of the opportunity of making many enquiries, which Jane was equally eager to satisfy. After joining in general lamentations over the dreadful sequel of this event, which Elizabeth considered as all but certain, and Miss Bennet could not assert to be wholly impossible; the former continued the subject, by saying, "But tell me all and every thing about it, which I have not already heard. Give me farther particulars. What did Colonel Forster say? Had they no apprehension of any thing before the elopement took place? They must have seen them together for ever."

"Colonel Forster did own that he had often suspected some partiality, especially on Lydia's side, but nothing to give him any alarm. I am so grieved for him. His behaviour was attentive and kind to the utmost. He *was* coming to us, in order to assure us

---

1 Mary's unforgiving theses come straight from the conduct books: see the opening paragraphs from Fordyce in Appendix B, and More's stance on "fallen women" in the extracts from pp. 53–5 of the *Strictures* in Appendix D.

of his concern, before he had any idea of their not being gone to Scotland: when that apprehension first got abroad, it hastened his journey."

"And was Denny convinced that Wickham would not marry? Did he know of their intending to go off? Had Colonel Forster seen Denny himself?"

"Yes; but when questioned by *him* Denny denied knowing any thing of their plan, and would not give his real opinion about it. He did not repeat his persuasion of their not marrying—and from *that*, I am inclined to hope, he might have been misunderstood before."

"And till Colonel Forster came himself, not one of you entertained a doubt, I suppose, of their being really married?"

"How was it possible that such an idea should enter our brains! I felt a little uneasy—a little fearful of my sister's happiness with him in marriage, because I knew that his conduct had not been always quite right. My father and mother knew nothing of that, they only felt how imprudent a match it must be. Kitty then owned, with a very natural triumph on knowing more than the rest of us, that in Lydia's last letter, she had prepared her for such a step. She had known, it seems, of their being in love with each other, many weeks."

"But not before they went to Brighton?"

"No, I believe not."

"And did Colonel Forster appear to think ill of Wickham himself? Does he know his real character?"

"I must confess that he did not speak so well of Wickham as he formerly did. He believed him to be imprudent and extravagant. And since this sad affair has taken place, it is said, that he left Meryton greatly in debt; but I hope this may be false."

"Oh, Jane, had we been less secret, had we told what we knew of him, this could not have happened!"

"Perhaps it would have been better;" replied her sister. "But to expose the former faults of any person, without knowing what their present feelings were, seemed unjustifiable. We acted with the best intentions."

"Could Colonel Forster repeat the particulars of Lydia's note to his wife?"

"He brought it with him for us to see."

Jane then took it from her pocket-book, and gave it to Elizabeth. These were the contents:

"My dear Harriet,

"You will laugh when you know where I am gone, and I cannot help laughing myself at your surprise tomorrow morning, as soon as I am missed. I am going to Gretna Green, and if you cannot guess with who, I shall think you a simpleton, for there is but one man in the world I love, and he is an angel. I should never be happy without him, so think it no harm to be off. You need not send them word at Longbourn of my going, if you do not like it, for it will make the surprise the greater, when I write to them, and sign my name Lydia Wickham. What a good joke it will be! I can hardly write for laughing. Pray make my excuses to Pratt, for not keeping my engagement, and dancing with him to night. Tell him I hope he will excuse me when he knows all, and tell him I will dance with him at the next ball we meet, with great pleasure. I shall send for my clothes when I get to Longbourn; but I wish you would tell Sally to mend a great slit in my worked muslin gown, before they are packed up. Good bye. Give my love to Colonel Forster, I hope you will drink to our good journey.

"Your affectionate friend,

"Lydia Bennet."

"Oh! thoughtless, thoughtless Lydia!" cried Elizabeth when she had finished it. "What a letter is this, to be written at such a moment. But at least it shews, that *she* was serious in the object of her journey. Whatever he might afterwards persuade her to, it was not on her side a *scheme* of infamy. My poor father! how he must have felt it!"

"I never saw any one so shocked. He could not speak a word for full ten minutes. My mother was taken ill immediately, and the whole house in such confusion!"

"Oh! Jane!" cried Elizabeth, "was there a servant belonging to it, who did not know the whole story before the end of the day?"

"I do not know. — I hope there was. — But to be guarded at such a time, is very difficult. My mother was in hysterics, and though I endeavoured to give her every assistance in my power, I am afraid I did not do so much as I might have done! But the horror of what might possibly happen, almost took from me my faculties."

"Your attendance upon her, has been too much for you. You do not look well. Oh! that I had been with you, you have had every care and anxiety upon yourself alone."

"Mary and Kitty have been very kind, and would have shared in every fatigue, I am sure, but I did not think it right for either of them. Kitty is slight and delicate, and Mary studies so much, that her hours of repose should not be broken in on. My aunt Phillips came to Longbourn on Tuesday, after my father went away; and was so good as to stay till Thursday with me. She was of great use and comfort to us all, and Lady Lucas has been very kind; she walked here on Wednesday morning to condole with us, and offered her services, or any of her Daughters, if they could be of use to us."

"She had better have stayed at home," cried Elizabeth; "perhaps she *meant* well, but, under such a misfortune as this, one cannot see too little of one's neighbours. Assistance is impossible; condolence, insufferable. Let them triumph over us at a distance, and be satisfied."

She then proceeded to enquire into the measures which her father had intended to pursue, while in town, for the recovery of his daughter.

"He meant, I believe," replied Jane, "to go to Epsom, the place where they last changed horses, see the postillions, and try if any thing could be made out from them.[1] His principal object must be, to discover the number of the hackney coach which took them from Clapham. It had come with a fare from London; and as he thought the circumstance of a gentleman and lady's removing from one carriage into another, might be remarked, he meant to make enquiries at Clapham. If he could any how discover at what house the coachman had before set down his fare, he determined to make enquiries there, and hoped it might not be impossible to find out the stand and

---

1   That is, from the drivers of the mail-coaches in which Lydia and Wickham travelled.

number of the coach. I do not know of any other designs that he had formed: but he was in such a hurry to be gone, and his spirits so greatly discomposed, that I had difficulty in finding out even so much as this."

CHAPTER VI.

THE whole party were in hopes of a letter from Mr. Bennet the next morning, but the post came in without bringing a single line from him. His family knew him to be, on all common occasions, a most negligent and dilatory correspondent, but at such a time they had hoped for exertion. They were forced to conclude, that he had no pleasing intelligence to send, but even of *that* they would have been glad to be certain. Mr. Gardiner had waited only for the letters before he set off.

When he was gone, they were certain at least of receiving constant information of what was going on, and their uncle promised, at parting, to prevail on Mr. Bennet to return to Longbourn, as soon as he could, to the great consolation of his sister, who considered it as the only security for her husband's not being killed in a duel.

Mrs. Gardiner and the children were to remain in Hertford-shire a few days longer, as the former thought her presence might be serviceable to her nieces. She shared in their attendance on Mrs. Bennet, and was a great comfort to them, in their hours of freedom. Their other aunt also visited them frequently, and always, as she said, with the design of cheering and heartening them up, though as she never came without reporting some fresh instance of Wickham's extravagance or irregularity, she seldom went away without leaving them more dispirited than she found them.

All Meryton seemed striving to blacken the man, who, but three months before, had been almost an angel of light. He was declared to be in debt to every tradesman in the place, and his intrigues, all honoured with the title of seduction, had been extended into every tradesman's family. Every body declared that he was the wickedest young man in the world; and every body began to find out, that they had always distrusted the appearance of his goodness. Elizabeth, though she did not credit above half of what was said, believed enough to make her former assurance of her sister's ruin still more certain; and even Jane, who believed still less of it, became almost hopeless, more especially as the time was now come, when if they had gone to Scotland, which she had never before entirely despaired of, they must in all probability have gained some news of them.

Mr. Gardiner left Longbourn on Sunday; on Tuesday, his wife received a letter from him; it told them, that on his arrival, he had immediately found out his brother, and persuaded him to come to Gracechurch street. That Mr. Bennet had been to Epsom and Clapham, before his arrival, but without gaining any satisfactory information; and that he was now determined to enquire at all the principal hotels in town, as Mr. Bennet thought it possible they might have gone to one of them, on their first coming to London, before they procured lodgings. Mr. Gardiner himself did not expect any success from this measure, but as his brother was eager in it, he meant to assist him in pursuing it. He added, that Mr. Bennet seemed wholly disinclined at present, to leave London, and promised to write again very soon. There was also a postscript to this effect:

"I have written to Colonel Forster to desire him to find out, if possible, from some of the young man's intimates in the regiment, whether Wickham has any relations or connections, who would be likely to know in what part of the town he has now concealed himself. If there were any one, that one could apply to, with a probability of gaining such a clue as that, it might be of essential consequence. At present we have nothing to guide us. Colonel Forster will, I dare say, do every thing in his power to satisfy us on this head. But, on second thoughts, perhaps Lizzy could tell us, what relations he has now living, better than any other person."

Elizabeth was at no loss to understand from whence this deference for her authority proceeded; but it was not in her power to give any information of so satisfactory a nature, as the compliment deserved.

She had never heard of his having had any relations, except a father and mother, both of whom had been dead many years. It was possible, however, that some of his companions in the —— shire, might be able to give more information; and, though she was not very sanguine in expecting it, the application was a something to look forward to.

Every day at Longbourn was now a day of anxiety; but the most anxious part of each was when the post was expected. The arrival of letters was the first grand object of every morning's impatience. Through letters, whatever of good or bad was to be told, would be communicated, and every succeeding day was expected to bring some news of importance.

But before they heard again from Mr. Gardiner, a letter arrived for their father, from a different quarter, from Mr. Collins; which, as Jane had received directions to open all that came for him in his absence, she accordingly read; and Elizabeth, who knew what curiosities his letters always were, looked over her, and read it likewise. It was as follows:

"MY DEAR SIR,

"I feel myself called upon, by our relationship, and my situation in life, to condole with you on the grievous affliction you are now suffering under, of which we were yesterday informed by a letter from Hertfordshire. Be assured, my dear Sir, that Mrs. Collins and myself sincerely sympathise with you, and all your respectable family, in your present distress, which must be of the bitterest kind, because proceeding from a cause which no time can remove. No arguments shall be wanting on my part, that can alleviate so severe a misfortune; or that may comfort you, under a circumstance that must be of all others most afflicting to a parent's mind. The death of your daughter would have been a blessing in comparison of this. And it is the more to be lamented, because there is reason to suppose, as my dear Charlotte informs me, that this licentiousness of behaviour in your daughter, has proceeded from a faulty degree of indulgence, though, at the same time, for the consolation of yourself and Mrs. Bennet, I am inclined to think that her own disposition must be naturally bad, or she could not be guilty of such an enormity, at so early an age. Howsoever that may be, you are grievously to be pitied, in which opinion I am not only joined by Mrs. Collins, but likewise by Lady Catherine and her daughter, to whom I have related the affair. They agree with me in apprehending that this false step in one daughter, will be injurious to the fortunes of all the others, for who, as Lady Catherine herself condescendingly says, will connect themselves with such a family. And this consideration leads me moreover to reflect with augmented satisfaction on a certain event of last November, for had it been otherwise, I must have been involved in all your sorrow and disgrace. Let me advise you then, my dear Sir, to console yourself as much as possible, to throw off your unworthy child from your affection for ever, and leave her to reap the fruits of her own heinous offence.

"I am, dear Sir, &c. &c."

Mr. Gardiner did not write again, till he had received an answer from Colonel Forster; and then he had nothing of a pleasant nature to send. It was not known that Wickham had a single relation, with whom he kept up any connection, and it was certain that he had no near one living. His former acquaintance had been numerous; but since he had been in the militia, it did not appear that he was on terms of particular friendship with any of them. There was no one therefore who could be pointed out, as likely to give any news of him. And in the wretched state of his own finances, there was a very powerful motive for secrecy, in addition to his fear of discovery by Lydia's relations, for it had just transpired that he had left gaming debts behind him, to a very considerable amount. Colonel Forster believed that more than a thousand pounds would be necessary to clear his expences at Brighton. He owed a good deal in the town, but his debts of honour were still more formidable.[1] Mr. Gardiner did not attempt to conceal these particulars from the Longbourn family, Jane heard them with horror. "A gamester!" she cried. "This is wholly unexpected. I had not an idea of it."

Mr. Gardiner added in his letter, that they might expect to see their father at home on the following day, which was Satur-

---

1 The distinction being made here is between money owed to tradesmen, and gambling debts: the latter would be regarded by most gentlemen as far more pressing.

day. Rendered spiritless by the ill-success of all their endeavours, he had yielded to his brother-in-law's intreaty that he would return to his family, and leave it to him to do, whatever occasion might suggest to be advisable for continuing their pursuit. When Mrs. Bennet was told of this, she did not express so much satisfaction as her children expected, considering what her anxiety for his life had been before.

"What, is he coming home, and without poor Lydia!" she cried. "Sure he will not leave London before he has found them. Who is to fight Wickham, and make him marry her, if he comes away?"

As Mrs. Gardiner began to wish to be at home, it was settled that she and her children should go to London, at the same time that Mr. Bennet came from it. The coach, therefore, took them the first stage of their journey, and brought its master back to Longbourn.

Mrs. Gardiner went away in all the perplexity about Elizabeth and her Derbyshire friend, that had attended her from that part of the world. His name had never been voluntarily mentioned before them by her niece; and the kind of half-expectation which Mrs. Gardiner had formed, of their being followed by a letter from him, had ended in nothing. Elizabeth had received none since her return, that could come from Pemberley.

The present unhappy state of the family, rendered any other excuse for the lowness of her spirits unnecessary; nothing, therefore, could be fairly conjectured from *that*, though Elizabeth, who was by this time tolerably well acquainted with her own feelings, was perfectly aware, that, had she known nothing of Darcy, she could have borne the dread of Lydia's infamy somewhat better. It would have spared her, she thought, one sleepless night out of two.

When Mr. Bennet arrived, he had all the appearance of his usual philosophic composure. He said as little as he had ever been in the habit of saying; made no mention of the business that had taken him away, and it was some time before his daughters had courage to speak of it.

It was not till the afternoon, when he joined them at tea,

that Elizabeth ventured to introduce the subject; and then, on her briefly expressing her sorrow for what he must have endured, he replied, "Say nothing of that. Who would suffer but myself? It has been my own doing, and I ought to feel it."

"You must not be too severe upon yourself," replied Elizabeth.

"You may well warn me against such an evil. Human nature is so prone to fall into it! No, Lizzy, let me once in my life feel how much I have been to blame. I am not afraid of being overpowered by the impression. It will pass away soon enough."

"Do you suppose them to be in London?"

"Yes; where else can they be so well concealed?"

"And Lydia used to want to go to London," added Kitty.

"She is happy, then," said her father, drily; "and her residence there will probably be of some duration."

Then, after a short silence, he continued, "Lizzy, I bear you no ill-will for being justified in your advice to me last May, which, considering the event, shews some greatness of mind."

They were interrupted by Miss Bennet, who came to fetch her mother's tea.

"This is a parade," cried he, "which does one good; it gives such an elegance to misfortune! Another day I will do the same; I will sit in my library, in my night cap and powdering gown,[1] and give as much trouble as I can,—or, perhaps, I may defer it till Kitty runs away."

"I am not going to run away, Papa," said Kitty, fretfully; "if *I* should ever go to Brighton, I would behave better than Lydia."

"*You* go to Brighton!—I would not trust you so near it as East Bourne, for fifty pounds![2] No, Kitty, I have at last learnt to be cautious, and you will feel the effects of it. No officer is ever to enter my house again, nor even to pass through the village. Balls will be absolutely prohibited, unless you stand up with[3]

---

1 A powdering gown is a sort of dressing-gown.

2 The distance to which Mr. Bennet refers is social rather than geographic: while the two south-coast resorts are equidistant from Hertfordshire, Eastbourne did not attract the high society and moral decadence brought to Brighton by the Prince Regent's patronage long before the militia camps arrived there.

3 That is, dance with.

one of your sisters. And you are never to stir out of doors, till you can prove that you have spent ten minutes of every day in a rational manner."

Kitty, who took all these threats in a serious light, began to cry.

"Well, well," said he, "do not make yourself unhappy. If you are a good girl for the next ten years, I will take you to a review at the end of them."[1]

CHAPTER VII.

Two days after Mr. Bennet's return, as Jane and Elizabeth were walking together in the shrubbery behind the house, they saw the housekeeper coming towards them, and, concluding that she came to call them to their mother, went forward to meet her; but, instead of the expected summons, when they approached her, she said to Miss Bennet, "I beg your pardon, madam, for interrupting you, but I was in hopes you might have got some good news from town, so I took the liberty of coming to ask."

"What do you mean, Hill? We have heard nothing from town."

"Dear madam," cried Mrs. Hill, in great astonishment, "dont you know there is an express come for master from Mr. Gardiner? He has been here this half hour, and master has had a letter."

Away ran the girls, too eager to get in to have time for speech. They ran through the vestibule into the breakfast room; from thence to the library;—their father was in neither; and they were on the point of seeking him up stairs with their mother, when they were met by the butler, who said,

"If you are looking for my master, ma'am, he is walking towards the little copse."

Upon this information, they instantly passed through the

1　An army review consisted of large-scale exercises and parades, attended by a member of the royal family: a social event as much as a military one.

hall once more, and ran across the lawn after their father, who was deliberately pursuing his way towards a small wood on one side of the paddock.

Jane, who was not so light, nor so much in the habit of running as Elizabeth, soon lagged behind, while her sister, panting for breath, came up with him, and eagerly cried out,

"Oh, Papa, what news? what news? Have you heard from my uncle?"

"Yes, I have had a letter from him by express."

"Well, and what news does it bring? good or bad?"

"What is there of good to be expected?" said he, taking the letter from his pocket; "but perhaps you would like to read it."

Elizabeth impatiently caught it from his hand. Jane now came up.

"Read it aloud," said their father, "for I hardly know myself what it is about."

"Gracechurch-street, Monday,
August 2.

"MY DEAR BROTHER,

"At last I am able to send you some tidings of my niece, and such as, upon the whole, I hope will give you satisfaction. Soon after you left me on Saturday, I was fortunate enough to find out in what part of London they were. The particulars, I reserve till we meet. It is enough to know they are discovered, I have seen them both—"

"Then it is, as I always hoped," cried Jane; "they are married!"

Elizabeth read on; "I have seen them both. They are not married, nor can I find there was any intention of being so; but if you are willing to perform the engagements which I have ventured to make on your side, I hope it will not be long before they are. All that is required of you is, to assure to your daughter, by settlement, her equal share of the five thousand pounds, secured among your children after the decease of yourself and my sister; and, moreover, to enter into an engagement of allowing her, during your life, one hundred pounds per annum. These are conditions, which, considering every thing, I had no hesitation in complying with, as far as I thought myself privileged, for you. I shall send this by express, that no time may be lost in bringing me your answer. You will easily comprehend, from these particulars, that Mr. Wickham's circumstances are not so hopeless as they are generally believed to be. The world has been deceived in that respect; and I am happy to say, there will be some little money, even when all his debts are discharged, to settle on my niece, in addition to her own fortune. If, as I conclude will be the case, you send me full powers to act in your name, throughout the whole of this business, I will immediately give directions to Haggerston for preparing a proper settlement. There will not be the smallest occasion for your coming to town again; therefore, stay quietly at Longbourn, and depend on my diligence and care. Send back your answer as soon as you can, and be careful to write explicitly. We have judged it best, that my niece should be married from this house, of which I hope you will approve. She comes to us today. I shall write again as soon as any thing more is determined on. Your's, &c.

"Edw. Gardiner."

"Is it possible!" cried Elizabeth, when she had finished. "Can it be possible that he will marry her?"

"Wickham is not so undeserving, then, as we have thought him;" said her sister. "My dear father, I congratulate you."

"And have you answered the letter?" said Elizabeth.

"No; but it must be done soon."

Most earnestly did she then intreat him to lose no more time before he wrote.

"Oh! my dear father," she cried, "come back, and write immediately. Consider how important every moment is, in such a case."

"Let me write for you," said Jane, "if you dislike the trouble yourself."

"I dislike it very much," he replied; "but it must be done."

And so saying, he turned back with them, and walked towards the house.

"And may I ask?" said Elizabeth, "but the terms, I suppose, must be complied with."

"Complied with! I am only ashamed of his asking so little."

"And they *must* marry! Yet he is *such* a man."

"Yes, yes, they must marry. There is nothing else to be done. But there are two things that I want very much to know: — one is, how much money your uncle has laid down, to bring it about; and the other, how I am ever to pay him."

"Money! my uncle!" cried Jane, "what do you mean, Sir?" ·

"I mean, that no man in his senses, would marry Lydia on so slight a temptation as one hundred a-year during my life, and fifty after I am gone."

"That is very true," said Elizabeth; "though it had not occurred to me before. His debts to be discharged, and something still to remain! Oh! it must be my uncle's doings! Generous, good man, I am afraid he has distressed himself.[1] A small sum could not do all this."

"No," said her father, "Wickham's a fool, if he takes her with a farthing less than ten thousand pounds. I should be sorry to think so ill of him, in the very beginning of our relationship."

"Ten thousand pounds! Heaven forbid! How is half such a sum to be repaid?"

Mr. Bennet made no answer, and each of them, deep in thought, continued silent till they reached the house. Their father then went to the library to write, and the girls walked into the breakfast-room.

"And they are really to be married!" cried Elizabeth, as soon as they were by themselves. "How strange this is! And for *this* we are to be thankful. That they should marry, small as is their chance of happiness, and wretched as is his character, we are forced to rejoice! Oh, Lydia!"

"I comfort myself with thinking," replied Jane, "that he certainly would not marry Lydia, if he had not a real regard for her. Though our kind uncle has done something towards clearing him, I cannot believe that ten thousand pounds, or any thing like it, has been advanced. He has children of his own, and may have more. How could he spare half ten thousand pounds?"

---

1 That is, financially, by, for example, mortgaging his business.

"If we are ever able to learn what Wickham's debts have been," said Elizabeth, "and how much is settled on his side on our sister, we shall exactly know what Mr. Gardiner has done for them, because Wickham has not sixpence of his own. The kindness of my uncle and aunt can never be requited. Their taking her home, and affording her their personal protection and countenance, is such a sacrifice to her advantage, as years of gratitude cannot enough acknowledge. By this time she is actually with them! If such goodness does not make her miserable now, she will never deserve to be happy! What a meeting for her, when she first sees my aunt!"

"We must endeavour to forget all that has passed on either side," said Jane: "I hope and trust they will yet be happy. His consenting to marry her is a proof, I will believe, that he is come to a right way of thinking. Their mutual affection will steady them; and I flatter myself they will settle so quietly, and live in so rational a manner, as may in time make their past imprudence forgotten."

"Their conduct has been such," replied Elizabeth, "as neither you, nor I, nor any body, can ever forget. It is useless to talk of it."

It now occurred to the girls that their mother was in all likelihood, perfectly ignorant of what had happened. They went to the library, therefore, and asked their father, whether he would not wish them to make it known to her. He was writing, and, without raising his head, coolly replied,

"Just as you please."

"May we take my uncle's letter to read to her?"

"Take whatever you like, and get away."

Elizabeth took the letter from his writing table, and they went up stairs together. Mary and Kitty were both with Mrs. Bennet: one communication would, therefore, do for all. After a slight preparation for good news, the letter was read aloud. Mrs. Bennet could hardly contain herself. As soon as Jane had read Mr. Gardiner's hope of Lydia's being soon married, her joy burst forth, and every following sentence added to its exuberance. She was now in an irritation as violent from delight, as she had ever been fidgety from alarm and vexation. To know that her daughter would be married was enough. She was disturbed by no fear for her felicity, nor humbled by any remembrance of her misconduct.

"My dear, dear Lydia!" she cried: "This is delightful indeed!—She will be married!—I shall see her again!—She will be married at sixteen!—My good, kind brother!—I knew how it would be—I knew he would manage every thing. How I long to see her! and to see dear Wickham too! But the clothes, the wedding clothes! I will write to my sister Gardiner about them directly. Lizzy, my dear, run down to your father, and ask him how much he will give her. Stay, stay, I will go myself. Ring the bell, Kitty, for Hill. I will put on my things in a moment. My dear, dear Lydia!—How merry we shall be together when we meet!"

Her eldest daughter endeavoured to give some relief to the violence of these transports, by leading her thoughts to the obligations which Mr. Gardiner's behaviour laid them all under.

"For we must attribute this happy conclusion," she added, "in a great measure, to his kindness. We are persuaded that he has pledged himself to assist Mr. Wickham with money."

"Well," cried her mother, "it is all very right; who should do it but her own uncle? If he had not had a family of his own, I and my children must have had all his money you know, and it is the first time we have ever had any thing from him, except a few presents. Well! I am so happy. In a short time, I shall have a daughter married. Mrs. Wickham! How well it sounds. And she was only sixteen last June. My dear Jane, I am in such a flutter that I am sure I can't write; so I will dictate, and you write for me. We will settle with your father about the money afterwards; but the things should be ordered immediately."

She was then proceeding to all the particulars of calico, muslin, and cambric, and would shortly have dictated some very plentiful orders, had not Jane, though with some difficulty, persuaded her to wait, till her father was at leisure to be consulted. One day's delay she observed, would be of small importance; and her mother was too happy, to be quite so obstinate as usual. Other schemes too came into her head.

"I will go to Meryton," said she, "as soon as I am dressed, and tell the good, good news to my sister Phillips. And as I come back, I can call on Lady Lucas and Mrs. Long. Kitty, run down and order the carriage. An airing would do me a great deal of good, I am sure. Girls, can I do any thing for you in Meryton? Oh! here comes Hill. My dear Hill, have you heard the good news? Miss Lydia is going to be married; and you shall all have a bowl of punch, to make merry at her wedding."

Mrs. Hill began instantly to express her joy. Elizabeth received her congratulations amongst the rest, and then, sick of this folly, took refuge in her own room, that she might think with freedom.

Poor Lydia's situation must, at best, be bad enough; but that it was no worse, she had need to be thankful. She felt it so; and though, in looking forward, neither rational happiness nor worldly prosperity, could be justly expected for her sister, in looking back to what they had feared, only two hours ago, she felt all the advantages of what they had gained.

CHAPTER VIII.

MR. BENNET had very often wished, before this period of his life, that, instead of spending his whole income, he had laid by an annual sum, for the better provision of his children, and of his wife, if she survived him. He now wished it more than ever. Had he done his duty in that respect, Lydia need not have been indebted to her uncle, for whatever of honour or credit could now be purchased for her. The satisfaction of prevailing on one of the most worthless young men in Great Britain to be her husband, might then have rested in its proper place.

He was seriously concerned, that a cause of so little advantage to any one, should be forwarded at the sole expence of his brother-in-law, and he was determined, if possible, to find out the extent of his assistance, and to discharge the obligation as soon as he could.

When first Mr. Bennet had married, economy was held to be perfectly useless; for, of course, they were to have a son. This son was to join in cutting off the entail, as soon as he should be of age, and the widow and younger children would by that means be provided for. Five daughters successively entered the world, but yet the son was to come; and Mrs. Bennet, for many years after Lydia's birth, had been certain that he would. This event had at last been despaired of, but it was then too late to be saving. Mrs. Bennet had no turn for economy, and her husband's love of independence had alone prevented their exceeding their income.

Five thousand pounds was settled by marriage articles on Mrs. Bennet and the children. But in what proportions it should be divided amongst the latter, depended on the will of the parents. This was one point, with regard to Lydia at least, which was now to be settled, and Mr. Bennet could have no hesitation in acceding to the proposal before him. In terms of grateful acknowledgment for the kindness of his brother, though expressed most concisely, he then delivered on paper his perfect approbation of all that was done, and his willingness to fulfil the engagements that had been made for him. He had never before supposed that, could Wickham be prevailed on to marry his daughter, it would be done with so little inconvenience to himself, as by the present arrangement. He would scarcely be ten pounds a-year the loser, by the hundred that was to be paid them; for, what with her board and pocket allowance, and the continual presents in money, which passed to her, through her mother's hands, Lydia's expences had been very little within that sum.

That it would be done with such trifling exertion on his side, too, was another very welcome surprise; for his chief wish at present, was to have as little trouble in the business as possible. When the first transports of rage which had produced his activity in seeking her were over, he naturally returned to all his former indolence. His letter was soon dispatched; for though dilatory in undertaking business, he was quick in its execution. He begged to know farther particulars of what he was indebted to his brother; but was too angry with Lydia, to send any message to her.

The good news quickly spread through the house; and with

proportionate speed through the neighbourhood. It was borne in the latter with decent philosophy. To be sure it would have been more for the advantage of conversation, had Miss Lydia Bennet come upon the town;[1] or, as the happiest alternative, been secluded from the world in some distant farm house. But there was much to be talked of, in marrying her; and the good-natured wishes for her well-doing, which had proceeded before, from all the spiteful old ladies in Meryton, lost but little of their spirit in this change of circumstances, because with such an husband, her misery was considered certain.

It was a fortnight since Mrs. Bennet had been down stairs, but on this happy day, she again took her seat at the head of her table, and in spirits oppressively high. No sentiment of shame gave a damp to her triumph. The marriage of a daughter, which had been the first object of her wishes, since Jane was sixteen, was now on the point of accomplishment, and her thoughts and her words ran wholly on those attendants of elegant nuptials, fine muslins, new carriages, and servants. She was busily searching through the neighbourhood for a proper situation for her daughter, and, without knowing or considering what their income might be, rejected many as deficient in size and importance.

"Haye-Park might do," said she, "if the Gouldings would quit it, or the great house at Stoke, if the drawing-room were larger; but Ashworth is too far off! I could not bear to have her ten miles from me; and as for Purvis Lodge, the attics are dreadful."

Her husband allowed her to talk on without interruption, while the servants remained. But when they had withdrawn, he said to her, "Mrs. Bennet, before you take any, or all of these houses, for your son and daughter, let us come to a right understanding. Into *one* house in this neighbourhood, they shall never have admittance. I will not encourage the impudence of either, by receiving them at Longbourn."

A long dispute followed this declaration; but Mr. Bennet was firm: it soon led to another; and Mrs. Bennet found, with amazement and horror, that her husband would not advance a

---

1 That is, become a prostitute.

guinea to buy clothes for his daughter. He protested that she should receive from him no mark of affection whatever, on the occasion. Mrs. Bennet could hardly comprehend it. That his anger could be carried to such a point of inconceivable resentment, as to refuse his daughter a privilege, without which her marriage would scarcely seem valid, exceeded all that she could believe possible. She was more alive to the disgrace, which the want of new clothes must reflect on her daughter's nuptials, than to any sense of shame at her eloping and living with Wickham, a fortnight before they took place.

Elizabeth was now most heartily sorry that she had, from the distress of the moment, been led to make Mr. Darcy acquainted with their fears for her sister; for since her marriage would so shortly give the proper termination to the elopement, they might hope to conceal its unfavourable beginning, from all those who were not immediately on the spot.

She had no fear of its spreading farther, through his means. There were few people on whose secrecy she would have more confidently depended; but at the same time, there was no one, whose knowledge of a sister's frailty would have mortified her so much. Not, however, from any fear of disadvantage from it, individually to herself; for at any rate, there seemed a gulf impossible between them. Had Lydia's marriage been concluded on the most honourable terms, it was not to be supposed that Mr. Darcy would connect himself with a family, where to every other objection would now be added, an alliance and relationship of the nearest kind with the man whom he so justly scorned.

From such a connection she could not wonder that he should shrink. The wish of procuring her regard, which she had assured herself of his feeling in Derbyshire, could not in rational expectation survive such a blow as this. She was humbled, she was grieved; she repented, though she hardly knew of what. She became jealous of his esteem, when she could no longer hope to be benefited by it. She wanted to hear of him, when there seemed the least chance of gaining intelligence. She was convinced that she could have been happy with him; when it was no longer likely they should meet.

What a triumph for him, as she often thought, could he know that the proposals which she had proudly spurned only four months ago, would now have been gladly and gratefully received! He was as generous, she doubted not, as the most generous of his sex. But while he was mortal, there must be a triumph.

She began now to comprehend that he was exactly the man, who, in disposition and talents, would most suit her. His understanding and temper, though unlike her own, would have answered all her wishes. It was an union that must have been to the advantage of both; by her ease and liveliness, his mind might have been softened, his manners improved, and from his judgment, information, and knowledge of the world, she must have received benefit of greater importance.

But no such happy marriage could now teach the admiring multitude what connubial felicity really was. An union of a different tendency, and precluding the possibility of the other, was soon to be formed in their family.

How Wickham and Lydia were to be supported in tolerable independence, she could not imagine. But how little of permanent happiness could belong to a couple who were only brought together because their passions were stronger than their virtue, she could easily conjecture.

Mr. Gardiner soon wrote again to his brother. To Mr. Bennet's acknowledgments he briefly replied, with assurances of his eagerness to promote the welfare of any of his family; and concluded with intreaties that the subject might never be mentioned to him again. The principal purport of his letter was to inform them, that Mr. Wickham had resolved on quitting the Militia.

"It was greatly my wish that he should do so," he added, "as soon as his marriage was fixed on. And I think you will agree with me, in considering a removal from that corps as highly advisable, both on his account and my niece's. It is Mr. Wickham's intention to go into the regulars; and, among his former friends, there are still some who are able and willing to assist him in the army. He has the promise of an ensigncy in General ——'s regiment, now quartered in the North. It is an advantage to have it so far from this part of the kingdom. He promises fairly, and I hope among different people, where they may each have a character to preserve, they will both be more prudent. I have written to Colonel Forster, to inform him of our present arrangements, and to request that he will satisfy the various creditors of Mr. Wickham in and near Brighton, with assurances of speedy payment, for which I have pledged myself. And will you give yourself the trouble of carrying similar assurances to his creditors in Meryton, of whom I shall subjoin a list, according to his information. He has given in all his debts; I hope at least he has not deceived us. Haggerston has our directions, and all will be completed in a week. They will then join his regiment, unless they are first invited to Longbourn; and I understand from Mrs. Gardiner, that my niece is very desirous of seeing you all, before she leaves the South. She is well, and begs to be dutifully remembered to you and her mother. — Your's, &c.

"E. GARDINER."

Mr. Bennet and his daughters saw all the advantages of Wickham's removal from the ——shire, as clearly as Mr. Gardiner could do. But Mrs. Bennet, was not so well pleased with it. Lydia's being settled in the North, just when she had expected most pleasure and pride in her company, for she had by no means given up her plan of their residing in Hertfordshire, was a severe disappointment; and besides, it was such a pity that Lydia should be taken from a regiment where she was acquainted with every body, and had so many favourites.

"She is so fond of Mrs. Forster," said she, "it will be quite shocking to send her away! And there are several of the young men, too, that she likes very much. The officers may not be so pleasant in General ——'s regiment."

His daughter's request, for such it might be considered, of being admitted into her family again, before she set off for the North, received at first an absolute negative. But Jane and Elizabeth, who agreed in wishing, for the sake of their sister's feelings and consequence, that she should be noticed on her marriage by her parents, urged him so earnestly, yet so rationally and so mildly, to receive her and her husband at Longbourn, as soon as they were married, that he was prevailed on to think as they thought, and act as they wished. And their mother had the satisfaction of knowing, that she should be able to shew her married daughter in the neighbourhood, before she was banished to the North. When Mr. Bennet wrote again to his brother, therefore, he sent his permission for them to come; and it was settled, that as soon as the ceremony was over, they should proceed to Longbourn. Elizabeth was surprised, however, that Wickham should consent to such a scheme, and, had she consulted only her own inclination, any meeting with him would have been the last object of her wishes.

CHAPTER IX.

THEIR sister's wedding day arrived; and Jane and Elizabeth felt for her probably more than she felt for herself. The carriage was sent to meet them at ———, and they were to return in it, by dinner-time. Their arrival was dreaded by the elder Miss Bennets; and Jane more especially, who gave Lydia the feelings which would have attended herself, had *she* been the culprit, was wretched in the thought of what her sister must endure.

They came. The family were assembled in the breakfast room, to receive them. Smiles decked the face of Mrs. Bennet, as the carriage drove up to the door; her husband looked impenetrably grave; her daughters, alarmed, anxious, uneasy.

Lydia's voice was heard in the vestibule; the door was thrown open, and she ran into the room. Her mother stepped forwards, embraced her, and welcomed her with rapture; gave her hand with an affectionate smile to Wickham, who followed his lady, and wished them both joy, with an alacrity which shewed no doubt of their happiness.

Their reception from Mr. Bennet, to whom they then turned, was not quite so cordial. His countenance rather gained in austerity; and he scarcely opened his lips. The easy assurance of the young couple, indeed, was enough to provoke him. Elizabeth was disgusted, and even Miss Bennet was shocked. Lydia was Lydia still; untamed, unabashed, wild, noisy, and fearless. She turned from sister to sister, demanding their congratulations; and when at length they all sat down, looked eagerly round the room, took notice of some little alteration in it, and observed, with a laugh, that it was a great while since she had been there.

Wickham was not at all more distressed than herself, but his manners were always so pleasing, that had his character and his marriage been exactly what they ought, his smiles and his easy address, while he claimed their relationship, would have delighted them all. Elizabeth had not before believed him quite equal to such assurance; but she sat down, resolving within herself, to draw no limits in future to the impudence of an impudent man. *She* blushed, and Jane blushed; but the cheeks of the two who caused their confusion, suffered no variation of colour.

There was no want of discourse. The bride and her mother could neither of them talk fast enough; and Wickham, who happened to sit near Elizabeth, began enquiring after his acquaintance in that neighbourhood, with a good humoured ease which she felt very unable to equal in her replies. They seemed each of them to have the happiest memories in the world. Nothing of the past was recollected with pain; and Lydia led voluntarily to subjects, which her sisters would not have alluded to for the world.

"Only think of its being three months," she cried, "since I went away; it seems but a fortnight I declare; and yet there have been things enough happened in the time. Good gracious! when I went away, I am sure I had no more idea of being married till I came back again! though I thought it would be very good fun if I was."

Her father lifted up his eyes. Jane was distressed. Elizabeth looked expressively at Lydia; but she, who never heard nor saw any thing of which she chose to be insensible, gaily continued, "Oh! mamma, do the people here abouts know I am married to day? I was afraid they might not; and we overtook William Goulding in his curricle, so I was determined he should know it, and so I let down the side glass next to him, and took off my glove, and let my hand just rest upon the window frame, so that he might see the ring, and then I bowed and smiled like any thing."

Elizabeth could bear it no longer. She got up, and ran out of the room; and returned no more, till she heard them passing through the hall to the dining parlour. She then joined them soon enough to see Lydia, with anxious parade, walk up to her mother's right hand, and hear her say to her eldest sister, "Ah! Jane, I take your place now, and you must go lower, because I am a married woman."

It was not to be supposed that time would give Lydia that embarrassment, from which she had been so wholly free at first. Her ease and good spirits increased. She longed to see Mrs. Phillips, the Lucasses, and all their other neighbours, and to hear herself called "Mrs. Wickham" by each of them; and in the mean time, she went after dinner to shew her ring and boast of being married, to Mrs. Hill and the two housemaids.

"Well, mamma," said she, when they were all returned to the breakfast room, "and what do you think of my husband? Is not he a charming man? I am sure my sisters must all envy me. I only hope they may have half my good luck. They must all go to Brighton. That is the place to get husbands. What a pity it is, mamma, we did not all go."

"Very true; and if I had my will, we should. But my dear Lydia, I don't at all like your going such a way off. Must it be so?"

"Oh, lord! yes;—there is nothing in that. I shall like it of all things. You and papa, and my sisters, must come down and see us. We shall be at Newcastle all the winter, and I dare say there will be some balls, and I will take care to get good partners for them all."

"I should like it beyond any thing!" said her mother.

"And then when you go away, you may leave one or two of my sisters behind you; and I dare say I shall get husbands for them before the winter is over."

"I thank you for my share of the favour," said Elizabeth; "but I do not particularly like your way of getting husbands."

Their visitors were not to remain above ten days with them. Mr. Wickham had received his commission before he left London, and he was to join his regiment at the end of a fortnight.

No one but Mrs. Bennet, regretted that their stay would be so short; and she made the most of the time, by visiting about with her daughter, and having very frequent parties at home. These parties were acceptable to all; to avoid a family circle was even more desirable to such as did think, than such as did not.

Wickham's affection for Lydia, was just what Elizabeth had expected to find it; not equal to Lydia's for him. She had scarcely needed her present observation to be satisfied, from the reason of things, that their elopement had been brought on by the strength of her love, rather than by his; and she would have wondered why, without violently caring for her, he chose to elope with her at all had she not felt certain that his flight was rendered necessary by distress of circumstances; and if that were the case, he was not the young man to resist an opportunity of having a companion.

Lydia was exceedingly fond of him. He was her dear Wickham on every occasion; no one was to be put in competition with him. He did every thing best in the world; and she was sure he would kill more birds on the first of September,[1] than any body else in the country.

One morning, soon after their arrival, as she was sitting with her two elder sisters, she said to Elizabeth,

"Lizzy, I never gave *you* an account of my wedding, I believe. You were not by, when I told mamma, and the others, all about it. Are not you curious to hear how it was managed?"

"No really," replied Elizabeth; "I think there cannot be too little said on the subject."

"La! You are so strange! But I must tell you how it went off. We were married, you know, at St. Clement's, because Wickham's lodgings were in that parish.[2] And it was settled that we should all be there by eleven o'clock. My uncle and aunt and I were to go together; and the others were to meet us at the church. Well, Monday morning came, and I was in such a fuss!

---

1 The beginning of the open season for partridges and bustard.
2 For the regulations within which Lydia's marriage is arranged, see the introduction to Appendix A.

I was so afraid you know that something would happen to put it off, and then I should have gone quite distracted. And there was my aunt, all the time I was dressing, preaching and talking away just as if she was reading a sermon. However, I did not hear above one word in ten, for I was thinking, you may suppose, of my dear Wickham. I longed to know whether he would be married in his blue coat.

"Well, and so we breakfasted at ten as usual; I thought it would never be over; for, by the bye, you are to understand, that my uncle and aunt were horrid unpleasant all the time I was with them. If you'll believe me, I did not once put my foot out of doors, though I was there a fortnight. Not one party, or scheme, or any thing. To be sure London was rather thin, but however the Little Theatre was open. Well, and so just as the carriage came to the door, my uncle was called away upon business to that horrid man Mr. Stone. And then, you know, when once they get together, there is no end of it. Well, I was so frightened I did not know what to do, for my uncle was to give me away; and if we were beyond the hour, we could not be married all day. But, luckily, he came back again in ten minutes time, and then we all set out. However, I recollected afterwards, that if he *had* been prevented going, the wedding need not be put off, for Mr. Darcy might have done as well."

"Mr. Darcy!" repeated Elizabeth, in utter amazement.

"Oh, yes!—he was to come there with Wickham, you know. But gracious me! I quite forgot! I ought not to have said a word about it. I promised them so faithfully! What will Wickham say? It was to be such a secret!"

"If it was to be secret," said Jane, "say not another word on the subject. You may depend upon my seeking no further."

"Oh! certainly," said Elizabeth, though burning with curiosity; "we will ask you no questions."

"Thank you," said Lydia, "for if you did, I should certainly tell you all, and then Wickham would be angry."

On such encouragement to ask, Elizabeth was forced to put it out of her power, by running away.

But to live in ignorance on such a point was impossible; or at least it was impossible not to try for information. Mr. Darcy had been at her sister's wedding. It was exactly a scene, and exactly among people, where he had apparently least to do, and least temptation to go. Conjectures as to the meaning of it, rapid and wild, hurried into her brain; but she was satisfied with none. Those that best pleased her, as placing his conduct in the noblest light, seemed most improbable. She could not bear such suspense; and hastily seizing a sheet of paper, wrote a short letter to her aunt, to request an explanation of what Lydia had dropt, if it were compatible with the secrecy which had been intended.

"You may readily comprehend," she added, "what my curiosity must be to know how a person unconnected with any of us, and (comparatively speaking) a stranger to our family, should have been amongst you at such a time. Pray write instantly, and let me understand it — unless it is, for very cogent reasons, to remain in the secrecy which Lydia seems to think necessary; and then I must endeavour to be satisfied with ignorance."

"Not that I *shall*, though," she added to herself, as she finished the letter; "and my dear aunt, if you do not tell me in an honourable manner, I shall certainly be reduced to tricks and stratagems to find it out."

Jane's delicate sense of honour would not allow her to speak to Elizabeth privately of what Lydia had let fall; Elizabeth was glad of it;—till it appeared whether her inquiries would receive any satisfaction, she had rather be without a confidante.

CHAPTER X.

ELIZABETH had the satisfaction of receiving an answer to her letter, as soon as she possibly could. She was no sooner in possession of it, than hurrying into the little copse, where she was least likely to be interrupted, she sat down on one of the benches, and prepared to be happy; for the length of the letter convinced her that it did not contain a denial.

"My dear niece,

"I have just received your letter, and shall devote this whole morning to answering it, as I foresee that a *little* writing will not comprise what I have to tell you. I must confess myself surprised by your application; I did not expect it from *you*. Don't think me angry, however, for I only mean to let you know, that I had not imagined such enquiries to be necessary on *your* side. If you do not choose to understand me, forgive my impertinence. Your uncle is as much surprised as I am—and nothing but the belief of your being a party concerned, would have allowed him to act as he has done. But if you are really innocent and ignorant, I must be more explicit. On the very day of my coming home from Longbourn, your uncle had a most unexpected visitor. Mr. Darcy called, and was shut up with him several hours. It was all over before I arrived; so my curiosity was not so dreadfully racked as *your's* seems to have been. He came to tell Mr. Gardiner that he had found out where your sister and Mr. Wickham were, and that he had seen and talked with them both, Wickham repeatedly, Lydia once. From what I can collect, he left Derbyshire only one day after ourselves, and came to town with the resolution of hunting for them. The motive professed, was his conviction of its being owing to himself that Wickham's worthlessness had not been so well known, as to make it impossible for any young woman of character, to love or confide in him. He generously imputed the whole to his mistaken pride, and confessed that he had before thought it beneath him, to lay his private actions open to the world. His character was to speak for itself. He called it, therefore, his duty to step forward, and endeavour to remedy an evil, which had been brought on by himself. If he *had another* motive, I am sure it would never disgrace him. He had been some days in town, before he was able to discover them; but he had something to direct his search, which was more than *we* had; and the consciousness of this, was another reason for his resolving to follow us. There is a lady, it seems, a Mrs. Younge, who was some time ago governess to Miss Darcy, and was dismissed from her charge on some cause of disapprobation, though he did not say what.

She then took a large house in Edward-street,[1] and has since maintained herself by letting lodgings. This Mrs. Younge was, he knew, intimately acquainted with Wickham; and he went to her for intelligence of him, as soon as he got to town. But it was two or three days before he could get from her what he wanted. She would not betray her trust, I suppose, without bribery and corruption, for she really did know where her friend was to be found. Wickham indeed had gone to her, on their first arrival in London, and had she been able to receive them into her house, they would have taken up their abode with her. At length, however, our kind friend procured the wished-for direction. They were in ———— street. He saw Wickham, and afterwards insisted on seeing Lydia. His first object with her, he acknowledged, had been to persuade her to quit her present disgraceful situation, and return to her friends as soon as they could be prevailed on to receive her, offering his assistance, as far as it would go. But he found Lydia absolutely resolved on remaining where she was. She cared for none of her friends, she wanted no help of his, she would not hear of leaving Wickham. She was sure they should be married some time or other, and it did not much signify when. Since such were her feelings, it only remained, he thought, to secure and expedite a marriage, which, in his very first conversation with Wickham, he easily learnt, had never been *his* design. He confessed himself obliged to leave the regiment, on account of some debts of honour, which were very pressing; and scrupled not to lay all the ill-consequences of Lydia's flight, on her own folly alone. He meant to resign his commission immediately; and as to his future situation, he could conjecture very little about it. He must go somewhere, but he did not know where, and he knew he should have nothing to live on. Mr. Darcy asked him why he had not married your sister at once. Though Mr. Bennet was not imagined to be very rich, he would have been able to do something for him, and his situation must have been benefited by marriage. But he found, in reply to this question, that Wickham still cherished the hope of more effec-

---

1 Edward Street is another West End address.

tually making his fortune by marriage, in some other country. Under such circumstances, however, he was not likely to be proof against the temptation of immediate relief. They met several times, for there was much to be discussed. Wickham of course wanted more than he could get; but at length was reduced to be reasonable. Every thing being settled between *them*, Mr. Darcy's next step was to make your uncle acquainted with it, and he first called in Gracechurch-street the evening before I came home. But Mr. Gardiner could not be seen, and Mr. Darcy found, on farther enquiry, that your father was still with him, but would quit town the next morning. He did not judge your father to be a person whom he could so properly consult as your uncle, and therefore readily postponed seeing him, till after the departure of the former. He did not leave his name, and till the next day, it was only known that a gentleman had called on business. On Saturday he came again. Your father was gone, your uncle at home, and, as I said before, they had a great deal of talk together. They met again on Sunday, and then *I* saw him too. It was not all settled before Monday: as soon as it was, the express was sent off to Longbourn. But our visitor was very obstinate. I fancy, Lizzy, that obstinacy is the real defect of his character, after all. He has been accused of many faults at different times; but *this* is the true one. Nothing was to be done that he did not do himself; though I am sure (and I do not speak it to be thanked, therefore say nothing about it,) your uncle would most readily have settled the whole. They battled it together for a long time, which was more than either the gentleman or lady concerned in it deserved. But at last your uncle was forced to yield, and instead of being allowed to be of use to his niece, was forced to put up with only having the probable credit of it, which went sorely against the grain; and I really believe your letter this morning gave him great pleasure, because it required an explanation that would rob him of his borrowed feathers, and give the praise where it was due. But, Lizzy, this must go no farther than yourself, or Jane at most. You know pretty well, I suppose, what has been done for the young people. His debts are to be paid, amounting, I believe, to considerably more than a thousand pounds, another thousand in addition to her own settled upon *her*, and his commission purchased.[1] The reason why all this was to be done by him alone, was such as I have given above. It was owing to him, to his reserve, and want of proper consideration, that Wickham's character had been so misunderstood, and consequently that he had been received and noticed as he was. Perhaps there was some truth in *this;* though I doubt whether *his* reserve, or *anybody's* reserve, can be answerable for the event. But in spite of all this fine talking, my dear Lizzy, you may rest perfectly assured, that your uncle would never have yielded, if we had not given him credit for *another interest* in the affair. When all this was resolved on, he returned again to his friends, who were still staying at Pemberley; but it was agreed that he should be in London once more when the wedding took place, and all money matters were then to receive the last finish. I believe I have now told you every thing. It is a relation which you tell me is to give you great surprise; I hope at least it will not afford you any displeasure. Lydia came to us; and Wickham had constant admission to the house. *He* was exactly what he had been, when I knew him in Hertfordshire; but I would not tell you how little I was satisfied with *her* behaviour while she staid with us, if I had not perceived, by Jane's letter last Wednesday, that her conduct on coming home was exactly of a piece with it, and therefore what I now tell you can give you no fresh pain. I talked to her repeatedly in the most serious manner, representing to her all the wickedness of what she had done, and all the unhappiness she had brought on her family. If she heard me, it was by good luck, for I am sure she did not listen. I was sometimes quite provoked, but then I recollected my dear Elizabeth and Jane, and for their sakes had patience with her. Mr. Darcy was punctual in his return, and as Lydia informed you, attended the wedding. He dined with us the next day, and

---

1 Commissions in the regular army were in high demand and had to be purchased; promotion would require further payment and often the influence of a patron. The unpopular militia regiments, on the other hand, were so desperate for officers in this period that the requirement that they own a minimum amount of property, the *sine qua non* of power in eighteenth-century Britain, had to be dropped (this is how Wickham can join the ——shire in the first place).

was to leave town again on Wednesday or Thursday. Will you be very angry with me, my dear Lizzy, if I take this opportunity of saying (what I was never bold enough to say before) how much I like him. His behaviour to us has, in every respect, been as pleasing as when we were in Derbyshire. His understanding and opinions all please me; he wants nothing but a little more liveliness, and *that*, if he marry *prudently*, his wife may teach him. I thought him very sly;—he hardly ever mentioned your name. But slyness seems the fashion. Pray forgive me, if I have been very presuming, or at least do not punish me so far, as to exclude me from P. I shall never be quite happy till I have been all round the park. A low phaeton, with a nice little pair of ponies, would be the very thing. But I must write no more. The children have been wanting me this half hour.

Your's, very sincerely,

"M.GARDINER."

The contents of this letter threw Elizabeth into a flutter of spirits, in which it was difficult to determine whether pleasure or pain bore the greatest share. The vague and unsettled suspicions which uncertainty had produced of what Mr. Darcy might have been doing to forward her sister's match, which she had feared to encourage as an exertion of goodness too great to be probable, and at the same time dreaded to be just, from the pain of obligation, were proved beyond their greatest extent to be true! He had followed them purposely to town, he had taken on himself all the trouble and mortification attendant on such a research; in which supplication had been necessary to a woman whom he must abominate and despise, and where he was reduced to meet, frequently meet, reason with, persuade, and finally bribe, the man whom he always most wished to avoid, and whose very name it was punishment to him to pronounce. He had done all this for a girl whom he could neither regard nor esteem. Her heart did whisper, that he had done it for her. But it was a hope shortly checked by other considerations, and she soon felt that even her vanity was insufficient, when required to depend on his affection for her, for a woman who had already refused him, as able to overcome a sentiment so natural as abhorrence against relationship with Wickham. Brother in law of Wickham! Every kind of pride must revolt from the connection. He had to be sure done much. She was ashamed to think how much. But he had given a reason for his interference, which asked no extraordinary stretch of belief. It was reasonable that he should feel he had been wrong; he had liberality, and he had the means of exercising it; and though she would not place herself as his principal inducement, she could, perhaps, believe that remaining partiality for her, might assist his endeavours in a cause where her peace of mind must be materially concerned. It was painful, exceedingly painful, to know that they were under obligations to a person who could never receive a return. They owed the restoration of Lydia, her character, every thing to him. Oh! how heartily did she grieve over every ungracious sensation she had ever encouraged, every saucy speech she had ever directed towards him. For herself she was humbled; but she was proud of him. Proud that in a cause of compassion and honour, he had been able to get the better of himself. She read over her aunt's commendation of him again and again. It was hardly enough; but it pleased her. She was even sensible of some pleasure, though mixed with regret, on finding how steadfastly both she and her uncle had been persuaded that affection and confidence subsisted between Mr. Darcy and herself.

She was roused from her seat, and her reflections, by some one's approach; and before she could strike into another path, she was overtaken by Wickham.

"I am afraid I interrupt your solitary ramble, my dear sister?" said he, as he joined her.

"You certainly do," she replied with a smile; "but it does not follow that the interruption must be unwelcome."

"I should be sorry indeed, if it were. *We* were always good friends; and now we are better."

"True. Are the others coming out?"

"I do not know. Mrs. Bennet and Lydia are going in the carriage to Meryton. And so, my dear sister, I find, from our uncle and aunt, that you have actually seen Pemberley."

She replied in the affirmative.

"I almost envy you the pleasure, and yet I believe it would be too much for me, or else I could take it in my way to Newcastle. And you saw the old housekeeper, I suppose? Poor Reynolds, she was always very fond of me. But of course she did not mention my name to you."

"Yes, she did."

"And what did she say?"

"That you were gone into the army, and she was afraid had—not turned out well. At such a distance as *that*, you know, things are strangely misrepresented."

"Certainly," he replied, biting his lips. Elizabeth hoped she had silenced him; but he soon afterwards said,

"I was surprised to see Darcy in town last month. We passed each other several times. I wonder what he can be doing there."

"Perhaps preparing for his marriage with Miss de Bourgh," said Elizabeth. "It must be something particular, to take him there at this time of year."

"Undoubtedly. Did you see him while you were at Lambton? I thought I understood from the Gardiners that you had."

"Yes; he introduced us to his sister."

"And do you like her?"

"Very much."

"I have heard, indeed, that she is uncommonly improved within this year or two. When I last saw her, she was not very promising. I am very glad you liked her. I hope she will turn out well."

"I dare say she will; she has got over the most trying age."

"Did you go by the village of Kympton?"

"I do not recollect that we did."

"I mention it, because it is the living which I ought to have had. A most delightful place! Excellent Parsonage House! It would have suited me in every respect."

"How should you have liked making sermons?"

"Exceedingly well. I should have considered it as part of my duty, and the exertion would soon have been nothing. One ought not to repine;—but, to be sure, it would have been such a thing for me! The quiet, the retirement of such a life, would have answered all my ideas of happiness! But it was not to be. Did you ever hear Darcy mention the circumstance, when you were in Kent?"

"I *have* heard from authority, which I thought *as good*, that it was left you conditionally only, and at the will of the present patron."

"You have. Yes, there was something in *that*; I told you so from the first, you may remember."

"I *did* hear, too, that there was a time, when sermon-making was not so palatable to you, as it seems to be at present; that you actually declared your resolution of never taking orders, and that the business had been compromised accordingly."

"You did! and it was not wholly without foundation. You may remember what I told you on that point, when first we talked of it."

They were now almost at the door of the house, for she had walked fast to get rid of him; and unwilling, for her sister's sake, to provoke him, she only said in reply, with a good-humoured smile,

"Come, Mr. Wickham, we are brother and sister, you know. Do not let us quarrel about the past. In future, I hope we shall be always of one mind."

She held out her hand; he kissed it with affectionate gallantry, though he hardly knew how to look, and they entered the house.

CHAPTER XI.

MR. WICKHAM was so perfectly satisfied with this conversation, that he never again distressed himself, or provoked his dear sister Elizabeth, by introducing the subject of it; and she was pleased to find that she had said enough to keep him quiet.

The day of his and Lydia's departure soon came, and Mrs. Bennet was forced to submit to a separation, which, as her husband by no means entered into her scheme of their all going to Newcastle, was likely to continue at least a twelvemonth.

"Oh! my dear Lydia," she cried, "when shall we meet again?"

"Oh, lord! I don't know. Not these two or three years perhaps."

"Write to me very often, my dear."

"As often as I can. But you know married women have never much time for writing. My sisters may write to *me*. They will have nothing else to do."

Mr. Wickham's adieus were much more affectionate than his wife's. He smiled, looked handsome, and said many pretty things.

"He is as fine a fellow," said Mr. Bennet, as soon as they were out of the house, "as ever I saw. He simpers, and smirks, and makes love to us all. I am prodigiously proud of him. I defy even Sir William Lucas himself, to produce a more valuable son-in-law."

The loss of her daughter made Mrs. Bennet very dull for several days.

"I often think," said she, "that there is nothing so bad as parting with one's friends. One seems so forlorn without them."

"This is the consequence you see, Madam, of marrying a daughter," said Elizabeth. "It must make you better satisfied that your other four are single."

"It is no such thing. Lydia does not leave me because she is married; but only because her husband's regiment happens to be so far off. If that had been nearer, she would not have gone so soon."

But the spiritless condition which this event threw her into, was shortly relieved, and her mind opened again to the agitation of hope, by an article of news, which then began to be in circulation. The housekeeper at Netherfield had received orders to prepare for the arrival of her master, who was coming down in a day or two, to shoot there for several weeks. Mrs. Bennet was quite in the fidgets. She looked at Jane, and smiled, and shook her head by turns.

"Well, well, and so Mr. Bingley is coming down, sister," (for

Mrs. Phillips first brought her the news). "Well, so much the better. Not that I care about it, though. He is nothing to us, you know, and I am sure *I* never want to see him again. But, however, he is very welcome to come to Netherfield, if he likes it. And who knows what *may* happen? But that is nothing to us. You know, sister, we agreed long ago never to mention a word about it. And so, is it quite certain he is coming?"

"You may depend on it," replied the other, "for Mrs. Nicholls was in Meryton last night; I saw her passing by, and went out myself on purpose to know the truth of it; and she told me that it was certain true. He comes down on Thursday at the latest, very likely on Wednesday. She was going to the butcher's, she told me, on purpose to order in some meat on Wednesday, and she has got three couple of ducks, just fit to be killed."

Miss Bennet had not been able to hear of his coming, without changing colour. It was many months since she had mentioned his name to Elizabeth; but now, as soon as they were alone together, she said,

"I saw you look at me to day, Lizzy, when my aunt told us of the present report; and I know I appeared distressed. But don't imagine it was from any silly cause. I was only confused for the moment, because I felt that I *should* be looked at. I do assure you, that the news does not affect me either with pleasure or pain. I am glad of one thing, that he comes alone; because we shall see the less of him. Not that I am afraid of *myself*, but I dread other people's remarks."

Elizabeth did not know what to make of it. Had she not seen him in Derbyshire, she might have supposed him capable of coming there, with no other view than what was acknowledged; but she still thought him partial to Jane, and she wavered as to the greater probability of his coming there *with* his friend's permission, or being bold enough to come without it.

"Yet it is hard," she sometimes thought, "that this poor man cannot come to a house, which he has legally hired, without raising all this speculation! I *will* leave him to himself."

In spite of what her sister declared, and really believed to be her feelings, in the expectation of his arrival, Elizabeth could easily perceive that her spirits were affected by it. They were more disturbed, more unequal, than she had often seen them.

The subject which had been so warmly canvassed between their parents, about a twelvemonth ago, was now brought forward again.

"As soon as ever Mr. Bingley comes, my dear," said Mrs. Bennet, "you will wait on him of course."

"No, no. You forced me into visiting him last year, and promised if I went to see him, he should marry one of my daughters. But it ended in nothing, and I will not be sent on a fool's errand again."

His wife represented to him how absolutely necessary such an attention would be from all the neighbouring gentlemen, on his returning to Netherfield.

"'Tis an etiquette I despise," said he. "If he wants our society, let him seek it. He knows where we live. I will not spend *my* hours in running after my neighbours every time they go away, and come back again."

"Well, all I know is, that it will be abominably rude if you do not wait on him. But, however, that shan't prevent my asking him to dine here, I am determined. We must have Mrs. Long and the Gouldings soon. That will make thirteen with ourselves, so there will be just room at table for him."

Consoled by this resolution, she was the better able to bear her husband's incivility; though it was very mortifying to know that her neighbours might all see Mr. Bingley in consequence of it, before *they* did. As the day of his arrival drew near,

"I begin to be sorry that he comes at all," said Jane to her sister. "It would be nothing; I could see him with perfect indifference, but I can hardly bear to hear it thus perpetually talked of. My mother means well; but she does not know, no one can know how much I suffer from what she says. Happy shall I be, when his stay at Netherfield is over!"

"I wish I could say any thing to comfort you," replied Elizabeth; "but it is wholly out of my power. You must feel it; and the usual satisfaction of preaching patience to a sufferer is denied me, because you have always so much."

Mr. Bingley arrived. Mrs. Bennet, through the assistance of

servants, contrived to have the earliest tidings of it, that the period of anxiety and fretfulness on her side, might be as long as it could. She counted the days that must intervene before their invitation could be sent; hopeless of seeing him before. But on the third morning after his arrival in Hertfordshire, she saw him from her dressing-room window, enter the paddock, and ride towards the house.

Her daughters were eagerly called to partake of her joy. Jane resolutely kept her place at the table; but Elizabeth, to satisfy her mother, went to the window—she looked,—she saw Mr. Darcy with him, and sat down again by her sister.

"There is a gentleman with him, mamma," said Kitty; "who can it be?"

"Some acquaintance or other, my dear, I suppose; I am sure I do not know."

"La!" replied Kitty, "it looks just like that man that used to be with him before. Mr. what's his name. That tall, proud man."

"Good gracious! Mr. Darcy!—and so it does I vow. Well, any friend of Mr. Bingley's will always be welcome here to be sure; but else I must say that I hate the very sight of him."

Jane looked at Elizabeth with surprise and concern. She knew but little of their meeting in Derbyshire, and therefore felt for the awkwardness which must attend her sister, in seeing him almost for the first time after receiving his explanatory letter. Both sisters were uncomfortable enough. Each felt for the other, and of course for themselves; and their mother talked on, of her dislike of Mr. Darcy, and her resolution to be civil to him only as Mr. Bingley's friend, without being heard by either of them. But Elizabeth had sources of uneasiness which could not be suspected by Jane, to whom she had never yet had courage to shew Mrs. Gardiner's letter, or to relate her own change of sentiment towards him. To Jane, he could be only a man whose proposals she had refused, and whose merit she had undervalued; but to her own more extensive information, he was the person, to whom the whole family were indebted for the first of benefits, and whom she regarded herself with an interest, if not quite so tender, at least as reasonable and just, as what Jane felt for Bingley. Her astonishment at his coming—at his coming to Netherfield, to Longbourn, and voluntarily seeking her again, was almost equal to what she had known on first witnessing his altered behaviour in Derbyshire.

The colour which had been driven from her face, returned for half a minute with an additional glow, and a smile of delight added lustre to her eyes, as she thought for that space of time, that his affection and wishes must still be unshaken. But she would not be secure.

"Let me first see how he behaves," said she; "it will then be early enough for expectation."

She sat intently at work, striving to be composed, and without daring to lift up her eyes, till anxious curiosity carried them to the face of her sister, as the servant was approaching the door. Jane looked a little paler than usual, but more sedate than Elizabeth had expected. On the gentlemen's appearing, her colour increased; yet she received them with tolerable ease, and with a propriety of behaviour equally free from any symptom of resentment, or any unnecessary complaisance.

Elizabeth said as little to either as civility would allow, and sat down again to her work, with an eagerness which it did not often command. She had ventured only one glance at Darcy. He looked serious as usual; and she thought, more as he had been used to look in Hertfordshire, than as she had seen him at Pemberley. But, perhaps he could not in her mother's presence be what he was before her uncle and aunt. It was a painful, but not an improbable, conjecture.

Bingley, she had likewise seen for an instant, and in that short period saw him looking both pleased and embarrassed. He was received by Mrs. Bennet with a degree of civility, which made her two daughters ashamed, especially when contrasted with the cold and ceremonious politeness of her curtsey and address to his friend.

Elizabeth particularly, who knew that her mother owed to the latter the preservation of her favourite daughter from irremediable infamy, was hurt and distressed to a most painful degree by a distinction so ill applied.

Darcy, after enquiring of her how Mr. and Mrs. Gardiner

did, a question which she could not answer without confusion, said scarcely any thing. He was not seated by her; perhaps that was the reason of his silence; but it had not been so in Derbyshire. There he had talked to her friends, when he could not to herself. But now several minutes elapsed, without bringing the sound of his voice; and when occasionally, unable to resist the impulse of curiosity, she raised her eyes to his face, she as often found him looking at Jane, as at herself, and frequently on no object but the ground. More thoughtfulness, and less anxiety to please than when they last met, were plainly expressed. She was disappointed, and angry with herself for being so.

"Could I expect it to be otherwise!" said she. "Yet why did he come?"

She was in no humour for conversation with any one but himself; and to him she had hardly courage to speak.

She enquired after his sister, but could do no more.

"It is a long time, Mr. Bingley, since you went away," said Mrs. Bennet.

He readily agreed to it.

"I began to be afraid you would never come back again. People *did* say, you meant to quit the place entirely at Michaelmas; but, however, I hope it is not true. A great many changes have happened in the neighbourhood, since you went away. Miss Lucas is married and settled. And one of my own daughters. I suppose you have heard of it; indeed, you must have seen it in the papers. It was in the Times and the Courier, I know; though it was not put in as it ought to be. It was only said, 'Lately, George Wickham, Esq. to Miss Lydia Bennet,' without there being a syllable said of her father, or the place where she lived, or any thing. It was my brother Gardiner's drawing up too, and I wonder how he came to make such an awkward business of it. Did you see it?"

Bingley replied that he did, and made his congratulations. Elizabeth dared not lift up her eyes. How Mr. Darcy looked, therefore, she could not tell.

"It is a delightful thing, to be sure, to have a daughter well married," continued her mother; "but at the same time, Mr. Bingley, it is very hard to have her taken such a way from me.

They are gone down to Newcastle, a place quite northward, it seems, and there they are to stay, I do not know how long. His regiment is there; for I suppose you have heard of his leaving the ——shire, and of his being gone into the regulars. Thank Heaven! he has *some* friends, though perhaps not so many as he deserves."

Elizabeth, who knew this to be levelled at Mr. Darcy, was in such misery of shame, that she could hardly keep her seat. It drew from her, however, the exertion of speaking, which nothing else had so effectually done before; and she asked Bingley whether he meant to make any stay in the country at present. A few weeks, he believed.

"When you have killed all your own birds, Mr. Bingley," said her mother, "I beg you will come here, and shoot as many as you please, on Mr. Bennet's manor. I am sure he will be vastly happy to oblige you, and will save all the best of the covies for you."[1]

Elizabeth's misery increased, at such unnecessary, such officious attention! Were the same fair prospect to arise at present, as had flattered them a year ago, every thing, she was persuaded, would be hastening to the same vexatious conclusion. At that instant she felt, that years of happiness could not make Jane or herself amends, for moments of such painful confusion.

"The first wish of my heart," said she to herself, "is never more to be in company with either of them. Their society can afford no pleasure, that will atone for such wretchedness as this! Let me never see either one or the other again!"

Yet the misery, for which years of happiness were to offer no compensation, received soon afterwards material relief, from observing how much the beauty of her sister re-kindled the admiration of her former lover. When first he came in, he had spoken to her but little; but every five minutes seemed to be giving her more of his attention. He found her as handsome as she had been last year; as good natured, and as unaffected, though not quite so chatty. Jane was anxious that no difference should be perceived in her at all, and was really persuaded that

---

1   That is, families or flocks of partridges.

she talked as much as ever. But her mind was so busily engaged, that she did not always know when she was silent.

When the gentlemen rose to go away, Mrs. Bennet was mindful of her intended civility, and they were invited and engaged to dine at Longbourn in a few days time.

"You are quite a visit in my debt, Mr. Bingley," she added, "for when you went to town last winter, you promised to take a family dinner with us, as soon as you returned. I have not forgot, you see; and I assure you, I was very much disappointed that you did not come back and keep your engagement."

Bingley looked a little silly at this reflection, and said something of his concern, at having been prevented by business. They then went away.

Mrs. Bennet had been strongly inclined to ask them to stay and dine there, that day; but, though she always kept a very good table, she did not think any thing less than two courses, could be good enough for a man, on whom she had such anxious designs, or satisfy the appetite and pride of one who had ten thousand a-year.

CHAPTER XII.

As soon as they were gone, Elizabeth walked out to recover her spirits; or in other words, to dwell without interruption on those subjects that must deaden them more. Mr. Darcy's behaviour astonished and vexed her.

"Why, if he came only to be silent, grave, and indifferent," said she, "did he come at all?"

She could settle it in no way that gave her pleasure.

"He could be still amiable, still pleasing, to my uncle and aunt, when he was in town; and why not to me? If he fears me, why come hither? If he no longer cares for me, why silent? Teazing, teazing, man! I will think no more about him."

Her resolution was for a short time involuntarily kept by the approach of her sister, who joined her with a cheerful look, which shewed her better satisfied with their visitors, than Elizabeth.

"Now," said she, "that this first meeting is over, I feel perfect-ly easy. I know my own strength, and I shall never be embar-rassed again by his coming. I am glad he dines here on Tuesday. It will then be publicly seen, that on both sides, we meet only as common and indifferent acquaintance."

"Yes, very indifferent indeed," said Elizabeth, laughingly. "Oh, Jane, take care."

"My dear Lizzy, you cannot think me so weak, as to be in danger now."

"I think you are in very great danger of making him as much in love with you as ever."

They did not see the gentlemen again till Tuesday; and Mrs. Bennet, in the meanwhile, was giving way to all the happy schemes, which the good humour, and common politeness of Bingley, in half an hour's visit, had revived.

On Tuesday there was a large party assembled at Longbourn; and the two, who were most anxiously expected, to the credit of their punctuality as sportsmen, were in very good time. When they repaired to the dining-room, Elizabeth eagerly watched to see whether Bingley would take the place, which, in all their former parties, had belonged to him, by her sister. Her prudent mother, occupied by the same ideas, forbore to invite him to sit by herself. On entering the room, he seemed to hesitate; but Jane happened to look round, and happened to smile: it was decided. He placed himself by her.

Elizabeth, with a triumphant sensation, looked towards his friend. He bore it with noble indifference, and she would have imagined that Bingley had received his sanction to be happy, had she not seen his eyes likewise turned towards Mr. Darcy, with an expression of half-laughing alarm.

His behaviour to her sister was such, during dinner time, as shewed an admiration of her, which, though more guarded than formerly, persuaded Elizabeth, that if left wholly to him-self, Jane's happiness, and his own, would be speedily secured. Though she dared not depend upon the consequence, she yet received pleasure from observing his behaviour. It gave her all the animation that her spirits could boast; for she was in no cheerful humour. Mr. Darcy was almost as far from her, as the table could divide them. He was on one side of her mother. She knew how little such a situation would give pleasure to either, or make either appear to advantage. She was not near enough to hear any of their discourse, but she could see how seldom they spoke to each other, and how formal and cold was their manner, whenever they did. Her mother's ungraciousness, made the sense of what they owed him more painful to Elizabeth's mind; and she would, at times, have given any thing to be privileged to tell him, that his kindness was neither unknown nor unfelt by the whole of the family.

She was in hopes that the evening would afford some opportunity of bringing them together; that the whole of the visit would not pass away without enabling them to enter into something more of conversation, than the mere ceremonious salutation attending his entrance. Anxious and uneasy, the period which passed in the drawing-room, before the gentlemen came, was wearisome and dull to a degree, that almost made her uncivil. She looked forward to their entrance, as the point on which all her chance of pleasure for the evening must depend.

"If he does not come to me, *then*," said she, "I shall give him up for ever."

The gentlemen came; and she thought he looked as if he would have answered her hopes; but, alas! the ladies had crowded round the table, where Miss Bennet was making tea, and Elizabeth pouring out the coffee, in so close a confederacy, that there was not a single vacancy near her, which would admit of a chair. And on the gentlemen's approaching, one of the girls moved closer to her than ever, and said, in a whisper,

"The men shan't come and part us, I am determined. We want none of them; do we?"

Darcy had walked away to another part of the room. She followed him with her eyes, envied every one to whom he spoke, had scarcely patience enough to help anybody to coffee; and then was enraged against herself for being so silly!

"A man who has once been refused! How could I ever be foolish enough to expect a renewal of his love? Is there one among the sex, who would not protest against such a weakness as a second proposal to the same woman? There is no indignity so abhorrent to their feelings!"

She was a little revived, however, by his bringing back his coffee cup himself; and she seized the opportunity of saying,

"Is your sister at Pemberley still?"

"Yes, she will remain there till Christmas."

"And quite alone? Have all her friends left her?"

"Mrs. Annesley is with her. The others have been gone on to Scarborough[1] these three weeks."

She could think of nothing more to say; but if he wished to converse with her, he might have better success. He stood by her, however, for some minutes, in silence; and, at last, on the young lady's whispering to Elizabeth again, he walked away.

When the tea-things were removed, and the card tables placed, the ladies all rose, and Elizabeth was then hoping to be soon joined by him, when all her views were overthrown, by seeing him fall a victim to her mother's rapacity for whist players, and in a few moments after seated with the rest of the party. She now lost every expectation of pleasure. They were confined for the evening at different tables, and she had nothing to hope, but that his eyes were so often turned towards her side of the room, as to make him play as unsuccessfully as herself.

Mrs. Bennet had designed to keep the two Netherfield gentlemen to supper; but their carriage was unluckily ordered before any of the others, and she had no opportunity of detaining them.

"Well girls," said she, as soon as they were left to themselves, "What say you to the day? I think every thing has passed off uncommonly well, I assure you. The dinner was as well dressed as any I ever saw. The venison was roasted to a turn—and everybody said, they never saw so fat a haunch. The soup was fifty times better than what we had at the Lucas's last week; and even Mr. Darcy acknowledged, that the partridges were remarkably well done; and I suppose he has two or three French cooks at least. And, my dear Jane, I never saw you look in greater beauty. Mrs. Long said so too, for I asked her

---

1 A fashionable spa town on the East coast, in Yorkshire.

whether you did not. And what do you think she said besides? 'Ah! Mrs. Bennet, we shall have her at Netherfield at last.' She did indeed. I do think Mrs. Long is as good a creature as ever lived—and her nieces are very pretty behaved girls, and not at all handsome: I like them prodigiously."

Mrs. Bennet, in short, was in very great spirits; she had seen enough of Bingley's behaviour to Jane, to be convinced that she would get him at last; and her expectations of advantage to her family, when in a happy humour, were so far beyond reason, that she was quite disappointed at not seeing him there again the next day, to make his proposals.

"It has been a very agreeable day," said Miss Bennet to Elizabeth. "The party seemed so well selected, so suitable one with the other. I hope we may often meet again."

Elizabeth smiled.

"Lizzy, you must not do so. You must not suspect me. It mortifies me. I assure you that I have now learnt to enjoy his conversation as an agreeable and sensible young man, without having a wish beyond it. I am perfectly satisfied from what his manners now are, that he never had any design of engaging my affection. It is only that he is blessed with greater sweetness of address, and a stronger desire of generally pleasing than any other man."

"You are very cruel," said her sister, "you will not let me smile, and are provoking me to it every moment."

"How hard it is in some cases to be believed!"

"And how impossible in others!"

"But why should you wish to persuade me that I feel more than I acknowledge?"

"That is a question which I hardly know how to answer. We all love to instruct, though we can teach only what is not worth knowing. Forgive me; and if you persist in indifference, do not make *me* your confidante."

CHAPTER XIII

A few days after this visit, Mr. Bingley called again, and alone. His friend had left him that morning for London, but was to return home in ten days time. He sat with them above an hour, and was in remarkably good spirits. Mrs. Bennet invited him to dine with them; but, with many expressions of concern, he confessed himself engaged elsewhere.

"Next time you call," said she, "I hope we shall be more lucky."

He should be particularly happy at any time, &c. &c.; and if she would give him leave, would take an early opportunity of waiting on them.

"Can you come to-morrow?"

Yes, he had no engagement at all for to-morrow; and her invitation was accepted with alacrity.

He came, and in such very good time, that the ladies were none of them dressed. In ran Mrs. Bennet to her daughter's room, in her dressing gown, and with her hair half finished, crying out,

"My dear Jane, make haste and hurry down. He is come — Mr. Bingley is come. — He is, indeed. Make haste, make haste. Here, Sarah, come to Miss Bennet this moment, and help her on with her gown. Never mind Miss Lizzy's hair."

"We will be down as soon as we can," said Jane; "but I dare say Kitty is forwarder than either of us, for she went up stairs half an hour ago."

"Oh! hang Kitty! what has she to do with it? Come be quick, be quick! Where is your sash my dear?"

But when her mother was gone, Jane would not be prevailed on to go down without one of her sisters.

The same anxiety to get them by themselves, was visible again in the evening. After tea, Mr. Bennet retired to the library, as was his custom, and Mary went up stairs to her instrument. Two obstacles of the five being thus removed, Mrs. Bennet sat looking and winking at Elizabeth and Catherine for a considerable time, without making any impression on them. Elizabeth would not observe her; and when at last Kitty did, she very innocently said, "What is the matter mamma? What do you keep winking at me for? What am I to do?"

"Nothing child, nothing. I did not wink at you." She then sat still five minutes longer; but unable to waste such a precious occasion, she suddenly got up, and saying to Kitty,

"Come here, my love, I want to speak to you," took her out of the room. Jane instantly gave a look at Elizabeth, which spoke her distress at such premeditation, and her intreaty that *she* would not give into it. In a few minutes, Mrs. Bennet half-opened the door and called out,

"Lizzy, my dear, I want to speak with you."

Elizabeth was forced to go.

"We may as well leave them by themselves you know;" said her mother, as soon as she was in the hall. "Kitty and I are going up stairs to sit in my dressing room."

Elizabeth made no attempt to reason with her mother, but remained quietly in the hall, till she and Kitty were out of sight, then returned into the drawing room.

Mrs. Bennet's schemes for this day were ineffectual. Bingley was every thing that was charming, except the professed lover of her daughter. His ease and cheerfulness rendered him a most agreeable addition to their evening party; and he bore with the ill-judged officiousness of the mother, and heard all her silly remarks with a forbearance and command of countenance, particularly grateful to the daughter.

He scarcely needed an invitation to stay supper; and before he went away, an engagement was formed, chiefly through his own and Mrs. Bennet's means, for his coming next morning to shoot with her husband.

After this day, Jane said no more of her indifference. Not a word passed between the sisters concerning Bingley; but Elizabeth went to bed in the happy belief that all must speedily be concluded, unless Mr. Darcy returned within the stated time. Seriously, however, she felt tolerably persuaded that all this must have taken place with that gentleman's concurrence.

Bingley was punctual to his appointment; and he and Mr. Bennet spent the morning together, as had been agreed on. The latter was much more agreeable than his companion expected. There was nothing of presumption or folly in Bingley, that could provoke his ridicule, or disgust him into silence; and he was more communicative, and less eccentric than the other had ever seen him. Bingley of course returned with him to dinner; and in the evening Mrs. Bennet's invention was again at work to get every body away from him and her daughter. Elizabeth, who had a letter to write, went into the breakfast room for that purpose soon after tea; for as the others were all going to sit down to cards, she could not be wanted to counteract her mother's schemes.

But on returning to the drawing room, when her letter was finished, she saw, to her infinite surprise, there was reason to fear that her mother had been too ingenious for her. On opening the door, she perceived her sister and Bingley standing together over the hearth, as if engaged in earnest conversation; and had this led to no suspicion, the faces of both as they hastily turned round, and moved away from each other, would have told it all. *Their* situation was awkward enough; but *her's* she thought was still worse. Not a syllable was uttered by either; and Elizabeth was on the point of going away again, when Bingley, who as well as the others had sat down, suddenly rose, and whispering a few words to her sister, ran out of the room.

Jane could have no reserves from Elizabeth, where confidence would give pleasure; and instantly embracing her, acknowledged, with the liveliest emotion, that she was the happiest creature in the world.

"'Tis too much!" she added, "by far too much. I do not deserve it. Oh! why is not every body as happy."

Elizabeth's congratulations were given with a sincerity, a warmth, a delight, which words could but poorly express. Every sentence of kindness was a fresh source of happiness to Jane. But she would not allow herself to stay with her sister, or say half that remained to be said, for the present.

"I must go instantly to my mother;" she cried. "I would not on any account trifle with her affectionate solicitude; or allow her to hear it from any one but myself. He is gone to my father already. Oh! Lizzy, to know that what I have to relate will give such pleasure to all my dear family! how shall I bear so much happiness!"

She then hastened away to her mother, who had purposely broken up the card party, and was sitting up stairs with Kitty.

Elizabeth, who was left by herself, now smiled at the rapidity and ease with which an affair was finally settled, that had given them so many previous months of suspense and vexation.

"And this," said she, "is the end of all his friend's anxious circumspection! of all his sister's falsehood and contrivance! the happiest, wisest, most reasonable end!"

In a few minutes she was joined by Bingley, whose conference with her father had been short and to the purpose.

"Where is your sister?" said he hastily, as he opened the door.

"With my mother up stairs. She will be down in a moment I dare say."

He then shut the door, and, coming up to her, claimed the good wishes and affection of a sister. Elizabeth honestly and heartily expressed her delight in the prospect of their relationship. They shook hands with great cordiality; and then till her sister came down, she had to listen to all he had to say, of his own happiness, and of Jane's perfections; and in spite of his being a lover, Elizabeth really believed all his expectations of felicity, to be rationally founded, because they had for basis the excellent understanding, and super-excellent disposition of Jane, and a general similarity of feeling and taste between her and himself.

It was an evening of no common delight to them all; the satisfaction of Miss Bennet's mind gave a glow of such sweet animation to her face, as made her look handsomer than ever. Kitty simpered and smiled, and hoped her turn was coming soon. Mrs. Bennet could not give her consent, or speak her approbation in terms warm enough to satisfy her feelings, though she talked to Bingley of nothing else, for half an hour; and when Mr. Bennet joined them at supper, his voice and manner plainly shewed how really happy he was.

Not a word, however, passed his lips in allusion to it, till their visitor took his leave for the night; but as soon as he was gone, he turned to his daughter and said,

"Jane, I congratulate you. You will be a very happy woman."

Jane went to him instantly, kissed him, and thanked him for his goodness.

"You are a good girl;" he replied, "and I have great pleasure in thinking you will be so happily settled. I have not a doubt of your doing very well together. Your tempers are by no means unlike. You are each of you so complying, that nothing will ever be resolved on; so easy, that every servant will cheat you; and so generous, that you will always exceed your income."

"I hope not so. Imprudence or thoughtlessness in money matters, would be unpardonable in *me*."

"Exceed their income! My dear Mr. Bennet," cried his wife, "what are you talking of? Why, he has four or five thousand a-year, and very likely more." Then addressing her daughter, "Oh! my dear, dear Jane, I am so happy! I am sure I shan't get a wink of sleep all night. I knew how it would be. I always said it must be so, at last. I was sure you could not be so beautiful for nothing! I remember, as soon as ever I saw him, when he first came into Hertfordshire last year, I thought how likely it was that you should come together. Oh! he is the handsomest young man that ever was seen!"

Wickham, Lydia, were all forgotten. Jane was beyond competition her favourite child. At that moment, she cared for no other. Her younger sisters soon began to make interest with her for objects of happiness which she might in future be able to dispense.

Mary petitioned for the use of the library at Netherfield; and Kitty begged very hard for a few balls there every winter.

Bingley, from this time, was of course a daily visitor at Longbourn; coming frequently before breakfast, and always remaining till after supper; unless when some barbarous neighbour, who could not be enough detested, had given him an invitation to dinner, which he thought himself obliged to accept.

Elizabeth had now but little time for conversation with her sister; for while he was present, Jane had no attention to bestow on any one else; but she found herself considerably useful to both of them, in those hours of separation that must sometimes occur. In the absence of Jane, he always attached himself to Elizabeth, for the pleasure of talking of her; and when Bingley was gone, Jane constantly sought the same means of relief.

"He has made me so happy," said she, one evening, "by telling me, that he was totally ignorant of my being in town last spring! I had not believed it possible."

"I suspected as much," replied Elizabeth. "But how did he account for it?"

"It must have been his sister's doing.[1] They were certainly no friends to his acquaintance with me, which I cannot wonder at, since he might have chosen so much more advantageously in many respects. But when they see, as I trust they will, that their brother is happy with me, they will learn to be contented, and we shall be on good terms again; though we can never be what we once were to each other."

"That is the most unforgiving speech," said Elizabeth, "that I ever heard you utter. Good girl! It would vex me, indeed, to see you again the dupe of Miss Bingley's pretended regard."

"Would you believe it, Lizzy, that when he went to town last November, he really loved me, and nothing but a persuasion of *my* being indifferent, would have prevented his coming down again!"

"He made a little mistake to be sure; but it is to the credit of his modesty."

This naturally introduced a panegyric from Jane on his diffidence, and the little value he put on his own good qualities.

Elizabeth was pleased to find, that he had not betrayed the interference of his friend, for, though Jane had the most generous and forgiving heart in the world, she knew it was a circumstance which must prejudice her against him.

"I am certainly the most fortunate creature that ever exist-

---

1   This probably should be *sisters'*: Jane goes on to talk of them as "they," and see note on the text for volume I, chapter xviii. But it is also possible that Jane attributes agency specifically to Miss Bingley, even if motivated by feelings she shares with Mrs. Hurst.

ed!" cried Jane. "Oh! Lizzy, why am I thus singled from my family, and blessed above them all! If I could but see *you* as happy! If there *were* but such another man for you!"

"If you were to give me forty such men, I never could be so happy as you. Till I have your disposition, your goodness, I never can have your happiness. No, no, let me shift for myself; and, perhaps, if I have very good luck, I may meet with another Mr. Collins in time."

The situation of affairs in the Longbourn family could not be long a secret. Mrs. Bennet was privileged to whisper it to Mrs. Philips, and *she* ventured, without any permission, to do the same by all her neighbours in Meryton.

The Bennets were speedily pronounced to be the luckiest family in the world, though only a few weeks before, when Lydia had first run away, they had been generally proved to be marked out for misfortune.

CHAPTER XIV.

ONE morning, about a week after Bingley's engagement with Jane had been formed, as he and the females of the family were sitting together in the dining room, their attention was suddenly drawn to the window, by the sound of a carriage; and they perceived a chaise and four driving up the lawn. It was too early in the morning for visitors, and besides, the equipage did not answer to that of any of their neighbours. The horses were post;[1] and neither the carriage, nor the livery of the servant who preceded it, were familiar to them. As it was certain, however, that somebody was coming, Bingley instantly prevailed on Miss Bennet to avoid the confinement of such an intrusion, and walk away with him into the shrubbery. They both set off, and the conjectures of the remaining three continued, though with little satisfaction, till the door was thrown open, and their visitor entered. It was Lady Catherine de Bourgh.

---

1   That is, hired at post-houses to take the carriage on by stages: a sign that it has travelled a long way.

They were of course all intending to be surprised; but their astonishment was beyond their expectation; and on the part of Mrs. Bennet and Kitty, though she was perfectly unknown to them, even inferior to what Elizabeth felt.

She entered the room with an air more than usually ungracious, made no other reply to Elizabeth's salutation, than a slight inclination of the head, and sat down without saying a word. Elizabeth had mentioned her name to her mother, on her ladyship's entrance, though no request of introduction had been made.

Mrs. Bennet all amazement, though flattered by having a guest of such high importance, received her with the utmost politeness. After sitting for a moment in silence, she said very stiffly to Elizabeth,

"I hope you are well, Miss Bennet. That lady I suppose is your mother."

Elizabeth replied very concisely that she was.

"And *that* I suppose is one of your sisters."

"Yes, madam," said Mrs. Bennet, delighted to speak to a lady Catherine. "She is my youngest girl but one. My youngest of all, is lately married, and my eldest is some-where about the grounds, walking with a young man, who I believe will soon become a part of the family."

"You have a very small park here," returned Lady Catherine after a short silence.

"It is nothing in comparison of Rosings, my lady, I dare say; but I assure you it is much larger than Sir William Lucas's."

"This must be a most inconvenient sitting room for the evening, in summer; the windows are full west."

Mrs. Bennet assured her that they never sat there after dinner; and then added,

"May I take the liberty of asking your ladyship whether you left Mr. and Mrs. Collins well."

"Yes, very well. I saw them the night before last."

Elizabeth now expected that she would produce a letter for her from Charlotte, as it seemed the only probable motive for her calling. But no letter appeared, and she was completely puzzled.

Mrs. Bennet, with great civility, begged her ladyship to take some refreshment; but Lady Catherine very resolutely, and not very politely, declined eating any thing; and then rising up, said to Elizabeth,

"Miss Bennet, there seemed to be a prettyish kind of a little wilderness on one side of your lawn. I should be glad to take a turn in it, if you will favour me with your company."

"Go, my dear," cried her mother, "and shew her ladyship about the different walks. I think she will be pleased with the hermitage."

Elizabeth obeyed, and running into her own room for her parasol, attended her noble guest down stairs. As they passed through the hall, Lady Catherine opened the doors into the dining-parlour and drawingroom, and pronouncing them, after a short survey, to be decent looking rooms, walked on.

Her carriage remained at the door, and Elizabeth saw that her waiting-woman was in it. They proceeded in silence along the gravel walk that led to the copse; Elizabeth was determined to make no effort for conversation with a woman, who was now more than usually insolent and disagreeable.

"How could I ever think her like her nephew?" said she, as she looked in her face.

As soon as they entered the copse, Lady Catherine began in the following manner: —

"You can be at no loss, Miss Bennet, to understand the reason of my journey hither. Your own heart, your own conscience, must tell you why I come."

Elizabeth looked with unaffected astonishment.

"Indeed, you are mistaken, Madam. I have not been at all able to account for the honour of seeing you here."

"Miss Bennet," replied her ladyship, in an angry tone, "you ought to know, that I am not to be trifled with. But however insincere *you* may choose to be, you shall not find *me* so. My character has ever been celebrated for its sincerity and frankness, and in a cause of such moment as this, I shall certainly not depart from it. A report of a most alarming nature, reached me two days ago. I was told, that not only your sister was on the point of being most advantageously married, but that *you*, that Miss Elizabeth Bennet, would, in all likelihood, be soon afterwards united to my nephew, my own nephew, Mr. Darcy. Though I *know* it must be a scandalous falsehood; though I would not injure him so much as to suppose the truth of it possible, I instantly resolved on setting off for this place, that I might make my sentiments known to you."

"If you believed it impossible to be true," said Elizabeth, colouring with astonishment and disdain, "I wonder you took the trouble of coming so far. What could your ladyship propose by it?"

"At once to insist upon having such a report universally contradicted."

"Your coming to Longbourn, to see me and my family," said Elizabeth, coolly, "will be rather a confirmation of it; if, indeed, such a report is in existence."

"If! Do you then pretend to be ignorant of it? Has it not been industriously circulated by yourselves? Do you not know that such a report is spread abroad?"

"I never heard that it was."

"And can you likewise declare, that there is no *foundation* for it?"

"I do not pretend to possess equal frankness with your ladyship. *You* may ask questions, which *I* shall not choose to answer."

"This is not to be borne. Miss Bennet, I insist on being satisfied. Has he, has my nephew, made you an offer of marriage?"

"Your ladyship has declared it to be impossible."

"It ought to be so; it must be so, while he retains the use of his reason. But *your* arts and allurements may, in a moment of infatuation, have made him forget what he owes to himself and to all his family. You may have drawn him in."

"If I have, I shall be the last person to confess it."

"Miss Bennet, do you know who I am? I have not been accustomed to such language as this. I am almost the nearest relation he has in the world, and am entitled to know all his dearest concerns."

"But you are not entitled to know *mine;* nor will such behaviour as this, ever induce me to be explicit."

"Let me be rightly understood. This match, to which you

have the presumption to aspire, can never take place. No, never. Mr. Darcy is engaged to *my daughter*. Now what have you to say?"

"Only this; that if he is so, you can have no reason to suppose he will make an offer to me."

Lady Catherine hesitated for a moment, and then replied,

"The engagement between them is of a peculiar kind. From their infancy, they have been intended for each other. It was the favourite wish of *his* mother, as well as of her's. While in their cradles, we planned the union: and now, at the moment when the wishes of both sisters would be accomplished, in their marriage, to be prevented by a young woman of inferior birth, of no importance in the world, and wholly unallied to the family! Do you pay no regard to the wishes of his friends? To his tacit engagement with Miss De Bourgh? Are you lost to every feeling of propriety and delicacy? Have you not heard me say, that from his earliest hours he was destined for his cousin?"

"Yes, and I had heard it before. But what is that to me? If there is no other objection to my marrying your nephew, I shall certainly not be kept from it, by knowing that his mother and aunt wished him to marry Miss De Bourgh. You both did as much as you could, in planning the marriage. Its completion depended on others. If Mr. Darcy is neither by honour nor inclination confined to his cousin, why is not he to make another choice? And if I am that choice, why may not I accept him?"

"Because honour, decorum, prudence, nay, interest, forbid it. Yes, Miss Bennet, interest; for do not expect to be noticed by his family or friends, if you wilfully act against the inclinations of all. You will be censured, slighted, and despised, by every one connected with him. Your alliance will be a disgrace; your name will never even be mentioned by any of us."

"These are heavy misfortunes," replied Elizabeth. "But the wife of Mr. Darcy must have such extraordinary sources of happiness necessarily attached to her situation, that she could, upon the whole, have no cause to repine."

"Obstinate, headstrong girl! I am ashamed of you! Is this

your gratitude for my attentions to you last spring? Is nothing due to me on that score?

"Let us sit down. You are to understand, Miss Bennet, that I came here with the determined resolution of carrying my purpose; nor will I be dissuaded from it. I have not been used to submit to any person's whims. I have not been in the habit of brooking disappointment."

"*That* will make your ladyship's situation at present more pitiable; but it will have no effect on *me*."

"I will not be interrupted. Hear me in silence. My daughter and my nephew are formed for each other. They are descended on the maternal side, from the same noble line; and, on the father's, from respectable, honourable, and ancient, though untitled families. Their fortune on both sides is splendid. They are destined for each other by the voice of every member of their respective houses; and what is to divide them? The upstart pretensions of a young woman without family, connections, or fortune. Is this to be endured! But it must not, shall not be. If you were sensible of your own good, you would not wish to quit the sphere, in which you have been brought up."

"In marrying your nephew, I should not consider myself as quitting that sphere. He is a gentleman; I am a gentleman's daughter; so far we are equal."

"True. You *are* a gentleman's daughter. But who was your mother? Who are your uncles and aunts? Do not imagine me ignorant of their condition."

"Whatever my connections may be," said Elizabeth, "if your nephew does not object to them, they can be nothing to *you*."

"Tell me once for all, are you engaged to him?"

Though Elizabeth would not, for the mere purpose of obliging Lady Catherine, have answered this question; she could not but say, after a moment's deliberation,

"I am not."

Lady Catherine seemed pleased.

"And will you promise me, never to enter into such an engagement?"

"I will make no promise of the kind."

"Miss Bennet, I am shocked and astonished. I expected to find a more reasonable young woman. But do not deceive yourself into a belief that I will ever recede. I shall not go away, till you have given me the assurance I require."

"And I certainly *never* shall give it. I am not to be intimidated into anything so wholly unreasonable. Your ladyship wants Mr. Darcy to marry your daughter; but would my giving you the wished-for promise, make *their* marriage at all more probable? Supposing him to be attached to me, would *my* refusing to accept his hand, make him wish to bestow it on his cousin? Allow me to say, Lady Catherine, that the arguments with which you have supported this extraordinary application, have been as frivolous as the application was ill-judged. You have widely mistaken my character, if you think I can be worked on by such persuasions as these. How far your nephew might approve of your interference in *his* affairs, I cannot tell; but you have certainly no right to concern yourself in mine. I must beg, therefore, to be importuned no farther on the subject."

"Not so hasty, if you please. I have by no means done. To all the objections I have already urged, I have still another to add. I am no stranger to the particulars of your youngest sister's infamous elopement. I know it all; that the young man's marrying her, was a patched-up business, at the expence of your father and uncles. And is *such* a girl to be my nephew's sister? Is *her* husband, is the son of his late father's steward, to be his brother? Heaven and earth!—of what are you thinking? Are the shades of Pemberley to be thus polluted?"

"You can *now* have nothing farther to say," she resentfully answered. "You have insulted me, in every possible method. I must beg to return to the house."

And she rose as she spoke. Lady Catherine rose also, and they turned back. Her ladyship was highly incensed.

"You have no regard, then, for the honour and credit of my nephew! Unfeeling, selfish girl! Do you not consider that a connection with you, must disgrace him in the eyes of everybody?"

"Lady Catherine, I have nothing farther to say. You know my sentiments."

"You are then resolved to have him?"

"I have said no such thing. I am only resolved to act in that manner, which will, in my own opinion, constitute my happiness, without reference to *you*, or to any person so wholly unconnected with me."

"It is well. You refuse, then, to oblige me. You refuse to obey the claims of duty, honour, and gratitude. You are determined to ruin him in the opinion of all his friends, and make him the contempt of the world."

"Neither duty, nor honour, nor gratitude," replied Elizabeth, "have any possible claim on me, in the present instance. No principle of either, would be violated by my marriage with Mr. Darcy. And with regard to the resentment of his family, or the indignation of the world, if the former *were* excited by his marrying me, it would not give me one moment's concern — and the world in general would have too much sense to join in the scorn."

"And this is your real opinion! This is your final resolve! Very well. I shall now know how to act. Do not imagine, Miss Bennet, that your ambition will ever be gratified. I came to try you. I hoped to find you reasonable; but depend upon it I will carry my point."

In this manner Lady Catherine talked on, till they were at the door of the carriage, when turning hastily round, she added,

"I take no leave of you, Miss Bennet. I send no compliments to your mother. You deserve no such attention. I am most seriously displeased."

Elizabeth made no answer; and without attempting to persuade her ladyship to return into the house, walked quietly into it herself. She heard the carriage drive away as she proceeded up stairs. Her mother impatiently met her at the door of the dressing-room, to ask why Lady Catherine would not come in again and rest herself.

"She did not choose it," said her daughter, "she would go."

"She is a very fine-looking woman! and her calling here was prodigiously civil! for she only came, I suppose, to tell us the Collinses were well. She is on her road somewhere, I dare say, and so passing through Meryton, thought she might as well call on you. I suppose she had nothing particular to say to you, Lizzy?"

Elizabeth was forced to give into a little falsehood here; for to acknowledge the substance of their conversation was impossible.

CHAPTER XV.

THE discomposure of spirits, which this extraordinary visit threw Elizabeth into, could not be easily overcome; nor could she for many hours, learn to think of it less than incessantly. Lady Catherine it appeared, had actually taken the trouble of this journey from Rosings, for the sole purpose of breaking off her supposed engagement with Mr. Darcy. It was a rational scheme to be sure! but from what the report of their engagement could originate, Elizabeth was at a loss to imagine; till she recollected that *his* being the intimate friend of Bingley, and *her* being the sister of Jane, was enough, at a time when the expectation of one wedding, made every body eager for another, to supply the idea. She had not herself forgotten to feel that the marriage of her sister must bring them more frequently together. And her neighbours at Lucas lodge, therefore, (for through their communication with the Collinses, the report she concluded had reached Lady Catherine) had only set *that* down, as almost certain and immediate, which *she* had looked forward to as possible, at some future time.

In revolving Lady Catherine's expressions, however, she could not help feeling some uneasiness as to the possible consequence of her persisting in this interference. From what she had said of her resolution to prevent their marriage, it occurred to Elizabeth that she must meditate an application to her nephew; and how *he* might take a similar representation of the evils attached to a connection with her, she dared not pronounce. She knew not the exact degree of his affection for his aunt, or his dependence on her judgment, but it was natural to suppose that he thought much higher of her ladyship than *she* could do; and it was certain, that in enumerating the miseries of a marriage with *one*, whose immediate connections were so unequal to his own, his aunt would address him on his weakest side. With his notions of dignity, he would probably feel that the arguments, which to Elizabeth had appeared weak and ridiculous, contained much good sense and solid reasoning.

If he had been wavering before, as to what he should do, which had often seemed likely, the advice and intreaty of so near a relation might settle every doubt, and determine him at once to be as happy, as dignity unblemished could make him. In that case he would return no more. Lady Catherine might see him in her way through town; and his engagement to Bingley of coming again to Netherfield must give way.

"If, therefore, an excuse for not keeping his promise, should come to his friend within a few days," she added, "I shall know how to understand it. I shall then give over every expectation, every wish of his constancy. If he is satisfied with only regretting me, when he might have obtained my affections and hand, I shall soon cease to regret him at all."

————

The surprise of the rest of the family, on hearing who their visitor had been, was very great; but they obligingly satisfied it, with the same kind of supposition, which had appeased Mrs. Bennet's curiosity; and Elizabeth was spared from much teazing on the subject.

The next morning, as she was going down stairs, she was met by her father, who came out of his library with a letter in his hand.

"Lizzy," said he, "I was going to look for you; come into my room."

She followed him thither; and her curiosity to know what he had to tell her, was heightened by the supposition of its being in some manner connected with the letter he held. It suddenly struck her that it might be from Lady Catherine; and she anticipated with dismay all the consequent explanations.

She followed her father to the fire place, and they both sat down. He then said,

"I have received a letter this morning that has astonished me exceedingly. As it principally concerns yourself, you ought to know its contents. I did not know before, that I had *two* daughters on the brink of matrimony. Let me congratulate you, on a very important conquest."

The colour now rushed into Elizabeth's cheeks in the instantaneous conviction of its being a letter from the nephew, instead of the aunt; and she was undetermined whether most to be pleased that he explained himself at all, or offended that his letter was not rather addressed to herself; when her father continued,

"You look conscious. Young ladies have great penetration in such matters as these; but I think I may defy even *your* sagacity, to discover the name of your admirer. This letter is from Mr. Collins."

"From Mr. Collins! and what can *he* have to say?"

"Something very much to the purpose of course. He begins with congratulations on the approaching nuptials of my eldest daughter, of which it seems he has been told, by some of the good-natured, gossiping Lucases. I shall not sport with your impatience, by reading what he says on that point. What relates to yourself, is as follows." "Having thus offered you the sincere congratulations of Mrs. Collins and myself on this happy event, let me now add a short hint on the subject of another; of which we have been advertised by the same authority. Your daughter Elizabeth, it is presumed, will not long bear the name of Bennet, after her elder sister has resigned it, and the chosen partner of her fate, may be reasonably looked up to, as one of the most illustrious personages in this land."

"Can you possibly guess, Lizzy, who is meant by this?" "This young gentleman is blessed in a peculiar way, with every thing the heart of mortal can most desire,—splendid property, noble kindred, and extensive patronage. Yet in spite of all these temptations, let me warn my cousin Elizabeth, and yourself, of what evils you may incur, by a precipitate closure with this gentleman's proposals, which, of course, you will be inclined to take immediate advantage of."

"Have you any idea, Lizzy, who this gentleman is? But now it comes out."

"My motive for cautioning you is as follows. We have reason to imagine that his aunt, lady Catherine de Bourgh, does not look on the match with a friendly eye."

"*Mr. Darcy*, you see, is the man! Now, Lizzy, I think I *have* surprised you. Could he, or the Lucases, have pitched on any man, within the circle of our acquaintance, whose name would have given the lie more effectually to what they related? Mr. Darcy, who never looks at any woman but to see a blemish, and who probably never looked at *you* in his life! It is admirable!"

Elizabeth tried to join in her father's pleasantry, but could only force one most reluctant smile. Never had his wit been directed in a manner so little agreeable to her.

"Are you not diverted?"

"Oh! yes. Pray read on."

"After mentioning the likelihood of this marriage to her ladyship last night, she immediately, with her usual condescension, expressed what she felt on the occasion; when it become apparent, that on the score of some family objections on the part of my cousin, she would never give her consent to what she termed so disgraceful a match. I thought it my duty to give the speediest intelligence of this to my cousin, that she and her noble admirer may be aware of what they are about, and not run hastily into a marriage which has not been properly sanctioned." "Mr. Collins moreover adds," "I am truly rejoiced that my cousin Lydia's sad business has been so well hushed up, and am only concerned that their living together before the marriage took place, should be so generally known. I must not, however, neglect the duties of my station, or refrain from declaring my amazement, at hearing that you received the young couple into your house as soon as they were married. It was an encouragement of vice; and had I been the rector of Longbourn, I should very strenuously have opposed it. You ought certainly to forgive them as a christian, but never to admit them in your sight, or allow their names to be mentioned in your hearing."[1] "*That* is his notion of christian forgiveness! The rest of his letter is only about his dear Charlotte's

---

[1] Mr. Collins adopts the stance taken by Hannah More in the third extract from chapter 1 of the *Strictures* (Appendix D.2).

situation, and his expectation of a young olive-branch. But, Lizzy, you look as if you did not enjoy it. You are not going to be *Missish*, I hope, and pretend to be affronted at an idle report. For what do we live, but to make sport for our neighbours, and laugh at them in our turn?"

"Oh!" cried Elizabeth, "I am excessively diverted. But it is so strange!"

"Yes—*that* is what makes it amusing. Had they fixed on any other man it would have been nothing; but *his* perfect indifference, and *your* pointed dislike, make it so delightfully absurd! Much as I abominate writing, I would not give up Mr. Collins's correspondence for any consideration. Nay, when I read a letter of his, I cannot help giving him the preference even over Wickham, much as I value the impudence and hypocrisy of my son-in-law. And pray, Lizzy, what said Lady Catherine about this report? Did she call to refuse her consent?"

To this question his daughter replied only with a laugh; and as it had been asked without the least suspicion, she was not distressed by his repeating it. Elizabeth had never been more at a loss to make her feelings appear what they were not. It was necessary to laugh, when she would rather have cried. Her father had most cruelly mortified her, by what he said of Mr. Darcy's indifference, and she could do nothing but wonder at such a want of penetration, or fear that perhaps, instead of his seeing too *little*, she might have fancied too *much*.

CHAPTER XVI.

INSTEAD of receiving any such letter of excuse from his friend, as Elizabeth half expected Mr. Bingley to do, he was able to bring Darcy with him to Longbourn before many days had passed after Lady Catherine's visit. The gentlemen arrived early; and, before Mrs. Bennet had time to tell him of their having seen his aunt, of which her daughter sat in momentary dread, Bingley, who wanted to be alone with Jane, proposed their all walking out. It was agreed to. Mrs. Bennet was not in the habit of walking, Mary could never spare time, but the

remaining five set off together. Bingley and Jane, however, soon allowed the others to outstrip them. They lagged behind, while Elizabeth, Kitty, and Darcy, were to entertain each other. Very little was said by either; Kitty was too much afraid of him to talk; Elizabeth was secretly forming a desperate resolution; and perhaps he might be doing the same.

They walked towards the Lucases, because Kitty wished to call upon Maria; and as Elizabeth saw no occasion for making it a general concern, when Kitty left them, she went boldly on with him alone. Now was the moment for her resolution to be executed, and, while her courage was high, she immediately said,

"Mr. Darcy, I am a very selfish creature; and, for the sake of giving relief to my own feelings, care not how much I may be wounding your's. I can no longer help thanking you for your unexampled kindness to my poor sister. Ever since I have known it, I have been most anxious to acknowledge to you how gratefully I feel it. Were it known to the rest of my family, I should not have merely my own gratitude to express."

"I am sorry, exceedingly sorry," replied Darcy, in a tone of surprise and emotion, "that you have ever been informed of what may, in a mistaken light, have given you uneasiness. I did not think Mrs. Gardiner was so little to be trusted."

"You must not blame my aunt. Lydia's thoughtlessness first betrayed to me that you had been concerned in the matter; and, of course, I could not rest till I knew the particulars. Let me thank you again and again, in the name of all my family, for that generous compassion which induced you to take so much trouble, and bear so many mortifications, for the sake of discovering them."

"If you *will* thank me," he replied, "let it be for yourself alone. That the wish of giving happiness to you, might add force to the other inducements which led me on, I shall not attempt to deny. But your *family* owe me nothing. Much as I respect them, I believe, I thought only of *you*."

Elizabeth was too much embarrassed to say a word. After a short pause, her companion added, "You are too generous to trifle with me. If your feelings are still what they were last

April, tell me so at once. *My* affections and wishes are unchanged, but one word from you will silence me on this subject for ever."

Elizabeth feeling all the more than common awkwardness and anxiety of his situation, now forced herself to speak; and immediately, though not very fluently, gave him to understand, that her sentiments had undergone so material a change, since the period to which he alluded, as to make her receive with gratitude and pleasure, his present assurances. The happiness which this reply produced, was such as he had probably never felt before; and he expressed himself on the occasion as sensibly and as warmly as a man violently in love can be supposed to do. Had Elizabeth been able to encounter his eye, she might have seen how well the expression of heartfelt delight, diffused over his face, became him; but, though she could not look, she could listen, and he told her of feelings, which, in proving of what importance she was to him, made his affection every moment more valuable.

They walked on, without knowing in what direction. There was too much to be thought, and felt, and said, for attention to any other objects. She soon learnt that they were indebted for their present good understanding to the efforts of his aunt, who *did* call on him in her return through London, and there relate her journey to Longbourn, its motive, and the substance of her conversation with Elizabeth; dwelling emphatically on every expression of the latter, which, in her ladyship's apprehension, peculiarly denoted her perverseness and assurance, in the belief that such a relation must assist her endeavours to obtain that promise from her nephew, which *she* had refused to give. But, unluckily for her ladyship, its effect had been exactly contrariwise.

"It taught me to hope," said he, "as I had scarcely ever allowed myself to hope before. I knew enough of your disposition to be certain, that, had you been absolutely, irrevocably decided against me, you would have acknowledged it to Lady Catherine, frankly and openly."

Elizabeth coloured and laughed as she replied, "Yes, you

know enough of my *frankness* to believe me capable of *that.* After abusing you so abominably to your face, I could have no scruple in abusing you to all your relations."

"What did you say of me, that I did not deserve? For, though your accusations were ill-founded, formed on mistaken premises, my behaviour to you at the time, had merited the severest reproof. It was unpardonable. I cannot think of it without abhorrence."

"We will not quarrel for the greater share of blame annexed to that evening," said Elizabeth. "The conduct of neither, if strictly examined, will be irreproachable; but since then, we have both, I hope, improved in civility."

"I cannot be so easily reconciled to myself. The recollection of what I then said, of my conduct, my manners, my expressions during the whole of it, is now, and has been many months, inexpressibly painful to me. Your reproof, so well applied, I shall never forget: 'had you behaved in a more gentleman-like manner.' Those were your words. You know not, you can scarcely conceive, how they have tortured me;— though it was some time, I confess, before I was reasonable enough to allow their justice."

"I was certainly very far from expecting them to make so strong an impression. I had not the smallest idea of their being ever felt in such a way."

"I can easily believe it. You thought me then devoid of every proper feeling, I am sure you did. The turn of your countenance I shall never forget, as you said that I could not have addressed you in any possible way, that would induce you to accept me."

"Oh! do not repeat what I then said. These recollections will not do at all. I assure you, that I have long been most heartily ashamed of it."

Darcy mentioned his letter. "Did it," said he, "did it *soon* make you think better of me? Did you, on reading it, give any credit to its contents?"

She explained what its effect on her had been, and how gradually all her former prejudices had been removed.

"I knew," said he, "that what I wrote must give you pain, but it was necessary. I hope you have destroyed the letter. There was one part especially, the opening of it, which I should dread your having the power of reading again. I can remember some expressions which might justly make you hate me."

"The letter shall certainly be burnt, if you believe it essential to the preservation of my regard; but, though we have both reason to think my opinions not entirely unalterable, they are not, I hope, quite so easily changed as that implies."

"When I wrote that letter," replied Darcy, "I believed myself perfectly calm and cool, but I am since convinced that it was written in a dreadful bitterness of spirit."

"The letter, perhaps, began in bitterness, but it did not end so. The adieu is charity itself. But think no more of the letter. The feelings of the person who wrote, and the person who received it, are now so widely different from what they were then, that every unpleasant circumstance attending it, ought to be forgotten. You must learn some of my philosophy. Think only of the past as its remembrance gives you pleasure."

"I cannot give you credit for any philosophy of the kind. *Your* retrospections must be so totally void of reproach, that the contentment arising from them, is not of philosophy, but what is much better, of ignorance. But with *me*, it is not so. Painful recollections will intrude, which cannot, which ought not to be repelled. I have been a selfish being all my life, in practice, though not in principle. As a child I was taught what was *right*, but I was not taught to correct my temper. I was given good principles, but left to follow them in pride and conceit. Unfortunately an only son, (for many years an only *child*) I was spoilt by my parents, who though good themselves (my father particularly, all that was benevolent and amiable,) allowed, encouraged, almost taught me to be selfish and overbearing, to care for none beyond my own family circle, to think meanly of all the rest of the world, to *wish* at least to think meanly of their sense and worth compared with my own. Such I was, from eight to eight and twenty; and such I might still have been but for you, dearest, loveliest Elizabeth! What do I not owe you! You taught me a lesson, hard indeed at first, but most advantageous. By you, I was properly humbled. I came to you without a doubt of my reception. You shewed me how insufficient were all my pretensions to please a woman worthy of being pleased."

"Had you then persuaded yourself that I should?"

"Indeed I had. What will you think of my vanity? I believed you to be wishing, expecting my addresses."

"My manners must have been in fault, but not intentionally, I assure you. I never meant to deceive you, but my spirits might often lead me wrong. How you must have hated me after *that* evening!"

"Hate you! I was angry perhaps at first, but my anger soon began to take a proper direction."

"I am almost afraid of asking what you thought of me; when we met at Pemberley. You blamed me for coming?"

"No indeed; I felt nothing but surprise."

"Your surprise could not be greater than *mine* in being noticed by you. My conscience told me that I deserved no extraordinary politeness, and I confess that I did not expect to receive *more* than my due."

"My object *then*," replied Darcy, "was to shew you, by every civility in my power, that I was not so mean as to resent the past; and I hoped to obtain your forgiveness, to lessen your ill opinion, by letting you see that your reproofs had been attended to. How soon any other wishes introduced themselves I can hardly tell, but I believe in about half an hour after I had seen you."

He then told her of Georgiana's delight in her acquaintance, and of her disappointment at its sudden interruption; which naturally leading to the cause of that interruption, she soon learnt that his resolution of following her from Derbyshire in quest of her sister, had been formed before he quitted the inn, and that his gravity and thoughtfulness there, had arisen from no other struggles than what such a purpose must comprehend.

She expressed her gratitude again, but it was too painful a subject to each, to be dwelt on farther.

After walking several miles in a leisurely manner, and too busy to know any thing about it, they found at last, on examining their watches, that it was time to be at home.

"What could become of Mr. Bingley and Jane!" was a wonder which introduced the discussion of *their* affairs. Darcy was delighted with their engagement; his friend had given him the earliest information of it.

"I must ask whether you were surprised?" said Elizabeth.

"Not at all. When I went away, I felt that it would soon happen."

"That is to say, you had given your permission. I guessed as much." And though he exclaimed at the term, she found that it had been pretty much the case.

"On the evening before my going to London," said he, "I made a confession to him, which I believe I ought to have made long ago. I told him of all that had occurred to make my former interference in his affairs, absurd and impertinent. His surprise was great. He had never had the slightest suspicion. I told him, moreover, that I believed myself mistaken in supposing, as I had done, that your sister was indifferent to him; and as I could easily perceive that his attachment to her was unabated, I felt no doubt of their happiness together."

Elizabeth could not help smiling at his easy manner of directing his friend.

"Did you speak from your own observation," said she, "when you told him that my sister loved him, or merely from my information last spring?"

"From the former. I had narrowly observed her during the two visits which I had lately made here; and I was convinced of her affection."

"And your assurance of it, I suppose, carried immediate conviction to him."

"It did. Bingley is most unaffectedly modest. His diffidence had prevented his depending on his own judgment in so anxious a case, but his reliance on mine, made every thing easy. I was obliged to confess one thing, which for a time, and not unjustly, offended him. I could not allow myself to conceal that your sister had been in town three months last winter, that I had known it, and purposely kept it from him. He was angry.

But his anger, I am persuaded, lasted no longer than he remained in any doubt of your sister's sentiments. He has heartily forgiven me now."

Elizabeth longed to observe that Mr. Bingley had been a most delightful friend; so easily guided that his worth was invaluable; but she checked herself. She remembered that he had yet to learn to be laught at, and it was rather too early to begin. In anticipating the happiness of Bingley, which of course was to be inferior only to his own, he continued the conversation till they reached the house. In the hall they parted.

CHAPTER XVII.

"My dear Lizzy, where can you have been walking to?" was a question which Elizabeth received from Jane as soon as she entered the room, and from all the others when they sat down to table. She had only to say in reply, that they had wandered about, till she was beyond her own knowledge. She coloured as she spoke; but neither that, nor any thing else, awakened a suspicion of the truth.

The evening passed quietly, unmarked by any thing extraordinary. The acknowledged lovers talked and laughed, the unacknowledged were silent. Darcy was not of a disposition in which happiness overflows in mirth; and Elizabeth, agitated and confused, rather *knew* that she was happy, than *felt* herself to be so; for, besides the immediate embarrassment, there were other evils before her. She anticipated what would be felt in the family when her situation became known; she was aware that no one liked him but Jane; and even feared that with the others it was a *dislike* which not all his fortune and consequence might do away.

At night she opened her heart to Jane. Though suspicion was very far from Miss Bennet's general habits, she was absolutely incredulous here.

"You are joking, Lizzy. This cannot be! — engaged to Mr. Darcy! No, no, you shall not deceive me. I know it to be impossible."

"This is a wretched beginning indeed! My sole dependence

was on you; and I am sure nobody else will believe me, if you do not. Yet, indeed, I am in earnest. I speak nothing but the truth. He still loves me, and we are engaged."

Jane looked at her doubtingly. "Oh, Lizzy! it cannot be. I know how much you dislike him."

"You know nothing of the matter. *That* is all to be forgot. Perhaps I did not always love him so well as I do now. But in such cases as these, a good memory is unpardonable. This is the last time I shall ever remember it myself."

Miss Bennet still looked all amazement. Elizabeth again, and more seriously assured her of its truth.

"Good Heaven! can it be really so! Yet now I must believe you," cried Jane. "My dear, dear Lizzy, I would—I do congratulate you—but are you certain? forgive the question — are you quite certain that you can be happy with him?"

"There can be no doubt of that. It is settled between us already, that we are to be the happiest couple in the world. But are you pleased, Jane? Shall you like to have such a brother?"

"Very, very much. Nothing could give either Bingley or myself more delight. But we considered it, we talked of it as impossible. And do you really love him quite well enough? Oh, Lizzy! do any thing rather than marry without affection. Are you quite sure that you feel what you ought to do?"

"Oh, yes! You will only think I feel *more* than I ought to do, when I tell you all."

"What do you mean?"

"Why, I must confess, that I love him better than I do Bingley. I am afraid you will be angry."

"My dearest sister, now *be* serious. I want to talk very seriously. Let me know every thing that I am to know, without delay. Will you tell me how long you have loved him?"

"It has been coming on so gradually, that I hardly know when it began. But I believe I must date it from my first seeing his beautiful grounds at Pemberley."

Another intreaty that she would be serious, however, produced the desired effect; and she soon satisfied Jane by her solemn assurances of attachment. When convinced on that article, Miss Bennet had nothing farther to wish.

"Now I am quite happy," said she, "for you will be as happy as myself. I always had a value for him. Were it for nothing but his love of you, I must always have esteemed him; but now, as Bingley's friend and your husband, there can be only Bingley and yourself more dear to me. But Lizzy, you have been very sly, very reserved with me. How little did you tell me of what passed at Pemberley and Lambton! I owe all that I know of it, to another, not to you."

Elizabeth told her the motives of her secrecy. She had been unwilling to mention Bingley; and the unsettled state of her own feelings had made her equally avoid the name of his friend. But now she would no longer conceal from her, his share in Lydia's marriage. All was acknowledged, and half the night spent in conversation.

––––––––

"Good gracious!" cried Mrs. Bennet, as she stood at a window the next morning, "if that disagreeable Mr. Darcy is not coming here again with our dear Bingley! What can he mean by being so tiresome as to be always coming here? I had no notion but he would go a shooting, or something or other, and not disturb us with his company. What shall we do with him? Lizzy, you must walk out with him again, that he may not be in Bingley's way."

Elizabeth could hardly help laughing at so convenient a proposal; yet was really vexed that her mother should be always giving him such an epithet.

As soon as they entered, Bingley looked at her so expressively, and shook hands with such warmth, as left no doubt of his good information; and he soon afterwards said aloud, "Mr. Bennet, have you no more lanes hereabouts in which Lizzy may lose her way again to-day."[1]

"I advise Mr. Darcy, and Lizzy, and Kitty," said Mrs. Bennet, "to walk to Oakham Mount this morning. It is a nice long walk, and Mr. Darcy has never seen the view."

---

1   As Chapman notes (p.397), this question should almost certainly be addressed to *Mrs.* Bennet: Bingley knows how much she wants to get Mr. Darcy out of the way, and there is no sign of her husband in this scene.

"It may do very well for the others," replied Mr. Bingley; "but I am sure it will be too much for Kitty. Wont it, Kitty?"

Kitty owned that she had rather stay at home. Darcy professed a great curiosity to see the view from the Mount, and Elizabeth silently consented. As she went up stairs to get ready, Mrs. Bennet followed her, saying,

"I am quite sorry, Lizzy, that you should be forced to have that disagreeable man all to yourself. But I hope you will not mind it: it is all for Jane's sake, you know; and there is no occasion for talking to him, except just now and then. So, do not put yourself to inconvenience."

During their walk, it was resolved that Mr. Bennet's consent should be asked in the course of the evening. Elizabeth reserved to herself the application for her mother's. She could not determine how her mother would take it; sometimes doubting whether all his wealth and grandeur would be enough to overcome her abhorrence of the man. But whether she were violently set against the match, or violently delighted with it, it was certain that her manner would be equally ill adapted to do credit to her sense; and she could no more bear that Mr. Darcy should hear the first raptures of her joy, than the first vehemence of her disapprobation.

In the evening, soon after Mr. Bennet withdrew to the library, she saw Mr. Darcy rise also and follow him, and her agitation on seeing it was extreme. She did not fear her father's opposition, but he was going to be made unhappy, and that it should be through her means, that *she*, his favourite child, should be distressing him by her choice, should be filling him with fears and regrets in disposing of her, was a wretched reflection, and she sat in misery till Mr. Darcy appeared again, when, looking at him, she was a little relieved by his smile. In a few minutes he approached the table where she was sitting with Kitty; and, while pretending to admire her work, said in a whisper, "Go to your father, he wants you in the library." She was gone directly.

Her father was walking about the room, looking grave and anxious. "Lizzy," said he, "what are you doing? Are you out of your senses, to be accepting this man? Have not you always hated him?"

How earnestly did she then wish that her former opinions had been more reasonable, her expressions more moderate! It would have spared her from explanations and professions which it was exceedingly awkward to give; but they were now necessary, and she assured him with some confusion, of her attachment to Mr. Darcy.

"Or in other words, you are determined to have him. He is rich, to be sure, and you may have more fine clothes and fine carriages than Jane. But will they make you happy?"

"Have you any other objection," said Elizabeth, "than your belief of my indifference?"

"None at all. We all know him to be a proud, unpleasant sort of man; but this would be nothing if you really liked him."

"I do, I do like him," she replied, with tears in her eyes, "I love him. Indeed he has no improper pride. He is perfectly amiable. You do not know what he really is; then pray do not pain me by speaking of him in such terms."

"Lizzy," said her father, "I have given him my consent. He is the kind of man, indeed, to whom I should never dare refuse any thing, which he condescended to ask. I now give it to *you*, if you are resolved on having him. But let me advise you to think better of it. I know your disposition, Lizzy. I know that you could be neither happy nor respectable, unless you truly esteemed your husband; unless you looked up to him as a superior. Your lively talents would place you in the greatest danger in an unequal marriage. You could scarcely escape discredit and misery. My child, let me not have the grief of seeing *you* unable to respect your partner in life. You know not what you are about."

Elizabeth, still more affected, was earnest and solemn in her reply; and at length, by repeated assurances that Mr. Darcy was really the object of her choice, by explaining the gradual change which her estimation of him had undergone, relating her absolute certainty that his affection was not the work of a day, but had stood the test of many months suspense, and enumerating with energy all his good qualities, she did conquer her father's incredulity, and reconcile him to the match.

"Well, my dear," said he, when she ceased speaking, "I have no more to say. If this be the case, he deserves you. I could not have parted with you, my Lizzy, to any one less worthy."

To complete the favourable impression, she then told him what Mr. Darcy had voluntarily done for Lydia. He heard her with astonishment.

"This is an evening of wonders, indeed! And so, Darcy did every thing; made up the match, gave the money, paid the fellow's debts, and got him his commission! So much the better. It will save me a world of trouble and economy. Had it been your uncle's doing, I must and *would* have paid him; but these violent young lovers carry every thing their own way. I shall offer to pay him to-morrow; he will rant and storm about his love for you, and there will be an end of the matter."

He then recollected her embarrassment a few days before, on his reading Mr. Collins's letter; and after laughing at her some time, allowed her at last to go — saying, as she quitted the room, "If any young men come for Mary or Kitty, send them in, for I am quite at leisure."

Elizabeth's mind was now relieved from a very heavy weight; and, after half an hour's quiet reflection in her own room, she was able to join the others with tolerable composure. Every thing was too recent for gaiety, but the evening passed tranquilly away; there was no longer any thing material to be dreaded, and the comfort of ease and familiarity would come in time.

When her mother went up to her dressing-room at night, she followed her, and made the important communication. Its effect was most extraordinary; for on first hearing it, Mrs. Bennet sat quite still, and unable to utter a syllable. Nor was it under many, many minutes, that she could comprehend what she heard; though not in general backward to credit what was for the advantage of her family, or that came in the shape of a lover to any of them. She began at length to recover, to fidget about in her chair, get up, sit down again, wonder, and bless herself.

"Good gracious! Lord bless me! only think! dear me! Mr. Darcy! Who would have thought it! And is it really true? Oh!

my sweetest Lizzy! how rich and how great you will be! What pin-money,[1] what jewels, what carriages you will have! Jane's is nothing to it—nothing at all. I am so pleased—so happy. Such a charming man!—so handsome! so tall!—Oh, my dear Lizzy! pray apologise for my having disliked him so much before. I hope he will overlook it. Dear, dear Lizzy. A house in town! Every thing that is charming! Three daughters married! Ten thousand a year! Oh, Lord! What will become of me. I shall go distracted."

This was enough to prove that her approbation need not be doubted: and Elizabeth, rejoicing that such an effusion was heard only by herself, soon went away. But before she had been three minutes in her own room, her mother followed her.

"My dearest child," she cried, "I can think of nothing else! Ten thousand a year, and very likely more! 'Tis as good as a Lord! And a special licence. You must and shall be married by a special licence. But my dearest love, tell me what dish Mr. Darcy is particularly fond of, that I may have it to-morrow."

This was a sad omen of what her mother's behaviour to the gentleman himself might be; and Elizabeth found, that though in the certain possession of his warmest affection, and secure of her relations' consent, there was still something to be wished for. But the morrow passed off much better than she expected; for Mrs. Bennet luckily stood in such awe of her intended son-in-law, that she ventured not to speak to him, unless it was in her power to offer him any attention, or mark her deference for his opinion.

Elizabeth had the satisfaction of seeing her father taking pains to get acquainted with him; and Mr. Bennet soon assured her that he was rising every hour in his esteem.

"I admire all my three sons-in-law highly," said he. "Wickham, perhaps, is my favourite; but I think I shall like *your* husband quite as well as Jane's."

---

1 Pin-money is a wife's pocket-money, to be spent as she pleases.

CHAPTER XVIII.

ELIZABETH'S spirits soon rising to playfulness again, she wanted Mr. Darcy to account for his having ever fallen in love with her. "How could you begin?" said she. "I can comprehend your going on charmingly, when you had once made a beginning; but what could set you off in the first place?"

"I cannot fix on the hour, or the spot, or the look, or the words, which laid the foundation. It is too long ago. I was in the middle before I knew that I *had* begun."

"My beauty you had early withstood, and as for my manners—my behaviour to *you* was at least always bordering on the uncivil, and I never spoke to you without rather wishing to give you pain than not. Now be sincere; did you admire me for my impertinence?"

"For the liveliness of your mind, I did."

"You may as well call it impertinence at once. It was very little less. The fact is, that you were sick of civility, of deference, of officious attention. You were disgusted with the women who were always speaking and looking, and thinking for *your* approbation alone. I roused, and interested you, because I was so unlike *them*. Had you not been really amiable you would have hated me for it; but in spite of the pains you took to disguise yourself, your feelings were always noble and just; and in your heart, you thoroughly despised the persons who so assiduously courted you. There—I have saved you the trouble of accounting for it; and really, all things considered, I begin to think it perfectly reasonable. To be sure, you knew no actual good of me—but nobody thinks of *that* when they fall in love."

"Was there no good in your affectionate behaviour to Jane, while she was ill at Netherfield?"

"Dearest Jane! who could have done less for her? But make a virtue of it by all means. My good qualities are under your protection, and you are to exaggerate them as much as possible; and, in return, it belongs to me to find occasions for teazing and quarrelling with you as often as may be; and I shall begin directly by asking you what made you so unwilling to come to the point at last. What made you so shy of me, when you first called, and afterwards dined here? Why, especially, when you called, did you look as if you did not care about me?"

"Because you were grave and silent, and gave me no encouragement."

"But I was embarrassed."

"And so was I."

"You might have talked to me more when you came to dinner."

"A man who had felt less, might."

"How unlucky that you should have a reasonable answer to give, and that I should be so reasonable as to admit it! But I wonder how long you *would* have gone on, if you had been left to yourself. I wonder when you *would* have spoken, if I had not asked you! My resolution of thanking you for your kindness to Lydia had certainly great effect. *Too much*, I am afraid; for what becomes of the moral, if our comfort springs from a breach of promise, for I ought not to have mentioned the subject? This will never do."

"You need not distress yourself. The moral will be perfectly fair. Lady Catherine's unjustifiable endeavours to separate us, were the means of removing all my doubts. I am not indebted for my present happiness to your eager desire of expressing your gratitude. I was not in a humour to wait for any opening of your's. My aunt's intelligence had given me hope, and I was determined at once to know every thing."

"Lady Catherine has been of infinite use, which ought to make her happy, for she loves to be of use. But tell me, what did you come down to Netherfield for? Was it merely to ride to Longbourn and be embarrassed? or had you intended any more serious consequence?"

"My real purpose was to see *you*, and to judge, if I could, whether I might ever hope to make you love me. My avowed one, or what I avowed to myself, was to see whether your sister were still partial to Bingley, and if she were, to make the confession to him which I have since made."

"Shall you ever have courage to announce to Lady Catherine, what is to befall her?"

"I am more likely to want time than courage, Elizabeth. But it ought to be done, and if you will give me a sheet of paper, it shall be done directly."

"And if I had not a letter to write myself, I might sit by you, and admire the evenness of your writing, as another young lady once did. But I have an aunt, too, who must not be longer neglected."

From an unwillingness to confess how much her intimacy with Mr. Darcy had been over-rated, Elizabeth had never yet answered Mrs. Gardiner's long letter, but now, having *that* to communicate which she knew would be most welcome, she was almost ashamed to find, that her uncle and aunt had already lost three days of happiness, and immediately wrote as follows:

"I would have thanked you before, my dear aunt, as I ought to have done, for your long, kind, satisfactory, detail of particulars; but to say the truth, I was too cross to write. You supposed more than really existed. But *now* suppose as much as you chuse; give a loose to your fancy, indulge your imagination in every possible flight which the subject will afford, and unless you believe me actually married, you cannot greatly err. You must write again very soon, and praise him a great deal more than you did in your last. I thank you, again and again, for not going to the Lakes. How could I be so silly as to wish it! Your idea of the ponies is delightful. We will go round the Park every day. I am the happiest creature in the world. Perhaps other people have said so before, but not one with such justice. I am happier even than Jane; she only smiles, I laugh. Mr. Darcy sends you all the love in the world, that he can spare from me. You are all to come to Pemberley at Christmas. Your's, &c."

Mr. Darcy's letter to Lady Catherine, was in a different style; and still different from either, was what Mr. Bennet sent to Mr. Collins, in reply to his last.

"Dear Sir,

"I must trouble you once more for congratulations. Elizabeth will soon be the wife of Mr. Darcy. Console Lady Catherine as well as you can. But, if I were you, I would stand by the nephew. He has more to give.

Your's sincerely, &c."

Miss Bingley's congratulations to her brother, on his approaching marriage, were all that was affectionate and insincere. She wrote even to Jane on the occasion, to express her delight, and repeat all her former professions of regard. Jane was not deceived, but she was affected; and though feeling no reliance on her, could not help writing her a much kinder answer than she knew was deserved.

The joy which Miss Darcy expressed on receiving similar information, was as sincere as her brother's in sending it. Four sides of paper were insufficient to contain all her delight, and all her earnest desire of being loved by her sister.

Before any answer could arrive from Mr. Collins, or any congratulations to Elizabeth, from his wife, the Longbourn family heard that the Collinses were come themselves to Lucas lodge. The reason of this sudden removal was soon evident. Lady Catherine had been rendered so exceedingly angry by the contents of her nephew's letter, that Charlotte, really rejoicing in the match, was anxious to get away till the storm was blown over. At such a moment, the arrival of her friend was a sincere pleasure to Elizabeth, though in the course of their meetings she must sometimes think the pleasure dearly bought, when she saw Mr. Darcy exposed to all the parading and obsequious civility of her husband. He bore it however with admirable calmness. He could even listen to Sir William Lucas, when he complimented him on carrying away the brightest jewel of the country, and expressed his hopes of their all meeting frequently at St. James's, with very decent composure. If he did shrug his shoulders, it was not till Sir William was out of sight.

Mrs. Philips's vulgarity was another, and perhaps a greater tax on his forbearance; and though Mrs. Philips, as well as her sister, stood in too much awe of him to speak with the familiarity which Bingley's good humour encouraged, yet, whenever she *did* speak, she must be vulgar. Nor was her respect for him, though it made her more quiet, at all likely to make her more elegant. Elizabeth did all she could, to shield him from the frequent notice of either, and was ever anxious to keep him to herself, and to those of her family with whom he might converse without mortification; and though the uncomfortable feelings arising from all this took from the season of courtship much of its pleasure, it added to the hope of the future; and she looked forward with delight to the time when they should be removed from society so little pleasing to either, to all the comfort and elegance of their family party at Pemberley.

CHAPTER XIX.

HAPPY for all her maternal feelings was the day on which Mrs. Bennet got rid of her two most deserving daughters. With what delighted pride she afterwards visited Mrs. Bingley and talked of Mrs. Darcy may be guessed. I wish I could say, for the sake of her family, that the accomplishment of her earnest desire in the establishment of so many of her children, produced so happy an effect as to make her a sensible, amiable, well-informed woman for the rest of her life; though perhaps it was lucky for her husband, who might not have relished domestic felicity in so unusual a form, that she still was occasionally nervous and invariably silly.

Mr. Bennet missed his second daughter exceedingly; his affection for her drew him oftener from home than any thing else could do. He delighted in going to Pemberley, especially when he was least expected.

Mr. Bingley and Jane remained at Netherfield only a twelvemonth. So near a vicinity to her mother and Meryton relations was not desirable even to *his* easy temper, or *her* affectionate heart. The darling wish of his sisters was then gratified; he bought an estate in a neighbouring county to Derbyshire, and Jane and Elizabeth, in addition to every other source of happiness, were within thirty miles of each other.

Kitty, to her very material advantage, spent the chief of her time with her two elder sisters. In society so superior to what she had generally known, her improvement was great. She was not of so ungovernable a temper as Lydia, and, removed from the influence of Lydia's example, she became, by proper attention and management, less irritable, less ignorant, and less insipid. From the farther disadvantage of Lydia's society she was of course carefully kept, and though Mrs. Wickham frequently invited her to come and stay with her, with the promise of balls and young men, her father would never consent to her going.

Mary was the only daughter who remained at home; and she was necessarily drawn from the pursuit of accomplishments by Mrs. Bennet's being quite unable to sit alone. Mary was obliged to mix more with the world, but she could still moralize over every morning visit; and as she was no longer mortified by comparisons between her sisters' beauty and her own, it was suspected by her father that she submitted to the change without much reluctance.

As for Wickham and Lydia, their characters suffered no revolution from the marriage of her sisters. He bore with philosophy the conviction that Elizabeth must now become acquainted with whatever of his ingratitude and falsehood had before been unknown to her; and in spite of every thing, was not wholly without hope that Darcy might yet be prevailed on to make his fortune. The congratulatory letter which Elizabeth received from Lydia on her marriage, explained to her that, by his wife at least, if not by himself, such a hope was cherished. The letter was to this effect:

"MY DEAR LIZZY,

"I wish you joy. If you love Mr. Darcy half as well as I do my dear Wickham, you must be very happy. It is a great comfort to have you so rich, and when you have nothing else to do, I hope you will think of us. I am sure Wickham would like a place at court very much, and I do not think we shall have quite money enough to live upon without some help. Any place would do, of about three or four hundred a year; but, however, do not speak to Mr. Darcy about it, if you had rather not.

"Your's, &c."

As it happened that Elizabeth had *much* rather not; she endeavoured in her answer to put an end to every intreaty and expectation of the kind. Such relief, however, as it was in her power to afford, by the practice of what might be called economy in her own private expences, she frequently sent them. It had always been evident to her that such an income as theirs, under the direction of two persons so extravagant in their wants, and heedless of the future, must be very insufficient to their support; and whenever they changed their quarters, either Jane or herself were sure of being applied to, for some little assistance towards discharging their bills. Their manner of living, even when the restoration of peace dismissed them to a home, was unsettled in the extreme.[1] They were always moving from place to place in quest of a cheap situation, and always spending more than they ought. His affection for her soon sunk into indifference; her's lasted a little longer; and in spite of her youth and her manners, she retained all the claims to reputation which her marriage had given her.

Though Darcy could never receive *him* at Pemberley, yet, for Elizabeth's sake, he assisted him farther in his profession. Lydia was occasionally a visitor there, when her husband was gone to enjoy himself in London or Bath; and with the Bingleys they both of them frequently staid so long, that even Bingley's good humour was overcome, and he proceeded so far as to *talk* of giving them a hint to be gone.

Miss Bingley was very deeply mortified by Darcy's marriage; but as she thought it advisable to retain the right of visiting at Pemberley, she dropt all her resentment; was fonder than ever of Georgiana, almost as attentive to Darcy as heretofore, and paid off every arrear of civility to Elizabeth.

Pemberley was now Georgiana's home; and the attachment of the sisters was exactly what Darcy had hoped to see. They were able to love each other, even as well as they intended. Georgiana had the highest opinion in the world of Elizabeth; though at first she often listened with an astonishment bordering on alarm, at her lively, sportive, manner of talking to her

---

1 The "peace" referred to is presumably the temporary one of the Treaty of Amiens, which lasted from March 1802 till May 1803: see introduction to Appendix F.

brother. He, who had always inspired in herself a respect which almost overcame her affection, she now saw the object of open pleasantry. Her mind received knowledge which had never before fallen in her way. By Elizabeth's instructions she began to comprehend that a woman may take liberties with her husband, which a brother will not always allow in a sister more than ten years younger than himself.

Lady Catherine was extremely indignant on the marriage of her nephew; and as she gave way to all the genuine frankness of her character, in her reply to the letter which announced its arrangement, she sent him language so very abusive, especially of Elizabeth, that for some time all intercourse was at an end. But at length, by Elizabeth's persuasion, he was prevailed on to overlook the offence, and seek a reconciliation; and, after a little farther resistance on the part of his aunt, her resentment gave way, either to her affection for him, or her curiosity to see how his wife conducted herself; and she condescended to wait on them at Pemberley, in spite of that pollution which its woods had received, not merely from the presence of such a mistress, but the visits of her uncle and aunt from the city.

With the Gardiners, they were always on the most intimate terms. Darcy, as well as Elizabeth, really loved them; and they were both ever sensible of the warmest gratitude towards the persons who, by bringing her into Derbyshire, had been the means of uniting them.

FINIS

Appendix A: Parliamentary Debate on the Marriage Act of 1754

From **The Parliamentary History of England, from the earliest period to the year 1803. Volume XV: 1753–1765. London: T.C. Hansard, 1813.**

[Until the middle of the eighteenth century, it was very easy for young people to enter into legally binding marriages without the consent of their parents by simply exchanging vows, with or without the presence of one of the many clerics who would conduct ceremonies for cash. In 1753 Lord Hardwicke introduced a Bill to Parliament which would make such marriages invalid in England and Wales. The consent of parents or guardians would be required for all persons under 21, for example; marriages would have to be conducted in the parish church of one of the parties, unless a special licence was obtained to marry "privately" in, usually, their house (a common practice of the rich); the service must be held between eight o'clock and noon; a month's notice would have to be given, and the proposed marriage announced in church on the three preceding Sundays.

The ensuing debate in the House of Commons, after the Bill had been passed in much altered form by the House of Lords, reveals the extent to which intermarriage between the landowning classes and the new money of trade and speculation was perceived as (a) essential to the good of the nation, and (b) a distinctively English practice, with "English" understood here, as usual, in opposition to "French": compare this with Burke's comments in Appendix C, pp.417–18. Despite the fears that the Bill would stop this practice, it was passed into law, and there is no evidence that these fears were realised as a result. However, as Scotland retained its own legal and religious institutions in the 1707 Treaty of Union, Hardwicke's Act did not apply there, and Gretna Green, the first village across the border, developed a brisk business in marrying well-off young lovers fleeing parental opposition in the South.]

26 George the Second, A.D. 1753: Sixth Session of the Tenth Parliament of Great Britain.

May 7, 1753. A Cause having been brought before the House of Lords by appeal, which was founded upon an alleged Clandestine Marriage, it set the bad consequences of such marriages in so strong a light, that their lordships ordered the judges to prepare and bring in "a Bill for the better preventing of Clandestine Marriages;" which they accordingly did: but the Bill met with so many alterations and amendments in that House, that it was not sent down to the Commons till this day.

May 14. The said Bill was read a second time, and on the motion that it be committed,[1] the following Debate took place:

Mr. Attorney General *Ryder*:[2]
Sir; the Bill which has been now read a second time, is designed for putting an end to an evil which has been long and grievously complained of, an evil by which many of our best families have often suffered, and which our laws have often endeavoured to prevent, but always hitherto without success; and yet it is an evil which, one would think, should rarely happen, if we consider that duty and respect which children ought to shew towards their parents, and that indulgence and affection parents ought to have for their children, especially in that affair of their marriage, which is generally the first step that people of all ranks make into the world, and a step upon which their future happiness, prosperity and success almost entirely depends. In this step the happiness both of the parents and children is so intimately concerned, that children ought never to make it without the approbation of their parents, nor ought the parent to refuse his approbation, when the match proposed is not such as apparently tends to the dishonour of his family, or may probably bring on the ruin of his child. Yet we often find the passion called love triumphing over the duty of children to their parents, and on the other hand we some-

---

1 Committed: that is, passed on to the scrutiny of a committee of the whole House. This is the normal procedure if the bill is passed at a second reading.
2 Sir Dudley Ryder (1691–1756), the government's chief law officer and M.P. for Tiverton. This was Ryder's last speech in Parliament.

times find the passion of pride or avarice triumphing over the duty of parents to their children. And when a young gentleman or lady happens to be born to a good fortune, they are so beset with selfish designing people, and so many arts made use of for engaging their affection, that their innocence often becomes a prey to the lowest and vilest seducer. How often have we known the heir of a good family seduced, and engaged in a clandestine marriage, perhaps with a common strumpet? How often have we known a rich heiress carried off by a man of low birth, or perhaps by an infamous sharper? What distress some of our best families have been brought into, what ruin some of their sons or daughters have been involved in, by such means, every gentleman may from his own knowledge recollect; and every gentleman must allow, that such misfortunes ought to be prevented, if possible.

[columns 1–3]

* * * * *

Mr. *Robert Nugent:*[1]

... But now, Sir, supposing that the legislature has power, or rather a right, to prescribe what forms and ceremonies it pleases to the marriage contract, and to declare every marriage void and null, where all the punctilios prescribed are not exactly observed, which, notwithstanding the authority of the reverend bench, I am far from being satisfied about, yet the Bill now before us I must be against, because I think it absolutely inconsistent with the public good of this kingdom. The other House had some reason, and some sort of right, to agree to it, because they represent themselves and those of their own body only, and because, should the Bill be passed into a law, they will thereby gain a very considerable and a very particular advantage; for they will in a great measure secure all the rich heiresses in the kingdom to those of their own body. An old miser, even of the lowest birth, is

---

1   Robert Nugent (1702–88), the charismatic M.P. for St. Mawes in Cornwall. A commoner of comparatively humble Irish origins, Nugent ended his life as an Earl, and a very wealthy man indeed; famously flexible in his political principles, he may have felt uncharacteristic conviction in the present case, as his wealth had been gained "by his skill in marrying rich widows" (*Dictionary of National Biography*).

generally ambitious of having his only daughter married to a lord, and a guardian has generally some selfish view, or some interest to serve, by getting his rich ward married to the eldest son of some duke, marquiss [sic], or earl; so that when a young commoner makes his addresses to a rich heiress, he has no friend but his superior merit, and that little deity called love, whose influence over a young lady always decreases as she increases in years; for by the time she comes of age, pride and ambition seizes possession of her breast likewise, and banishes from thence the little deity called love, or if he preserve a corner for his friend, it is only to introduce him as a gallant, not a husband. Therefore I may prophesy, that if this Bill passes into a law, no commoner will ever marry a rich heiress, unless his father be a minister of state, nor will a peer's eldest son marry the daughter of a commoner, unless she be a rich heiress.

From hence will appear, Sir, the particular advantage which the other House had in passing this Bill, and as they are not chosen by the people, we have often found that they shew no great regard to the interest of the people, when it happens to come in competition with the particular interest of their own body. But we in this House, Sir, represent the people, and as the interest of the people and that of the nation must always be the same, whatever advantage may accrue to our noble and rich families from this Bill, if it be against the national interest and that of the people, we ought not to consent to its being passed into a law. As to the national interest, I think it is allowed, that to prevent the accumulation of wealth, and to disperse it as much as possible through the whole body of the people, is a maxim religiously observed in every well-regulated society. Riches is the blood of the body politic: it must be made to circulate: if you allow it to stagnate, or if too much of it be thrown into any one part, it will destroy the body politic, as the same cause often does the body natural: if this Bill passes, our quality and rich families will daily accumulate riches by marrying only one another;[1] and what sort of breed their offspring will be, we may easily judge: if the gout, the gravel, the pox and madness are always to wed together, what a hopeful generation of quality and rich commoners shall we have amongst us?[2] What a fine appear-

---

1 "Quality families": i.e., the nobility: those who inherit the right to exercise political power in the House of Lords, and thus to be distinguished from the merely rich.

2 The gout and the gravel, related and agonising conditions involving the formation of crystals in the joints and urinary tract respectively, were linked to an excessive

ance will they make at the head of an army, should we ever happen to be invaded by a foreign enemy?

Besides this, Sir, the Bill plainly tends towards introducing into this country a distinction, which is inconsistent with our constitution. In other countries they have distinctions established and still kept up, between what they call their noblesse and their burghers, boors, and *roturiers*.[1] In some countries a nobleman loses his estate if he marries below his rank; and in France one of their noblesse must not marry a *rotourier*. What is the consequence, especially in France? The marriages of their quality are something like the marriages of sovereign princes: the bride and bridegroom sometimes have never seen one another, till they meet to be married. Can any love or affection be expected between such a married couple? Accordingly, it for the most part happens: the bride goes to bed, perhaps, the first night with the bridegroom, but the next, if not before, with her gallant; and conjugal love or fidelity is now become so rare in that country, that it is deemed scandalous for a lady of quality not to have a gallant, or for a man of quality to be seen at any public diversion with his wife, unless his mistress be known to be in company. Can any man be desirous of introducing such customs into this country? Yet such customs will certainly be the consequence, as our quality and rich people will by this Bill acquire the absolute disposal of their children in marriage; for whilst the father is alive, even the court of Chancery is to have no power to authorize a proper marriage without his consent, let his refusal be never so whimsical or selfish.

In this country, Sir, we as yet know of no distinctions with regard to marriage: a gentleman's, a farmer's daughter is a match for the eldest son of the best lord in the land, and perhaps a better match than his father would chuse for him, because she will bring good and wholesome blood into the family. It is this equality that gives such spirit to our middling sort of gentlemen, and to our common people in general: it is this that makes the infantry of our armies superior to any in the world. And I believe it would no way derogate from the

---

consumption of rich food and alcohol and thus perceived as maladies specific to wealthy males. As the group with the money and leisure to indulge in prostitutes, the pox (syphilis) was common in the same class: the general paralysis of the tertiary stage of syphilis was understood as a form of madness.

1   *Roturiers*: persons of low social rank.

health, strength or spirit of our nobility, if, out of pure love, they married the daughters of our middling sort of gentlemen oftener than they do; for the offspring of conjugal love have generally more spirit, and more sense too, than the offspring of conjugal duty. But such marriages will be rendered almost impossible by this Bill. At present, indeed, our nobility are not quite so squeamish as those of France or Germany: they do not think, nor do our laws render it beneath them to marry the daughter of a tradesman or merchant, if she be one whose father has heaped up, by whatever means, a large sum of money, and has no child but her; and if the father was become rich before, or soon after she was born, she is generally bred up to be good for as little, and to be as proud, expensive, and whimsical as any lady of quality whatsoever.

[columns 14–16]

* * * * *

Mr. *Charles Townsend* [sic]:[1]

... Let us consider, Sir, that the flower of a youth, the highest bloom of a woman's beauty, is, from 16 to 21: it is then that a young woman of little or no fortune has the best chance for disposing of herself to advantage in marriage; shall we make it impossible for her to do so, without the consent of an indigent and mercenary father? Shall we render it next to impossible for her to do so, even though she has neither father nor mother alive? For a gentleman marrying a beautiful young girl of little or no fortune, is generally so much laughed at by his companions, that no man would chuse to have it made public before-hand, by a proclamation of banns, or an application to the court of Chancery for appointing her a guardian; and the necessity of his doing so may very probably prevent his making her happy, or induce him to render her miserable by debauching her. Sir, I must look upon this Bill as one of the most cruel enterprizes against

---

1   Charles Townshend (1725–67) M.P. for Great Yarmouth. With this speech Townshend first made his mark in the Commons. He would end his career as the Chancellor of the Exchequer responsible for suspending the New York legislature and imposing port duties on glass, lead, paper, and tea on the American colonies, actions which made a rather greater mark on history.

the fair sex that ever entered into the heart of man, and if I were concerned in promoting it, I should expect to have my eyes torn out by
the women of the first country town I passed through; for against
such an enemy I could not surely hope for the protection of the gentlemen of our army.

[columns 59–60]

✳ ✳ ✳ ✳ ✳

Mr. *William Beckford*:[1]

... [H]ow comes it, Sir, that the fair sex are so often deceived,
deluded and ruined by promises of marriage? Is it not because the
betrayer pretends some difficulty or anther in going directly to be
married? Either he cannot get a license, or he cannot find a parson, or
he has some relation from whom he expects a great fortune, and cannot publicly marry till his death. These are the pretences made use of
by men who intend to seduce and betray: these are the pretences by
which women are persuaded not to insist upon a previous marriage,
but consent to yield upon a promise; for no woman, I believe, ever
yielded upon a promise, [but] in hopes of her being able to compel a
performance of that promise. Will not these pretences be rendered
much more probable and convincing after this Bill is passed into a
law? Will not young women oftener be thereby induced to trust a
promise of marriage? And will not deceitful men be more ready to
make such promises than they ever were heretofore?

This Bill may therefore, Sir, most justly be entitled a Bill for the
ruin of the fair sex ...

[column 80]

---

1 William Beckford (1709–70), the fabulously wealthy merchant and West Indian
plantation owner, twice Lord Mayor of London, father of his namesake the author
of the gothic novel *Vathek*, and at this point M.P. for Shaftesbury.

Appendix B: From the Conduct Books

1. From James Fordyce, D.D., *Sermons to Young Women*. In two volumes. Third edition, corrected. London: A. Miller and T. Cadell, J. Dodsley, and J. Payne, 1766.

[James Fordyce (1720–96) was a Presbyterian minister who left his native Scotland in 1760 to seek his fortune in London, in a period when it was possible for a clergyman possessed of both energy and "politeness" to shine in fashionable society. He retreated to the country in 1782, long after the collapse of his brother's banking concerns had diminished his popularity, but the *Sermons to Young Women* are the product of his ascendancy.]

Volume I.

From Sermon I. On the Importance of the Female Sex, especially the Younger Part.

... When a daughter, it may be a favourite daughter, turns out unruly, foolish, wanton; when she disobeys her parents, disgraces her education, dishonours her sex, disappoints the hopes she has raised; when she throws herself away on a man unworthy of her, or if disposed, yet by his or her situation unqualified, to make her happy; what her parents in any of these cases must necessarily suffer, we may conjecture, they alone can feel.

The world, I know not how, overlooks in our sex a thousand irregularities, which it never forgives in yours; so that the honour and peace of a family are, in this view, much more dependant on the conduct of daughters than of sons; and one young lady going astray shall subject her relations to such discredit and distress, as the united good conduct of all her brothers and sisters, supposing them numerous, shall scarce ever be able to repair. But I press not any further an argument so exceedingly plain. We can prognosticate nothing virtuous, nothing happy, concerning those wretched creatures of either sex, that do not feel for the satisfaction, ease, or honour of their parents.

Another and a principal source of your importance is the very great and extensive influence which you, in general, have with Our sex. There is in female youth an attraction, which every man of the least sensibility must perceive. If assisted by beauty, it becomes in the first impression irresistible. Your power so far we do not affect to conceal. That He who made us meant it thus, is manifest from his having attempered our hearts to such emotions. Would to God you knew how to improve this power to its noblest ends! We should then rejoice to see it increased: then indeed it would be increased of course. Youth and beauty set off with sweetness and virtue, capacity and discretion — what have not they accomplished?

Far be it from me, my fair hearers, to damp your spirits, or to wish in the least to abridge your triumphs: on the contrary, by assisting you to direct, we would contribute to exalt and extend them. We are always sorry when we see them misplaced or abused; and — I was going to add, there is nothing more common. To give them their just direction, is truly a nice point. Power, from whatever source derived, is always in danger of turning the head. It has turned many an old one. What then shall become of a young woman, placed on such a precipice? What can balance or preserve her, but sobriety and caution, a good providence, and good advice?

There are few young women who do not appear agreeable in the eyes of some men. And what might not be done by the greater part of you to secure solid esteem, and to promote general reformation, among our sex? Are such objects unworthy of your pursuit? or will ye say, that those which frequently engage it are of superior or equal importance?

If men discover that you study to captivate them by an outside only, or by little frivolous arts, there are, it must be confessed, many of them who will rejoice at the discovery; and while they themselves seem taken by the lure, they will endeavour in reality to make you their prey. Some more sentimental spirits, who might be dazzled in the beginning, will be soon disabused; and a few more honourable characters will scorn to take advantage of your folly. Folly most undoubtedly it is, by a wrong application of your force, to lose the substance for the shadow.

Now and then a giddy youth may be caught. But what is the shallow admiration of an hundred such, or the smooth address of artful destroyers, to the heart-felt respect of men of worth and discernment, or the well-earned praise of reclaiming were it but one offender? I verily believe you might reclaim a multitude. I can hardly conceive that any man would be able to withstand the soft persuasion of your words, but chiefly of your looks and actions, habitually exerted on the side of goodness.

"Were Virtue," said an ancient philosopher, "to appear amongst men in visible shape, what vehement desires would she enkindle!" Virtue exhibited without affectation by a lovely young person, of improved understanding and gentle manners, may be said to appear with the most alluring aspect, surrounded by the Graces; and that breast must be cold indeed which does not take fire at the sight!

The influence of the sexes is, no doubt, reciprocal; but I must ever be of opinion, that yours is the greatest. How often have I seen a company of men who were disposed to be riotous, checked all at once into decency by the accidental entrance of an amiable woman; while her good sense and obliging deportment charmed them into at least a temporary conviction, that there is nothing so beautiful as female excellence, nothing so delightful as female conversation in its best form!

Were such conviction frequently repeated, (and it would be frequently repeated, if such excellence and such conversation were more general) what might we not expect from it at last? In the mean time, it were easy to point out instances of the most evident reformation wrought on particular men, by their having happily conceived a passion for virtuous women: but among the least valuable of your sex, when have you known any that were amended by the society or example of the better part of ours?

To form the manners of men various causes contribute; but nothing, I apprehend, so much as the turn of the women with whom they converse. Those who are most conversant with women of virtue and understanding will be always found the most amiable characters, other circumstances being supposed alike. Such society, beyond everything else, rubs off the corners that give many of our sex an ungracious roughness. It produces a polish much more perfect, and more pleasing, than that which is received from a general commerce with the world. This last is often specious, but commonly superficial. The other is the result of gentler feelings, and a more elegant humanity: the heart itself is moulded; habits of undissembled courtesy are formed; a certain flowing urbanity is acquired; violent passions, rash oaths, course jests, indelicate language of every kind, are precluded and disrelished. Understanding and virtue, by being often contemplated in the most engaging lights, have a sort of assimilating power. I do not mean, that the men I speak of will become feminine; but their sentiments and deportment will contract a grace. Their principles will have nothing ferocious or forbidding; their affections will be chaste and soothing at the same instant.

[pp.16–23]

From Sermon V. On Female Virtue, Friendship, and Conversation.

... The more intimate reciprocations of a close friendship are now, as you know, out of the question. That at your time of life you should be particularly fond of sprightly conversation, where all is enlivened and joyful, and where Wisdom when allowed to enter puts on her gayest garb, is perfectly natural. To advise you against it were as weak, as it would be unfriendly. Such sprightliness and freedom, when supported by sense, and chastened by decency, have always, I frankly acknowledge, appeared to me delightful. Dulness and insipidity, moroseness and rigour, are dead weights on every kind of social intercourse; nor will I conceal it from you that I wish, as much as any of you can do, to make my escape from them on all occasions. But tell me, my lively friends; when the heart overflows with gaiety, is there no danger of its bursting the proper bounds? Is not extreme vivacity a near borderer on folly? To prevent its breaking loose, and throwing itself into very serious inconveniencies, into a very hurtful conduct, will surely require the check of self-command. But how is that to be attained? By associating only with the fanciful, the vivacious, or the witty? Is hazard to be shunned by rushing into the field of battle? Or, to represent things at the best, is familiarity with Wisdom to be contracted most readily, where Wisdom appears most seldom? Would ye form habits of sobriety, a spirit of sedateness, no way inconsistent with innocent mirth, you must frequently resort to the company of the sober and the sedate. But will not these be chiefly found among such as are farther advanced in years than yourselves? Should not you be ambitious of profiting by their experience and knowledge? And will not a respect for superior age, when possessed of superior discretion, often prove a seasonable restraint on the wildness of more youthful sallies? "He that walketh with wise men shall be wise," said the wisest of mortals.[1] Is not the maxim equally applicable to women?

Will you give me leave on this occasion to mention, what is much to the honour of our sex, that all the most sensible and worthy of yours have ever professed a particular relish for the conversation of men of sense and worth? Such men, I presume, are attached to the society of such women beyond everything else in the world. And when such circumstances favour, this mutual tendency cannot fail to be a rich source of mutual improvement. Was not such a reciprocal aid a great part of Nature's intention in that mental and moral difference of sex, which she has marked by characters no less distinguishable than those that diversify their outward forms?

[pp. 172–5]

* * * * *

Having mentioned Wit, let me proceed to warn you against the affectation and the abuse of it. Here our text from the Colossians comes in with propriety, "Let your Speech be always with Grace, seasoned with Salt."[2] These remarkable words were addressed to christians in general. They are considered by the best commentators, as an exhortation to that kind of converse, which, both for matter and manner, shall appear most graceful, and prove most acceptable; being tempered by courteousness and modesty, seasoned with wisdom and discretion, that like salt will serve, at the same instant, to prevent its corruption and heighten its flavour. How beautiful this precept in itself! How useful and pleasing in the practice! How peculiarly fit to be practised by you, my female friends, on the turn of whose conversation and deportment so much depends to yourselves, and all about you! From what I have now to offer, it will be found likewise to come, with advantage, in aid of our leading doctrine; since there are not perhaps many worse foes to that of Sobriety of spirit, which we would still inculcate, than the abuse and affectation already mentioned.

It is not my design to gather up, if I could, the profusion of flowers that have been scattered by innumerable hands on this tempting

---

1   Proverbs 13.20: "He that walketh with wise men shall be wise; but a companion of fools shall be destroyed." The "wisest of mortals" is of course Solomon.

2   Epistle to the Colossians 4.6: "Let your speech be alway with grace, seasoned with salt, that ye may know how ye ought to answer every man."

theme; and by which those very hands have, in their own case, shown how difficult it is to resist the temptation. I would only observe, that the dangerous talent in question has been well compared to the dancing of a meteor, that blazes, allures, and misleads.[1] Most certainly it alone can never be a steady light; and too probably it is often a fatal one. Of those who have resigned themselves to its guidance, how few has it not betrayed into great indiscretions at least, by inflaming their thirst of applause; by rendering them little nice in their choice of company; by seducing them into strokes of satire, too offensive to the persons against whom they were levelled, not to be repelled upon the authors with full vengeance; and finally, by making them, in consequence of that heat which produces, and that vanity which fosters it, forgetful of those cool and moderate rules that ought to regulate their conduct!

A very few there may have been, endowed with judgment and temper sufficient to restrain them from indulging "the rash dexterity of wit," and to direct it to purposes equally agreeable and beneficial.[2] But one thing is certain, that witty men for the most part have had few friends, though many admirers. Their conversation has been

---

1 If Fordyce has in mind the apocalypse that closes the fourth and final book of Alexander Pope's poem *The Dunciad* (1742), he is mis-remembering the point of Pope's metaphor. Wit for Pope is still a positive "art," not a misleading vanity; but it is an art rendered powerless by the onset of an invincible (and feminine) Chaos:

> Before her, *Fancy's* gilded clouds decay,
> And all its varying Rain-bows die away.
> *Wit* shoots in vain its momentary fires,
> The meteor drops, and in a flash expires.
> ...
> Thus at her felt approach, and secret might,
> Art after Art goes out, and all is Night.
>
> (ll.631–4, 639–40)

2 Another spectacularly inapposite allusion to Pope. *An Essay on Man* Epistle II (1733) argues for the complementary relation between "self-love" and "reason" where Fordyce continually cautions against the former. "Wit," in the passage quoted, names the ingenuity of those who, like Fordyce, try to pull these two principles of human nature apart:

> Let subtle schoolmen teach these friends to fight,
> More studious to divide than to unite,
> And Grace and Virtue, Sense and Reason split,
> With all the rash dexterity of Wit ...
>
> (ll.81–4)

courted, while their abilities have been feared, or their characters hated, or both. In truth the last have seldom merited affection, even when the first have excited esteem. Sometimes their hearts have been so bad, as at length to bring their heads into disgrace. At any rate, the faculty termed Wit is commonly looked upon with a suspicious eye, as a two-edged sword, from which not even the sacredness of friendship can secure. It is especially, I think, dreaded in women. In a Mrs. Rowe, I dare say, it was not.[1] To great brilliancy of imagination that female angel joined yet greater goodness of disposition; and never wrote, nor, as I have been told, was ever supposed to have said, in her whole life, an ill-natured, or even an indelicate thing. Of such a woman, with all her talents, none could be afraid. In her company, it must have been impossible not to feel respect; but then it would be like that, which the pious man entertains for a ministring spirit from heaven, a respect full of confidence and joy. If aught on earth can present the image of celestial excellence in its softest array, it is surely an Accomplished Woman, in whom purity and meekness, intelligence and modesty, mingle their charms. But when I speak on this subject, need I tell you, that men of the best sense have been usually averse to the thought of marrying a witty female?

You will probably tell me, they were afraid of being outshone; and some of them perhaps might be so. But I am apt to believe, that many of them acted on different motives. Men who understand the science of domestic happiness, know that its very first principle is ease. Of that indeed we grow fonder, in whatever condition, as we advance in life, and as the heat of youth abates. But we cannot be easy, where we are not safe. We are never safe in the company of a critic; and almost every wit is a critic by profession. In such company we are not at liberty to unbend ourselves. All must be the straining of a study, or the anxiety of apprehension: how painful! Where the heart may not expand and open itself with freedom, farewel to real friendship, farewel to convivial delight! But to suffer this restraint at home, what misery! From the brandishings of wit in the hand of ill nature, of imperious passion, or of unbounded vanity, who would not flee? But

---

1   Elizabeth Rowe (1674–1737). A very successful author of poetry and epistolary fiction of a religious-moral-didactic nature, Rowe is the paradigmatic example of a woman writer who won cultural authority for the feminine literary voice by turning it to consistently pious ends: hence Fordyce's admiration.

when that weapon is pointed at a husband, is it to be wondered if from his own house he takes shelter in the tavern? He sought a soft friend; he expected to be happy in a reasonable companion. He has found a perpetual satirist, or a self-sufficient prattler. How have I pitied such a man, when I have seen him in continual fear on his own account, and that of his friends, and for the poor lady herself; lest, in the run of her discourse, she should be guilty of some petulance, or some indiscretion, that would expose her and hurt them all! But take the matter at the best; there is still all the difference in the world between the entertainer of an evening, and a partner for life. Of the latter a sober mind, steady attachment, and gentle manners, joined to a good understanding, will ever be the chief recommendations; whereas the qualities that sparkle will be often sufficient for the former.

As to the affectation of wit, one can hardly say, whether it be most ridiculous or hurtful. The abuse of it, which we have been just considering, we are sometimes, perhaps too often, inclined to forgive, for the sake of that amusement which in spite of all the improprieties mentioned it yet affords. The other is universally contemptible and odious. Who is not shocked by the flippant impertinence of the self-conceited woman, that wants to dazzle by the supposed superiority of her powers? If you, my fair ones, have knowledge and capacity; let it be seen, by your not affecting to show them, that you have something much more valuable, humility and wisdom.

> "Naked in nothing should a woman be,
> "But veil her very wit with modesty.
> "Let man discover, let not her display,
> "But yield her charms of mind with sweet delay."[1]

Must women then keep silence in the house, as well as in the church?[2] By no means. There may indeed be many cases, in which it will particularly become a young lady to observe the apostolic rule,

---

1 I have been unable to find a source for these verses, and since Fordyce published a volume of poetry later in life, they may well be his own.
2 First Epistle to the Corinthians 14.34, 35: "Let your women keep silence in the churches: for it is not permitted unto them to speak; but they are commanded to be under obedience, as also saith the law. / And if they will learn any thing, let them ask their husbands at home: for it is a shame for women to speak in the church."

"Be swift to hear, and slow to speak:"[1] but there are many too, where-in it will be no less fit, that with an unassuming air she should endeavour to support and enliven the conversation. It is the opinion of some, that girls should never speak before company, when their parents are present; and parents there are, so deficient in understanding, as to make this a rule. How then shall those girls learn to acquit themselves properly in their absence? It is hard if you cannot distinguish, and teach your daughters to distinguish, between good breeding and pertness, between an obliging study to please and an indecent desire to put themselves forward, between a laudable inquisitiveness and an improper curiosity. But this, I confess, is not the most common mistake in the education of young women; and they must permit me to say, that it were well if the generality of mothers were careful, by prudent instruction in private, to repress that talkative humour which runs away with so many of them, and never quits them all their life after, for want of being curbed in their early years. But what words can express the impertinence of a female tongue let loose into boundless loquacity? Nothing can be more stunning, except where a number of Fine Ladies open at once—Protect us, ye powers and gentleness and decorum, protect us from the disgust of such a scene—Ah! my dear hearers, if ye knew how terrible it appears to a male ear of the least delicacy, I think you would take care never to practise it.

[pp.188–197]

2. From Dr. John Gregory, *A Father's Legacy to his Daughters.* The second edition. London: W. Strahan and T. Cadell; Edinburgh: W. Creech, 1774.

[John Gregory (1724–73) followed the same path south from Scotland as Fordyce, as a medical doctor and thinker, and moved in similar literary circles in London. But he returned to take up the chair of medicine first at Aberdeen, then, from 1764, at Edinburgh, where he was at the centre of the intellectual life of that city at that time. *A Father's Legacy* seems (see footnote 1 on page 404) to have been written in the 1760s, but was only published, in accordance with its stated aim, after his death.]

---

1 James 1.19: "Wherefore, my beloved brethren, let every man be swift to hear, slow to speak, slow to wrath."

[Introduction]

MY DEAR GIRLS,

You had the misfortune to be deprived of your mother, at a time of life when you were insensitive of your loss, and could receive little benefit, either from her instruction, or her example. — Before this comes to your hands, you will likewise have lost your father.

I have had many melancholy reflections on the forlorn and help-less situation you must be in, if it should please God to remove me from you, before you arrive at that period of life, when you will be able to think and act for yourselves. I know mankind too well. I know their falsehood, their dissipation, their coldness to all the duties of friendship and humanity. I know the little attention paid to help-less infancy. — You will meet with few friends disinterested enough to do you good offices, when you are incapable of making them any return by contributing to their interest or their pleasure, or even to the gratification of their vanity.

I have been supported under the gloom naturally arising from these reflections, by a reliance on the goodness of that Providence which has hitherto preserved you, and given me the most pleasing prospect of the goodness of your dispositions; and by the secret hope that your mother's virtues will entail a blessing on her children.

The anxiety I have for your happiness has made me resolve to throw together my sentiments relating to your future conduct in life. If I live for some years, you will receive them with much greater advantage, suited to your different geniuses and dispositions. If I die sooner, you must receive them in this very imperfect manner,— the last proof of my affection.

You will all remember your father's fondness, when perhaps every other circumstance relating to him is forgotten. This remembrance, I hope, will induce you to give a serious attention to the advices I am now going to leave with you. — I can request this attention with the greater confidence, as my sentiments on the most interesting points that regard life and manners, were entirely correspondent to your mother's, whose judgment and taste I trusted much more than my own.

You must expect, that the advices which I shall give you will be very imperfect, as there are many nameless delicacies, in female manners, of which none but a woman can judge. — You will have one advantage by attending to what I am going to leave to you; you will hear, at least for once in your lives, the genuine sentiments of a man who has no interest in flattering or deceiving you. — I shall throw my reflections together without any studied order, and shall only, to avoid confusion, range them under a few general heads.

You will see, in a little treatise of mine just published, in what an honourable point of view I have considered your sex;[1] not as domestic drudges, or the slave of our pleasures; but as our companions and equals; as designed to soften our hearts and polish our manners; and, as Thomson finely says,

> To raise the virtues, animate the bliss,
> And sweeten all the toils of human life.[2]

I shall not repeat what I have there said on this subject; and shall only observe, that from the view I have given of your natural character and place in society, there arises a certain propriety of conduct peculiar to your sex. It is this peculiar propriety of female manners of which I intend to give you my sentiments, without touching on those general rules of conduct by which men and women are equally bound.

While I explain to you that system of conduct which I think will tend most to your honour and happiness, I shall, at the same time, endeavour to point out those virtues and accomplishments which render you most respectable and most amiable in the eyes of my own sex.

[pp. 1–8]

---

1 *A Comparative View of the State and Faculties of Man with those of the Animal World.* London: J. Dodsley, 1766. Section II of this primer in the Scottish Enlightenment allocates women an important role in fostering the "Social Principle" by which individuals are attached to one another "by sympathy and affection" (p.87). See pp.92–94 for a list of qualities which allow them to do this.

2 James Thomson, *The Seasons* (1730): "Autumn":

> To raise the virtues, animate the bliss,
> Even charm the pains to something more than joy,
> And sweeten all the toils of human life:
> This be the female dignity and praise.

[ll.606–9]

One of the chief beauties in a female character is that modest reserve, that retiring delicacy, which avoids the public eye, and is disconcerted even at the gaze of admiration. — I do not wish you to be insensible to applause. If you were, you must become, if not worse, at least less amiable women. But you may be dazzled by that admiration, which yet rejoices your hearts.

When a girl ceases to blush, she has lost the most powerful charm of her beauty. That extreme sensibility which it indicates, may be a weakness and incumbrance in our sex, as I have too often felt; but in yours it is peculiarly engaging. Pedants, who think themselves philosophers, ask why a woman should blush when she is conscious of no crime. It is a sufficient answer, that Nature has made you to blush when you are guilty of no fault, and has forced us to love you because you do so. — Blushing is so far from being necessarily an attendant on guilt, that it is the usual companion of innocence.

This modesty, which I think so essential in your sex, will naturally dispose you to be rather silent in company, especially in a large one. — People of sense and discernment will never mistake such silence for dulness. One may take a share in conversation without uttering a syllable. The expression in the countenance shews it; and this never escapes an observing eye.

I should be glad that you had an easy dignity in your behaviour at public places, but not that confident ease, that unabashed countenance, which seems to set the company at defiance. — If, while a gentleman is speaking to you, one of superior rank addresses you, do not let your eager attention and visible preference betray the flutter of your heart. Let your pride on this occasion preserve you from that meanness into which your vanity would sink you. Consider that you expose yourself to the ridicule of the company, and affront one gentleman, only to swell the triumph of another, who perhaps thinks he does you an honour in speaking to you.

Converse with men even of the first rank with that dignified modesty, which may prevent the approach of the most distant familiarity, and consequently prevent them from feeling themselves your superiors.

Wit is the most dangerous talent that you can possess. It must be guarded with great discretion and good-nature, otherwise it will create you many enemies. Wit is perfectly consistent with softness and delicacy; yet they are seldom found united. Wit is so flattering to vanity, that they who possess it become intoxicated, and lose all self-command.

Humour is a different quality. It will make your company much solicited; but be cautious how you indulge it. — It is often a great enemy to delicacy, and a still greater one to dignity of character. It may sometimes gain you applause, but will never procure you respect.

Be even cautious in displaying your good sense. It will be thought you assume a superiority over the rest of the company. — But if you happen to have any learning, keep it a profound secret, especially from the men, who generally look with a jealous and malignant eye on a woman of great parts, and cultivated understanding.

A man of real genius and candour is far superior to this meanness. But such a one will seldom fall in your way; and if by accident he should, do not be anxious to shew the full extent of your knowledge. If he has any opportunities of seeing you, he will soon discover it himself; and if you have any advantages of person or manner, and keep your own secret, he will probably give you credit for a great deal more than you possess. The great art of pleasing in conversation consists in making the company pleased with themselves. You will more readily hear than talk yourselves into their good graces.

Beware of detraction, especially where your own sex are concerned. You are generally accused of being particularly addicted to this vice. — I think unjustly. Men are fully as guilty of it when their interests interfere. — As your feelings are quicker than ours, your temptations to it are more frequent. For this reason, be particularly tender of the reputation of your own sex, especially when they happen to rival you in our regards. We look on this as the strongest proof of dignity and true greatness of mind.

Shew a compassionate sympathy to unfortunate women, especially to those who are rendered so by the villainy [sic] of men. Indulge a secret pleasure, I may say pride, in being the friends and refuge of the unhappy, but without the vanity of shewing it.

[pp. 26–34]

... I would particularly recommend to you those exercises that oblige you to be much abroad in the open air, such as walking, and riding on horse-back. This will give vigour to your constitutions, and a bloom to your complexions. If you accustom yourselves to go abroad always in chairs and carriages, you will soon become so enervated, as to be unable to go out of doors without them. They are, like most articles of luxury, useful and agreeable when judiciously used; but when made habitual, they become both insipid and pernicious.

An attention to your health is a duty you owe to yourselves and to your friends. Bad health seldom fails to have an influence on the spirits and temper. The finest geniuses, the most delicate minds, have very frequently a correspondent delicacy of bodily constitution, which they are too apt to neglect. Their luxury lies in reading and late hours, equal enemies to health and beauty.

But, though good health be one of the greatest blessings in life, never make a boast of it, but enjoy it in grateful silence. We so naturally associate the idea of female softness and delicacy with a correspondent delicacy of constitution, that when a woman speaks of her great strength, her extraordinary appetite, her ability to bear excessive fatigue, we recoil at the description in a way she is little aware of.

[pp. 48–51]

FRIENDSHIP, LOVE, MARRIAGE

... People whose sentiments, and particularly whose tastes, correspond, naturally like to associate together, although neither of them have the most distant view of any further connection. But as this similarity of minds often gives rise to a more tender attachment than friendship, it will be prudent to keep a watchful eye over yourselves, lest your hearts become too far engaged before you are aware of it. At the same time, I do not think that your sex, at least in this part of the world, have much of that sensibility which disposes to such attachments. What is commonly called love among you is rather gratitude, and a partiality to the man who prefers you to the rest of your sex: and such a man you often marry, with little of either personal esteem or affection. Indeed, without an unusual share of natural sensibility, and very peculiar good fortune, a woman in this country has very little probability of marrying for love.

It is a maxim laid down among you, and a very prudent one it is, That love is not to begin on your part, but is entirely to be the consequence of our attachment to you. Now, supposing a woman to have sense and taste, she will not find many men to whom she can possibly be supposed to bear any considerable share of esteem. Among these few, it is a very great chance if any of them distinguishes her particularly. Love, at least with us, is exceedingly capricious, and will not always fix where reason says it should. But supposing one of them should become particularly attached to her, it is still extremely improbable, that he should be the man in the world her heart most approved of.

As, therefore, Nature has not given you that unlimited range in your choice which we enjoy, she has wisely and benevolently assigned to you a greater flexibility of taste on this subject. Some agreeable qualities recommend a gentleman to your common good liking and friendship. In the course of his acquaintance, he contracts an attachment to you. When you perceive it, it excites your gratitude; this gratitude rises into a preference, and this preference perhaps at last advances to some degree of attachment, especially if it meets with crosses and difficulties; for these, and a state of suspense, are very great incitements to attachment, and are the food of love in both sexes. If attachment was not excited in your sex in this manner, there is not one of a million of you that could ever marry with any degree of love.

[pp. 79–83]

＊ ＊ ＊ ＊ ＊

His heart and his character will be improved in every respect by his attachment. His manners will become more gentle, and his conversation more agreeable; but diffidence and embarrassment will always make him appear to disadvantage in the company of his mistress. If the fascination continue long, it will totally depress his spirit, and extinguish every active, vigorous, and manly principle of his mind. You will find this subject beautifully and pathetically painted in Thomson's *Spring*.[1]

---

1 James Thomson, *Spring* (1728): ll. 1004–73 describe "the charming agonies of love" (1074).

When you observe in a gentleman's behaviour these marks which I have described above, reflect seriously what you are to do. If his attachment is agreeable to you, I leave you to do as nature, good sense, and delicacy, shall direct you. If you love him, let me advise you never to discover to him the full extent of your love, no not although you marry him. That sufficiently shews your preference; which is all he is intitled to know. If he has delicacy, he will ask for no stronger proof of your affection, for your sake; if he has sense, he will not ask it for his own. This is an unpleasant truth; but it is my duty to let you know it. Violent love cannot subsist, at least cannot be expressed, for any time together, on both sides; otherwise the certain consequence, however concealed, is satiety and disgust. Nature in this case has laid the reserve on you.

[pp.86–8]

* * * * *

... [In the event of unreciprocated attachment,] [A]t least do not shun opportunities of letting him explain himself. If you do this, you act barbarously and unjustly. If he brings you to an explanation, give him a polite, but resolute and decisive answer. In whatever way you convey your sentiments to him, if he is a man of spirit and delicacy, he will give you no further trouble, nor apply to your friends for their intercession. This last is a method of courtship which every man of spirit will disdain. — He will never whine nor sue for your pity. That would mortify him almost as much as your scorn. In short, you may possibly break such a heart; but you can never bend it. — Great pride always accompanies delicacy, however concealed under the appearance of the utmost gentleness and modesty, and is the passion of all others the most difficult to conquer.

There is a case where a woman may coquette justifiably to the utmost verge which her conscience will allow. It is, where a gentleman purposely declines to make his addresses, till such time as he thinks himself perfectly sure of her consent. This at bottom is intended to force a woman to give up the undoubted privilege of her sex, the privilege of refusing; it is intended to force her to explain herself, in effect, before the gentleman deigns to do it, and by this means to violate the modesty and delicacy of her sex, and to invert the clearest order of nature. All this sacrifice is proposed to be made merely to gratify a most despicable vanity in a man who would degrade the very woman whom he wishes to make his wife.

[pp.91–3]

* * * * *

A woman, in this country, may easily prevent the first impressions of love, and every motive of prudence and delicacy should make her guard her heart against them, till such time as she has received the most convincing proofs of the attachment of a man of such merit, as will justify a reciprocal regard. Your hearts indeed may be shut inflexibly and permanently against all the merit a man can possess. That may be your misfortune, but cannot be your fault. In such a situation, you would be equally unjust to yourself and your lover, if you gave him your hand when your heart revolted against him. But miserable will be your fate, if you allow an attachment to steal on you before you are sure of a return; or, what is infinitely worse, where there are wanting those qualities which alone can ensure happiness in a married state.

I know nothing that renders a woman more despicable, than her thinking it essential to happiness to be married. Besides the gross indelicacy of the sentiment, it is a false one, as thousands of women have experienced. But if it was true, the belief that it is so, and the consequent impatience to be married, is the most effectual way to prevent it.[1]

---

1 A passage difficult in itself, and, as Gregory acknowledges, in some tension with the three paragraphs that follow. It is possible to read the phrase, "thinking it essential to happiness to be married" to mean, not that marriage is a necessary condition for happiness, but that from marriage, happiness necessarily flows: what "thousands of women have experienced" is then not happy spinsterhood (which the following text deems extremely unlikely) but unhappy marriage. The last sentence might be paraphrased as, "Rushing into marriage because you think your happiness depends on it ensures you will end up in an unhappy marriage": the fate of Lydia Wickham as of her mother before her. In any case, the first sentence locates the problem with this opinion not in its factual error, but in its rendering the woman who holds it "despicable" (to men), suggesting that the problem only arises if this opinion (that it is "essential to happiness to be married") is one she is known (by men) to hold. Thus the tension between this paragraph and the following discussion is an expression of the double bind in which the conduct books routinely place the young woman: her choice of a husband is of enormous moral importance, yet she only retains that choice if her preference for any one man is never openly expressed. What renders a woman despicable is, as so often in conduct literature, the open acknowledgement of her own desire.

You must not think from this, that I do not wish you to marry. On the contrary, I am of opinion, that you may attain a superior degree of happiness in a married state, to what you can possibly find in any other. I know the forlorn and unprotected situation of the old maid, the chagrin and peevishness which are apt to infect their tempers, and the great difficulty of making a transition, with dignity and cheerfulness, from the period of youth, beauty, admiration, and respect, into the calm, silent, unnoticed retreat of declining years.

I see some unmarried women of active vigorous minds, and great vivacity of spirits, degrading themselves, sometimes by entering into a dissipated course of life, unsuitable to their years, and exposing themselves to the ridicule of girls, who might have been their grandchildren; sometimes by oppressing their acquaintances by impertinent instructions into their private affairs; and sometimes by being the propagators of scandal and defamation. And this is owing to an exuberant activity of spirit, which, if it had found employment at home, would have rendered them respectable and useful members of society.

I see other women, in the same situation, gentle, modest, blessed with sense, taste, delicacy, and every milder feminine virtue of the heart, but of weak spirits, bashful, and timid: I see such women sinking into obscurity and insignificance, and gradually losing every elegant accomplishment; for this evident reason, that they are not united to a partner who has sense, and worth, and taste, to know their value; one who is able to draw forth their concealed qualities, and shew them to advantage; who can give that support to their feeble spirits which they stand so much in need of; and who, by his affection and tenderness, might make such a woman happy in exerting every talent, and accomplishing herself in every elegant art that could contribute to his amusement.[1]

In short, I am of opinion, that a married state, if entered into from proper motives of esteem and affection, will be the happiest for yourselves, make you most respectable in the eyes of the world, and the most useful members of society. But I confess, I am not enough of a

---

1 The ambiguity continues: were it not for that phrase "in the same situation," which on the face of it marks this passage as a continuation of the discussion of spinsterhood, this passage would read convincingly as a description of marriage to an inadequate husband, understood as an outcome equally morally disastrous. This is after all the equivalence with which the following paragraph ends the discussion.

patriot to wish you to marry for the good of the public. I wish you to marry for no other reason but to make yourselves happier. When I am so particular in my advices about your conduct, I own my heart beats with the fond hope of making you worthy the attachment of men who will deserve you, and be sensible of your merit. But Heaven forbid you should ever relinquish the ease and independence of a single life, to become the slaves of a fool or a tyrant's caprice.

[pp.103–10]

Appendix C: Burke on the French Revolution

From Edmund Burke, *Reflections on the Revolution in France, and on the proceedings of certain societies in London relative to that event. In a letter intended to have been sent to a gentleman in Paris.* London: J. Dodsley, 1790.

[Edmund Burke (1729–97) was a lawyer, politician, and writer. He was a passionate advocate of greater political liberty for Ireland and, before their secession, for the American colonies, and a fierce defender of the autonomy of the House of Commons from the Crown; yet the *Reflections* denounced the overthrow of the monarchy in France, at a time when many of his political allies were still celebrating it as a triumph for just this sort of liberty. For Burke, the institutions of society, including political liberty, are founded on what he calls "feeling" or "prejudice" of the sort that we have in favour of family members or neighbours, and not the abstract reasoning on which he sees the revolutionaries trying to found their new order.]

* * * * *

You will observe, that from Magna Charta to the Declaration of Right, it has been the uniform policy of our constitution to claim and assert our liberties, as an *entailed inheritance* derived to us from our forefathers, and to be transmitted to posterity; as an estate specially belonging to the people of this kingdom without any reference whatever to any other more general or prior right.[1] By this means

---

1 The Magna Carta (1215) and the Bill of Rights (1689) both set limits to the powers of the crown. In the former, King John grants "to all freemen of our kingdom, for us and our heirs forever, all the liberties herein under written, to be had and held by them and their heirs of us and our heirs" (trans. from the Latin by Stephenson and Marcham); in the latter, lords and commons "in the first place (as their Auncestors in like Case have usually done) for the Vindicating and Asserting their auntient Rights and Liberties" subordinate royal authority to the law. Just how "ancient" the rights asserted in 1689 really were was a subject of some controversy in eighteenth-century Britain, but it is this language of "ancestors" and "heirs" that Burke has in mind here.

our constitution preserves an unity in so great a diversity of its parts. We have an inheritable crown; an inheritable peerage; and an house of commons and a people inheriting privileges, franchises, and liberties, from a long line of ancestors.

This policy appears to me to be the result of profound reflection; or rather the happy effect of following nature, which is wisdom without reflection, and above it. A spirit of innovation is generally the result of a selfish temper and confined views. People will not look forward to posterity, who never look backward to their ancestors. Besides, the people of England well know, that the idea of inheritance furnishes a sure principle of conservation, and a sure principle of transmission; without at all excluding a principle of improvement. It leaves acquisition free; but it secures what it acquires. Whatever advantages are obtained by a state proceeding on these maxims, are locked fast as in a sort of family settlement; grasped as in a kind of mortmain[1] for ever. By a constitutional policy, working after the pattern of nature, we receive, we hold, we transmit our government and our privileges, in the same manner in which we enjoy and transmit our property and our lives. The institutions of policy, the goods of fortune, the gifts of Providence, are handed down, to us and from us, in the same course and order. Our political system is placed in a just correspondence and symmetry with the order of the world, and with the mode of existence decreed to a permanent body composed of transitory parts; wherein, by the disposition of a stupendous wisdom, moulding together the great mysterious incorporation of the human race, the whole, at one time, is never old, or middle-aged, or young, but in a condition of unchangeable constancy, moves on through the varied tenour of perpetual decay, fall, renovation, and progression. Thus, by preserving the method of nature in the conduct of the state, in what we improve we are never wholly new; in what we retain we are never wholly obsolete. By adhering in this manner and on those principles to our forefathers, we are guided not by the superstition of antiquarians, but by the spirit of philosophic analogy. In this choice of inheritance we have given to our frame of polity the image of a relation in blood; binding up the constitution of our country with our

---

1 Lands held in mortmain are, like those bound by entail, not available to the possessor to dispose of as he likes; the possessor in this case being a corporation (e.g. the church) rather than an individual.

dearest domestic ties; adopting our fundamental laws into the bosom of our family affections; keeping inseparable, and cherishing with the warmth of all their combined and mutually reflected charities, our state, our hearths, our sepulchres, and our altars.

Through the same plan of a conformity to nature in our artificial institutions, and by calling in the aid of her unerring and powerful instincts, to fortify the fallible and feeble contrivances of our reason, we have derived several other, and these no small benefits, from considering our liberties in the light of an inheritance. Always acting as if in the presence of our canonized forefathers, the spirit of freedom, leading in itself to misrule and excess, is tempered with an awful gravity. This idea of a liberal descent inspires us with a sense of habitual native dignity, which prevents that upstart insolence almost inevitably adhering to and disgracing those who are the first acquirers of any distinction. By this means our liberty becomes a noble freedom. It carries an imposing and majestic aspect. It has a pedigree, and illustrating ancestors. It has its bearings, and its ensigns armorial. It has its gallery of portraits; its monumental inscriptions; its records, evidences, and titles. We procure reverence to our civil institutions on the principle upon which nature teaches us to revere individual men; on account of their age; and on account of those from whom they are descended. All your sophisters cannot produce any thing better adapted to preserve a rational and manly freedom than the course that we have pursued, who have chosen our nature rather than our speculations, our breasts rather than our inventions, for the great conservatories and magazines of our rights and privileges.

[pp.47–50]

* * * * *

…We preserve the whole of our feelings still native and entire, unsophisticated by pedantry and infidelity. We have real hearts of flesh and blood beating in our bosoms. We fear God; we look up with awe to kings; with affection to parliaments; with duty to magistrates; with reverence to priests; and with respect to nobility. Why? Because when such ideas are brought before our minds, it is *natural* to be so affected; because all other feelings are false and spurious, and tend to corrupt our minds, to vitiate our primary morals, to render us unfit for rational liberty; and, by teaching us a servile, licentious, and abandoned insolence, to be our low sport for a few holidays, to make us perfectly fit for, and justly deserving of slavery, through the whole course of our lives.

You see, Sir, that in this enlightened age I am bold enough to confess, that we are generally men of untaught feelings; that instead of casting away all our old prejudices, we cherish them to a very considerable degree, and, to take more shame to ourselves, we cherish them because they are prejudices; and the longer they have lasted, and the more generally they have prevailed, the more we cherish them. We are afraid to put men to live and trade each on his own private stock of reason; because we suspect that this stock in each man is small, and that the individuals would do better to avail themselves of the general bank and capital of nations, and of ages. Many of our men of speculation, instead of exploding general prejudices, employ their sagacity to discover the latent wisdom which prevails in them. If they find what they seek, and they seldom fail, they think it more wise to continue the prejudice, with the reason involved, than to cast away the coat of prejudice, and to leave nothing but the naked reason; because prejudice, with its reason, has a motive to give action to that reason, and an affection which will give it permanence. Prejudice is of ready application in the emergency; it previously engages the mind in a steady course of wisdom and virtue, and does not leave the man hesitating in the moment of decision, sceptical, puzzled, and unresolved. Prejudice renders a man's virtue his habit; and not a series of unconnected acts. Through just prejudice, his duty becomes a part of his nature.

Your literary men, and your politicians, and so do the whole clan of the enlightened among us, essentially differ in these points.[1] They have no respect for the wisdom of others; but they pay it off by a very full measure of confidence in their own. With them it is a sufficient

---

1   The opposition Burke is constructing here is between the economists and "common sense" philosophers of the Scottish school such as Adam Smith (1723–90) and Thomas Reid (1710–96), who were concerned to show how the human mind and society actually worked, and in doing to so to explain (and, broadly, *justify*) the existing commercial/oligarchic political arrangements of the United Kingdom; and thinkers such as Voltaire (1694–1778) and Denis Diderot (1713–84) and their English admirers, who attempted to demystify the absolutist alliance of church and monarchy in their native France with the aim of *replacing* it with a more rational order. Burke holds the *philosophes* and their critical project responsible for the revolution. Despite the differences of their respective institutional situations, there was of course a great deal of mutual interest and influence between the Scottish and French schools.

motive to destroy an old scheme of things, because it is an old one. As to the new, they are in no sort of fear with regard to the duration of a building run up in haste; because duration is no object to those who think little or nothing has been done before their time, and who place all their hopes in discovery. They conceive, very systematically, that all things which give perpetuity are mischievous, and therefore they are at inexpiable war with all establishments.

[pp. 128–30]

* * * * *

... [O]ne of the first and most leading principles on which the commonwealth and the laws are consecrated, is lest the temporary possessors and life-renters in it, unmindful of what they have received from their ancestors, or of what is due to their posterity, should act as if they were the entire masters; that they should not think it amongst their rights to cut off the entail, or commit waste on the inheritance, by destroying at their pleasure the whole original fabric of their society; hazarding to leave to those who come after them, a ruin instead of an habitation — and teaching these successors as little to respect their contrivances, as they had themselves respected the institutions of their forefathers. By this unprincipled facility of changing the state as often, and as much, and in as many ways as there are floating fancies or fashions, the whole chain and continuity of the commonwealth would be broken. No one generation could link with the other. Men would become little better than the flies of a summer.

[p. 141]

* * * * *

By the vast debt of France a great monied interest had insensibly grown up, and with it a great power. By the ancient usages which prevailed in that kingdom, the general circulation of property, and in particular the mutual convertability of land into money, and of money into land, had always been a matter of difficulty. Family settlements, rather more general and more strict than they are in England, the *jus retractus*,[1] the great mass of landed property held by the crown, and by a maxim of the French law held unalienably, the vast estates of

---

1   The "right of retraction" whereby the heirs of a landowner who has sold some of his land can force the buyer to sell it back. In pre-revolutionary French law, this rule prevented a free market in land even more thoroughly than strict settlements did in England: see Introduction.

the ecclesiastic corporations,—all these had kept the landed and monied interests more separated in France, less miscible, and the owners of the two distinct species of property not so well disposed to each other as they are in this country.

The monied property was long looked on with rather an evil eye by the people. They saw it connected with their distresses, and aggravating them. It was no less envied by the old landed interests, partly for the same reasons that rendered it obnoxious to the people, but much more so as it eclipsed, by the splendour of ostentatious luxury, the unendowed pedigrees and naked titles of several among the nobility. Even when the nobility, which represented the more permanent landed interest, united themselves by marriage (which sometimes was the case) with the other description, the wealth which saved the family from ruin, was supposed to contaminate and degrade it. Thus the enmities and heart-burnings of these parties were encreased even by the usual means by which discord is made to cease, and quarrels are turned into friendship. In the mean time, the pride of the wealthy men, not noble or newly noble, encreased with its cause. They felt with resentment an inferiority, the grounds of which they did not acknowledge. There was no measure to which they were not willing to lend themselves, in order to be revenged of the outrages of this rival pride, and to exalt their wealth to what they considered as its natural rank and estimation... .

[pp. 163–64]

Appendix D: Discussion of Women's Role after the French Revolution

1. From Mary Wollstonecraft, *A Vindication of the Rights of Woman: with strictures on political and moral subjects*. London: J. Johnson, 1792.

[Mary Wollstonecraft (1759–97) had published, in 1790, a radical counterblast to Burke, entitled *A Vindication of the Rights of Men. A Vindication of the Rights of Woman* is both a continuation and a departure from that project, turning a revolutionary eye on the subordinated position of women in society, a position that male radicals and conservatives alike left unquestioned. She finds the cause of that subordination in the poor education that middle-class girls receive, leaving them unable to fulfill any useful function in society. In 1798 her widower, William Godwin, published a memoir in which he revealed the facts of her unconventional private life, including her illegitimate child with the American writer Gilbert Imlay. This pretty much ruined her reputation among those concerned, like Austen, to appear "respectable," yet her emphasis on the need for young women to be treated as and thus become rational creatures is one that Austen shares.]

From Chapter 2. The Prevailing Opinion of a Sexual Character Discussed

... To do everything in an orderly manner is a most important precept, which women, who, generally speaking, receive only a disorderly kind of education, seldom attend to with that degree of exactness that men, who from their infancy are broken into method, observe. This negligent kind of guesswork—for what other epithet can be used to point out the random exertions of a sort of instinctive common sense never brought to the test of reason?—prevents their generalizing matters of fact; so they do today what they did yesterday, merely because they did it yesterday.

This contempt of the understanding in early life has more baneful consequences than is commonly supposed; for the little knowledge which young women of strong minds attain is, from various circumstances, of a more desultory kind than the knowledge of men, and it is acquired more by sheer observations of real life than from comparing what has been individually observed with the results of experience generalized by speculation. Led by their dependent situation and domestic employments more into society, what they learn is rather by snatches; and as learning is with them in general only a secondary thing, they do not pursue any one branch with that persevering ardour necessary to give vigour to the faculties and clearness to the judgement.

[pp.40–41]

* * * * *

As a proof that education gives this appearance of weakness to females, we may instance the example of military men, who are, like them, sent into the world before their minds have been stored with knowledge, or fortified by principles. The consequences are similar; soldiers acquire a little superficial knowledge, snatched from the muddy current of conversation, and from continually mixing with society, they gain what is termed a knowledge of the world; and this acquaintance with manners and customs has frequently been confounded with a knowledge of the human heart. But can the crude fruit of casual observation, never brought to the test of judgement, formed by comparing speculation and experience, deserve such a distinction? Soldiers, as well as women, practise the minor virtues with punctilious politeness. Where is then the sexual difference, when the education has been the same? All the difference that I can discern arises from the superior advantage of liberty which enables the former to see more of life.

It is wandering from my present subject, perhaps, to make a political remark; but as it was produced naturally by the train of my reflections, I shall not pass it silently over.

Standing armies can never consist of resolute robust men;[1] they

---

1 Note that Wollstonecraft is here discussing specifically *professional* soldiers, rather than the militias. Her comments stand in a long line of objections to professional standing armies originating in late seventeenth- and early eighteenth-century anxieties about their expense and gift of greater power to the monarch and his or her ministers — objections only finally silenced by the long years of war that Britain, in 1792, was about to enter.

may be well-disciplined machines, but they will seldom contain men under the influence of strong passions, or with very vigorous faculties; and as for any depth of understanding, I will venture to affirm that it is as rarely to be found in the army as amongst women. And the cause, I maintain, is the same. It may be further observed that officers are also particularly attentive to their persons, fond of dancing, crowded rooms, adventures, and ridicule. Like the *fair* sex, the business of their lives is gallantry; they were taught to please, and they only live to please. Yet they do not lose their rank in the distinction of sexes, for they are still reckoned superior to women, though in what their superiority consists, beyond what I have just mentioned, it is difficult to discover.

The great misfortune is this, that both acquire manners before morals, and a knowledge of life before they have from reflection any acquaintance with the grand ideal outline of human nature. The consequence is natural. Satisfied with common nature, they become a prey to prejudices, and taking all their opinions on credit, they blindly submit to authority. So that if they have any sense, it is a kind of instinctive glance that catches proportions, and decides with respect to manners, but falls when arguments are to be pursued below the surface, or opinions analysed.

[pp.42–44]

* * * * *

... Do passive indolent women make the best wives? Confining our discussion to the present moment of existence, let us see how such weak creatures perform their part? Do the women who, by the attainment of a few superficial accomplishments, have strengthened the prevailing prejudice, merely contribute to the happiness of their husbands? Do they display their charms merely to amuse them? And have women who have early imbibed notions of passive obedience, sufficient character to manage a family or educate children? So far from it, that, after surveying the history of woman, I cannot help agreeing with the severest satirist, considering the sex as the weakest as well as the most oppressed half of the species. What does history disclose but marks of inferiority, and how few women have emancipated themselves from the galling yoke of sovereign man? So few that the exceptions remind me of an ingenious conjecture respecting Newton—that he was probably a being of a *superiour* order accidentally caged in a human body. Following the same train of thinking, I have been led to imagine that the few extraordinary women who have rushed in eccentrical directions out of the orbit prescribed to their sex, were *male* spirits, confined by mistake in female frames. But if it be not philosophical to think of sex when the soul is mentioned, the inferiority must depend on the organs; or the heavenly fire, which is to ferment the clay, is not given in equal portions.

But avoiding, as I have hitherto done, any direct comparison of the two sexes collectively, or frankly acknowledging the inferiority of woman, according to the present appearance of things, I shall only insist that men have increased that inferiority till women are almost sunk below the standing of rational creatures. Let their faculties have room to unfold, and their virtues to gain strength, and then determine where the whole sex must stand in the intellectual scale. Yet let it be remembered that for a small number of distinguished women I do not ask a place.

It is difficult for us purblind mortals to say to what height human discoveries and improvements may arrive, when the gloom of despotism subsides, which makes us stumble at every step; but, when morality shall be settled on a more solid basis, then, without being gifted with a prophetic spirit, I will venture to predict that woman will be either the friend or the slave of man.

[pp.67–69]

* * * * *

From Chapter 3. The Same Subject continued.

... I will venture to affirm, that a girl, whose spirits have not been damped by inactivity, or innocence tainted by false shame, will always be a romp, and the doll will never excite attention unless confinement allows her no alternative. Girls and boys, in short, would play harmlessly together, if the distinction of sex was not inculcated long before nature makes any difference. I will go further, and affirm, as an indisputable fact, that most of the women, in the circle of my observation, who have acted like rational creatures, or shown any vigour of intellect, have accidentally been allowed to run wild, as some of the elegant formers of the fair sex would insinuate.

The baneful consequences which flow from inattention to health during infancy and youth, extend further than is supposed—dependence of body naturally produces dependence of mind; and how can she be a good wife or mother, the greater part of whose time is employed to guard against or endure sickness? Nor can it be expected that a woman will resolutely endeavour to strengthen her constitution and abstain from enervating indulgences, if artificial notions of beauty, and false descriptions of sensibility, have been early entangled with her motives of action. Most men are sometimes obliged to bear with bodily inconveniences, and to endure, occasionally, the inclemency of the elements; but genteel women are, literally speaking, slaves to their bodies, and glory in their subjection.

[pp.87–88]

* * * * *

From Chapter 4. Observations on the State of Degradation to which Woman is Reduced by Various Causes.

… A fine lady, on the contrary, has been taught to look down with contempt on the vulgar employments of life, though she had only been incited to acquire accomplishments that rise a degree above sense; for even corporeal accomplishments cannot be acquired with any degree of precision unless the understanding has been strengthened by exercise. Without a foundation of principles taste is superficial; grace must arise from something deeper than imitation. The imagination, however, is heated, and the feelings rendered fastidious, if not sophisticated, or a counter poise of judgement is not acquired when the heart still remains artless, though it becomes too tender.

These women are often amiable, and their hearts are really more sensible to general benevolence, more alive to the sentiments that civilize life, than the square-elbowed family drudge, but, wanting a due proportion of reflection and self-government, they only inspire love, and are the mistresses of their husbands, whilst they have any hold on their affections, and the Platonic friends of his male acquaintance. These are the fair defects in Nature; the women who appear to be created not to enjoy the fellowship of man, but to save him from sinking into absolute brutality, by rubbing off the rough angles of his character, and by playful dalliance to give some dignity to the appetite that draws him to them. Gracious Creator of the whole human race! hast Thou created such a being as woman, who can trace Thy wisdom in Thy works, and feel that Thou alone art served by Thy nature exalted above her, for no better purpose? Can she believe that she was only made to submit to man, her equal—a being, who, like her, was sent into the world to acquire virtue? Can she consent to be occupied merely to please him—merely to adorn the earth—when her soul is capable of rising to Thee? And can she rest supinely dependent on man for reason, when she ought to mount with him the arduous steeps of knowledge?

Yet if love be the supreme good, let woman be only educated to inspire it, and let every charm be polished to intoxicate the senses; but if they be moral beings, let them have a chance to become intelligent; and let love to man be only a part of that glowing flame of universal love, which, after encircling humanity, mounts in grateful incense to God.

[pp.144–46]

✳ ✳ ✳ ✳ ✳

From Chapter 5. Animadversions on Some Writers Who Have Rendered Women Objects of Pity.

Section III [Dr. Gregory].

Such paternal solicitude pervades Dr. Gregory's *Legacy to his Daughters*, that I enter on the task of criticism with affectionate respect; but as this little volume has many attractions to recommend it to the notice of the most respectable part of my sex, I cannot silently pass over arguments that so speciously support opinions which, I think, have had the most baneful effect on the morals and manners of the female world.

His easy familiar style is particularly suited to the tenor of his advice, and the melancholy tenderness which his respect for the memory of a beloved wife, diffuses through the whole work, renders it very interesting; yet there is a degree of concise elegance conspicuous in many passages that disturbs this sympathy; and we pop on the author, when we only expected to meet the—father.

Besides, having two objects in view, he seldom adhered steadily to either; for wishing to make his daughters amiable, and fearing lest unhappiness should only be the consequence, of instilling sentiments that might draw them out of the track of common life without enabling them to act with consonant independence and dignity, he checks the natural flow of his thoughts, and neither advises one thing nor the other.

[pp.215–16]

* * * * *

The remarks relative to behaviour, though many of them very sensible, I entirely disapprove of, because it appears to me to be beginning, as it were, at the wrong end. A cultivated understanding, and an affectionate heart, will never want starched rules of decorum—something more substantial than seemliness will be the result; and, without understanding the behaviour here recommended, would be rank affectation. Decorum, indeed, is the one thing needful!—decorum is to supplant nature, and banish all simplicity and variety of character out of the female world. Yet what good end can all this superficial counsel produce? It is, however, much easier to point out this or that mode of behaviour, than to set the reason to work; but, when the mind has been stored with useful knowledge, and strengthened by being employed, the regulation of the behaviour may safely be left to its guidance.

Why, for instance, should the following caution be given when art of every kind must contaminate the mind; and why entangle the grand motives of action, which reason and religion equally combine to enforce, with pitiful worldly shifts and slight-of-hand tricks to gain the applause of gaping tasteless fools? 'Be even cautious in displaying your good sense. It will be thought you assume a superiority over the rest of the company—But if you happen to have any learning, keep it a profound secret, especially from the men, who generally look with a jealous and malignant eye on a woman of great parts, and a cultivated understanding.'[1] If men of real merit, as he afterwards observes, are superiour to this meanness, where is the necessity that the behaviour of the whole sex should be modulated to please fools, or men, who having little claim to respect as individuals, choose to keep close in their phalanx. Men, indeed, who insist on their common superiority, having only this sexual superiority, are certainly very excusable.

There would be no end to rules for behaviour, if it be proper

---

1   More quotes John Gregory: see p.406.

always to adopt the tone of the company; for thus, for ever varying the key, a *flat* would often pass for a *natural* note.

Surely it would have been wiser to have advised women to improve themselves till they rose above the fumes of vanity; and then to let the public opinion come round—for where are rules of accommodation to stop? The narrow path of truth and virtue inclines neither to the right nor left—it is a straight-forward business, and they who are earnestly pursuing their road, may bound over many decorous prejudices, without leaving modesty behind. Make the heart clean, and give the head employment, and I will venture to predict that there will be nothing offensive in the behaviour.

The air of fashion, which many young people are so eager to attain, always strikes me like the studied attitudes of some modern prints, copied with tasteless servility after the antiques;—the soul is left out, and none of the parts are tied together by what may properly be termed character. This varnish of fashion, which seldom sticks very close to sense, may dazzle the weak; but leave nature to itself, and it will seldom disgust the wise. Besides, when a woman has sufficient sense not to pretend to any thing which she does not understand in some degree, there is no need of determining to hide her talents under a bushel. Let things take their natural course, and all will be well.

It is this system of dissimulation, throughout the volume, that I despise. Women are always to seem to be this and that—yet virtue might apostrophize them, in the words of Hamlet—Seems! I know not seems! Have that within that passeth show!—[1]

[pp.217–21]

✳ ✳ ✳ ✳ ✳

From Chapter 6. The Effect which an Early Association of Ideas Has upon the Character.

… [T]here is an habitual association of ideas, that grows 'with our growth,' which has a great effect on the moral character of mankind;

---

1 Hamlet, questioned by his mother on his protracted mourning for his father: "'Seems', madam? Nay, it is. I know not 'seems'. / … / … I have that within which passes show— / These but the trappings and the suits of woe" (I.ii.76, 85–6).

and by which a turn is given to the mind that commonly remains throughout life. So ductile is the understanding, and yet so stubborn, that the associations which depend on adventitious circumstances, during the period that the body takes to arrive at maturity, can seldom be disentangled by reason. One idea calls up another, its old associate, and memory, faithful to the first impressions, particularly when the intellectual powers are not employed to cool our sensations, retraces them with mechanical exactness.

This habitual slavery, to first impressions, has a more baneful effect on the female than the male character, because business and other dry employments of the understanding, tend to deaden the feelings and break associations that do violence to reason. But females, who are made women of when they are mere children, and brought back to childhood when they ought to leave the go-cart for ever, have not sufficient strength of mind to efface the superinductions of art that have smothered nature.

Every thing that they see or hear serves to fix impressions, call forth emotions, and associate ideas, that give a sexual character to the mind. False notions of beauty and delicacy stop the growth of their limbs and produce a sickly soreness, rather than delicacy of organs; and thus weakened by being employed in unfolding instead of examining the first associations, forced on them by every surrounding object, how can they attain the vigour necessary to enable them to throw off their factitious character? — where find strength to recur to reason and rise superiour to a system of oppression, that blasts the fair promises of spring? This cruel association of ideas, which every thing conspires to twist into all their habits of thinking, or, to speak with more precision, of feeling, receives new force when they begin to act a little for themselves; for they then perceive that it is only through their address to excite emotions in men, that pleasure and power are to be obtained. Besides, the books professedly written for their instruction, which make the first impression on their minds, all inculcate the same opinions. Educated then in worse than Egyptian bondage, it is unreasonable, as well as cruel, to upbraid them with faults that can scarcely be avoided, unless a degree of native vigour be supposed, that falls to the lot of very few amongst mankind.

For instance, the severest sarcasms have been levelled against the sex, and they have been ridiculed for repeating 'a set of phrases learnt by rote,' when nothing could be more natural, considering the education they receive, and that their 'highest praise is to obey, unargued'—the will of man. If they are not allowed to have reason sufficient to govern their own conduct—why, all they learn—must be learned by rote! And when all their ingenuity is called forth to adjust their dress, 'a passion for a scarlet coat,'[1] is so natural, that it never surprised me; and, allowing Pope's summary of their character to be just, 'that every woman is at heart a rake,' why should they be bitterly censured for seeking a congenial mind, and preferring a rake to a man of sense?[2]

Rakes know how to work on their sensibility, whilst the modest merit of reasonable men has, of course, less effect on their feelings, and they cannot reach the heart by the way of the understanding, because they have few sentiments in common.

It seems a little absurd to expect women to be more reasonable than men in their *likings*, and still to deny them the uncontrouled use of reason. When do men *fall-in-love* with sense? When do they, with their superiour powers and advantages, turn from the person to the mind? And how can they then expect women, who are only taught to observe behaviour, and acquire manners rather than morals, to despise what they have been all their lives labouring to attain? Where are they suddenly to find *judgment* enough to weigh patiently the sense of an awkward virtuous man, when his manners, of which they are made critical judges, are rebuffing, and his conversation cold and dull, because it does not consist of pretty repartees, or well turned compliments? In order to admire or esteem any thing for a continuance, we must, at least, have our curiosity excited by knowing, in some degree, what we admire; for we are unable to estimate the value of qualities and virtues above our comprehension. Such a respect, when it is felt, may be very sublime; and the confused consciousness of humility may render the dependent creature an interesting object, in some points of view; but human love must have grosser ingredients; and the person

---

1 "A scarlet coat": i.e., a soldier: exactly as Mrs. Bennett expresses herself in Volume I chapter vii. Wollstonecraft takes the phrase from Jonathan Swift's satirical poem "The Furniture of a Woman's Mind" (c.1735) which begins its list with "A set of phrases learnt by rote; / A passion for a scarlet coat ...".

2   Men, some to Bus'ness, some to Pleasure take;
        But ev'ry Woman is at heart a Rake:
        Men, some to Quiet, some to public Strife;
        But ev'ry Lady would be Queen for life.
Pope, *Moral Essays. Epistle II: To a Lady. Of the Characters of Women* (1735) ll.215–18.

very naturally will come in for its share—and, an ample share it mostly has!

Love is, in a great degree, an arbitrary passion, and will reign, like some other stalking mischiefs, by its own authority, without deigning to reason; and it may also be easily distinguished from esteem, the foundation of friendship, because it is often excited by evanescent beauties and graces, though to give an energy to the sentiment, something more solid must deepen their impression and set the imagination to work, to make the most fair—the first good.

[pp.262–66]

2. From Hannah More, *Strictures on the Modern System of Female Education, with a view of the principles and conduct prevalent among women of rank and fortune*. Two volumes. London: T. Cadell Jun. and W. Davies, 1799

[Hannah More (1745–1833) began her working life running a boarding school in Bristol; in the 1770s she was a literary star in London among the "Bluestockings" (educated, well-connected literary women), and in the circle around Samuel Johnson, writing successful plays and poetry. But in the 1780s, driven by deepening religious convictions, she once again became active in education, and particularly the setting up of Sunday schools for the poor. She put her skills as a writer to work in various popular works of religious and moral didacticism, and in the aftermath of the French Revolution, in the service of the anti-Jacobin cause (she argued against teaching the poor to write, for example, as this would only lead to discontent with their station: not an unusual position in late eighteenth-century England, by any means). In *Strictures* she turns her attention to the morality of the wealthy, but this text shares with her other later work an emphasis on the *political* importance that the behaviour of women is now supposed to have, and in this *Strictures* is set apart from earlier conduct manuals such as those by Fordyce and Gregory.]

From Chapter 1. *Address to women of rank and fortune, on the effect of their influence on society.—Suggestions for the exertion of it in various instances.*

Among the talents for the application of which women of the higher class will be peculiarly accountable, there is one, the importance of which they can scarcely rate too highly. This talent is influence. We read of the greatest orator of antiquity, that the wisest plans which it had cost him years to frame, a woman could overturn in a single day;[1] and when one considers the variety of mischiefs which an ill-directed influence has been known to produce, one is lead to reflect with the most sanguine hope on the beneficial effects to be expected from the same powerful force when exerted in its true direction.

The general state of civilized society depends more than those are aware, who are not accustomed to scrutinize into the springs of human action, on the prevailing sentiments and habits of women, and on the nature and degree of the estimation in which they are held. Even those who admit the power of female elegance on the manners of men, do not always attend to the influence of female principles on their character. In the former case, indeed, women are apt to be sufficiently conscious of their power, and not backward in turning it to account. But there are nobler objects to be effected by the exertion of their powers, and unfortunately, ladies, who are often unreasonably confident where they ought to be diffident, are sometimes capriciously diffident just when they ought to feel their true importance lies; and, feeling, to exert it. To use their boasted power over mankind to no higher purpose than the gratification of vanity or the indulgence of pleasure, is the degrading triumph of those fair victims to luxury, caprice, and despotism, whom the laws and the religion of the voluptuous prophet of Arabia exclude from light, and liberty, and knowledge; and it is humbling to reflect, that in those countries in which fondness for the mere persons of women is carried to the highest

---

1 I have been unable to trace this: "the greatest orator" was usually taken as the 4th century B.C.E. Athenian statesman Demosthenes. More may have no more in mind than the standard clause in Athenian law, often alluded to by Demosthenes in his speeches, that a man is not legally responsible for his actions if "under the influence of a woman" at the time, as equally if under the influence of drugs, or madness, or senility.

excess, *they are slaves;* and that their moral and intellectual degradation increases in direct proportion to the adoration which is paid to mere external charms.

But I turn to the bright reverse of this mortifying scene; to a country where our sex enjoys the blessing of liberal instruction, of reasonable laws, of a pure religion, and all the endearing pleasures of an equal, social, virtuous, and delightful intercourse: I turn with an earnest hope, that women, thus richly endowed with the bounties of Providence, will not content themselves with polishing, when they are able to reform; with entertaining, when they may awaken; and with captivating for a day, when they may bring into action powers of which the effects may be commensurate with eternity.

In this moment of alarm and peril, I would call on them with a "warning voice,"[1] which would stir up every latent principle in their minds, and kindle every slumbering energy in their hearts; I would call on them to come forward, and contribute their full and fair proportion towards the saving of their country. But I would call on them to come forward, without departing from the refinement of their character, without derogating from the dignity of their rank, without blemishing the delicacy of their sex: I would call them to the best and most appropriate exertion of their power, to raise the depressed tone of public morals, and to awaken the drowsy spirit of religious principle. They know all too well how arbitrarily they give the law to manners, and with how despotic a sway they fix the standard of fashion. But this is not enough; this is a low mark, a prize not worthy of their high and holy calling. For, on the use which women of the superior class may be disposed to make of that power delegated to them by the courtesy of custom, by the honest gallantry of the heart, by the imperious control of virtuous affections, by the habits of civilized states, by the usages of polished society; on the use, I say, which they shall hereafter make of this influence, will depend, in no low degree, the well-being of those states, and the virtue and happiness, nay perhaps the very existence of that society.

At this period, when our country can only hope to stand by opposing a bold and noble *unanimity* to the most tremendous confed-

---

1   "O for that warning voice, which he who saw / The Apocalypse, heard cry in heaven aloud": the opening of Book IV of John Milton's *Paradise Lost* (1667).

eracies against religion, and order, and governments, which the world ever saw;[1] what an accession would it bring to the public strength, could we prevail on beauty, and rank, and talents, and virtue, confederating their several powers, to come forward with a patriotism at once firm and feminine for the general good! I am not sounding an alarm to female warriors, or exciting female politicians; I hardly know which of the two is the most disgusting and unnatural character. Propriety is to a woman what the great Roman critic says action is to an orator; it is the first, the second, the third requisite.[2] A woman may be knowing, active, witty, and amusing; but without propriety she cannot be amiable. Propriety is the centre in which all the lines of duty and of agreeableness meet. It is to character what proportion is to figure, and grace to attitude. It does not depend on any one perfection; but it is the result of general excellence. It shows itself by a regular, orderly, undeviating course; and never starts from its sober orbit into any splendid eccentricities; for it would be ashamed of such praise as it might extort by any aberrations from its proper path. It renounces all commendation but what is characteristic; and I would make it the criterion of true taste, right principle, and genuine feeling, in a woman, whether she would be less touched with all the flattery of romantic and exaggerated panegyric than with that beautiful picture of correct and elegant propriety, which Milton draws of our first mother, when he delineates

"Those thousand *decencies* which daily flow
"From all her words and actions."[3]

[pp. 1–7]

* * * * *

How then is it to be reconciled with the decisions of principle, that delicate women should receive with complacency the successful libertine, who has been detected by the wretched father or the

---

1 That is, revolutionary France and its allies.

2 The idea occurs in *De oratore* (Book III, lvi [213]) by the Roman orator Cicero, although it is there attributed to the Greek Demosthenes; this is the text cited by Mrs Thrale in debate with Samuel Johnson in James Boswell, *Life of Johnson* (3 April 1773).

3 Adam on Eve in *Paradise Lost* Book VIII, ll.601–3: "Those thousand decencies that daily flow / From all her words and actions mixed with love / And sweet compliance …"

injured husband in a criminal commerce, the discovery of which has too justly banished the unhappy partner of his crime from virtuous society? Nay, if he happen to be very handsome, or very brave, or very fashionable, is there not sometimes a kind of dishonourable competition for his favour? But, whether his popularity be derived from birth, or parts, or person, or (what is a substitute for all) from his having made his way into *good company*, women of distinction sully the sanctity of virtue by the too visible pleasure they sometimes express at the attentions of such a popular libertine, whose voluble small-talk they admire, and whose sprightly nothings they quote, and whom perhaps their favour tends to prevent from becoming a better character, because he finds himself more acceptable as he is.

[pp.28–29]

* * * * *

O ye to whom this address is particularly directed! an awful charge is, in this instance, committed to your hands; as you discharge it or shrink from it, you promote or injure the honour and the happiness of your sons, of both which you are the depositories. And, while you resolutely persevere in making a stand against the encroachments of this crime, suffer not your firmness to be shaken by that affectation of charity, which is growing into a general substitute for principle. Abuse not so noble a quality as Christian candour, by misemploying it in instances to which it does not apply. Pity the wretched woman you dare not countenance; and bless HIM who has "made you to differ."[1] If unhappily she be your relation or your friend, anxiously watch for the period when she shall be deserted by her betrayer; and see if, by your Christian offices, she can be snatched from a perpetuity of vice. But if, through the Divine blessing on your patient endeavours, she should ever be awakened to remorse, be not anxious to restore the forlorn penitent to that society against whose laws she has so grievously offended; and remember, that her soliciting such a restoration, furnishes but too plain a proof that she is not the penitent your partiality would believe; since penitence is more anxious to make its peace with Heaven than with the world. Joyfully would a truly contrite spirit commute an earthly for an everlasting reprobation! To restore a criminal to public society, is perhaps to tempt her to repeat her crime, or

---

1   First Epistle to the Corinthians 4.7: "For who maketh thee to differ from another?"

to deaden her repentance for having committed it, as well as to injure that society; while to restore a strayed soul to God will add lustre to your Christian character, and brighten your eternal crown.

[pp. 53–5]

* * * * *

But the great object to which YOU who are, or may be mothers, are more especially called, is the education of your children. If we are responsible for the use of influence in the case of those over whom we have no immediate control, in the case of our children we are responsible for the exercise of an acknowledged *power:* a power wide in its extent, indefinite in its effects, and inestimable in its importance. On YOU, depend in no small degree the principles of the whole rising generation. To your direction the daughters are almost exclusively committed; and until a certain age, to you also is consigned the mighty privilege of forming the hearts and minds of your infant sons. By the blessing of God on the principles you shall, as far as it depends on you, infuse into both sons and daughters, they will hereafter "arise and call you blessed."[1] And in the great day of general account, may every Christian mother be enabled through divine grace to say, with humble confidence, to her Maker and Redeemer, "Behold the children whom thou hast given me!"[2]

Christianity, driven out from the rest of the world, has still, blessed be God! a "strong hold"[3] in this country. And though it be the special duty of the appointed "watchman, *now* that he seeth the sword come upon the land, to blow the trumpet and warn the people, which if he neglect to do, their blood shall be required of the watchman's hand:"[4] yet, in this sacred garrison, *impregnable but by neglect,* YOU too have an awful post, that of arming the minds of the rising generation "with the shield of faith, whereby they shall be able to quench the fiery darts of the wicked;" that of girding them with "that sword of the Spirit which is the word of the God."[5] If you neglect this your

---

1 Proverbs 31.28, describing the virtuous woman: "Her children arise up, and call her blessed; her husband also, and he praiseth her."

2 These words appear to be More's own: they do not occur in either the King James Bible or the Anglican Liturgy.

3 The common form of "stronghold" in the King James Bible.

4 Ezekial, xxxiii. 6 [More's note].

5 Epistle to the Ephesians 6.16–17: "Above all, taking the shield of faith, wherewith ye shall be able to quench all the fiery darts of the wicked. / And take the helmet of salvation, and the sword of the Spirit, which is the word of God."

bounden duty, you will have effectually contributed to expel Christianity from her last citadel. And, remember, that the dignity of the work to which you are called, is no less than that of preserving the ark of the Lord.

[pp.59–61]

From chapter XIII.   *The practical uses of female knowledge —A comparative view of both sexes.*

… The contest [for women's equality] has recently been revived with added fury, and with multiplied exactions; for whereas the ancient demand [for literary patronage and authority in the sixteenth and seventeenth centuries] was merely a kind of imaginary prerogative, a speculative importance, a mere titular right, a shadowy claim to a few unreal acres of Parnassian territory; the revived contention has taken a more serious turn, and brings forward political as well as intellectual pretensions: and among the innovations of this innovating period, the imposing term of *rights* has been produced to sanctify the claim of our female pretenders, with a view not only to rekindle in the minds of women a presumptuous vanity dishonourable to their sex, but produced with a view to excite in their hearts an impious discontent with the post which God has assigned to them in this world.

But *they* little understand the true interests of women who would lift her from the important duties of her allotted station, to fill with fantastic dignity a loftier but less appropriate niche. Nor do they understand her true happiness, who seek to annihilate distinctions from which she derives advantages, and to attempt innovations which would depreciate her real value. Each sex has its proper excellencies, which would be lost were they melted down into the common character by the fusion of the new philosophy. Why should we do away distinctions which increase the mutual benefits and enhance the satisfaction of life? Whence, but by carefully preserving the original marks of difference stamped by the hand of the Creator, would be derived the superior advantage of mixed society? Have men no need to have their harshnesses and asperities smoothed and polished by assimilating with beings of more softness and refinement? Are the ideas of women naturally so *very* judicious, are their principles so *invincibly* firm, are their views so *perfectly* correct, are their judgments so *completely* exact, that there is occasion for no additional weight, no superadded strength, no increased clearness, none of that enlargement of mind, none of that additional invigoration which may be derived from the aids of the stronger sex? What identity could advantageously supersede an enlivening opposition and an interesting variety of character? Is it not then more wise as well as more honourable to move contentedly in the plain path which Providence has obviously marked out to the sex, and in which custom has for the most part rationally confirmed them, than to stray awkwardly, unbecomingly, and unsuccessfully, in a forbidden road? Is it not desirable to be the lawful possessors of a lesser domestic territory, rather than the turbulent usurpers of a wider foreign empire? to be good originals, rather than bad imitators? to be the best thing of one's own kind, rather than an inferior thing even if it were of an higher kind? to be excellent women rather than indifferent men?

Is the author then undervaluing her own sex?—No. It is her zeal for their true *interests* which leads her to oppose their imaginary *rights*... .

[pp.20–23]

From chapter XIV. CONVERSATION. —*Hints suggested on the subject.—On the tempers and dispositions to be introduced in it.— Errors to be avoided.—Vanity under various shapes the cause of those errors.*

But conversation must not be considered as a stage for the display of our talents, so much as a field for the exercise and improvement of our virtues; as a means for promoting the glory of our Creator, and the good and happiness of our fellow-creatures. Well-bred and intelligent Christians are not, when they join in society, to consider themselves as entering the lists like intellectual prize-fighters, in order to exhibit their own vigour and dexterity, to discomfit their adversary, and to bear away the palm of victory. Truth and not triumph should be the object; and there are few occasions in life, in which we are more unremittingly called upon to watch ourselves narrowly, and to resist the assaults of various temptations, than in conversation. Vanity, jealousy, envy, misrepresentation, resentment, disdain, levity, impatience, insincerity, will in turn solicit to be gratified. Constantly to struggle against the desire of being thought more wise, more witty, and more knowing, than those with whom we associate, demands the incessant exertion of Christian vigilance, a vigilance which the generality are so far from suspecting necessary in the intercourse of common society, that cheerful conversation is rather considered as an exemption and release from it, than as an additional obligation to it.

But society, as was observed before, is not a stage on which to throw down our gauntlet, and prove our own prowess by the number of falls we give to our adversary; so far from it, good breeding as well as Christianity, considers as an indispensable requisite for conversation, the disposition to bring forward to notice any talent in others, which their own modesty, or conscious inferiority, would lead them to keep back. To do this with effect requires a penetration exercised to discern merit, and a generous candour which delights in drawing it out. There are few who cannot converse tolerably on some one topic; what that is, we should try to find out, and in general introduce that topic, though to the suppression of any one on which we ourselves are supposed to excel: and however superior we may be in other respects to the persons in question, we may, perhaps, in that particular point, improve by them; and if we do not gain information, we shall at least gain a wholesome exercise to our humility and self-denial; we shall be restraining our own impetuosity; we shall, if we take this course on just occasions only, and so as to beware lest we gratify the vanity of others, be giving confidence to a doubting, or cheerfulness to a depressed spirit. And to place a just remark, hazarded by the diffident, in the most advantageous point of view; to call the attention of the inattentive, the forward and the self-sufficient, to some quiet person in the company, who, though of much worth, is perhaps of little note; these are requisites for conversation, less brilliant, but far more valuable, than the power of exciting bursts of laughter by the brightest wit, or of extorting admiration by the most poignant sallies of ridicule.

For wit is of all the qualities of the female mind that which requires the severest castigation; yet the temperate exercise of this fascinating quality throws an additional lustre round the character of an amiable woman; for to manage with discreet modesty a dangerous talent, confers a higher praise than can be claimed by those in whom the absence of the talent takes away the temptation to misemploy it. To women, wit is a particularly perilous possession, which nothing short of the sober-mindedness of Christianity can keep in order. Intemperate wit craves admiration as its natural aliment; it lives on flattery as on its daily bread. The professed wit is a hungry beggar, that subsists on the extorted alms of perpetual panegyric; and like the vulture in the Greek fable, its appetite increases by indulgence.[1] Simple truth and sober approbation become tasteless and insipid to the palate, daily vitiated by the delicious poignancies of exaggerated commendation. Under the above restrictions, however, wit may be safely and pleasantly exercised; for *chastised wit* is an elegant and well-bred, and not unfeminine quality. But *humour*, especially if it degenerate into imitation, or mimicry, is very sparingly to be ventured on; for it is so difficult totally to detach it from the suspicion of buffoonery, that a woman will be likely to lose more of that delicacy which is her appropriate grace, than she will gain in the eyes of the judicious, by the most successful display of humour.

But if it be true that some women are too apt to affect brilliancy and display in their own discourse, and to undervalue the more humble pretensions of less showy characters; it must be confessed also, that some of more ordinary abilities are now and then guilty of the opposite error, and foolishly affect to value themselves on not making use of the understanding they really possess. They exhibit no small satisfaction in ridiculing women of high intellectual endowments, while they exclaim with much affected humility, and much real envy, that "they are thankful *they* are not geniuses." Now, although one is glad to hear gratitude expressed on any occasion, yet the want of sense is really no such great mercy to be thankful for; and it would indicate a better spirit, were they to pray to be enabled to make a right use of the moderate understanding they possess, instead of exposing with a visible pleasure the imaginary or real defects of their more shining acquaintance. Women of the brightest faculties should not only "bear those faculties meekly,"[2] but consider it as no derogation, cheerfully to

---

1 Perhaps alluding to the eagle sent by the gods to feast daily on the (continually renewed) liver of the chained Titan Prometheus.
2 Macbeth's description of Duncan at I.vii.16–18: "this Duncan / Hath borne his faculties so meek, hath been / So clear in his great office …"

fulfil those humbler duties which make up the business of common life, always taking into account the higher responsibility attached to higher gifts. While women of lower attainments should exert to the utmost such abilities as Providence has assigned them; and while they should not deride excellencies which are above their reach, they should not despond at an inferiority which did not depend on themselves; nor, because God has denied them ten talents, should they forget that they are equally responsible for the one he *has* allotted them, but set about devoting that one with humble diligence to the glory of the Giver.

Vanity, however, is not the monopoly of talents; let not a young lady, therefore, fancy that she is humble, merely because she is not ingenious. Humility is not the exclusive privilege of dulness. Folly is as conceited as wit, and ignorance many a time outstrips knowledge in the race of vanity. Equally earnest competitions spring from causes less worthy to excite them than wit and genius. Vanity insinuates itself into the female heart under a variety of unsuspected forms, and seizes on many a little pass which was not thought worth guarding.

[pp. 68–74]

From Chapter XVI. *On dissipation, and the modern habits of fashionable life.*

... First then, as has been observed before, the showy education of women tends chiefly to qualify them for the glare of public assemblies: secondly, they seem in many instances to be so educated, with a view to the greater possibility of their being splendidly married: thirdly, it is alleged in vindication of those dissipated practices, that daughters can only be seen, and admirers procured at balls, operas, and assemblies: and that therefore, by a natural consequence, balls, operas and assemblies must be followed up without intermission till the object be effected. For the accomplishment of this object it is that all this complicated machinery had been previously set a-going, and kept in motion with an activity not at all slackened by the disordered state of the system; for some machines, instead of being stopped, go faster because the true spring is out of order; the only difference being that they go wrong, and so the increased rapidity adds only to the quantity of the error.

It is also, as we have already remarked, an error to fancy that the love of pleasure exhausts itself by indulgence, and that the very young are chiefly addicted to it. The contrary appears to be true. The desire often grows with the pursuit in the same degree as motion quickened by the continuance of the gravitating force.

First then, it cannot be thought unfair to trace back the excessive fondness for amusement to that mode of education we have elsewhere reprobated. Few of the accomplishments, falsely so called, assist the development of the faculties: they do not exercise the judgment, nor bring into action those powers which fit the heart and mind for the occupations of life; they do not prepare women to love home, to understand its occupations, to enliven its uniformity, to fulfil its duties, to multiply its comforts: they do not lead to that sort of experimental logic, if I may so speak, compounded of observation and reflection, which makes up the moral science of life and manners. Talents which have *display* for their object despise the narrow stage of home: they demand mankind for their spectators, and the world for their theatre.

While one cannot help shrinking a little from the idea of a delicate young creature, lovely in person, and engaging in mind and manners, sacrificing nightly at the public shrine of Fashion, at once the votary and the victim; one cannot help figuring to oneself how much more interesting she would appear in the eyes of a man of feeling, did he behold her in the more endearing situations of domestic life. And who can forbear wishing, that the good sense, good taste, and delicacy of the men had rather led them to prefer seeking companions for life in the almost sacred quiet of a virtuous home? *There* they might have had the means of seeing and admiring those amiable beings in the best point of view: *there* they might have been enabled to form a juster estimate of female worth, than is likely to be obtained in scenes where such qualities and talents as might be expected to add to the stock of domestic comfort must necessarily be kept in the back ground, and where such only *can* be brought into view as are not particularly calculated to insure the certainty of home delights.

O! did they keep their persons fresh and new,
How would they pluck allegiance from men's hearts,
And win by rareness![1]

But by what unaccountable infatuation is it that men too, even men of sense, join in the confederacy against their own happiness, by looking for their home companions in the resorts of vanity? Why do not such men rise superior to the illusions of fashions? why do they not uniformly seek her who is to preside in *their* families in the bosom of their own? in the practice of every domestic duty, in the exercise of every amiable virtue, in the exertion of every elegant accomplishment? those accomplishments of which we have been reprobating, not the possession, but the application? *there* they would find her exerting them to their true end, to enliven business, to ani-mate retirement, to embellish the charming scene of family delights, to heighten the interesting pleasures of social intercourse, and, rising to their noblest object, to adorn the doctrine of God the Saviour.

If, indeed, woman were mere outside, form and face only, if *mind* made up no part of her composition, it would follow that a ball-room was quite as appropriate a place for choosing a wife, as an exhibition room for choosing a picture. But, inasmuch as women are not mere portraits, their value not being determinable by a glance of the eye, it follows that a different mode of appreciating their value, and a differ-ent place for viewing them antecedent to their being individually selected, is desirable. The two cases differ also in this, that if a man select a picture for himself from among all its exhibited competitors, and bring it to his own house, the picture being passive, he is able to *fix* it there: while the wife, picked up at a public place, and accus-tomed to incessant display, will not, it is probable, when brought home stick so quietly to the spot where he fixes her; but will escape to the exhibition-room again, and continue to be displayed at every

---

1 A clever domestic appropriation of Henry IV's description of his own carefully rationed pomp, who "dress'd myself in such humility / That I did pluck allegiance from men's hearts, / ... / Thus did I keep my person fresh and new, / ... / ... and so my state, / Seldom, but sumptuous, show'd like a feast, / And won by rareness such solemnity" (Shakespeare, *The First Part of King Henry IV* III.ii.50–1, 55, 57–9). More at the start of chapter XIII compares women to the classical orator, now to the renaissance absolutist monarch.

subsequent exhibition, just as if she were not become private property, and had never been definitively disposed of.

[pp.161–66]

Appendix E: Domestic Tourism

1. From William Watts, *The Seats of the Nobility and Gentry. In a collection of the most interesting and picturesque views engraved by William Watts. With descriptions of each view.* Chelsea: William Watts, 1779.

[In contrast to William Bray's *Sketch of a Tour*, extracted below, it is very unlikely that anyone took Watts's *Seats of the Nobility* with them on a trip round the country: an expensively produced collection of engraved reproductions of paintings of country houses, it might have been bought as a souvenir of such a tour on one's return home. However, it taps into a more general curiosity on the part of the newly wealthy regarding the taste and lifestyles of an established élite with whom they could claim a common culture. In productions such as that of Watts, a professional printer and engraver, houses designed to express the power and wealth of an oligarchy are turned into aesthetic objects to be sold on the open market to a paying public.

It is in their appropriation of the signs of aristocratic power by a commercial middle class that books such as this prefigure Elizabeth Bennett's visit to Pemberley (see Introduction). I have selected Kedleston as my example as the epitome of late eighteenth-century taste, one situated in the same county as Darcy's fictional pile, and the subject of some interesting description in Bray's *Sketch*; but it is also the seat of a titled nobleman as Pemberley is not, and one should not imagine Mr. Darcy's house to be built on anything like Kedleston's impressive scale.]

Kedleston House *in Derbyshire, the Seat of* Lord Scarsdale.

PLATE XXII
KEDLESTON HOUSE
IN DERBYSHIRE
The Seat of the Right Honourable Lord SCARSDALE
(Drawn by G. BARRET, Esq. R. A.)

KEDLESTON HOUSE, we may venture to assert (if not unequalled) is inferior to none in this Kingdom, in any respect; the style of Architecture is uncommonly beautiful, and worthy of Admiration: the proportion of the Wings, as well as the Portico, to the Center, are judiciously observed, and produce a pleasing Effect. The Portico consists of six Corinthian Columns with their corresponding Pilaster, three Feet in Diameter, which support a handsome Pediment, decorated with light Statues. The Center is united to the Wings with Corridors, which project an agreeable sweep, forming together one magnificent Front, three hundred and sixty feet in Extent. The Entrance to the principal Story, is by a double Flight of Steps, which lead through the Portico to a noble Hall, sixty-nine Feet by forty-two, adorned with eighteen Columns of Alabaster, of the Corinthian Order, twenty-nine Feet in height, the Entablature richly ornamented, nothing can surpass this Room in Elegance; between the Columns are fine antique Statues in Niches, over which are Basso Relievos in Compartments, crowned with Festoons; the Ceiling is arched, and highly finished in Stucco; in the Center is a large Window, by which the whole receives Light; the height to the Top of this Window is forty-seven Feet. The Saloon to which the Hall communicates is a circular Room, forty-two Feet in Diameter, and fifty-five in height, terminating in a Dome; the Ceiling finished in Mosaic Work; it contains some good Statues, and Basso Relievos, and is light in the same Manner as the Hall, by a Window from the Summit. The Dimensions of the other principal Apartments, are as follow:

Drawing Room	44	by	28	Feet
Dining Room	36	—	24	
Music Room	36	—	24	
Library	36	—	24	

These Rooms are finished in the most superb taste, and embellished with several valuable Paintings by *Raphael, Guido, N. Poussin, Rembrandt, Annibal Carracci, Claude Lorraine,* and other Eminent Masters.

Kedleston is situated upon a gentle Rise, in the Center of a fine Park, about four Miles from *Derby,* and commands from every Part the most delightful Prospects. The Pleasure-Grounds are laid out with great Taste, in a style answerable to the Magnificence of the Building, and the Park abounds with noble Plantations of Oak and other Timber agreeably interspersed.

This Building was erected from the designs of *Robert Adam,* Esq.

2. From William Bray, F.A.S.. *Sketch of a Tour into Derbyshire and Yorkshire, including part of Buckingham, Warwick, Leicester, Nottingham, Bedford, and Hertford-shires.* 2nd edition. London: B. White, 1783.

[William Bray (1736–1832) was a lawyer by profession but an antiquary by vocation. This, his first book (originally published anonymously in 1777), was a consistently popular contribution to a thriving late eighteenth-century genre, the description of a tour through the various nations and regions of the British Isles. Such tours had been made possible for the well-to-do by improvements in communications, and desirable by the new enthusiasm for picturesque landscape. Descriptions such as this had both a practical function, suggesting itineraries, accommodation and so on, and a didactic one, teaching tourists how to look at and appreciate landscape, architecture, or (central to Bray's interests) the traces of the historical past.]

* * * * *

... About two miles and an half from *Derby*, in the road to *Buxton*, is *Kedleston*, the seat of Lord *Scarsdale*, which may properly be called the glory of *Derbyshire*, eclipsing *Chatsworth*, the ancient boast of the country. It was built from the designs of Mr. Robert Adam. The front is magnificent and beautiful, the apartments elegant, and at the same time useful, a circumstance not always to be met with in a great house. It is the ancient seat of the *Curzon's* [sic], a family of great antiquity, wealth, and interest in this country. This house has been built by the present lord (created Lord Scarsdale in 1761) partly on the spot where the old house stood, but the ground has been so much altered, that there is no resemblance of what it was. In the front stood a village with a small inn for the accomodation of those who came to drink of a medicinal well, which has the virtues of the *Harrowgate* water; a rivulet turned a water-mill, and the high road went by the gate. The village is now removed (not destroyed, as is too often done) the road is thrown to a considerable distance, out of the sight of the house, the scanty stream is encreased into a large piece of water, and the ground disposed in the finest order.

The entrance from the turnpike road is thro' a grove of noble and venerable oaks (something hurt by a few small circular clumps of firs planted amongst them) after which, crossing a fine lawn, and passing the water by an elegant stone bridge, of three arches, a gentle ascent leads to the house.

[pp. 111–12]

* * * * *

From the principal front of the house, which is the north, the eye is conducted by a beautiful slope to the water, which is seen tumbling down a cascade, encircling an island planted with firs, and at the bridge falling over rough rocks, and then forming a large river, on which is a yatch [sic]. Below is a small rustic building over the well and bath, which are used by many persons, who are accommodated at an inn, built by his lordship in the road, and from which a pleasant walk thro' the park leads to the bath.

In the back front of the house is the pleasure ground, stretching up to the edge of the rising ground, on which is a fine and extensive plantation, beginning to show itself in great beauty. The walk is about three miles in the whole.

Of all the houses I ever saw, I do not recollect any one which pleased me as this did, and the uncommon politeness and attention of the housekeeper who showed it, added not a little to the entertainment.

[p.116]

* * * * *

[Visiting Chatsworth, belonging to the Duke of Devonshire:]

So much has been said of this house, at a time when there was no house in the country to be compared with it, that it is no wonder if the visitor is disappointed. It was built in the reign of *William* 3. and is certainly magnificent, but you look in vain for those beautiful productions of the pencil, which now so frequently adorn the seats of our nobility and gentry: a few whole-length portraits in one of the state apartments are nearly all you see.... The manner in which you are shewn the house, does not prejudice you much in its favor. Nor can I say anything in praise of the garden, *as it is now kept*; the conceits in the water-works might be deemed wonderful when they were made, but those who have contemplated the water-falls which nature exhibits in this country, and in various parts of the kingdom, will receive little pleasure from seeing a temporary stream falling down a flight of steps, spouted out of the mouths of dolphins or dragons, or squirted from the leaves of a copper tree. The little current in the wood above, which descends in a perpetual rill from the reservoir on the hills, would, if properly exhibited, furnish a much more pleasing scene, tho' it could not be said to be in the style of the house, magnificent. [168–70]

* * * * *

However little the noble owner may be inclined to lay out his money in disposing his grounds according to the modern simple and beautiful style, he is not backward, when he is here, in distributing it to the distressed. The poor, the widow, and the fatherless, bless the providence which has bestowed such wealth on one so ready to relieve their wants. [173–4]

Appendix F: The Militia Regiments on the South Coast of England in 1793–95

[The following passages are all extracted from *The Sussex Weekly Advertiser; or, Lewes Journal,* the local newspaper for the county. They give some idea of the problems created by the deployment of militia regiments in the southern counties of England to meet the perceived threat of invasion by France in the first years of the war. Militia regiments drafted men by lot from their respective counties (wealthier draftees could escape service by paying a fine); once mobilised, as they were in 1792 in anticipation of war, they were usually posted outside their home counties to avoid local attachments getting in the way of military duty, but could not be sent abroad. Until 1795, the militia regiments spent the winter billeted on inland towns such as Austen's fictional Meryton (Sir William Lucas is central to the social scene because, as the local bigwig, he would be responsible for liasing between military and residents), then assembled at a series of large camps along the coast during the summer months. The ——shire's departure for the biggest, at Brighton, at the end of May (as anticipated at the start of Volume II, chapter xvi) places the action of *Pride and Prejudice* in 1794 or 1795: the Brighton camp was not operational until August 1793. The Oxfordshire regiment, staying in barracks throughout the year (see section 3 below) were at this period unusual, but barracks were in place for all regiments from 1796.

To the largely self-contained communities on which they were billeted the militias brought unfamiliar voices and customs and, perhaps, an increased consciousness of belonging to a national community, governed from London and engaged in world-historical events, beyond the boundaries of parish or county. In the passages below, one can glimpse clashes between these two perspectives. A soldier accuses a town constable, secure in his *local* authority, of not calling for peace "in the King's name" (see section 2 below); the people of Lewes are unaware of the *metropolitan* practice of standing and removing hats for the national anthem (see section 3 below), and so on (see also Introduction).]

1. Women at the Brighton camp.

From Vol. XLVII, no. 2452: August 19, 1793.

The CAMP. A new Song.

Tune. *"Johnny's return'd from the Fair."*

My Kate was all love, and no turtle more true,
Till the Soldiers, with baggage & guns came in view;
Then she put her best gown on, and after them flew;
    Whilst I, left to rave and to stamp,
Cry'd, dear! dear! what can the matter be?
O dear! what can the matter be?
G—d z—ds! what can the matter be?
    Why has she gone to *the Camp?*

At eve, to my cottage fair KITTY repair'd,
And told me of strange things she'd seen, and what heard;
How noble the *Prince, Duke,* and *Captains* appear'd!
    Then sighing, the sweet little *Tramp*
Cry'd, dear! dear! what can the matter be?
Good lack! what can the matter be?
Heigh ho! what can the matter be?
    Sure I'm possess'd, with *this Camp!*

Next morning, quite cheerly, my charmer again,
For *Brighton* set out, tho' the cloud threaten'd rain,
And all I could urge to prevent her prov'd vain,
    Tho' I told her the grass would be damp!
Dear! dear! what can the matter be?
O dear! what can the matter be?
Dear! dear! what can the matter be?
    KITTY would live in *the Camp!*

At night-fall, returning I met my fair Queen,
Her head bore a *helmet* she call'd *Valenciennes,**
Her gown, (for 'twas moon-light) I saw was quite green,
    This quickly extinguish'd Love's lamp;
Dear! dear! *Roger*, pray look, said she,
What a fine bonnet! —'twas given me,
Under the *Captain*'s nice warm marqué,
    All in the mid'st of *the Camp!*

Said I, my dear KATE, since the Captain you've kiss'd
I'd have you go back to his tent child, and list;
You'll fight well as him,— or my mark I have miss'd!
    She smil'd, 'saucy Roger decamp;
'O dear! what could the matter be?
'Dear, dear, what could the matter be?
'Good-lack! when I first look'd on *thee*
    'I'd never once been at *the Camp!*'

From Vol. XLVII, no 2457: September 30, 1793

On the GIRL who walks the STEINE WITHOUT PETTICOATS.[1]
HOR. ODE XIII. LIB. II.

——— *Illis carminibus stupens*
Demittit atras Bellua centiceps
Aures, &c.
Nec curat Orion *Leones*
Aut timidos agitare Lynces.[2]

ALCÆUS sounds the golden lyre,
Around the list'ning shades admire;

---

* The present fashionable camp bonnets, are call'd, the *Valenciennes' helmet-bonnets.*
[original note]

---

1 The Steine is the central square in Brighton.
2 The following six lines give the gist of these extracts from the last stanzas from Book
II, Ode 13 of the Roman poet Horace (65–8 BCE). Alcæus was a Greek lyric poet
from around 600 BCE; Cerberus the many-headed dog who guards the entrance to
the underworld, and Orion the mighty hunter, both in Greek mythology.

E'en CERBERUS attentive hears
The harmony, and drops his ears.
And now no more the fierce ORION
Pursues the timid Lynx, or Lion.

So, whilst Miss ———— walks the *Steine,*
The Soldiers, stiff as stakes, are seen;
All gazing at the novel sight,
Forget to wheel to left or right;
The Col'nel too, like *Peeping Tom,*
Can't keep his eyes from off her b——m.
Meanwhile, their horses, Coachmen stop;
And GREGORY forgets his shop. —
Save that some boys can't hold their laughter,
And frightened curs come barking after,
All things, as if by magic wand,
Are put completely to a stand.

Let Frenchmen boast their *sans culottes,*[1]
We'll sing the Girls *sans petticoats,*
For what so much true spunk denotes
As walking *without petticoats?*

BRIGHTON, SEPT. 27.

From Vol. XLVII, no 2458: October 7, 1793

The Girl who walks the Steine *without petticoats* it should not be
understood, appears there as our Mother *Eve* is pictured, *quite naked,*
but habited in a gown and shift, *only,* through which her shapes are
displayed in a manner not a little gratifying to all her male-admirers,
who, taking advantage of every rude blast of the sportive wind, have
been often observed to *stand,* in raptures, gazing at the *milk white
Linen,* of this enchanting, but eccentrick female. She is, we under-

---

1 "Sans culottes" ("without breeches") was the adopted name of the armed protesters
who stormed the Tuileries Palace in Paris on 20 June 1792 to confront Louis XVI;
breeches and stockings being the preserve of the wealthy, it signified their membership of the (trousered) urban poor and artisanal classes. Thereafter a general name
for the militant urban mob.

stand, a girl of good character, and an upper servant in a family of fashion.

From Vol. XLVII, no. 2552: July 20, 1795

Nine unfortunate young prostitutes whose activity in their baleful profession is said to have greatly swelled the SICK-LIST at Brighton Camp, were re-committed till the next Sessions, and one of them named Sarah Mitchell, was also ordered to be privately whipped.

2. Officers: the trial of Lord Bateman.

From Vol. XLVII, no. 2540: April 27, 1795.

COMMON PLEAS. LEE against Lord BATEMAN.

On Friday last a cause of considerable importance to the civil polity of this country, was tried in the Court of Common Pleas, Westminster, before Lord Chief Justice Eyre, in which Arthur Lee, Printer, was Plaintiff, and Lord Viscount Bateman, Colonel of the Herefordshire Militia, Defendant.

The action was brought to recover a compensation in damages, for a violent assault and battery committed on the person of the Plaintiff, in the execution of his office as Constable of the Borough of Lewes, on the 21st of May last, by some soldiers belonging to the above regiment acting under the immediate command and direction of the Defendant.

The Plaintiff's case was opened by Mr. Serjeant Le Blanc,[1] who in a very neat and able address, of about an hour and a half's continuance, stated to the Court and Jury the wrongs his client had sustained; he did not complain, he said, of the Defendant's having with his own hands assaulted the person of the Plaintiff, but with having instigated others under his immediate controul to beat and otherwise ill-treat the Defendant, whilst in the due and proper execution of a very necessary and serviceable office. His client, he said, did not bring this action to create jealousy, or to foment animosity betwixt the civil and

---

1   Serjeant Le Blanc is a serjeant at law, the highest rank of barrister and nothing to do with the army. The second "Defendant" in this sentence is clearly a mistake for "Plaintiff."

military powers of this country, but for the purpose of obtaining substantial justice, by a compensation in damages, for a grievous and unprovoked assault upon his person, whilst employed on a public duty.

The Defendant, (he should be enabled to prove,) had so far forgotten his duty on this occasion, that instead of preventing the interference of the soldiers under his command, in a trifling dispute, which had taken place betwixt a townsman and an orderly man belonging to the regiment, that he threatened to drive the whole town before him; and, at length, actually ordered them to break the ranks and fall upon the people; in consequence of which order the Plaintiff received the injury of which he so justly complains; and for which the Jury, he doubted not, would allow him ample and sufficient compensation in damages.

The first witness called on the part of the Plaintiff was Mr. Henry Verrall, Surgeon. — Examined by Serjeant Clayton.

On the evening of the 11th of May last, the Herefordshire Militia were parading before his door in the High Street of Lewes; he was looking out of window, and saw a little bustle occasioned by soldiers pushing a man, named William Kennard, belonging to the town. He went down for the purpose of preventing mischief; saw Lord Bateman talking to the crowd, which was composed, as usual, of men, women, and children, (which had collected, he supposed, for the purpose of hearing the regimental band;) he desired Lord Bateman who was using warm language, to put a stop to the bustle, as he did not know to what extent it might go. The Defendant laid hold of Kennard, who was before held by a soldier. At this period, several persons said the Constable was coming, and he (the witness) saw Mr. Lee; he then said, addressing himself to Lord Bateman, "My Lord, here is the Civil Magistrate of the Borough; if you will keep your soldiers quiet, I am sure he will keep the town's-people quiet, for he is much respected." The defendant answered, "No d—n you, I'll call my men forth, and drive the whole town." Witness took hold of his coat and said, "Do my Lord keep them quiet." Defendant flew from him in a passion, and again said, "D—n you I'll drive your town." The witness then spoke to the town's people, and desired them to remain quiet and not to mind any insult; he then looked round, and found that the ranks were broken; he saw a soldier strike the Constable a severe blow; and amongst the men who were out of the ranks, he saw the Defendant pushing and striking about. Witness cried mind, what you are doing, you are striking the Constable. Afterwards saw Mr. Lee raised from the ground, with his face much bruised, and his nose considerably laid open; he seemed confounded by the blow or blows he had received, and could hardly answer the witness when he asked him how he was. The Constable was taken to a neighbouring shop. The witness a considerable time afterwards, heard the drum beat, immediately on which the soldiers fell into their ranks. He did not hear that Lord Bateman had ordered the soldiers to fall on.

Cross examined by Serj. Bond. — He had heard of a proceeding which was to have come on at the Quarter Sessions; and that the matter had been referred to Colonel Pelham. — He remembered the Defendant's saying, "if he is a Constable let him take this man, (meaning Kennard,) into custody;" to which Mr. Lee replied, "I do not think myself authorized; as I have not seen him commit any breach of the peace; but if I do see any man assault another, I will take him into custody." — Witness did not see Kennard shove either Lord Bateman or the soldier who had hold of him. Lord Bateman assisted the men in beating the townsmen; he did fight away as well as the common soldiers; saw him strike in places where there was no occasion; where people did not use their hands in the like acts of violence. Did not believe there were more than 130 men, women, and children, belonging to the town, present. Disturbance lasted about fifteen minutes.

Thomas Lindfield, Brewer, examined by Mr. Holroyd. — Was a few minutes after seven o'clock, on the 21st of May last, seeing the Herefordshire Regiment parade. Some of the soldiers and town's people had words; Lord Bateman came up, said, "Which is the rascal," and took Kennard by the collar; did not hear Kennard say any thing to the Defendant; Mr. Lee came up and said he was Constable, and demanded the peace to be kept; Lord Bateman said, "If you be Constable take this man into custody." Plaintiff answered, "My Lord, I doubt my authority; for I have not seen him do any thing amiss. If you will keep your men quiet, I will answer for the town's people." Defendant said, "D—n the town, I'll drive your town."

The Plaintiff turned a little aside; Defendant said, speaking to his men, "Break the ranks and fall upon them." The soldiers immediately broke their ranks, and at least ten or twelve went and struck away upon many people; saw two strike Mr. Lee; saw him knocked down; had a violent blow on the face; and was very bloody. Drum afterwards beat for men to fall into ranks; they immediately obeyed.

* * * * *

William Kennard, examined by Mr. Holroyd. —Orderly man came up, and told him to stand back; he did so, a first and second time, till he could get no further, the soldier then pushed him; witness told him it was an indecent way of proceeding; in half a minute repeated his thrust when witness told him, if he did so again, he must take the consequences, for, in that case he would knock him down; soldier said, that if he durst he would thrash him; witness replied, he would make no disturbance on the parade, but if he would meet him out of town, he would try his strength. Lord Bateman came at the end of this altercation, and seized him by the collar, as did also two or three other men. Verrall came up, and said keep yourself peaceable. Witness said this is ungentleman-like usage. At this period the Constable arrived; Mr. Verrall said to the Defendant there is the Constable; Defendant said take him into custody, meaning the witness; Mr. Lee replied, he doubted his authority, as he had not seen him riotous; said he would insist on having the peace kept, for that if he saw any man riotous, he would take him into custody. Defendant said d—n your town, I'll drive your town before me. A few words and some little bustle ensued, but no blows that he saw, till Lord Bateman said, turning to his men, break the ranks and fall on them; which orders the men instantly obeyed. There might have been 40 or 50 of them out, could not say how many. Saw a townsman struck by an officer; saw also the Constable struck seemingly senseless, bled a great deal.

On his cross-examination, said he had his hands in his pockets till after he was collared. Did not put his elbow in the breast of Lord Bateman. Was further back at last, than almost any other spectator.

* * * * *

Serjeant Bond proceeded in his observations; which he finished by saying, he should bring an host of witnesses, to contradict the principal parts of the evidence for the Plaintiff.

Abraham Charles. He was a pioneer, and employed when the affair happened at Lewes, in front of the rank to keep off the people; Davis was Lord Bateman's orderly man. Band was playing; mob crouded round. Kennard would not go back, said the street was as free for him as for them; and if he provoked him, he would knock him down. Drum-Major went for Defendant. He was about the centre. Lord Bateman said which is the man? Drum-Major shewed him, his Lordship said to Kennard, my friend, you and I will go along to some Magistrate; Kennard pushed at him; Lord Bateman likely to fall, and caught by Kennard's coat; a man knocked the Adjutant down; and the ranks were broken. Defendant ordered the roll to beat as soon as he could. Defendant did not order ranks to be broken; said keep peace, for if ranks are broken cannot say what may be the consequence. Men were in ranks till the Adjutant was knocked down.

Cross-examination. — Does not know Mr. Lee; stood within a yard of Lord Bateman. Did not hear any thing pass between the Plaintiff and Defendant.

John Simpson, Drum Major. The last witness was ordered to keep the mob from drums; he could not keep them back. The Baker [Thomas, William Kennard's brother] said don't push me, I will knock you down; told Kennard, if he could not go back, he might go about his business. Said he supposed he had 18d. a day. If he attempted to put him back he would break his mouth. Went to my Lord, he came, and said "Which is the man." The people behind were pressing. Lord Bateman said, you and I must go to a Magistrate together." He said, "What have you to do with me?" The others said, "you shan't go with him." The crowd got close to him. I did not see any blow struck. My Lord said, "Fall in men, what are you about," and ordered me to beat the long roll immediately; two or three minutes before the drummers could beat, being mixed with crowd. When it was beat the men instantly fell in. Did not hear the order to break ranks.

Cross examination. He heard nothing said, but, fall in.

Wm. Rudge, Musician, deposed to nearly the same purpose as the former witness in respect to the commencement of the affray. Kennard pushed Lord Bateman, who would have fallen if Serjeant Cole had not prevented him. Riot ten yards below where he stood, caused by Captain Roworth's hat having been knocked off; when the men saw it they broke their ranks; formed again in three or four minutes.

Lord Bateman immediately ordered the men to fall in, and the Drum Major to beat the long roll.

Cross examination. Saw a man who said he was Constable, but he had no stick; nor did he demand peace in the King's name. Lord Bateman ordered him to take Kennard into custody; he answered, "I doubt your authority."

* * * * *

The evidence on both sides being closed, the LORD CHIEF JUSTICE very accurately summed it up; towards the end of which, he observed, that the CIVIL POWER must be protected; it was for that the military fought.

We are sorry we have not room to follow him through his observations. The law which he laid down on the subject, we shall not, however, in this hasty sketch, pass over, but give it nearly in his Lordship's own words:

"A Commanding Officer who does not check, but encourages his men, by ordering them to break their ranks and commit disorder, is answerable for the consequences. — I go further: If a Commanding Officer, seeing a disposition in them to break their ranks (though he does not order or encourage them) does not every thing in his power to restrain them, and prevent disorder, he is answerable for the consequences."

He concluded by stating to the Jury, that the Plaintiff had certainly been much injured; and that if they thought Lord Bateman had made use of the words ascribed to him, they must think there was great intemperance in his behaviour, and would in course give a verdict for the Plaintiff; if, on the other hand, they thought Capt. Roworth's scuffle had brought the men forth, and that the Defendant had used every means to bring them back to their duty, they must, though he should be sorry for the Plaintiff, find for the Defendant.

Verdict for the Plaintiff, damages FORTY POUNDS.

Counsel for the Plaintiff, Serjeant Le Blanc, Serjeant Clayton, and Mr. Holroyd. — Attorneys, Mr. Walter, Cuckfield, and Mr. Cocker, London.

Counsel for the Defendant, Serjeant Bond, Serjeant Cockle, and Mr. Leach. — Attorneys, Tourle and Palmer, Bartlett's Buildings, London.

The above trial lasted from a quarter before one o'clock till near seven in the evening; and was declared by the Crier to have been the longest in that Court, during the time he had been in office, which was three years.

3. Men: the Mutiny of the Oxfordshire militia.

[Militia soldiers were not at first issued rations, but given a cash allowance to buy food and other necessities. But the economic consequences of the war and a poor harvest in 1794 (and, the soldiers alleged, profiteering by local merchants) drove up prices in early 1795 until this allowance was pitifully inadequate. To the great anxiety of an already paranoid government, militiamen frequently made common cause with the local poor to force lower, in their eyes fairer, prices on shopkeepers and wholesalers, and blockade supplies intended for export. The following describes one of the more dramatic instances of such action, the mutiny of the Oxfordshire Militia stationed at Blatchington barracks near Seaford on the Sussex coast: it was this event that forced the government to introduce a system of rations. Henry Austen, Jane's favourite brother, was an officer in the Oxfordshire from 1793–1801, and it is very unlikely that she did not hear of these events through him.

The extracts here also give glimpses into the local power wielded by the provincial gentry to which Austen's characters belong, in, for example, setting prices for foodstuffs; and into their relation to London authority, although the frequent presence of the Prince of Wales at Brighton, a very fashionable resort where he had a holiday residence, the Pavilion, constructed (see extract for 25 May), makes the Sussex experience to some extent atypical in this last regard.]

From Vol. XLVII, no. 2539: April 20, 1795.

Last Thursday evening a most alarming spirit of mutiny broke out amongst the Oxfordshire Regiment of Militia, at Bletchington barracks, near Seaford, for which place the men had set out to lower the price of provisions, but where [sic] by their officers soon afterwards prevailed on to return to their barracks. The next morning, however, they assembled again in number about 500, attended even by some men from the hospital, when they took their arms, fixed their bayonets, and marched to Seaford, where they seized all the flour, bread, and meat they could find, and sold it at reduced prices. From thence they proceeded to the Tide Mill between Bishopstone and Newhaven, where they found a considerable quantity of wheat and flour, about 200 sacks of which they seized and marked, and having pressed waggons and horses from the neighbouring farmers, and horses from the Train of Artillery, they regularly loaded the grain and meal, and conveyed the same under an escort to Seaford. They next obliged some men who were employed in loading a sloop with flour from the mill, to work her down to Newhaven, to which place they marched immediately, took possession of the town, and helped themselves to whatever they thought proper. The sloop being safely moored, they ordered the men to unload her, which was accordingly done, and the flour, about 300 sacks, stored in a warehouse belonging to Mr. Brown, where they placed a guard over it, and sold it to those who chose to purchase at a rate of about 15s. the sack.

Soon after LORD SHEFFIELD had taken the Chair at our Quarter Sessions,[1] in this town [i.e. Lewes], about ten o'clock on Friday morning, the Constable of Newhaven applied to the Bench for succour. His Lordship immediately wrote to General Ainslie, who commands in this town, requesting he would send such force as he should think proper, to restore order; and in the afternoon, his Lordship accompanied by the HIGH SHERIFF, went to Newhaven, where he found that the great body of the Militia had retired to their Barracks, declaring they should return in the morning, and leaving a guard of 60 men to take care of the flour, who were all drunk and very riotous. LORD SHEFFIELD put the fort and ammunition under the care of Lieutenant JAMES COOK, of the Navy, and directed him to moor an Ordnance vessel laden with stores and ammunition (which lay in the river) under the battery. The Militia, it seems, had only one non-commissioned officer with them, a Serjeant of Grenadiers. At night

---

1 "Quarter Sessions": the regular local court of law, of limited criminal and civil jurisdiction, held four times a year, and presided over by a (usually) visiting judge such as Lord Sheffield; Mr. Newbury, as High Sheriff, is the highest *resident* law-officer in the county.

LORD SHEFFIELD returned to this town, and reported to General Ainslie, the state of Newhaven and its neighbourhood, and early on Saturday morning the Lancashire Fencibles at Brighton, and the Horse Artillery stationed in this town, with two field pieces, marched to the scene of action, where on their first appearance the Mutineers formed, as if they were determined to dispute the point with them, but being thrown into confusion by two cannon balls discharged at them, and having no ammunition, they were in about an hour all overcome and disarmed, happily without the loss of any lives, though two or three of the militia were severely wounded by the Fencibles,[1] many of whom broke their swords in the skirmish, and appeared greatly exasperated at seeing their Colonel (Bishop) knocked off his horse, by a man against whom his sword was uplifted. The Col. received no hurt; but a Cornet had a finger broken. A private fencible was severely wounded, but, we hear, not dangerously. One of the cannon balls stuck a militiaman's musket and carried away the butt end of it.

Twenty-one prisoners, including two countrymen, were conducted, under a strong escort of the Fencibles, to this town, and committed by G. L. Newnham, Esq. to the House of Correction, for further examination. The rest were marched back to their barracks, where they are strongly guarded by a troop of Fencibles. 'Tis expected that a Court-Martial will this day be assembled to try them.

Their arms were all conveyed, in waggons, to this town, and lodged in the store-room belonging to the Royal Artillery.

Immediately after the Newhaven Constable had arrived here with his disagreeable intelligence, expresses were dispatched to Mr. Pitt, the War-Office, and the Duke of Richmond.[2]

On Saturday morning Lord Spencer, Colonel of the Oxford Militia, arrived at Blatchington, and shewed great concern for the defection of his regiment.

Near one hundred who returned to the barracks on Friday night, and did not assemble the next morning, have been liberated.

There was no truth in the report that a serjeant had been run

---

1 Lancashire Fencibles, Horse Artillery, and the Highland Regiments referred to later on, are all units of the regular, professional, army.

2 Pitt was Prime Minister; Richmond was in overall command of the militia forces.

through the body and thrown into the river; but one of them was very ill treated by the men for being averse to their measures.

Soon after the regiment had commenced its violences at Seaford, CAPT. HARBEN. obtained a hearing and forcibly exhorted the men to return to their duty, at the same time assuring them, that he would purchase ten loads of wheat and retail it to them at four pounds a load less than it should cost him, for which they gave him three cheers, and the majority seemed inclined to disperse, but some, the most desperate and disaffected objected, saying they should obtain their ends more effectually by getting on and threatening the rest, when they proceeded, and pursued their mad career as above-stated.

CAPTAIN HARBEN, on Saturday assembled his Corps of Volunteers,[1] who cheerfully submitted to perform the duty of common soldiers, by taking charge of the battery and ammunition, and all the corn and flour that could be found, over which they have constantly kept guard night and day ever since.

Nearly fifty pounds were subscribed in our corn market on Saturday to be distributed amongst the Soldiers of the Artillery and Fencibles as a reward for their good behaviour in suppressing the above-mentioned riot and mutiny. See Advertisement.

We are sorry to hear that other militiamen stationed in this county, have betrayed strong marks of discontent and revolt.

Not any thing could exceed the readiness, cheerfulness and alertness with which the North Fencible regiment, quartered at Shoreham, assembled and hurried out on Friday, in case their services had been required.

As reports have been circulated in some parts of this county, that the SUSSEX MILITIA have been concerned in riots in the town of READING, where they are quartered, on account of the high cost of provisions, it is but justice both to the regiment and to the people of READING, and its vicinity to declare, and this we do from the most indubitable authority, that no kind of disturbance has hitherto happened amongst them, nor does there appear the smallest symptom of discontent.

The several corn-buyers resident in the town and neighbourhood of ARUNDEL, had a meeting at the Norfolk Arms Inn, in that town,

---

1   The Volunteers were local residents organised into a home defence force.

on Thursday last, pursuant to a Requisition from the Mayor, for the purpose of adopting some resolutions, relative to the present high price of Wheat, when an agreement was unanimously entered into, not to purchase at a higher price than FOURTEEN POUNDS per load, for three months from that day; the merchants also agreed to cease buying entirely, for one month, and to enforce these agreements, they have mutually bound themselves in the penalty of ONE HUNDRED POUNDS to be applied to the relief of the poor.

The above well-timed and spirited resolutions have had the desired effect by producing an immediate reduction of the price of this most necessary article of subsistence, from SEVENTEEN POUNDS FIVE SHILLINGS, to FOURTEEN POUNDS the load.

Similar resolutions have been recommended to the BUTCHERS, which it is to be hoped will be followed, and attended, with equal success.

At Arundel market, on Thursday last, the current price of wheat was FOURTEEN POUNDS the load. Mr. Hern, proprieter of the water-mill, purchased nine loads, at that rate; and Mr. Ibbetson bought a great deal for the same price. The Mayor, in consequence, ordered the assize of bread to be lowered accordingly.

The inhabitants of Horsham, at their Easter vestry, agreed to sell flour to their poor neighbours at 10d. per gallon for some time to come, the expence of which is to be defrayed out of their Poor's Rate.[1]

The dread of an ACTUAL scarcity of wheat in this kingdom appears less and less every day, for in the inland counties it seems, there is a great plenty, if not superabundance, and this we state upon the authority of the best information.

F. NEWBURY, Esq. HIGH SHERIFF for this county, has set a most laudable example to gentlemen, farmers, and others who give employment to labourers, by having directed his steward, in consequence of the increased price of provisions, to augment the weekly wages of every man employed in the business of agriculture or husbandry, at HEATHFIELD PARK; and this has been done accordingly ever since MICHAELMAS last.

Samuel Whitbread, Esq, of Portman-Square, has generously pre-

---

1 A local tax designed to relieve poverty on a parish by parish basis; only available to the propertyless, as the following extract observes.

sented Twenty Pounds, for the relief of the poor of the parish of Nin-field. — The parish has likewise received distinguished favors from several other gentlemen.

From Vol. XLVII, no. 2540: April 27, 1795

The spirit of turbulence and discontent that has within the last few weeks manifested itself very openly and very generally among the lower ranks of men in this country, has been occasioned by very complicated and some unavoidable causes. But these causes, we apprehend, will not be removed by riot, tumult, or rapine.

If the poorer class of the community considered the situation of their neighbours, they would observe, that the little farmers and tradesmen were in a worse situation than themselves, with the inward suffering of perhaps needing the parish relief more, though not liable to receive (from some trifling possession) that assistance, which their less worthy but meaner spirited neighbours scruple not to partake of.

In the present situation we cannot sufficiently praise the comfort we receive from the plan for internal defence, and we look up to the YEOMANRY CORPS,[1] as the foremost to support order and good government.

From Vol. XLVII, no. 2542: May 11, 1795

Last Wednesday our HIGH SHERIFF, accompanied by the DUKE of RICHMOND, LORD SELSEA, SIR CECIL BISSHOPP, COUNSELLOR NEWNHAM, LIEUT. COLONEL NEWTON, Mr. POYNTZ, &c. &c. attended at St. James's and presented the following Address to his Majesty.

To the KING's Most Excellent Majesty.
"We, the Nobility, Gentry, Clergy, Freeholders and other Inhabitants of the County of Sussex, request leave to present to your Majesty this unfeigned testimony of joy upon the nuptials of His Royal Highness the Prince of Wales. This happy event we consider as an additional security to the many blessings derived to us from your mild and

---

1 Yet another locally-raised and based unit.

parental government. Deign then, Sire, we humbly intreat you, to accept these cordial effusions of loyalty and gratitude; they prove how sincerely we revere that benevolent wisdom of your Majesty, which thus connects the dearest interests of the community with the firmest pledges of domestic union.

"May you long continue to reign in the hearts of your faithful subjects, and may the British Throne be filled, to the latest posterity, by your descendants, emulous of your Royal virtues, and proud to deserve that character which so justly distinguishes your Majesty's reign,—the beloved Father of a grateful people."

The next day the SHERIFF had the honour of being introduced to the QUEEN in her Drawing-Room, where he presented the following address to her Majesty.

To the QUEEN's Most Excellent Majesty.

"At this season of national exultation, when the public heart expands with the prospect of manifold blessings accruing to the British empire, from the nuptials of His Royal Highness the Prince of Wales; permit us, Madam, the Nobility, Gentry, Clergy, Freeholders and other Inhabitants of the County of Sussex, to join our warmest congratulations to the general voice.[1] Impressed, as we are, with the deepest veneration for your Majesty, we rejoice in this addition to your domestic happiness; for while we contemplate, with the utmost deference, your Majesty ever most eminently uniting the splendid functions of Royal dignity, with the lovely virtues of the conjugal and maternal character, we look forward with glad confidence to the influence of so bright an example upon these, your dearest connections, being firmly persuaded, that the nearer the resemblance, the greater will be the source, both of private and public felicity."

The above Addresses were most graciously received.

Mr. NEWBERY refused the honour of Knighthood; but he received the distinguished gratification of being applauded, by the KING in person, for the readiness he had evinced in endeavouring to suppress

---

1 George Prince of Wales had recently been married off for political reasons to Princess Caroline of Brunswick (despite his secret, and illegal, marriage to his mistress, a Roman Catholic widow, 10 years before). By the time *Pride and Prejudice* was published, George was Prince Regent, acting monarch during the long illness of his father, George III; his admiration obliged Austen to dedicate *Emma* to him.

the late riot at Newhaven: for which his Majesty, at the same time, signified the country was obliged to him.

* * * * *

Last Monday the Court-Martial for the trial of the Oxford Militiamen charged with mutiny, was opened at the Old Ship Tavern, in Brighton ...

The first prisoner arraigned before the court, was Edward Cook, commonly called Capt. Cook, whose trial lasted three days, and produced strong evidence against him; but his defence was accompanied by some favorable circumstances, and his character, abstracted from the offence he stood charged with, merited the approbation and praise of his captain.

Richard Blake, John Cox, and John Haddocks, were next tried. — The principal evidence against Blake was Mr. Inskip, master of the White Hart Inn, Newhaven: he had noticed the prisoner, at his house among the rest at the time of the riot, but observed nothing conspicuous in his conduct; he made no defence, but committed himself entirely to the mercy of the court — Cox had been much mis-represented, his defence seemed to do away the criminality that was imputed to him, and furthermore his Colonel, his Captain, and the Serj. Major spoke greatly in favor of his general character. — Haddocks, feasibly accounted for his conduct on the first day, but produced no evidence to contradict what was alleged against him on the second day of the riot.

The prisoners, after trial, are remanded to the House of Correction in this town, and conducted hither under an escort of the Lancashire Fencibles.

This morning the court will proceed on the trial of Parish, who was arraigned on Saturday.

The court is quite public, free admission being given to all who choose to witness its proceedings, which are strictly regular, perfectly candid, and truly honourable; in short, whatever may be the fate of the prisoners, we venture to affirm, that not one of them, will impute it to a WANT OF JUSTICE on his trial....

We have with pleasure noticed the quiet disposition and orderly behaviour of the North Fencibles, or Highlanders stationed in this town; and thus publicly acknowledge the fact, because we think them entitled to it, and that it redounds much to their credit both as men and soldiers.

From Vol. XLVII, no. 2543: May 18, 1795

Last Thursday the Court Martial assembled at Brighton to try the Oxford Militiamen, broke up, having tried all the prisoners who on their examinations were declared capitally punishable by martial law.

The following are the prisoners who took their trials last week; viz. on Monday, Henry Parish, and William Harper.

On Tuesday, Corporal Richard Day; William Warren, bugleman; and Samuel Hermitage.

On Wednesday and Thursday Sergt. Drake; Richard Weaver; John Woodmarshal; and Richard Johnson, drummer. Against Johnson there appeared hardly any ground for accusation; the only evidence examined on the part of the prosecution, was a Serjeant's LADY, whose uncorroberated testimony seemed to have little or no weight with the Court; not did it deserve any, for she was evidently more under the influence of PIQUE than of JUSTICE.

The other military prisoners confined in the house of correction in this town, were on Saturday morning removed, under a strong guard, to Blatchington, to be tried by a regimental court-martial.

The sentences of the prisoners found guilty will not be made public, until the proceedings of the Court have been laid before the King, and received his Majesty's confirmations.

From Vol. XLVII, no. 2544: May 25, 1795

A number of painters and other workmen are now busily employed in decorating the MARINE PAVILION, at BRIGHTON; at which place their Royal Highnesses the PRINCE and PRINCESS of WALES are expected in about a fortnight.

The Cheshire, Wilts, West Essex, and Herefordshire regiments of Militia are now encamped at Brighthelmston,[1] on nearly the same ground as they occupied in the year 1793, a little more to the west-

---

1   The old name, still current in the 1790s, for Brighton.

ward of the Brick-kilns, on the road to Hove; a situation far more convenient than the spot made use of last year. The regiments are all placed in a line, the Cheshire on the right. The Dorset are expected to take their ground on Tuesday; The Prince's regiment, and Park of Artillery, in the course of next week.

The fineness of the weather and the attraction of the camp has put the inhabitants of the above highly-favored watering-place in a considerable degree of bustle, by causing a larger influx of company than is usual at this early part of the season.

Last Monday morning the first division of North-Fencibles that had marched into this town from Shoreham, for Hastings, proceeded on their route. The same morning the other division arrived here and on Tuesday continued their route as above.

On Saturday one division of the South-Devon Regiment, marched into town from Surrey, on their route to Warley camp; they halted that day and yesterday, and about two o'clock this morning proceeded on their march.

On Saturday evening the officers very politely ordered their band into the Bowling-Green for the entertainment of the town, were [sic] many excellent pieces of music were performed, and though the band was without one of its best supports, the trumpet, it obtained great credit for its excellence among the best judges, and particularly from the MASTER of our VOLUNTEER Band, who, though he may turn his deaf ear to *discordant* sounds, will never lavish praises where they are not due.

All the officers were present, who rose from their seats and stood uncovered while God save the King was playing. The circumstance of none of the bye-standers having followed their example, proceeded from their being unaccustomed to such a ceremony, and by no means from any lack of loyalty or proper respect for their Sovereign.

In the Bowling-Green yesterday evening, there were few if any short of two thousand people assembled to hear the above Band again perform.

* * * * *

On Wednesday next a Special Commission of Oyer and Terminer will be opened before Judges BULLER and LAWRENCE, at the Town-Hall in this town, for the trial of the following prisoners, viz.

JAMES SYKES, charged with riotously and tumultuously assembling, with diverse other persons, on the 17th of April last at Bishopstone, and stealing and carrying away ten hempen sacks and 50 bushels of flour, the property of Thomas Barton and Edmund Catt, value 13 l.

WILLIAM SANSOM, charged with tumultuously assembling at Bishopstone, as aforesaid, on the 17th of April, and stealing and carrying away three bottles and three quarts of rum, value 6s. 6d; and also with stealing and carrying away out of the mill and granary of said Barton and Carr, several sacks, and large quantities of wheat flour, the goods of said Barton and Carr, value 10 l.

WILLIAM AVERY, charged with riotously assembling on the said 17th of April, at Newhaven, with divers others, and stealing and carrying away out of the sloop Lucy, upwards of 200 sacks and 1000 bushels of flour, the goods of said Barton and Carr, value 250 l.

WILLIAM MIDWINTER, charged with the like offence.

And HENRY BROOK and JOHN ETHERINGTON, charged with riotously and tumultuously assembling, on said 17th of April, at Newhaven aforesaid, and stealing, taking, and carrying away from and out of the dwelling-house of John Greathead, at Newhaven aforesaid, a silver watch, value 20s, and two woollen jackets and other things, value 1 l. 5s. 6d. the property of the said John Greathead.

Sykes, Sanson, Avery and Midwinter, were all soldiers lately of the OXFORDSHIRE MILITIA; Brook and Etherington are labourers, and to the credit of the country people, the only two we have heard of at all implicated in the riots on account of which the above Special Commission has been issued.[1]

* * * * *

In addition to what we stated in a former Paper, touching the evidence of Mr. Inskip, who was called on the part of the prosecution against Blake, on the late Court Martial held at Brighton, should be added, in favor of the prisoner, that on hearing Mrs. Inskip had not

---

1   Sykes, Sanson, Avery and Midwinter were all arrested by the civil authorities and therefore tried under ordinary criminal rather than military law. Assizes were, like Quarter Sessions, periodical courts, but could also be specially convened to try specific crimes, as here.

lain in more than three days, he placed himself as centinel at the top of the stairs, and there continued during the time of the riot at Newhaven, to prevent anyone approaching her chamber, or doing anything that might alarm or disturb her.

From vol. XLVII, no. 2545: June 1, 1795

The Assizes appointed to be held here under a Special Commission of Oyer and Terminer on the 17th inst. before the Judges BULLER and LAWRENCE, ended on Friday last, at which four prisoners were tried, two of whom were capitally convicted and received sentence of death, viz.

James Sykes [on the charges made above]

And William Sansom [on the charges made above].

Henry Brook and John Etherington ... were found guilty of stealing to the value of THIRTY-NINE SHILLINGS; but, an objection being made by the prisoners counsel to the indictment, which set forth that certain persons in the prosecutor's house had been put in FEAR, without stating by WHOM, their sentences were respited till our next Assizes, in order that the objection may be previously submitted to the opinion of the rest of the Judges. The prisoners were of course remanded to Horsham Jail....

William Avery and William Midwinter were arraigned, but on an affadavit of the Solicitor for the prosecution, read in Court, stating that he had not been able to secure the attendance of two of his principal witnesses, the Captain and Mate of the sloop Lucy, their trials were put off till the next Assizes.

Judgment of death was pronounced against the two capital convicts by JUDGE BULLER, in a very solemn and emphatical manner, accompanied with observations that tended to shew the enormity of the offence of which the unhappy men stood convicted. It was, his Lordship said, the bounden duty of Judges, to watch evidence with peculiar attention, that no part of it which could operate in favor of the prisoners arraigned before him, might escape their notice; he had so watched the evidence just given, and sorry was he to say, he could discover nothing in it that would afford the prisoners the smallest hope of mercy in this world; on the contrary, the case was attended with some very aggravated circumstances, particularly that of having asserted to one of the witnesses, servant to Mr. Carr, near the mill, that if his master were present, his body should be stuck as full of bay-onets as it would hold; which proved an intention to murder, and though prevented, by Mr. Carr's absence, it nevertheless fixed the fate of the prisoners beyond the possibility of alteration. They had indeed set up a sort of defence, that the prosecutors had been in the practice of exporting flour to France, but not the least shadow of evidence had appeared in support of it. If however there should be persons con-cerned in such a trade, they were highly criminal, and ought to be placed where the prisoners stood; there they would be sure to meet the most severe and exemplary punishment. His Lordship made many other observations, touching the offence and the nature of it, one of which was, that the AMPLE PROVISION made for Militiamen, should have been one consideration to have restrain'd the prisoners in their violent pursuits; and concluded his awful address, in the usual way of passing sentence of death.

The prisoners called many persons of respectability to their char-acters, who all spoke highly in praise of them, but the Judge observed, character could have no weight, but in cases of doubt, when it ought always to operate on the side of mercy.

After the assizes, the Judges accompanied the High-Sheriff to Heathfield-Park, where their Lordships purposed staying three or four days, previous to their visiting Tunbridge-Wells.[1]

The Assize sermon was preached at St. Michael's Church by the Rev. Mr. CONSTABLE, Chaplain to the Sheriff, from 1. Epistle ST. PETER, ch. ii. v. 13. *"Submit yourselves to every ordinance of man, for the Lord's sake."* From the above text the Rev. Gentleman delivered an apposite and well connected discourse of about 25 minutes continu-ance, in which he shewed, both in a religious and moral point of view, the comforts which result from an obedience to the Laws, and the absolute necessity of using the strong arm of Justice to punish such as wilfully and wickedly attempted to overthrow them: He drew a lively picture of the happiness deriving to the inhabitants of these realms from the excellence of the British Constitution, which he contrasted with the wretchedness of the people of a neighbouring country: He pointed out the absurdity of supposing, if a scarcity was

---

1   A spa-town and, like Brighton, a resort popular among the wealthy.

really to be apprehended, that the outrageous proceedings of a mob, (always accompanied by wastefulness) were likely to produce plenty! —and concluded by exhorting those among his auditory immediately concerned in the trials of the deluded men, on account of whom they were then specially assembled, to recollect, that the lives, security, and property of their fellow-creatures, were in their hands; and with beseeching, that they might be guided in their determinations by the superintendence of the Almighty.

We cannot but regret the indisposition of Mr. CONSTABLE, which occasioned his voice to be so low, as to render parts of the above Sermon difficult to be heard at the extremities of the Church.

'Tis rather singular, that the above assizes were not honoured with the attendance of one single Nobleman; nor did the occasion bring together more Gentlemen than were necessary to form the Grand Jury.

* * * * *

Last Wednesday the 13 Oxford Militiamen, who were lately tried by a General Court-Martial at Brighton, were taken from the House of Correction in this town, and conducted in two Artillery waggons, under a strong guard of the Lancashire Fencibles, to Brighton, where two of them are to be shot on Friday se'nnight the 12th instant. Three were condemned, but one has been since pardoned on condition of being transported to Botany Bay.[1] Four were liberated on Friday, one of which was Johnson, the drummer, against whom we observed in a former paper, that no case to which criminality attached, had been made out. What is to be done with the remaining six that are under confinement, we have not yet learnt.

From Vol. XLVII, no. 2546: June 8, 1795

Edward Cook and Henry Parish, the two unfortunate men of the Oxford Militia, condemned to be shot for Mutiny, are daily attended by two Clergymen. They are truly penitent, and thoroughly resigned to their unhappy fate. The place appointed for executing the awful

---

1   In Australia: an increasingly common commutation of the death penalty.

sentence, is Brighton; the day, 'tis generally believed, Friday next the 12th inst. as stated in our last, and early in the morning.

The other man who was adjudged death, and ordered to be shot, but pardoned on condition of being transported to Botany-Bay for ten years, is named Haddocks.

Of the six that are sentenced to be flogged, one is to receive 500 lashes, one 1500, and the rest 1000 each.

Sykes and Sansom, condemned to be hanged at our late Special Assizes, 'tis expected will suffer at Horsham, on Saturday.

Last Tuesday the arms belonging to the Oxfordshire Militia were removed, in six Artillery waggons, from this town to Blatchington, for the purpose, we apprehend, of being restored to that regiment, which 'tis said is to march to Brighton early on Friday morning to attend the execution of their unhappy comrades.

The 10th or Prince of Wales's Light Dragoons, are expected at Brighton Camp, in the course of this week, probably in time to be present at the intended execution.

The Militia Forces at the above Camp are all perfectly quiet, and without betraying the smallest disposition to be otherwise; which sufficiently evinces the fallacy of the late ridiculous reports.

From Vol. XLVII, no. 2547: June 15, 1795

On Friday, about noon, the 10th, or Prince of Wales's own Light Dragoons, headed by Lieut. Col. Churchill, took their ground on the right of the Brighton camp. This regiment consists of nine complete troops, and is supposed, in every point of view, as respectable a body of cavalry as any in Europe.

Last Friday being the day appointed for the execution of Edward Cook and Henry Parish, privates in the Oxford militia, condemned by a general Court-Martial to be shot for mutiny, the death warrant accordingly arrived, by express, early in the morning, but according to some informality in making it out, General Lascelles did not think it such as would justify him in shooting the men, for we understand it did not specify either the time of execution, nor the mode of performing it; the General therefore found it necessary to dispatch his Aid-de-Camp to town on the subject, which occasioned a delay that agreeably flattered the public with the hope of a reprieve, for it seemed to be the wish of almost every one in the neighbourhood, that the lives of the men should be saved: all who spoke of it during the course of the day seemed interested in the event, and there were but few who did not conceive the suspension favorable to the prisoners.

The next morning, however, proved the fallacy of their conceptions, for at six o'clock a strong guard of horse and foot appeared before the prison, which was announced to the unhappy objects within by the sound of drum, and immediately afterwards the prisoners were brought out, first the six sentenced to be flogged, who were placed on foot in the centre of the guard, and then the two under sentence of death, in a cart, attended by a clergyman, and being placed in front of the others, the whole proceeded with slow and solemn pace, through the Camp on their way to Goldstone Bottom the place of execution, where the whole line had already been formed into an oblong square half a mile in length, but before it appeared in view the guard was halted, and the men to be flogged taken by a file of men to be punished first; on arriving at the spot, they were marched from one end of the square to the other, and back again to the centre, where three of them received 300 lashes each; Blake was next tied up, but let down again and forgiven, for which he returned the General thanks on his knees. Warren, whose sentence was 500 lashes was also forgiven, and Hermitage went unpunished, but was marched back a prisoner.

The guard now moved forward with the condemned men, who being arrived at the head of the square quitted the cart, and were marched, still attended by the clergyman, to the other end of it, where the Oxford regiment was stationed. Here they spent a short time in prayer, and having declared themselves ready to meet their fate, their coffins were brought and placed before them, which they viewed very attentively, and having taken leave of each other, pulled their caps over their faces and knelt as they were directed, on their coffins, immediately after which the fatal triggers were pulled, and they both dropped at the same instant; Cook pitched forward over his coffin upon his head, turned upon his back, and moved no more; Parish fell upon his back, and turned on his left side, and after lying motionless near five minutes he turned again upon his back, when one of the two men who kept his fire in reserve, ran up, and placing the muzzle of his gun to his ear, shot him through the head; the other then went up to Cook, and shot him in like manner.

The troops were then marched close by the bodies, and many of the Oxford regiment wept much as they passed their dead comrades. The deceased were after put into their coffins, with all their clothes on, and conveyed in one of the Artillery waggons to Hove church-yard, and there interred.

These unfortunate men throughout the whole of their trying situations, conducted themselves with the utmost decency, firmness, and fortitude; they kept their step accurately with the guard between the lines, and knelt, unshackled, upon their coffins to meet their doom, without betraying the smallest timidity or agitation.

They were shot at half past eight by 12 men selected for the purpose from their own regiment, ten of whom fired at first, five at each object; the other two were kept in reserve, and discharged their musquets as before-mentioned. They stood at the distance of about ten yards, and took good aim, as we observed two balls had entered the body of Parish a little below the left breast, and as many that of Cook, who at the instant must have been sensible of it, as he was observed, at the time he fell, to raise and apply his right hand to the part.

The execution was attended by Lieut. Generals LASCELLES, HULSE, and JONES, and conducted with the utmost solemnity and order; it exhibited a scene awfully grand, which was heightened by the Regiments of Cavalry, placed in squadrons on rising ground in the rear of the Infantry, and a number of loaded cannon pointed at the spot where the unhappy men suffered. Not the smallest symptom of opposition, resistance, or revenge appeared, on the contrary, we believe, a due regard to subordination, never appeared more manifest in so large a body of men assembled on any occasion whatever. But few country people were present.

The same day, between one and two o'clock, James Sykes and William Sansom, privates in the above regiment, who were capitally convicted and received sentence of death at the late Special Assizes, held at this town, were executed at Horsham, pursuant to their sentence. Their behaviour since condemnation and at the gallows, was truly becoming men in their unhappy situations; they said they were prepared to meet their fate, and should die in charity with all mankind, and lastly exhorted the spectators to beware of drunkenness and mobs. Two hangmen from the Old-Bailey attended, who notwithstanding their practice, made but a bungling job of it, for having carelessly taken Sansom's hair into the noose, the poor fellow in consequence died extremely hard. The HIGH SHERIFF himself was present, attended by Captain SEWELL's and Mr. FULLER's Troops of Yeomanry Cavalry.

On Saturday, after the execution, the first and Cinque Port regiment of Fencibles left the above camp, on their route to the place of their original destination, the ground of encampment near Goodwood.

Same day the Corps of Horse Artillery left this town, on their route to Goodwood. They halted at Brighton camp, and attended the punishment of the unfortunate culprits of the Oxfordshire regiment.

Same day the Lancashire Fencibles, after witnessing the execution, left Brighthelmston, on their route to Barham Downs; two troops of which halted in this town on Saturday and Sunday; the other four troops marched forward to Uckfield, Tunbridge-Wells, and adjacents.

From Vol. XLVII, no. 2548: June 22, 1795

Their Royal Highnesses the Prince and Princess of Wales arrived at Brighton between one and two o'clock on Thursday morning last. They alighted at the house of Mr. Hamilton, on the Steine, which is to be made the royal residence, till the alteration [sic], that are going forward at the Pavilion, can be completed.

In the evening the whole town was illuminated, in honour of their Royal Highnesses arrival, but the effect of the illumination was greatly lessened by the wetness of the night, as it prevented the lamps with which the Castle, the Libraries, and other houses were decorated, from burning.

The Prince, we are informed, perambulated the town, in his great coat, to view the different devices.

Though the untowardness of the weather has hitherto obscured the beauties of Brighton from the Princess of Wales, it has had no effect on her Royal Highness's spirits; on the contrary, her cheerfulness and pleasantry, strongly bespeak her approbation of the place.

The Prince, about noon yesterday, set off for town, but we understand his Royal Highness signified his intention of returning to Brighton some time in the course of the day.

On Wednesday morning, should the weather prove favorable, the Prince and Princess of Wales intend visiting the camp, when the whole line will be drawn up, and fire a Royal Salute on the occasion. After which there will be a grand field–day.[1]

Last Thursday morning the Wiltshire Militia encamped at Brighton, struck their tents and marched on their route to Danbury, in Essex, to augment the encampment there. The regiment was much disgusted at being obliged to quit their ground at Brighton, and the Officers petitioned the DUKE of YORK not to be removed, but in vain, as the DUKE of RICHMOND, who commands the district, had thought it necessary.

---

1   That is, military exercises.

Appendix G: Austen's Letters to her Sister on the Publication of Pride and Prejudice[1]

[Austen's letters, particularly to her elder sister Cassandra, are the source of much of what we know about her life and attitudes. In early 1813 when *Pride and Prejudice* appeared, Cassandra was staying with their eldest brother James and his (second) wife Mary at Steventon in Hampshire where he was rector, while Jane remained with her mother at Chawton.]

To Cassandra Austen.
Chawton Friday Jany 29. [1813]
I hope you received my little parcel by J. Bond[2] on Wednesday evening my dear Cassandra, & that you will be ready to hear from me again on Sunday, for I feel that I must write to you to day. Your parcel is safely arrived & everything shall be delivered as it ought. Thank you for your note. As you had not heard from me at that time it was very good in you to write, but I shall not be so much your debtor soon. — I want to tell you that I have got my own darling Child from London; — on Wednesday I received one Copy, sent down by Falknor,[3] with three lines from Henry to say that he had given another to Charles & sent a 3d by the Coach to Godmersham;[4] just the two Sets which I was least eager for the disposal of. I wrote to him immediately to beg for my two other Sets, unless he would take the trouble of forwarding them at once to Steventon & Portsmouth[5]—not having an idea of his leaving Town before to-day; — by your account how-

---

1 © Déirdre Le Faye, 1995. Reprinted from *Jane Austen's Letters*, collected and edited by Déirdre Le Faye (3rd ed., 1995) by permission of Oxford University Press.
2 John Bond was steward of the farm at Steventon.
3 This seems to refer to a local coaching agent.
4 Austen refers to three of her brothers: Henry was at this stage a banker in London; Charles was her youngest brother, a naval officer; and Godmersham was Edward's substantial estate in Kent.
5 If copies are sent to James and Cassandra at Steventon, and via the naval base at Portsmouth to Frank (like Charles an officer in the service), this would complete the distribution of the novel among Jane's siblings — except for the mentally-handicapped George, who is not mentioned.

ever he was gone before my Letter was written. The only evil is the delay, nothing more can be done till his return. Tell James & Mary so, with my love. — For *your* sake I am as well pleased that it should be so, as it might be unpleasant to you to be in the Neighbourhood at the first burst of business. — The Advertisement is in our paper to day for the first time; *18s.* He shall ask £1. 1. for my two next & £1. 8 for my stupidest of all.[1] I shall write to Frank that he may not think himself neglected. Miss Benn[2] dined with us on the very day of the books coming & in the evening we fairly set at it, and read half the first vol. to her, prefacing that, having intelligence from Henry that such a work would soon appear, we had desired him to send it when-ever it came out, and I believe it passed with her unsuspected. She was amused, poor soul! *That* she could not help, you know, with two such people to lead the way, but she really does seem to admire Eliza-beth. I must confess I think her as delightful a creature as ever appeared in print, and how I shall be able to tolerate those who do not like *her* at least I do not know. There are a few typical errors; and a 'said he,' or a 'said she,' would sometimes make the dialogue more immediately clear; but

> I do not write for such dull elves
> As have not a great deal of ingenuity themselves.[3]

The second volume is shorter than I could wish, but the difference is not so much in reality as in look, there being a larger proportion of

---

1 Austen is alluding here to her publisher Thomas Egerton's canny pricing tactics. *Sense and Sensibility* was published at the author's own risk: that is, Austen, an unknown quantity as far as the market was concerned, would bear any losses, but also be entitled to all profits once the costs of production were covered. Egerton turned it into a quality product and sold it at 15 shillings (20 shillings = £1). Before it became clear that *Sense and Sensibility* would be a success (it made Austen £140), she agreed to sell the copyright of *Pride and Prejudice* outright for £110. Egerson cut costs on paper and binding, set the price at 18s, and pocketed the substantial profits. Austen imagines his prices continuing to rise, as her novels (to correspond with their declining material quality? out of pique?) get worse.

2 A neighbour at Chawton, the impoverished younger sister of a local rector.

3 Paraphrases the penultimate verse of *Marmion* by Walter Scott (see below), which, describing a character at the battle of Flodden, begins: "I do not rhyme to that dull elf, / Who cannot image to himself, / That, all through Flodden's dismal night, / Wilton was foremost in the fight."

narrative in that part. I have lop't and crop't so successfully, however, that I imagine it must be rather shorter than S. & S. altogether. Now I will try to write of something else, & it shall be a complete change of subject—ordination—I am glad to find your enquiries have ended so well. If you could discover whether Northamptonshire is a country of Hedgerows I should be glad again.[1] We admire your Charades excessively—but as yet have guessed only the 1st. The others seem very difficult. There is so much beauty in the versification however, that the finding them out is but a secondary pleasure. I grant you that *this is* a cold day, & am sorry to think how cold you will be through the process of your visit at Manydown.[2] I hope you will wear your China crape. Poor wretch! I can see you shivering away in your miserable feeling feet. What a vile character Mr Digweed turns out, quite beyond anything & everything—instead of going to Steventon, they are to have a dinner-party next Tuesday! I am sorry to say that I cd not eat a mince-pie at Mr Papillon's;[3] I was rather headachey that day & could not venture on anything sweet except jelly, and *that* was excellent. There were no stewed pears—but Miss Benn had some almonds & raisins. By the bye she desired to be kindly remembered to you when I wrote last & I forgot it. Betsy sends her duty to you & hopes you are well[4]—& her love to Miss Caroline & hopes she has got rid of her cough. It was such a pleasure to her to think her oranges were so well timed that I daresay she was rather glad to hear of the cough. Since I wrote this letter we have been visited by Mrs Digweed, her sister and Miss Benn. I gave Mrs D. her little parcel which she opened here, & seemed much pleased with—and she desired me to make her best thanks etc. to Miss Lloyd for it. Martha may guess how full of wonder and gratitude she was.[5]

---

1 Austen is currently writing her next novel, *Mansfield Park*, set in Northamptonshire and in which the hero becomes a clergyman.
2 The home of the Bigg family, not far from Steventon.
3 The Digweed family were tenants of the Steventon manor-house, but currently, it seems, on a visit to Chawton, where John-Rawston Papillon was rector.
4 Betsy was a maidservant in the Chawton household; Caroline was the daughter of James and Mary.
5 Martha Lloyd was Mary's sister and living at Steventon.

To Cassandra Austen.
Chawton, Thursday Feb. 4 [1813]
My dear Cassandra

Your letter was truly welcome, and I am much obliged to you all for your praise; it came at a right time, for I had had some fits of disgust. Our second evening's reading to Miss Benn had not pleased me so well, but I believe something must be attributed to my mother's too rapid way of getting on: and though she perfectly understands the characters herself, she cannot speak as they ought. Upon the whole, however, I am quite vain enough and well satisfied enough. The work is rather too light, and bright, and sparkling; it wants shade; it wants to be stretched out here and there with a long chapter of sense, if it could be had; if not, of solemn specious nonsense, about something unconnected with the story; an essay on writing, a critique on Walter Scott, or the history of Buonaparté,[1] or anything that would form a contrast, and bring the reader with increased delight to the playfulness and epigrammatism of the general style. I doubt your quite agreeing with me here. I know your starched notions. The caution observed at Steventon with regard to the possession of the book is an agreeable surprise to me, & I heartily wish it may be the means of saving you from everything unpleasant—but you must be prepared for the neighbourhood being perhaps already informed of there being such a Work in the World & in the Chawton World! Dummer[2] will do that you know. It was spoken of here one morning when Mrs D. called with Miss Benn. The greatest blunder in the printing that I have met with is in page 220, v.3, where two speeches are made into one.[3] There might as well have been no suppers at Longbourn; but I suppose it was the remains of Mrs. Bennet's old Meryton habits....

---

1   Austen names the two giants of the worlds of politics and literature respectively, the French Emperor and Europe's most successful poet. Both were losing their dominance in 1813: Napoleon after a disastrous Russian campaign and defeats in Spain, Scott after the appearance of Byron's *Childe Harold's Pilgrimage*. The following year, Napoleon abdicates, and Scott becomes a novelist (with the publication of *Waverley*).
2   Dummer House was the nearby home of the Terry family, whose five sons and six daughters perhaps constituted a particularly effective news service.
3   See note on the text to p.345 of this edition (p.40).

Appendix H: Contemporary Periodical Reviews of Pride and Prejudice

1. From *The British Critic* XLI no.2 (February 1813). London: F.C. and J. Rivington.

British Catalogue: Novels

Art.17. *Pride and Prejudice, a Novel, in three Volumes. By the Author of Sense and Sensibility*

We had occasion to speak favorably of the former production of this author or authoress, specified above, and we readily do the same of the present. It is very far superior to almost all the publications of the kind which have lately come before us. It has a very unexceptionable tendency, the story is well told, the characters remarkably well drawn and supported, and written with great spirit as well as vigour. The story has no great variety, it is simply this. The hero is a young man of large fortune and fashionable manners, whose distinguishing characteristic is personal pride. The heroine, on the first introduction, conceives a most violent prejudice against Darcy, which a variety of circumstances well imagined and happily represented, tend to strengthen and confirm. The under plot is an attachment between the friend of Darcy and the elder sister of the principal female character; other personages, of greater or less interest and importance, complete the dramatis personæ, some of whose characters are exceedingly well drawn. Explanations of the different perplexities and seeming contrarieties, are gradually unfolded, and the two principal performers are happily united.

Of the characters, Elizabeth Bennet, the heroine, is supported with great spirit and consistency throughout; there seems no defect in the portrait; this is not precisely the case with Darcy her lover; his easy unconcern and fashionable indifference, somewhat abruptly changes to the ardent lover. The character of Mr. Collins, the obsequious rector, is excellent. Fancy presents us with many such, who consider the patron of exalted rank as the model of all that is excellent on earth, and the patron's smiles and condescension as the sum of human happiness. Mr. Bennet, the father of Elizabeth, presents us with some novelty of character; a reserved, acute, and satirical, but indolent personage, who sees and laughs at the follies and indiscretions of his dependents, without making any exertions to correct them. The picture of the younger Miss Bennets, their perpetual visits to the market town where officers are quartered, and the result, is perhaps exemplified in every provincial town in the kingdom.

It is unnecessary to add, that we have perused these volumes with much satisfaction and amusement, and entertain very little doubt that their successful circulation will induce the author to similar exertions.

[189–90]

2. From the *Critical Review: or, Annals of Literature.* 4th series, Vol. III, no.3 (March 1813). London: J. Mawman.

Instead of the whole interest of the tale hanging upon one or two characters, as is generally the case in novels, the fair author of the present introduces us, at once, to a whole family, every individual of which excites the interest, and very agreeably divides the attention of the reader.

Mr. Bennet, the father of this family, is represented as a man of abilities, but of a sarcastic humour, and combining a good deal of caprice and reserve in his composition. He possesses an estate of about two thousand a year, and lives at Longbourne, in Hertfordshire, a pleasant walk from the market town of Meryton. This gentleman's estate is made to descend, in default of male issue, to a distant relation. Mr. Bennet, captivated by a handsome face and the appearance of good temper, had married early in life the daughter of a country attorney.

'A woman of mean understanding, little information, and uncertain temper. When she was discontented, she fancied herself nervous. The business of her life was to get her daughters married; its solace was visiting and news.'

At a very early period of his marriage, Mr. Bennett finds, that a pretty face is but a sorry compensation for the absence of common sense; and that youth and the appearance of good nature, with the want of other good qualities, will not make a rational companion or an estimable wife. The consequence of this discovery of the ill effects of an unequal marriage, is the defalcation of all real affection, confidence, and respect on the side of Mr. Bennet towards his wife. His views of domestic comfort being overthrown, he seeks consolation for a disappointment, which he had brought upon himself, by indulging his fondness for a country life and his love of study. Being, as we said, a man of abilities and sense, though with some peculiarities and eccentricities, he contrives not to be out of temper with the follies which his wife discovers,[1] and is contented to laugh and be amused with her want of decorum and propriety.

"This," as our sensible author remarks, "is not the sort of happiness which a man would, in general, wish to owe to his wife; but where other powers of entertainment are wanting, the true philosopher will derive benefit from such as are given."

However this may be, though Mr. Bennet finds amusement in absurdity, it is by no means of advantage to his five daughters, who, with the help of their silly mother, are looking out for husbands. Jane, the eldest daughter, is very beautiful, and possesses great feeling, good sense, equanimity, cheerfulness, and elegance of manners. Elizabeth, the second, is represented as combining quickness of perception and strength of mind, with a playful vivacity something like that of her father, joined with a handsome person. Mary is a female pedant, affecting great wisdom, though saturated with stupidity. "She is a lady," (as Mr. Bennet says), "of deep reflection, who reads great books and makes extracts." Kitty is weak-spirited and fretful; but Miss Lydia, the youngest,

'is a stout, well-grown girl of fifteen, with a fine complexion and good humoured countenance; a favourite with her mother, whose affection had brought her into public at an early age. She had high animal spirits, and a sort of self-consequence.'

This young lady is mad after the officers who are quartered at Meryton; and from the attentions of these *beaux garçons*, Miss Lydia becomes a most decided flirt.

Although these young ladies claim a great share of the reader's interest and attention, none calls forth our admiration so much as Elizabeth, whose archness and sweetness of manner render her a very

---

1 "Discovers": that is, reveals.

attractive object in the family piece.¹ She is the *Beatrice* of the tale;²
and falls in love on much the same principles of contrariety. This
family of worthies are informed, that Netherfield Park, which is situated near to the Longbourn estate, is let to a young single gentleman
of good fortune. The intelligence puts Mrs. Bennet on the *Qui vive*;³
or, in a more homely phrase, quite on the *high fidgets*. In her own
mind, Mrs. B. augers not only great good from this occurrence, but
secretly determines, that the said gentleman *shall and must* fix upon
one of her girls for a wife. She therefore exhorts her husband to visit
the new-comer without delay; but perhaps the following conjugal
dialogue will exhibit Mr. and Mrs. Bennet to the best advantage.

[Quotes Volume 1, chapter 1, from "My dear Mr. Bennet" to "visit
them all" (pp.44–45 in this edition).]

The desired object of Mrs. Bennet's wishes at length arrives; and
Mr. Bennet, though he continues to teaze his lady, by refusing to go
to Netherfield, is among the first to welcome Mr. Bingley. Mrs. Bennet is delighted to find, that not only has her husband complied with
her wishes; but that Mr. Bingley is a charming handsome man, that
he intends to be at the next county ball, and that he is fond of dancing, "which was a certain step towards falling in love." At the ball her
raptures know no bounds, when Mr. Bingley evidently gives the preference to her eldest daughter before any lady in the room by dancing
twice with her in the course of the evening. This is not all; for Mr.
Bingley, according to the wishes and desires of Mrs. Bennet, does
really and truly fall in love with the beautiful and amiable Jane. Mr.
Bingley is, however, prevented from making his proposals of marriage
by the interference of his friend, Mr. Darcy, a man of high birth and
great fortune. Mr. Darcy represents to his friend the disgrace not only
of being allied to a family, who had relations in trade, but particularly
where the chief members of it were so wanting in the common
forms of decorum and propriety as Mrs. Bennet and her younger
daughters were. Mr. Bingley has great respect for his friend's judgment; and, being given to understand, that Jane did not return his pas-

---

1   That is, family portrait.
2   Shakespeare's feisty heroine in *Much Ado About Nothing*.
3   That is, on the alert (French for "who goes there?").

sion, absents himself from Netherfield, and leaves Jane to wear the willow.[1]

Mr. Darcy, who has, in his manners, the greatest reserve and hauteur, and a prodigious quantity of family pride, becomes, in spite of his determination to the contrary, captivated with the lively and sensible Elizabeth; who, thinking him the proudest of his species, takes great delight in playing *the Beatrice* upon him; and, finding his manners so very unbending, sets him down as a most disagreeable man. This dislike is heightened almost into hate by her being made acquainted with the part which he took in separating Mr. Bingley from her sister. She is also prejudiced against him for some cruel conduct, of which she believes him guilty towards a young man who was left to his protection. Whilst thinking of him with great bitterness and dislike, and believing herself also to be equally disliked in turn by him, she is surprised by a visit from Mr. Darcy, who formally declares himself her admirer. This gentleman, at the same time, owns, that his pride was hurt by the contemplation of her inferiority; and he acknowledges, that he loves her against his will, his reason, and even his character. This provocation, aided by her fixed dislike, makes her refuse him with very little ceremony. Darcy is highly offended; and during their conversation, Elizabeth upbraids him for his conduct towards her sister, in separating her from Mr. Bingley. She accuses him also of having, in defiance of honour and humanity, ruined the immediate prosperity, and blasted the prospects of the young man who was left under his protection. Darcy parts from her in anger, and Elizabeth retains her abhorrence of his character.

The next day comes an explanation in a letter of Darcy's conduct, which so entirely exculpates him from the crimes which have been alleged against him, and to which Elizabeth had given credit, that she is obliged to condemn herself for her precipitancy in believing the calumnies to which she had given ear, and exclaims: "How despicably have I acted! I who valued myself on my abilities! who have often disdained the generous candour of my sister, and gratified my vanity in useless or blameable distrust."

From this moment, Elizabeth's prejudice and dislike gradually subside; and the *sly little god* shoots one of his sharpest arrows very dex-

---

1   To "wear the willow" is to lament the loss of a lover.

terously into her heart. On the character of Elizabeth, the main interest of the novel depends; and the fair author has shewn considerable
ingenuity in the mode of bringing about the final *eclairissment*
between her and Darcy. Elizabeth's sense and conduct are of superior
order to those of the common heroines of novels. From her independence of character, which is kept within the proper line of decorum,
and her well-timed sprightliness, she teaches the man of Family-Pride
to know himself. He owns:

[Quotes Volume III, chapter xvi, from "I have been" to "being
pleased" (pp.368–69 in this edition).]

The above is merely the brief outline of this very agreeable novel.
An excellent lesson may be learned from the elopement of Lydia: —
the work also shows the folly of letting young girls have their own
way, and the danger which they incur in associating with the officers,
who may be quartered in or near their residence. The character of
Wickham is very well pourtrayed;— we fancy, that our authoress had
Joseph Surface before her eyes when she sketched it;[1] as well as the
lively Beatrice, when she drew the portrait of Elizabeth. Many such
silly women as Mrs. Bennet may be found; and numerous parsons like
Mr. Collins, who are every thing to every body; and servile in the
extreme to their superiors. Mr. Collins is indeed a notable object.

The sentiments, which are dispersed over the work, do great credit to the *sense* and *sensibility* of the authoress. The line she draws
between the prudent and the mercenary in matrimonial concerns,
may be useful to our fair readers — therefore we extract the part.

[Quotes Volume II, chapter iv, from "Mrs. Gardiner then rallied" to
"shall be foolish" (p.180 in this edition).]

This also may serve as a specimen of the lively manner in which
Elizabeth supports an argument.

We cannot conclude, without repeating our approbation of this
performance, which rises very superior to any novel we have lately
met with in the delineation of domestic scenes. Nor is there one

---

1 Joseph Surface is the superficially charming but really cynical character in Sheri-
dan's play, *The School for Scandal* (1777).

character which appears flat, or obtrudes itself upon the notice of the readers with troublesome impertinence. There is not one person in the drama with whom we could readily dispense;—they have all their proper places; and fill their several stations, with great credit to themselves, and much satisfaction to the reader.

Select Bibliography

Editions:

Chapman, R.W. *The Novels of Jane Austen: The Text Based on Collation of the Early Editions.* Vol. II: *Pride and Prejudice.* Oxford: Clarendon Press, 1923.

There are also useful editions from Oxford World's Classics (introduction by Isobel Armstrong, 1990, but otherwise a reissue of a much older edition); Penguin (ed. Vivien Jones, 1997); and Norton (3rd edition ed. Donald Gray, 2000: includes a selection of critical essays on the novel).

Biographical:

Chapman, R.W. (ed.) *Jane Austen's Letters to Her Sister Cassandra and Others.* Oxford: Oxford UP, 1932.

Fergus, Jan. *Jane Austen: A Literary Life.* New York: St. Martin's Press, 1991.

Halperin, John. *The Life of Jane Austen.* Baltimore: Johns Hopkins UP, 1996.

Honan, Park. *Jane Austen: Her Life.* 1987; London: Phoenix, 1997.

Jenkins, Elizabeth. *Jane Austen: A Biography.* 1938; London: Indigo, 1996.

Le Faye, Deirdre (ed.). *Jane Austen's Letters.* 3rd edition. Oxford: Oxford UP, 1995.

Nokes, Davis. *Jane Austen: A Life.* London: Fourth Estate, 1997.

Tomalin, Claire. *Jane Austen: A Life.* Harmondsworth: Viking, 1997.

On Austen's relation to literary antecedents:

Bradbrook, Frank. *Jane Austen and Her Predecessors.* Cambridge: Cambridge UP, 1966.

Harris, Jocelyn. *Jane Austen's Art of Memory.* Cambridge: Cambridge UP, 1989.

Litz, A. Walton. *Jane Austen: A Study in Her Artistic Development*. London: Chatto and Windus, 1965.

Moler, Kenneth. *Jane Austen's Art of Allusion*. Lincoln: U of Nebraska P, 1968.

Spencer, Jane. *The Rise of the Woman Novelist: From Aphra Behn to Jane Austen*. Oxford: Blackwell, 1986.

On gender and politics in Austen's novels:

Aers, David. "Community and Morality: Towards Reading Jane Austen." In David Aers et al ed., *Romanticism and Ideology: Studies in English Writing 1765–1830*. London: Routledge and Kegan Paul, 1981.

Armstrong, Nancy. *Desire and Domestic Fiction: A Political History of the Novel*. Oxford: Oxford UP, 1987.

Brown, Lloyd W. "Jane Austen and the Feminist Tradition." *Nineteenth-Century Fiction* 28 (1973): 321–38.

Butler, Marilyn. *Jane Austen and the War of Ideas*. Oxford: Oxford UP, 1975.

Cohen, Paula Marantz. *The Daughter's Dilemma: Family Process and the Nineteenth-century Domestic Novel*. Ann Arbor: U of Michigan P, 1991.

Copeland, Edward. *Women Writing about Money: Women's Fiction in England, 1790–1820*. Cambridge: Cambridge UP, 1995.

Duckworth, Alistair M. *The Improvement of the Estate: A Study of Jane Austen's Novels*. 1971; Baltimore: Johns Hopkins UP, 1994.

Evans, Mary. *Jane Austen and the State*. London: Tavistock, 1987.

Fraiman, Susan. "The Humiliation of Elizabeth Bennet." *Refiguring the Father: New Feminist Readings of Patriarchy*, ed. Patricia Yaeger and Beth Kowaleski-Wallace. Carbondale: South Illinois UP, 1989. 168–87.

Green, Katherine Sobba. *The Courtship Novel 1740–1820: A Feminized Genre*. Lexington: UP of Kentucky, 1991.

Horowitz, J. Barbara. *Jane Austen and the Question of Women's Education*. New York: Peter Lang, 1991.

Hunt, Linda C. *A Woman's Portion: Ideology, Culture and the British Female Novel Tradition*. New York: Garland, 1988.

Johnson, Claudia L. *Jane Austen: Women, Politics and the Novel*. Chicago: U of Chicago P, 1988.

—. *Equivocal Beings: Politics, Gender, and Sentimentality in the 1790s. A Study of Wollstonecraft, Radcliffe, Burney, and Austen*. Chicago: U of Chicago P, 1995.

Kelly, Gary. "Jane Austen and the English Novel of the 1790s." In Schofield and Mecheski, eds., *Fetter'd or Free? British Women Novelists 1670–1815*. Athens: Ohio UP, 1986. 285–306.

Kirkham, Margaret. *Jane Austen, Feminism and Fiction*. Brighton: Harvester, 1983.

Langbauer, Laurie. *Women and Romance: the Consolations of Gender in the English Novel*. Ithaca: Cornell UP, 1990.

Looser, Devoney (ed.). *Jane Austen and Discourses of Feminism*. Basingstoke: Macmillan, 1995.

Lovell, Terry. "Jane Austen and Gentry Society." In Francis Barker et al, ed., *Literature, Society, and the Sociology of Literature*. Colchester: University of Essex, 1977. 118–32.

Newton, Judith Lowder. *Women, Power, and Subversion: Social Strategies in British Fiction, 1778–1860*. Athens: U of Georgia P, 1981; NY and London: Methuen, 1985.

Poovey, Mary. *The Proper Lady and the Woman Writer*. Chicago and London: U of Chicago P, 1984.

Roberts, Warren. *Jane Austen and the French Revolution*. New York: St. Martin's Press, 1979.

Schofield, Mary Ann, (ed.). *Fetter'd or Free? British Women Novelists, 1670–1815*. Athens, Ohio: Ohio UP, 1986.

Shaffer, Julie. "Not Subordinate: Empowering Women in the Marriage-Plot. The Novels of Frances Burney, Maria Edgeworth, Jane Austen." *Criticism: A Quarterly for Literature and the Arts* XXXIV. 1 (Winter 1992): 51–73.

Siskin, Clifford. *The Historicity of Romantic Discourse*. Oxford: Oxford UP, 1988.

—. *The Work of Writing: Literature and Social Change, 1700–1830*. Baltimore: Johns Hopkins UP, 1998.

Spacks, Patricia Meyer. "Austen's Laughter." *Women's Studies* 15 (1988): 71–85.

—. *Desire and Truth: Functions of Plot in Eighteenth-Century English Novels.* Chicago and London: U of Chicago P, 1990 (ch.8 is on Austen and Scott).

Stewart, Maaja A. *Domestic Realities and Imperial Fictions: Jane Austen's Novels in Eighteenth-Century Contexts.* Athens: U of Georgia P, 1993.

Stratton, Jon. *The Virgin Text: Fiction, Sexuality, and Ideology.* Sussex: Harvester Press, 1987.

Spring, David A. "Interpreters of Jane Austen's Social World." In Janet Todd, ed., *Jane Austen: New Perspectives.* New York: Holmes and Meier, 1983. 53–72.

Sulloway, Alison. *Jane Austen and the Province of Womanhood.* Philadelphia: U of Philadelphia P, 1989.

Yeazell, Ruth Bernard. *Fictions of Modesty: Women and Courtship in the English Novel.* Chicago and London: Chicago UP, 1991.

For discussion of Austen's relation to the conduct books, see particularly Armstrong 1987, Newton 1981, Poovey 1984, and Yeazell 1991.

On rank, land-ownership, and inheritance:

Perkin, Harold. *The Origins of Modern English Society 1780–1880.* London: Routledge and Kegan Paul, 1969.

Spring, Eileen. *Law, Land, and Family: Aristocratic Inheritance in England, 1300 to 1800.* Chapel Hill: U of North Carolina P, 1993.

Stone, Lawrence, and Jeanne C. Fawtier Stone, *An Open Elite? England 1540–1880.* Oxford: Oxford UP, 1984.

—. *Family, Sex and Marriage in England, 1500–1800.* New York: Harper and Row, 1977.

Gillis, John R. *For Better, for Worse: British Marriages, 1600 to the Present.* Oxford: Clarendon, 1985.

Habakkuk, H. J. "Marriage Settlements in the Eighteenth Century." *Transactions of the Royal Historical Society,* 4th series 32 (1950). 15–30.

Trumbach, Randolph. *The Rise of the Egalitarian Family: Aristocratic Kinship and Domestic Relations in Eighteenth-Century England.* New York: Academic Press, 1978.

On Domestic Tourism:

Harris, John. "English Country House Guides, 1740–1840." In John Summerson, ed., *Concerning Architecture*. London: Allan Lane, 1968. 58–74.

Tinniswood, Adrian. *A History of Country House Visiting: Five Centuries of Tourism and Taste*. Oxford: Basil Blackwell and the National Trust, 1989.

On the Militia:

Breihan, John and Clive Caplan. "Jane Austen and the Militia." *Persuasions* 14 (December 1992): 16–26.

Wells, Roger. "The Militia Mutinies of 1795." In John Rule, ed., *Outside the Law: Studies in Crime and Order 1650–1850*. U of Exeter P, 1982. 35–64.

Other texts cited:

Bond, Donald F. (ed.). *The Spectator.* 5 vols. Oxford: Clarendon, 1965.

Klein, Lawrence E. "The Third Earl of Shaftesbury and the Progress of Politeness." *Eighteenth-Century Studies* 18 (1984–5): 186–214.

Potkay, Adam. *The Fate of Eloquence in the Age of Hume*. Ithaca: Cornell UP, 1994.

Stephenson, Carl, and F.G. Marcham. *Sources of English Constitutional History: a selection of documents from A.D. 600 to the present*. New York and London: Harper, 1937.